This book belongs to:

....

....

....

OXFORD CHILDREN'S CLASSICS

Alice's Adventures *in* Wonderland
Anne *of* Green Gables
Black Beauty
Flambards
Jack Holborn
Little Women
Party Shoes
The Adventures *of* Huckleberry Finn
The Adventures *of* Tom Sawyer
The Call *of the* Wild
The Hound *of the* Baskervilles
The Jungle Book
The Secret Garden
The Wind *in the* Willows
The Wonderful Wizard *of* Oz
Treasure Island

Louisa May Alcott

LITTLE WOMEN

OXFORD

UNIVERSITY PRESS

OXFORD
UNIVERSITY PRESS

Great Clarendon Street, Oxford OX2 6DP

Oxford University Press is a department of the University of Oxford.
It furthers the University's objective of excellence in research, scholarship,
and education by publishing worldwide in

Oxford   New York

Auckland   Cape Town   Dar es Salaam   Hong Kong   Karachi
Kuala Lumpur   Madrid   Melbourne   Mexico City   Nairobi
New Delhi   Shanghai   Taipei   Toronto

With offices in

Argentina   Austria   Brazil   Chile   Czech Republic   France   Greece
Guatemala   Hungary   Italy   Japan   Poland   Portugal   Singapore
South Korea   Switzerland   Thailand   Turkey   Ukraine   Vietnam

Oxford is a registered trade mark of Oxford University Press
in the UK and in certain other countries

Database right Oxford University Press (maker)

First published 1868
First published in Oxford Children's Classics 2007

British Library Cataloguing in Publication Data

Data available

ISBN: 978-0-19-272001-6

5 7 9 10 8 6

Printed in China

Paper used in the production of this book is a natural,
recyclable product made from wood grown in sustainable forests.
The manufacturing process conforms to the environmental
regulations of the country of origin.

PREFACE

Go then, my little Book, and show to all
That entertain and bid thee welcome shall,
What thou dost keep close shut up in thy breast;
And wish what thou dost show them may be blest
To them for good, may make them choose to be
Pilgrims better by far, than thee or me.
Tell them of Mercy; she is one
Who early hath her pilgrimage begun.
Yea, let young damsels learn of her to prize
The world which is to come, and so be wise;
For little tripping maids may follow God
Along the ways which saintly feet have trod.

Adapted from JOHN BUNYAN

CONTENTS

CHAPTER ONE

——•——

Playing Pilgrims

'Christmas won't be Christmas without any presents,' grumbled Jo, lying on the rug.

'It's so dreadful to be poor!' sighed Meg, looking down at her old dress.

'I don't think it's fair for some girls to have lots of pretty things, and other girls nothing at all,' added little Amy, with an injured sniff.

'We've got father and mother, and each other, anyhow,' said Beth, contentedly, from her corner.

The four young faces on which the firelight shone brightened at the cheerful words, but darkened again as Jo said sadly,—

'We haven't got father, and shall not have him for a long time.' She didn't say 'perhaps never', but each silently added it, thinking of father far away, where the fighting was.

Nobody spoke for a minute; then Meg said in an altered tone,—

'You know the reason mother proposed not having any presents this Christmas, was because it's going to be a hard winter for every one; and she thinks we ought not to spend money for pleasure, when our men are suffering so in the army. We can't do much, but we can make our little sacrifices, and ought to do it gladly. But I am afraid I don't;' and Meg shook her head, as she thought regretfully of all the pretty things she wanted.

'But I don't think the little we should spend would do any good. We've each got a dollar, and the army wouldn't be much helped by our giving that. I agree not to expect anything from mother or you, but I do want to buy *Undine and Sintram* for myself; I've wanted it *so* long,' said Jo, who was a bookworm.

'I planned to spend mine in new music,' said Beth, with a little sigh, which no one heard but the hearth-brush and kettle-holder.

'I shall get a nice box of Faber's drawing pencils; I really need them,' said Amy, decidedly.

'Mother didn't say anything about our money, and she won't wish us to give up everything. Let's each buy what we want, and have a little fun; I'm sure we grub hard enough to earn it,' cried Jo, examining the heels of her boots in a gentlemanly manner.

'I know *I* do,—teaching those dreadful children nearly all day, when I'm longing to enjoy myself at home,' began Meg, in the complaining tone again.

'You don't have half such a hard time as I do,' said Jo. 'How would you like to be shut up for hours with a nervous, fussy old lady, who keeps you trotting, is never satisfied, and worries you till you're ready to fly out of the window or box her ears?'

'It's naughty to fret,—but I do think washing dishes and keeping things tidy is the worst work in the world. It makes me cross; and my hands get so stiff, I can't practise good a bit.' And Beth looked at her rough hands with a sigh that any one could hear that time.

'I don't believe any of you suffer as I do,' cried Amy; 'for you don't have to go to school with impertinent girls, who plague you if you don't know your lessons, and laugh at your dresses, and label your father if he isn't rich, and insult you when your nose isn't nice.'

'If you mean *libel* I'd say so, and not talk about *labels*, as if pa was a pickle-bottle,' advised Jo, laughing.

'I know what I mean, and you needn't be "statirical" about it. It's proper to use good words, and improve your *vocabilary*,' returned Amy, with dignity.

'Don't peck at one another, children. Don't you wish we had the money papa lost when we were little, Jo? Dear me, how happy and good we'd be, if we had no worries,' said Meg, who could remember better times.

'You said the other day you thought we were a deal happier than the King children, for they were fighting and fretting all the time, in spite of their money.'

'So I did, Beth. Well, I guess we are; for though we do have to work, we make fun for ourselves, and are a pretty jolly set, as Jo would say.'

'Jo does use such slang words,' observed Amy, with a reproving look at the long figure stretched on the rug. Jo immediately sat up, put her hands in her apron pockets, and began to whistle.

'Don't, Jo; it's so boyish.'

'That's why I do it.'

'I detest rude, unlady-like girls.'

'I hate affected, niminy piminy chits.'

'Birds in their little nests agree,' sang Beth, the peace-maker, with such a funny face that both sharp voices softened to a laugh, and the 'pecking' ended for that time.

'Really, girls, you are both to be blamed,' said Meg, beginning to lecture in her elder sisterly fashion. 'You are old enough to leave off boyish tricks, and behave better, Josephine. It didn't matter so much when you were a little girl; but now you are so tall, and turn up your hair, you should remember that you are a young lady.'

'I ain't! and if turning up my hair makes me one, I'll wear it in two tails till I'm twenty,' cried Jo, pulling off her net, and shaking down a chestnut mane. 'I hate to think I've got to grow up and be Miss March, and wear long gowns, and look as prim as a China-aster. It's bad enough to be a girl, any-way, when I like boy's games, and work, and manners. I can't get over my disappointment in not being a boy, and it's worse than ever now, for I'm dying to go and fight with papa, and I can only stay at home and knit like a poky old woman;' and Jo shook the blue army-sock till the needles rattled like castanets, and her ball bounded across the room.

'Poor Jo; it's too bad! But it can't be helped, so you must try to be contented with making your name boyish, and playing brother to us girls,' said Beth, stroking the rough head at her knee with a hand that all the dishwashing and dusting in the world could not make ungentle in its touch.

'As for you, Amy,' continued Meg, 'you are altogether too particular and prim. Your airs are funny now, but you'll grow up an affected little goose if you don't take care. I like your nice manners, and refined ways of speaking, when you don't try to be elegant; but your absurd words are as bad as Jo's slang.'

'If Joe is a tom-boy, and Amy a goose, what am I, please?' asked Beth, ready to share the lecture.

'You're a dear, and nothing else,' answered Meg, warmly; and no one contradicted her, for the 'Mouse' was the pet of the family.

As young readers like to know 'how people look', we will take this moment to give them a little sketch of the four sisters, who sat knitting away in the twilight, while the December snow fell quietly without, and the fire crackled cheerfully within. It was a comfortable old room, though the carpet was faded and the furniture very plain, for a good picture or two hung on the walls, books filled the recesses, chrysanthemums and Christmas roses bloomed in the windows, and a pleasant atmosphere of home-peace pervaded it.

Margaret, the eldest of the four, was sixteen, and very pretty, being plump and fair, with large eyes, plenty of soft brown hair, a sweet mouth, and white hands, of which she was rather vain. Fifteen-year-old Jo was very tall, thin and brown, and reminded one of a colt; for she never seemed to know what to do with her long limbs, which were very much in her way. She had a decided mouth, a comical nose, and sharp gray eyes, which appeared to see everything, and were by turns fierce, funny, or thoughtful. Her long, thick hair was her one beauty; but it was usually bundled into a net, to be out of her way. Round shoulders had Jo, big hands and feet, a fly-away look to her clothes, and the uncomfortable appearance of a girl who was rapidly shooting up into a woman, and didn't like it. Elizabeth,—or Beth, as every one called her,—was a rosy, smooth-haired, bright-eyed girl of thirteen, with a shy manner, a timid voice, and a peaceful expression, which was seldom disturbed. Her father called her 'Little Tranquillity', and the name suited her excellently; for she seemed to live in a happy world of her own, only venturing out to meet the few whom she trusted and loved. Amy, though the youngest, was a most important person, in her own opinion at least. A regular snow maiden, with blue eyes, and yellow hair curling on her shoulders; pale and slender, and always carrying herself like a young lady mindful of her manners. What the characters of the four sisters were, we will leave to be found out.

The clock struck six; and, having swept up the hearth, Beth put a pair of slippers down to warm. Somehow the sight of the old shoes had a good effect upon the girls, for mother was coming, and every one brightened to welcome her. Meg stopped lecturing, and lit the lamp, Amy got out of the easy-chair without being asked, and Jo forgot how tired she was as she sat up to hold the slippers nearer to the blaze.

'They are quite worn out; Marmee must have a new pair.'

'I thought I'd get her some with my dollar,' said Beth.

'No, I shall!' cried Amy.

'I'm the oldest,' began Meg, but Joe cut in with a decided—

'I'm the man of the family now papa is away, and *I* shall provide the slippers, for he told me to take special care of mother while he was gone.'

'I'll tell you what we'll do,' said Beth; 'let's each get her something for Christmas, and not get anything for ourselves.'

'That's like you, dear! What will we get?' exclaimed Jo.

Every one thought soberly for a minute; then Meg announced, as if the idea was suggested by the sight of her own pretty hands, 'I shall give her a nice pair of gloves.'

'Army shoes, best to be had,' cried Jo.

'Some handkerchiefs, all hemmed,' said Beth.

'I'll get a little bottle of Cologne; she likes it, and it won't cost much, so I'll have some left to buy something for me,' added Amy.

'How will we give the things?' asked Meg.

'Put 'em on the table, and bring her in and see her open the bundles. Don't you remember how we used to do on our birthdays?' answered Jo.

'I used to be so frightened when it was my turn to sit in the big chair with a crown on, and see you all come marching round to give the presents, with a kiss. I liked the things and the kisses, but it was dreadful to have you sit looking at me while I opened the bundles,' said Beth, who was toasting her face and the bread for tea, at the same time.

'Let Marmee think we are getting things for ourselves, and then surprise her. We must go shopping to-morrow afternoon, Meg; there is lots to do about the play for Christmas night,' said Jo, marching up and down with her hands behind her back, and her nose in the air.

'I don't mean to act any more after this time; I'm getting too old for such things,' observed Meg, who was as much a child as ever about 'dressing up' frolics.

'You won't stop, I know, as long as you can trail round in a white gown with your hair down, and wear gold-paper jewelry. You are the best actress we've got, and there'll be an end of everything if you quit the boards,' said Jo. 'We ought to rehearse to-night; come here, Amy, and do the fainting scene, for you are as stiff as a poker in that.'

'I can't help it; I never saw any one faint, and I don't choose to make myself all black and blue, tumbling flat as you do. If I can go down easily, I'll drop; if I can't, I shall fall into a chair and be graceful; I don't care if Hugo does come at me with a pistol,' returned Amy, who was not gifted with dramatic power, but was chosen because she was small enough to be borne out shrieking by the hero of the piece.

'Do it this way; clasp your hands so, and stagger across the room, crying frantically, "Roderigo! save me! save me!"' and away went Jo, with a melodramatic scream which was truly thrilling.

Amy followed, but she poked her hands out stiffly before her, and jerked herself along as if she went by machinery; and her 'Ow!' was more suggestive of pins being run into her than of fear and anguish. Jo gave a despairing groan, and Meg laughed outright, while Beth let her bread burn as she watched the fun, with interest.

'It's no use! do the best you can when the time comes, and if the audience shout, don't blame me. Come on, Meg.'

Then things went smoothly, for Don Pedro defied the world in a speech of two pages without a single break; Hagar, the witch, chanted an awful incantation over her kettleful of simmering toads, with weird effect; Roderigo rent his chains asunder manfully, and Hugo died in agonies of remorse and arsenic, with a wild 'Ha! ha!'

'It's the best we've had yet,' said Meg, as the dead villain sat up and rubbed his elbows.

'I don't see how you can write and act such splendid

things, Jo. You're a regular Shakespeare!' exclaimed Beth, who firmly believed that her sisters were gifted with wonderful genius in all things.

'Not quite,' replied Jo, modestly. 'I do think "The Witch's Curse, an Operatic Tragedy", is rather a nice thing; but I'd like to try *Macbeth*, if we only had a trapdoor for Banquo. I always wanted to do the killing part. "Is that a dagger that I see before me?"' muttered Jo, rolling her eyes and clutching at the air, as she had seen a famous tragedian do.

'No, it's the toasting fork, with ma's shoe on it instead of the bread. Beth's stage struck!' cried Meg, and the rehearsal ended in a general burst of laughter.

'Glad to find you so merry, my girls,' said a cheery voice at the door, and actors and audience turned to welcome a stout, motherly lady, with a 'can-I-help-you' look about her which was truly delightful. She wasn't a particularly handsome person, but mothers are always lovely to their children, and the girls thought the gray cloak and unfashionable bonnet covered the most splendid woman in the world.

'Well, dearies, how have you got on to-day? There was so much to do, getting the boxes ready to go to-morrow, that I didn't come home to dinner. Has any one called, Beth? How is your cold, Meg? Jo, you look tired to death. Come and kiss me, baby.'

While making these maternal inquiries Mrs March got her wet things off, her hot slippers on, and sitting down in the easy-chair, drew Amy to her lap, preparing to enjoy the happiest hour of her busy day. The girls flew about, trying to make things comfortable, each in her own way. Meg arranged the tea-table; Jo brought wood and set chairs, dropping, overturning, and clattering everything she touched; Beth trotted to and fro between parlor and kitchen, quiet and busy; while Amy gave directions to every one, as she sat with her hands folded.

As they gathered about the table, Mrs March said, with a particularly happy face, 'I've got a treat for you after supper.'

A quick, bright smile went round like a streak of sunshine. Beth clapped her hands, regardless of the hot biscuit she held, and Jo tossed up her napkin, crying, 'A letter! a letter! Three cheers for father!'

'Yes, a nice long letter. He is well, and thinks he shall get through the cold season better than we feared. He sends all sorts of loving wishes for Christmas, and an especial message to you girls,' said Mrs March, patting her pocket as if she had got a treasure there.

'Hurry up, and get done. Don't stop to quirk your little finger, and prink over your plate, Amy,' cried Jo, choking in her tea, and dropping her bread, butter side down, on the carpet, in her haste to get at the treat.

Beth ate no more, but crept away, to sit in her shadowy corner and brood over the delight to come, till the others were ready.

'I think it was so splendid in father to go as a chaplain when he was too old to be drafted, and not strong enough for a soldier,' said Meg, warmly.

'Don't I wish I could go as a drummer, a *vivan*—what's its name? or a nurse, so I could be near him and help him,' exclaimed Jo, with a groan.

'It must be very disagreeable to sleep in a tent, and eat all sorts of bad-tasting things, and drink out of a tin mug,' sighed Amy.

'When will he come home, Marmee?' asked Beth, with a little quiver in her voice.

'Not for many months, dear, unless he is sick. He will stay and do his work faithfully as long as he can, and we won't ask for him back a minute sooner than he can be spared. Now come and hear the letter.'

They all drew to the fire, mother in the big chair with Beth at her feet, Meg and Amy perched on either arm of the chair, and Jo leaning on the back, where no one would see any sign of emotion if the letter should happen to be touching.

Very few letters were written in those hard times that were not touching, especially those which fathers sent home. In this one little was said of the hardships endured, the dangers faced, or the homesickness conquered; it was a cheerful, hopeful letter, full of lively descriptions of camp life, marches, and military news; and only at the end did the writer's heart overflow with fatherly love and longing for the little girls at home.

'Give them all my dear love and a kiss. Tell them I think of them by day, pray for them by night, and find my best comfort in their affection at all times. A year seems very long to wait before I see them, but remind them that while we wait we may all work, so that these hard days need not be wasted. I know they will remember all I said to them, that they will be loving children to you, will do their duty faithfully, fight their bosom enemies bravely, and conquer themselves so beautifully, that when I come back to them I may be fonder and prouder than ever of my little women.'

Everybody sniffed when they came to that part; Jo wasn't ashamed of the great tear that dropped off the end of her nose, and Amy never minded the rumpling of her curls as she hid her face on her mother's shoulder and sobbed out, 'I *am* a selfish pig! but I'll truly try to be better, so he mayn't be disappointed in me by and by.'

'We all will!' cried Meg. 'I think too much of my looks, and hate to work, but won't any more, if I can help it.'

'I'll try and be what he loves to call me, "a little woman," and not be rough and wild; but do my duty here instead of wanting to be somewhere else,' said Jo, thinking that keeping her temper at home was a much harder task than facing a rebel or two down South.

Beth said nothing, but wiped away her tears with the blue army-sock, and began to knit with all her might, losing no time in doing the duty that lay nearest her, while she resolved in her quiet little soul to be all that father hoped to find her when the year brought round the happy coming home.

Mrs March broke the silence that followed Jo's words, by saying in her cheery voice, 'Do you remember how you used to play *Pilgrim's Progress* when you were little things? Nothing delighted you more than to have me tie my piece-bags on your backs for burdens, give you hats and sticks, and rolls of paper, and let you travel through the house from the cellar, which was the City of Destruction, up, up, to the house-top, where you had all the lovely things you could collect to make a Celestial City.'

'What fun it was, especially going by the lions, fighting Apollyon, and passing through the Valley where the hobgoblins were,' said Jo.

'I liked the place where the bundles fell off and tumbled down stairs,' said Meg.

'My favorite part was when we came out on the flat roof

where our flowers and arbors, and pretty things were, and all stood and sung for joy up there in the sunshine,' said Beth, smiling, as if that pleasant moment had come back to her.

'I don't remember much about it, except that I was afraid of the cellar and the dark entry, and always liked the cake and milk we had up at the top. If I wasn't too old for such things, I'd rather like to play it over again,' said Amy, who began to talk of renouncing childish things at the mature age of twelve.

'We never are too old for this, my dear, because it is a play we are playing all the time in one way or another. Our burdens are here, our road is before us, and the longing for goodness and happiness is the guide that leads us through many troubles and mistakes to the peace which is a true Celestial City. Now, my little pilgrims, suppose you begin again, not in play, but in earnest, and see how far on you can get before father comes home.'

'Really, mother? where are our bundles?' asked Amy, who was a very literal young lady.

'Each of you told what your burden was just now, except Beth; I rather think she hasn't got any,' said her mother.

'Yes, I have; mine is dishes and dusters, and envying girls with nice pianos, and being afraid of people.'

Beth's bundle was such a funny one that everybody wanted to laugh; but nobody did, for it would have hurt her feelings very much.

'Let us do it,' said Meg, thoughtfully. 'It is only another name for trying to be good, and the story may help us; for though we do want to be good, it's hard work, and we forget, and don't do our best.'

'We were in the Slough of Despond to-night, and mother came and pulled us out as Help did in the book. We ought to have our roll of directions, like Christian. What shall we do about that?' asked Jo, delighted with the fancy which lent a little romance to the very dull task of doing her duty.

'Look under your pillows, Christmas morning, and you will find your guide-book,' replied Mrs March.

They talked over the new plan while old Hannah cleared the table; then out came the four little workbaskets, and the needles flew as the girls made sheets for Aunt March. It was un-interesting sewing, but to-night no one grumbled. They adopted Jo's plan of dividing the long seams into four parts, and calling the quarters Europe, Asia, Africa and America, and in that way got on capitally, especially when they talked about the different countries as they stitched their way through them.

At nine they stopped work, and sung, as usual, before they went to bed. No one but Beth could get much music out of the old piano; but she had a way of softly touching the yellow keys, and making a pleasant accompaniment to the simple songs they sung. Meg had a voice like a flute, and she and her mother led the little choir. Amy chirped like a cricket, and Jo wandered through the airs at her own sweet will, always com-ing out at the wrong place with a crook or a quaver that spoilt the most pensive tune. They had always done this from the time they could lisp

'Crinkle, crinkle, 'ittle 'tar',

and it had become a household custom, for the mother was a born singer. The first sound in the morning was her voice, as she went about the house singing like a lark; and the last sound at night was the same cheery sound, for the girls never grew too old for that familiar lullaby.

CHAPTER TWO

A Merry Christmas

Jo was the first to wake in the gray dawn of Christmas morning. No stockings hung at the fireplace, and for a moment she felt as much disappointed as she did long ago, when her little sock fell down because it was so crammed with goodies. Then she remembered her mother's promise, and slipping her hand under her pillow, drew out a little crimson-covered book. She knew it very well, for it was that beautiful old story of the best life ever lived, and Jo felt that it was a true guide-book for any pilgrim going the long journey. She woke Meg with a 'Merry Christmas', and bade her see what was under her pillow. A green-covered book appeared, with the same picture inside, and a few words written by their mother, which made their one present very precious in their eyes. Presently Beth and Amy woke, to rummage and find their little books also,—one dove-colored, the other blue; and all sat looking at and talking about them, while the East grew rosy with the coming day.

In spite of her small vanities, Margaret had a sweet and pious nature, which unconsciously influenced her sisters, especially Jo, who loved her very tenderly, and obeyed her because her advice was so gently given.

'Girls,' said Meg, seriously, looking from the tumbled head beside her to the two little night-capped ones in the room beyond, 'mother wants us to read and love and mind these books, and we must begin at once. We used to be faithful about it; but since father went away, and all this war trouble unsettled us, we have neglected many things. You can do as you please; but *I* shall keep my book on the table here, and read a little every morning as soon as I wake, for I know it will do me good, and help me through the day.'

Then she opened her new book and began to read. Jo put her arm round her, and, leaning cheek to cheek, read also, with the quiet expression so seldom seen on her restless face.

'How good Meg is! Come, Amy, let's do as they do. I'll help you with the hard words, and they'll explain things if we don't understand,' whispered Beth, very much impressed by the pretty books and her sisters' example.

'I'm glad mine is blue,' said Amy; and then the rooms were very still while the pages were softly turned, and the winter sun-shine crept in to touch the bright heads and serious faces with a Christmas greeting.

'Where is mother?' asked Meg, as she and Jo ran down to thank her for their gifts, half an hour later.

'Goodness only knows. Some poor creeter come a-beggin', and your ma went straight off to see what was needed. There never *was* such a woman for givin' away vittles and drink, clothes and firin',' replied Hannah, who had lived with the family since Meg was born, and was considered by them all more as a friend than a servant.

'She will be back soon, I guess; so do your cakes, and have everything ready,' said Meg, looking over the presents which were collected in a basket and kept under the sofa, ready to be produced at the proper time. 'Why, where is Amy's bottle of Cologne?' she added, as the little flask did not appear.

'She took it out a minute ago, and went off with it to put a ribbon on it, or some such notion,' replied Jo, dancing about the room to take the first stiffness off the new army-slippers.

'How nice my handkerchiefs look, don't they? Hannah washed and ironed them for me, and I marked them all myself,' said Beth, looking proudly at the somewhat uneven letters which had cost her such labor.

'Bless the child, she's gone and put "Mother" on them instead of "M. March"; how funny!' cried Jo, taking up one.

'Isn't it right? I thought it was better to do it so, because Meg's initials are "M. M.", and I don't want any one to use these but Marmee,' said Beth, looking troubled.

'It's all right, dear, and a very pretty idea; quite sensible, too, for no one can ever mistake now. It will please her very much, I know,' said Meg, with a frown for Jo, and a smile for Beth.

'There's mother; hide the basket, quick!' cried Jo, as a door slammed, and steps sounded in the hall.

Amy came in hastily, and looked rather abashed when she saw her sisters all waiting for her.

'Where have you been, and what are you hiding behind you?' asked Meg, surprised to see, by her hood and cloak, that lazy Amy had been out so early.

'Don't laugh at me, Jo, I didn't mean any one should know till the time came. I only meant to change the little bottle for a big one, and I gave *all* my money to get it, and I'm truly trying not to be selfish any more.'

As she spoke, Amy showed the handsome flask which replaced the cheap one; and looked so earnest and humble in her little effort to forget herself, that Meg hugged her on the spot, and Jo pronounced her 'a trump,' while Beth ran to the window, and picked her finest rose to ornament the stately bottle.

'You see I felt ashamed of my present, after reading and talking about being good this morning, so I ran round the corner and changed it the minute I was up; and I'm *so* glad, for mine is the handsomest now.'

Another bang of the street-door sent the basket under the sofa, and the girls to the table eager for breakfast.

'Merry Christmas, Marmee! Lots of them! Thank you for our books; we read some, and mean to every day,' they cried, in chorus.

'Merry Christmas, little daughters! I'm glad you began at once, and hope you will keep on. But I want to say one word before we sit down. Not far away from here lies a poor woman with a little newborn baby. Six children are huddled into one bed to keep from freezing, for they have no fire. There is nothing to eat over there; and the oldest boy came to tell me they were suffering hunger and cold. My girls, will you give them your breakfast as a Christmas present?'

They were all unusually hungry, having waited nearly an hour, and for a minute no one spoke; only a minute, for Jo exclaimed impetuously,—

'I'm so glad you came before we began!'

'May I go and help carry the things to the poor little children?' asked Beth, eagerly.

'*I* shall take the cream and the muffins,' added Amy, heroically giving up the articles she most liked.

Meg was already covering the buckwheats, and piling the bread into one big plate.

'I thought you'd do it,' said Mrs March, smiling as if satisfied. 'You shall all go and help me, and when we come back we will have bread and milk for breakfast, and make it up at dinner-time.'

They were soon ready, and the procession set out. Fortunately it was early, and they went through back streets, so few people saw them, and no one laughed at the funny party.

A poor, bare, miserable room it was, with broken windows, no fire, ragged bed-clothes, a sick mother, wailing baby, and a group of pale, hungry children cuddled under one old quilt, trying to keep warm. How the big eyes stared, and the blue lips smiled, as the girls went in!

'Ach, mein Gott! it is good angels come to us!' cried the poor woman, crying for joy.

'Funny angels in hoods and mittens,' said Jo, and set them laughing.

In a few minutes it really did seem as if kind spirits had been at work there. Hannah, who had carried wood, made a fire, and stopped up the broken panes with old hats, and her own shawl. Mrs March gave the mother tea and gruel, and comforted her with promises of help, while she dressed the little baby as tenderly as if it had been her own. The girls, meantime, spread the table, set the children round the fire, and fed them like so many hungry birds; laughing, talking, and trying to understand the funny broken English.

'Das ist gute!' 'Der angel-kinder!' cried the poor things, as they ate, and warmed their purple hands at the comfortable blaze. The girls had never been called angel children before, and thought it very agreeable, especially Jo, who had been considered 'a Sancho' ever since she was born. That was a very happy breakfast, though they didn't get any of it; and when they went away, leaving comfort behind, I think there were not in all the city four merrier people than the hungry little girls who gave away their breakfasts, and contented themselves with bread and milk on Christmas morning.

'That's loving our neighbor better than ourselves, and I like it,' said Meg, as they set out their presents, while their mother was upstairs collecting clothes for the poor Hummels.

Not a very splendid show, but there was a great deal of love done up in the few little bundles; and the tall vase of red roses, white chrysanthemums, and trailing vines, which stood in the middle, gave quite an elegant air to the table.

'She's coming! strike up, Beth, open the door, Amy. Three cheers for Marmee!' cried Jo, prancing about, while Meg went to conduct mother to the seat of honor.

Beth played her gayest march, Amy threw open the door, and Meg enacted escort with great dignity. Mrs March was both surprised and touched; and smiled with her eyes full as she examined her presents, and read the little notes which accompanied them. The slippers went on at once, a new handkerchief was slipped into her pocket, well scented with Amy's Cologne, the rose was fastened in her bosom, and the nice gloves were pronounced 'a perfect fit'.

There was a good deal of laughing, and kissing, and explaining, in the simple, loving fashion which makes these home-festivals so pleasant at the time, so sweet to remember long afterward, and then all fell to work.

The morning charities and ceremonies took so much time, that the rest of the day was devoted to preparations for the evening festivities. Being still too young to go often to the theatre, and not rich enough to afford any great outlay for private performances, the girls put their wits to work, and, necessity being the mother of invention, made whatever they needed. Very clever were some of their productions; paste-board guitars, antique lamps made of old-fashioned butter-boats, covered with silver paper, gorgeous robes of old cotton, glittering with tin spangles from a pickle factory, and armor covered with the same useful diamond-shaped bits, left in sheets when the lids of tin preserve-pots were cut out. The furniture was used to being turned topsy-turvy, and the big chamber was the scene of many innocent revels.

No gentlemen were admitted; so Jo played male parts to her heart's content, and took immense satisfaction in a pair of russet-leather boots given her by a friend, who knew a lady who knew an actor. These boots, an old foil, and a slashed doublet once used by an artist for some picture, were Jo's chief treasures, and appeared on all occasions. The smallness of the company made it necessary for the two principal actors to take several parts apiece; and they certainly deserved some credit for the hard work they did in learning three or four different parts, whisking in and out of various costumes, and managing the stage besides. It was excellent drill for their memories, a harmless amusement, and employed many hours which otherwise would have been idle, lonely, or spent in less profitable society.

On Christmas night, a dozen girls piled on to the bed, which was the dress circle, and sat before the blue and yellow chintz curtains, in a most flattering state of expectancy. There was a good deal of rustling and whispering behind the curtain, a trifle of lamp-smoke, and an occasional giggle from Amy, who was apt to get hysterical in the excitement of the moment. Presently a bell sounded, the curtains flew apart, and the Operatic Tragedy began.

'A gloomy wood,' according to the one play-bill, was represented by a few shrubs in pots, a green baize on the floor, and a cave in the distance. This cave was made with a clothes-horse for a roof, bureaus for walls; and in it was a small furnace in full blast, with a black pot on it, and an old witch bending over it. The stage was dark, and the glow of the furnace had a fine effect, especially as real steam issued from the kettle when the witch took off the cover. A moment was allowed for the first thrill to subside; then Hugo, the villain, stalked in with a clanking sword at his side, a slouched hat, black beard, mysterious cloak, and the boots. After pacing to and fro in much agitation, he struck his forehead, and burst out in a wild strain, singing of his hatred for Roderigo, his love for Zara, and his pleasing resolution to kill the one and win the other. The gruff tones of Hugo's voice, with an occasional shout when his feelings overcame him, were very impressive, and the audience applauded the moment he paused for breath. Bowing with the air of one accustomed to public praise, he stole to the cavern and ordered Hagar to come forth with a commanding 'What ho! minion! I need thee!'

Out came Meg, with gray horse-hair hanging about her face, a red and black robe, a staff, and cabalistic signs upon her cloak. Hugo demanded a potion to make Zara adore him, and one to destroy Roderigo. Hagar, in a fine dramatic melody, promised both, and proceeded to call up the spirit who would bring the love philter:—

> 'Hither, hither, from thy home,
> Airy sprite, I bid thee come!
> Born of roses, fed on dew,
> Charms and potions canst thou brew?
> Bring me here, with elfin speed,
> The fragrant philter which I need;
> Make it sweet, and swift and strong;
> Spirit, answer now my song!'

A soft strain of music sounded, and then at the back of the cave appeared a little figure in cloudy white, with glittering wings, golden hair, and a garland of roses on its head. Waving a wand, it sung:—

> 'Hither I come,
> From my airy home,
> Afar in the silver moon;
> Take the magic spell,
> Oh, use it well!
> Or its power will vanish soon!'

and dropping a small gilded bottle at the witch's feet, the spirit vanished. Another chant from Hagar produced another apparition,—not a lovely one, for, with a bang, an ugly, black imp appeared, and having croaked a reply, tossed a dark bottle

at Hugo, and disappeared with a mocking laugh. Having warbled his thanks, and put the potions in his boots, Hugo departed; and Hagar informed the audience that, as he had killed
a few of her friends in times past, she has cursed him, and in-
tends to thwart his plans, and be revenged on him. Then the
curtain fell, and the audience reposed and ate candy while discussing the merits of the play.

A good deal of hammering went on before the curtain rose
again; but when it became evident what a masterpiece of
stage carpentering had been got up, no one murmured at the
delay. It was truly superb! A tower rose to the ceiling; half-way
up appeared a window with a lamp burning at it, and behind
the white curtain appeared Zara in a lovely blue and silver
dress, waiting for Roderigo. He came, in gorgeous array, with
plumed cap, red cloak, chestnut love-locks, a guitar, and the
boots, of course. Kneeling at the foot of the tower, he sung a
serenade in melting tones. Zara replied, and after a musical di-
alogue, consented to fly. Then came the grand effect of the
play. Roderigo produced a rope-ladder with five steps to it,
threw up one end, and invited Zara to descend. Timidly she
crept from her lattice, put her hand on Roderigo's shoulder,
and was about to leap gracefully down, when, 'alas, alas for
Zara!' she forgot her train,—it caught in the window; the
tower tottered, leaned forward, fell with a crash, and buried
the unhappy lovers in the ruins!

A universal shriek arose as the russet boots waved wildly
from the wreck, and a golden head emerged, exclaiming, 'I
told you so! I told you so!' With wonderful presence of mind
Don Pedro, the cruel sire, rushed in, dragged out his daughter
with a hasty aside,—

'Don't laugh, act as if it was all right!' and ordering Roderigo up, banished him from the kingdom with wrath and scorn. Though decidedly shaken by the fall of the tower upon him, Roderigo defied the old gentleman, and refused to stir. This dauntless example fired Zara; she also defied her sire, and he ordered them both to the deepest dungeons of the castle. A stout little retainer came in with chains, and led them away, looking very much frightened, and evidently forgetting the speech he ought to have made.

Act third was the castle hall; and here Hagar appeared, having come to free the lovers and finish Hugo. She hears him coming, and hides; sees him put the potions into two cups of wine, and bid the timid little servant 'Bear them to the captives in their cells, and tell them I shall come anon.' The servant takes Hugo aside to tell him something, and Hagar changes the cups for two others which are harmless. Ferdinando, the 'minion', carries them away, and Hagar puts back the cup which holds the poison meant for Roderigo. Hugo, getting thirsty after a long warble, drinks it, loses his wits, and after a good deal of clutching and stamping, falls flat and dies; while Hagar informs him what she has done in a song of exquisite power and melody.

This was a truly thrilling scene; though some persons might have thought that the sudden tumbling down of a quantity of long hair rather marred the effect of the villain's death. He was called before the curtain, and with great propriety appeared leading Hagar, whose singing was considered more wonderful than all the rest of the performance put together.

Act fourth displayed the despairing Roderigo on the point of stabbing himself, because he has been told that Zara has deserted him. Just as the dagger is at his heart, a lovely song is

25

sung under his window, informing him that Zara is true, but in danger, and he can save her if he will. A key is thrown in, which unlocks the door, and in a spasm of rapture he tears off his chains, and rushes away to find and rescue his lady-love.

Act fifth opened with a stormy scene between Zara and Don Pedro. He wishes her to go into a convent, but she won't hear of it; and, after a touching appeal, is about to faint, when Roderigo dashes in and demands her hand. Don Pedro refuses, because he is not rich. They shout and gesticulate tremendously, but cannot agree, and Roderigo is about to bear away the exhausted Zara, when the timid servant enters with a letter and a bag from Hagar, who has mysteriously disappeared. The latter informs the party that she bequeaths untold wealth to the young pair, and an awful doom to Don Pedro if he doesn't make them happy. The bag is opened and several quarts of tin money shower down upon the stage, till it is quite glorified with the glitter. This entirely softens the 'stern sire'; he consents without a murmur, all join in a joyful chorus and the curtain falls upon the lovers kneeling to receive Don Pedro's blessing, in attitudes of the most romantic grace.

Tumultuous applause followed, but received an unexpected check; for the cot-bed on which the 'dress circle' was built, suddenly shut up, and extinguished the enthusiastic audience. Roderigo and Don Pedro flew to the rescue, and all were taken out unhurt, though many were speechless with laughter. The excitement had hardly subsided when Hannah appeared, with 'Mrs March's compliments, and would the ladies walk down to supper.'

This was a surprise, even to the actors; and when they saw the table they looked at one another in rapturous amazement.

It was like 'Marmee' to get up a little treat for them, but anything so fine as this was unheard of since the departed days of plenty. There was ice cream, actually two dishes of it,—pink and white,—and cake, and fruit, and distracting French bonbons, and in the middle of the table four great bouquets of hot-house flowers!

It quite took their breath away; and they stared first at the table and then at their mother, who looked as if she enjoyed it immensely.

'Is it fairies?' asked Amy.

'It's Santa Claus,' said Beth.

'Mother did it;' and Meg smiled her sweetest, in spite of her gray beard and white eyebrows.

'Aunt March had a good fit, and sent the supper,' cried Jo, with a sudden inspiration.

'All wrong; old Mr Laurence sent it,' replied Mrs March.

'The Laurence boy's grandfather! What in the world put such a thing into his head? We don't know him,' exclaimed Meg.

'Hannah told one of his servants about your breakfast party; he is an odd old gentleman, but that pleased him. He knew my father, years ago, and he sent me a polite note this afternoon, saying he hoped I would allow him to express his friendly feeling toward my children by sending them a few trifles in honor of the day. I could not refuse, and so you have a little feast at night to make up for the bread and milk breakfast.'

'That boy put it into his head, I know he did! He's a capital fellow, and I wish we could get acquainted. He looks as if he'd like to know us; but he's bashful, and Meg is so prim she won't let me speak to him when we pass,' said Jo as the plates went round, and the ice began to melt out of sight, with ohs! and ahs! of satisfaction.

'You mean the people who live in the big house next door, don't you?' asked one of the girls. 'My mother knows old Mr Laurence, but says he's very proud, and don't like to mix with his neighbors. He keeps his grandson shut up when he isn't riding or walking with his tutor, and makes him study dreadful hard. We invited him to our party, but he didn't come. Mother says he's very nice, though he never speaks to us girls.'

'Our cat ran away once, and he brought her back, and we talked over the fence, and were getting on capitally, all about cricket, and so on, when he saw Meg coming, and walked off. I mean to know him some day, for he needs fun, I'm sure he does,' said Jo, decidedly.

'I like his manners, and he looks like a little gentleman, so I've no objection to your knowing him if a proper opportunity comes. He brought the flowers himself, and I should have asked him in if I had been sure what was going on upstairs. He looked so wistful as he went away, hearing the frolic, and evidently having none of his own.'

'It's a mercy you didn't, mother,' laughed Jo, looking at her boots. 'But we'll have another play some time, that he *can* see. Maybe he'll help act; wouldn't that be jolly?'

'I never had a bouquet before; how pretty it is,' and Meg examined her flowers with great interest.

'They *are* lovely, but Beth's roses are sweeter to me,' said Mrs March, sniffing at the half dead posy in her belt.

Beth nestled up to her, and whispered, softly, 'I wish I could send my bunch to father. I'm afraid he isn't having such a merry Christmas as we are.'

CHAPTER THREE

———— •• ————

The Laurence Boy

'Jo! Jo! where are you?' cried Meg, at the foot of the garret stairs.

'Here,' answered a husky voice from above; and running up, Meg found her sister eating apples and crying over the *Heir of Redcliffe*, wrapped up in a comforter on an old three-legged sofa by the sunny window. This was Jo's favorite refuge; and here she loved to retire with half a dozen russets and a nice book, to enjoy the quiet and the society of a pet rat who lived near by, and didn't mind her a particle. As Meg appeared, Scrabble whisked into his hole. Jo shook the tears off her cheeks, and waited to hear the news.

'Such fun! only see! a regular note of invitation from Mrs Gardiner for to-morrow night!' cried Meg, waving the precious paper, and then proceeding to read it, with girlish delight.

'"Mrs Gardiner would be happy to see Miss March and Miss Josephine at a little dance on New-Year's-Eve." Marmee is willing we should go; now what *shall* we wear?'

'What's the use of asking that, when you know we shall wear our poplins, because we haven't got anything else,' answered Jo, with her mouth full.

'If I only had a silk!' sighed Meg; 'mother says I may when I'm eighteen, perhaps; but two years is an everlasting time to wait.'

'I'm sure our pops look like silk, and they are nice enough for us. Yours is as good as new, but I forgot the burn and the tear in mine; whatever shall I do? the burn shows horridly, and I can't take any out.'

'You must sit still all you can, and keep your back out of sight; the front is all right. I shall have a new ribbon for my hair, and Marmee will lend me her little pearl pin, and my new slippers are lovely, and my gloves will do, though they aren't as nice as I'd like.'

'Mine are spoilt with lemonade, and I can't get any new ones, so I shall have to go without,' said Jo, who never troubled herself much about dress.

'You *must* have gloves, or I won't go,' cried Meg, decidedly. 'Gloves are more important than anything else; you can't dance without them, and if you don't I should be *so* mortified.'

'Then I'll stay still; I don't care much for company dancing; it's no fun to go sailing round, I like to fly about and cut capers.'

'You can't ask mother for new ones, they are so expensive, and you are so careless. She said, when you spoilt the others, that she shouldn't get you any more this winter. Can't you fix them any way?' asked Meg, anxiously.

'I can hold them crunched up in my hand, so no one will know how stained they are; that's all I can do. No! I'll tell you how we can manage—each wear one good one and carry a bad one; don't you see?'

'Your hands are bigger than mine, and you will stretch my glove dreadfully,' began Meg, whose gloves were a tender point with her.

'Then I'll go without. I don't care what people say,' cried Jo, taking up her book.

'You may have it, you may! only don't stain it, and do behave nicely; don't put your hands behind you, or stare, or say "Christopher Columbus!" will you?'

'Don't worry about me; I'll be as prim as a dish, and not get into any scrapes, if I can help it. Now go and answer your note, and let me finish this splendid story.'

So Meg went away to 'accept with thanks', look over her dress, and sing blithely as she did up her one real lace frill; while Jo finished her story, her four apples, and had a game of romps with Scrabble.

On New-Year's-Eve the parlor was deserted, for the two younger girls played dressing maids, and the two elder were absorbed in the all-important business of 'getting ready for the party'. Simple as the toilets were, there was a great deal of running up and down, laughing and talking, and at one time a strong smell of burnt hair pervaded the house. Meg wanted a few curls about her face, and Jo undertook to pinch the papered locks with a pair of hot tongs.

'Ought they to smoke like that?' asked Beth, from her perch on the bed.

'It's the dampness drying,' replied Jo.

'What a queer smell! it's like burnt feathers,' observed Amy, smoothing her own pretty curls with a superior air.

31

'There, now I'll take off the papers and you'll see a cloud of little ringlets,' said Jo, putting down the tongs.

She did take off the papers, but no cloud of ringlets appeared, for the hair came with the papers, and the horrified hair-dresser laid a row of little scorched bundles on the bureau before her victim.

'Oh, oh, oh! what *have* you done? I'm spoilt! I can't go! my hair, oh my hair!' wailed Meg, looking with despair at the uneven frizzle on her forehead.

'Just my luck! you shouldn't have asked me to do it; I always spoil everything. I'm no end sorry, but the tongs were too hot, and so I've made a mess,' groaned poor Jo, regarding the black pancakes with tears of regret.

'It isn't spoilt; just frizzle it, and tie your ribbon so the ends come on your forehead a bit, and it will look like the last fashion. I've seen lots of girls do it so,' said Amy, consolingly.

'Serves me right for trying to be fine. I wish I'd let my hair alone,' cried Meg, petulantly.

'So do I, it was so smooth and pretty. But it will soon grow out again,' said Beth, coming to kiss and comfort the shorn sheep.

After various lesser mishaps, Meg was finished at last, and by the united exertions of the family Jo's hair was got up, and her dress on. They looked very well in their simple suits, Meg in silvery drab, with a blue velvet snood, lace frills, and the pearl pin; Jo in maroon, with a stiff, gentlemanly linen collar, and a white chrysanthemum or two for her only ornament. Each put on one nice light glove, and carried one soiled one, and all pronounced the effect 'quite easy and nice'. Meg's high-heeled slippers were dreadfully tight, and hurt her, though she would not own it, and Jo's nineteen hair-pins all seemed stuck straight into her head, which was not exactly comfortable; but, dear me, let us be elegant or die.

'Have a good time, dearies,' said Mrs March, as the sisters went daintily down the walk. 'Don't eat much supper, and come away at eleven, when I send Hannah for you.' As the gate clashed behind them, a voice cried from a window,—

'Girls, girls! *have* you both got nice pocket-handkerchiefs?'

'Yes, yes, spandy nice, and Meg has Cologne on hers,' cried Jo, adding, with a laugh, as they went on, 'I do believe Marmee would ask that if we were all running away from an earthquake.'

'It is one of her aristocratic tastes, and quite proper, for a real lady is always known by neat boots, gloves, and handkerchief,' replied Meg, who had a good many little 'aristocratic tastes' of her own.

'Now don't forget to keep the bad breadth out of sight, Jo. Is my sash right; and does my hair look *very* bad?' said Meg, as she turned from the glass in Mrs Gardiner's dressing-room, after a prolonged prink.

'I know I shall forget. If you see me doing anything wrong, you just remind me by a wink, will you?' returned Jo, giving her collar a twitch and her head a hasty brush.

'No, winking isn't lady-like; I'll lift my eyebrows if anything is wrong, and nod if you are all right. Now hold your shoulders straight, and take short steps, and don't shake hands if you are introduced to any one, it isn't the thing.'

'How *do* you learn all the proper quirks? I never can. Isn't that music gay?'

Down they went, feeling a trifle timid, for they seldom went to parties, and, informal as this little gathering was, it was an event to them. Mrs Gardiner, a stately old lady, greeted them kindly, and handed them over to the eldest of her six daughters. Meg knew Sallie, and was at her ease very soon; but Jo, who didn't care much for girls or girlish gossip, stood about with her back carefully against the wall, and felt as much out of place as a colt in a flower-garden. Half a dozen jovial lads were talking about skates in another part of the room, and she longed to go and join them, for skating was one of the joys of her life. She telegraphed her wish to Meg, but the eyebrows went up so alarmingly that she dared not stir. No one came to talk to her, and one by one the group near her dwindled away, till she was left alone. She could not roam about and amuse herself, for the burnt breadth would show, so she stared at people rather forlornly till the dancing began. Meg was asked at once, and the tight slippers tripped about so briskly that none would have guessed the pain their wearer suffered smilingly. Jo saw a big redheaded youth approaching her corner, and fearing he meant to engage her, she slipped into a curtained recess, intending to peep and enjoy herself in peace. Unfortunately, another bashful person had chosen the same refuge; for, as the curtain fell behind her, she found herself face to face with the 'Laurence boy'.

'Dear me, I didn't know any one was here!' stammered Jo, preparing to back out as speedily as she had bounced in.

But the boy laughed, and said, pleasantly, though he looked a little startled,—

'Don't mind me; stay, if you like.'

'Shan't I disturb you?'

'Not a bit; I only came here because I don't know many people, and felt rather strange at first, you know.'

'So did I. Don't go away, please, unless you'd rather.'

The boy sat down again and looked at his boots, till Jo said, trying to be polite and easy,—

'I think I've had the pleasure of seeing you before; you live near us, don't you?'

'Next door;' and he looked up and laughed outright, for Jo's prim manner was rather funny when he remembered how they had chatted about cricket when he brought the cat home.

That put Jo at her ease; and she laughed too, as she said, in her heartiest way,—

'We did have such a good time over your nice Christmas present.'

'Grandpa sent it.'

'But you put it into his head, didn't you, now?'

'How is your cat, Miss March?' asked the boy, trying to look sober, while his black eyes shone with fun.

'Nicely, thank you, Mr Laurence; but I ain't Miss March, I'm only Jo,' returned the young lady.

'I'm not Mr Laurence, I'm only Laurie.'

'Laurie Laurence; what an odd name.'

'My first name is Theodore, but I don't like it, for the fellows called me Dora, so I made them say Laurie instead.'

'I hate my name, too—so sentimental! I wish every one would say Jo, instead of Josephine. How did you make the boys stop calling you Dora?'

'I thrashed 'em.'

'I can't thrash Aunt March, so I suppose I shall have to bear it;' and Jo resigned herself with a sigh.

'Don't you like to dance, Miss Jo?' asked Laurie, looking as if he thought the name suited her.

'I like it well enough if there is plenty of room, and every one is lively. In a place like this I'm sure to upset something, tread on people's toes, or do something dreadful, so I keep out of mischief and let Meg do the pretty. Don't you dance?'

'Sometimes; you see I've been abroad a good many years and haven't been about enough yet to know how you do things here.'

'Abroad!' cried Jo, 'oh, tell me about it! I love dearly to hear people describe their travels.'

Laurie didn't seem to know where to begin; but Jo's eager questions soon set him going, and he told her how he had been at school in Vevey, where the boys never wore hats, and had a fleet of boats on the lake, and for holiday fun went on walking trips about Switzerland with their teachers.

'Don't I wish I'd been there!' cried Jo. 'Did you go to Paris?'

'We spent last winter there.'

'Can you talk French?'

'We were not allowed to speak anything else at Vevey.'

'Do say some. I can read it, but can't pronounce.'

'*Quel nom a cette jeune demoiselle en les pantoufles jolis?*' said Laurie, good-naturedly.

'How nicely you do it! Let me see—you said, "Who is the young lady in the pretty slippers", didn't you?'

'*Oui, mademoiselle.*'

'It's my sister Margaret, and you knew it was! Do you think she is pretty?'

'Yes; she makes me think of the German girls, she looks so fresh and quiet, and dances like a lady.'

Jo quite glowed with pleasure at this boyish praise of her sister, and stored it up to repeat to Meg. Both peeped, and criticized, and chatted, till they felt like old acquaintances. Laurie's bashfulness soon wore off, for Jo's gentlemanly demeanor amused and set him at his ease, and Jo was her merry self again, because her dress was forgotten, and nobody lifted their eyebrows at her. She liked the 'Laurence boy' better than ever, and took several good looks at him, so that she might describe him to the girls; for they had no brothers, very few male cousins, and boys were almost unknown creatures to them.

Curly black hair, brown skin, big black eyes, long nose, nice teeth, little hands and feet, tall as I am; very polite for a boy, and altogether jolly. Wonder how old he is?

It was on the tip of Jo's tongue to ask; but she checked herself in time, and, with unusual tact, tried to find out in a roundabout way.

'I suppose you are going to college soon? I see you pegging away at your books——no, I mean studying hard;' and Jo blushed at the dreadful 'pegging' which had escaped her.

Laurie smiled, but didn't seem shocked, and answered, with a shrug,——

'Not for two or three years yet; I won't go before seventeen any-way.'

'Aren't you but fifteen?' asked Jo, looking at the tall lad, whom she had imagined seventeen already.

'Sixteen, next month.'

'How I wish I was going to college; you don't look as if you liked it.'

'I hate it! nothing but grinding or sky-larking; and I don't like the way fellows do either, in this country.'

'What do you like?'

'To live in Italy, and to enjoy myself in my own way.'

Jo wanted very much to ask what his own way was; but his black brows looked rather threatening as he knit them, so she changed the subject by saying, as her foot kept time, 'That's a splendid polka; why don't you go and try it?'

'If you will come too,' he answered, with a queer little French bow.

'I can't; for I told Meg I wouldn't, because—' there Jo stopped, and looked undecided whether to tell or to laugh.

'Because what?' asked Laurie, curiously.

'You won't tell?'

'Never!'

'Well, I have a bad trick of standing before the fire, and so I burn my frocks, and I scorched this one; and, though it's nicely mended, it shows, and Meg told me to keep still, so no one would see it. You may laugh if you want to; it is funny, I know.'

But Laurie didn't laugh; he only looked down a minute, and the expression of his face puzzled Jo, when he said very gently,—

'Never mind that; I'll tell you how we can manage: there's a long hall out there, and we can dance grandly, and no one will see us. Please come.'

Jo thanked him, and gladly went, wishing she had two neat gloves, when she saw the nice pearl-colored ones her partner put on. The hall was empty, and they had a grand polka, for Laurie danced well, and taught her the German step, which delighted Jo, being full of swing and spring. When the music stopped they sat down on the stairs to get their breath, and Laurie was in the midst of an account of a students' festival at Heidelberg, when Meg appeared in search of her sister. She beckoned, and Jo reluctantly followed her into a side-room, where she found her on a sofa holding her foot, and looking pale.

'I've sprained my ankle. That stupid high heel turned, and gave me a horrid wrench. It aches so, I can hardly stand, and I don't know how I'm ever going to get home,' she said, rocking to and fro in pain.

'I knew you'd hurt your foot with those silly things. I'm sorry; but I don't see what you can do, except get a carriage, or stay here all night,' answered Jo, softly rubbing the poor ankle, as she spoke.

'I can't have a carriage without its costing ever so much; I dare say I can't get one at all, for most people come in their own, and it's a long way to the stable, and no one to send.'

'I'll go.'

'No, indeed; it's past ten, and dark as Egypt. I can't stop here, for the house is full; Sallie has some girls staying with her. I'll rest till Hannah comes, and then do the best I can.'

'I'll ask Laurie; he will go,' said Jo, looking relieved as the idea occurred to her.

'Mercy, no! don't ask or tell any one. Get me my rubbers, and put these slippers with our things. I can't dance any more; but as soon as supper is over, watch for Hannah, and tell me the minute she comes.'

'They are going out to supper now. I'll stay with you; I'd rather.'

'No, dear; run along, and bring me some coffee. I'm so tired, I can't stir.'

So Meg reclined, with the rubbers well hidden, and Jo went blundering away to the dining-room, which she found after going into a china-closet and opening the door of a room where old Mr Gardiner was taking a little private refreshment. Making a dive at the table, she secured the coffee, which she immediately spilt, thereby making the front of her dress as bad as the back.

'Oh dear! what a blunderbuss I am!' exclaimed Jo, finishing Meg's glove by scrubbing her gown with it.

'Can I help you?' said a friendly voice; and there was Laurie, with a full cup in one hand and a plate of ice in the other.

'I was trying to get something for Meg, who is very tired, and some one shook me, and here I am, in a nice state,' answered Jo, glancing, dismally, from the stained skirt to the coffee-colored glove.

'Too bad! I was looking for some one to give this to; may I take it to your sister?'

'Oh, thank you; I'll show you where she is. I don't offer to take it myself, for I should only get into another scrape if I did.'

Jo led the way; and, as if used to waiting on ladies, Laurie drew up a little table, brought a second instalment of coffee and ice for Jo, and was so obliging that even particular Meg pronounced him a 'nice boy'. They had a merry time over the bonbons and mottos, and were in the midst of a quiet game of 'buzz' with two or three other young people who had strayed in, when Hannah appeared. Meg forgot her foot, and rose so quickly that she was forced to catch hold of Jo, with an exclamation of pain.

'Hush! don't say anything,' she whispered; adding aloud, 'It's nothing; I turned my foot a little,—that's all,' and limped up stairs to put her things on.

Hannah scolded, Meg cried, and Jo was at her wits' end, till she decided to take things into her own hands. Slipping out, she ran down, and finding a servant, asked if he could get her a carriage. It happened to be a hired waiter, who knew nothing about the neighborhood; and Jo was looking round for help, when Laurie, who had heard what she did, came up and offered his grandfather's carriage, which had just come for him, he said.

'It's so early,—you can't mean to go yet,' began Jo, looking relieved, but hesitating to accept the offer.

'I always go early,—I do, truly. Please let me take you home; it's all on my way, you know, and it rains, they say.'

That settled it; and telling him of Meg's mishap, Jo gratefully accepted, and rushed up to bring down the rest of the party. Hannah hated rain as much as a cat does; so she made no trouble, and they rolled away in the luxurious close carriage, feeling very festive and elegant. Laurie went on the box, so Meg could keep her foot up, and the girls talked over their party in freedom.

'I had a capital time; did you?' asked Jo, rumpling up her hair, and making herself comfortable.

'Yes, till I hurt myself. Sallie's friend, Annie Moffat, took a fancy to me, and asked me to come and spend a week with her when Sallie does. She is going in the spring, when the opera comes, and it will be perfectly splendid if mother only lets me go,' answered Meg, cheering up at the thought.

'I saw you dancing with the red-headed man I ran away from; was he nice?'

'Oh, very! his hair is auburn, not red; and he was very polite, and I had a delicious *redowa* with him!'

'He looked like a grasshopper in a fit, when he did the new step. Laurie and I couldn't help laughing; did you hear us?'

'No, but it was very rude. What *were* you about all that time, hidden away there?'

Jo told her adventures, and by the time she had finished they were at home. With many thanks, they said 'Good-night', and crept in, hoping to disturb no one; but the instant their door creaked, two little night-caps bobbed up, and two sleepy but eager voices cried out,—

'Tell about the party! tell about the party!'

With what Meg called 'a great want of manners', Jo had saved some bonbons for the little girls, and they soon subsided, after hearing the most thrilling events of the evening.

'I declare, it really seems like being a fine young lady, to come home from my party in my carriage, and sit in my dressing-gown with a maid to wait on me,' said Meg, as Jo bound up her foot with arnica, and brushed her hair.

'I don't believe fine young ladies enjoy themselves a bit more than we do, in spite of our burnt hair, old gowns, one glove apiece, and tight slippers, that sprain our ankles when we are silly enough to wear them.' And I think Jo was quite right.

CHAPTER FOUR

—•—

Burdens

'Oh dear, how hard it does seem to take up our packs and go on,' sighed Meg, the morning after the party; for now the holidays were over, the week of merry-making did not fit her for going on easily with the task she never liked.

'I wish it was Christmas or New-Year all the time; wouldn't it be fun?' answered Jo, yawning dismally.

'We shouldn't enjoy ourselves half so much as we do now. But it does seem so nice to have little suppers and bouquets, and go to parties, and drive home in a carriage, and read and rest, and not grub. It's like other people, you know, and I always envy girls who do such things; I'm so fond of luxury,' said Meg, trying to decide which of two shabby gowns was the least shabby.

'Well, we can't have it, so don't let's grumble, but shoulder our bundles and trudge along as cheerfully as Marmee does. I'm sure Aunt March is a regular Old Man of the Sea to me, but I suppose when I've learned to carry her without complaining, she will tumble off, or get so light that I shan't mind her.'

This idea tickled Jo's fancy, and put her in good spirits; but Meg didn't brighten, for her burden, consisting of four spoilt children, seemed heavier than ever. She hadn't heart enough to make herself pretty, as usual, by putting on a blue neck-ribbon, and dressing her hair in the most becoming way.

'Where's the use of looking nice, when no one sees me but those cross midgets, and no one cares whether I'm pretty or not,' she muttered, shutting her drawer with a jerk. 'I shall have to toil and moil all my days, with only little bits of fun now and then, and get old and ugly and sour, because I'm poor, and can't enjoy my life as other girls do. It's a shame!'

So Meg went down, wearing an injured look, and wasn't at all agreeable at breakfast-time. Every one seemed rather out of sorts, and inclined to croak. Beth had a headache, and lay on the sofa trying to comfort herself with the cat and three kittens; Amy was fretting because her lessons were not learned, and she couldn't find her rubbers; Jo *would* whistle, and make a great racket getting ready; Mrs March was very busy trying to finish a letter, which must go at once; and Hannah had the grumps, for being up late didn't suit her.

'There never *was* such a cross family!' cried Jo, losing her temper when she had upset an inkstand, broken both boot-lacings, and sat down upon her hat.

'You're the crossest person in it!' returned Amy, washing out the sum, that was all wrong, with the tears that had fallen on her slate.

'Beth, if you don't keep these horrid cats down cellar I'll have them drowned,' exclaimed Meg, angrily, as she tried to get rid of the kitten, who had swarmed up her back, and stuck like a burr just out of reach.

Jo laughed, Meg scolded, Beth implored, and Amy wailed, because she couldn't remember how much nine times twelve was.

'Girls! girls! do be quiet one minute. I *must* get this off by the early mail, and you drive me distracted with your worry,' cried Mrs March, crossing out the third spoilt sentence in her letter.

There was a momentary lull, broken by Hannah, who bounced in, laid two hot turn-overs on the table, and bounced out again. These turn-overs were an institution; and the girls called them 'muffs', for they had no others, and found the hot pies very comforting to their hands on cold mornings. Hannah never forgot to make them, no matter how busy or grumpy she might be, for the walk was long and bleak; the poor things got no other lunch, and were seldom home before three.

'Cuddle your cats, and get over your headache, Bethy. Good-by, Marmee; we are a set of rascals this morning, but we'll come home regular angels. Now then, Meg,' and Jo tramped away, feeling that the pilgrims were not setting out as they ought to do.

They always looked back before turning the corner, for their mother was always at the window, to nod, and smile, and wave her hand to them. Somehow it seemed as if they couldn't have got through the day without that, for whatever their mood might be, the last glimpse of that motherly face was sure to affect them like sunshine.

'If Marmee shook her fist instead of kissing her hand to us, it would serve us right, for more ungrateful minxes than we are were never seen,' cried Jo, taking a remorseful satisfaction in the slushy road and bitter wind.

'Don't use such dreadful expressions,' said Meg, from the depths of the veil in which she had shrouded herself like a nun sick of the world.

'I like good, strong words, that mean something,' replied Jo, catching her hat as it took a leap off her head, preparatory to flying away altogether.

'Call yourself any names you like; but *I* am neither a rascal nor a minx, and I don't choose to be called so.'

'You're a blighted being, and decidedly cross today, because you can't sit in the lap of luxury all the time. Poor dear! just wait till I make my fortune, and you shall revel in carriages, and ice-cream, and high-heeled slippers, and posies, and red-headed boys to dance with.'

'How ridiculous you are, Jo!' but Meg laughed at the nonsense, and felt better in spite of herself.

'Lucky for you I am; for if I put on crushed airs, and tried to be dismal, as you do, we should be in a nice state. Thank goodness, I can always find something funny to keep me up. Don't croak any more, but come home jolly, there's a dear.'

Jo gave her sister an encouraging pat on the shoulder as they parted for the day, each going a different way, each hugging her little warm turn-over, and each trying to be cheerful in spite of wintry weather, hard work, and the unsatisfied desires of pleasure-loving youth.

When Mr March lost his property in trying to help an unfortunate friend, the two oldest girls begged to be allowed to do something toward their own support, at least.

Believing that they could not begin too early to cultivate energy, industry, and independence, their parents consented, and both fell to work with the hearty good-will which, in spite of all obstacles, is sure to succeed at last. Margaret found a place as nursery governess, and felt rich with her small salary. As she said, she *was* 'fond of luxury', and her chief trouble was poverty. She found it harder to bear than the others, because she could remember a time when home was beautiful, life full of ease and pleasure, and want of any kind unknown. She tried not to be envious or discontented, but it was very natural that the young girl should long for pretty things, gay friends, accomplishments, and a happy life. At the Kings' she daily saw all she wanted, for the children's older sisters were just out, and Meg caught frequent glimpses of dainty ball-dresses and bouquets, heard lively gossip about theatres, concerts, sleighing parties and merrymakings of all kinds, and saw money lavished on trifles which would have been so precious to her. Poor Meg seldom complained, but a sense of injustice made her feel bitter toward every one sometimes, for she had not yet learned to know how rich she was in the blessings which alone can make life happy.

Jo happened to suit Aunt March, who was lame, and needed an active person to wait upon her. The childless old lady had offered to adopt one of the girls when the troubles came, and was much offended because her offer was declined. Other friends told the Marches that they had lost all chance of being remembered in the rich old lady's will; but the unworldly Marches only said,—

'We can't give up our girls for a dozen fortunes. Rich or poor, we will keep together and be happy in one another.'

The old lady wouldn't speak to them for a time, but, happening to meet Jo at a friend's, something in her comical face and blunt manners struck the old lady's fancy, and she proposed to take her for a companion. This did not suit Jo at all; but she accepted the place, since nothing better appeared, and, to every one's surprise, got on remarkably well with her irascible relative. There was an occasional tempest, and once Jo had marched home, declaring she couldn't bear it any longer; but Aunt March always cleared up quickly, and sent for her back again with such urgency that she could not refuse, for in her heart she rather liked the peppery old lady.

I suspect that the real attraction was a large library of fine books, which was left to dust and spiders since Uncle March died. Jo remembered the kind old gentleman who used to let her build railroads and bridges with his big dictionaries, tell her stories about the queer pictures in his Latin books, and buy her cards of gingerbread whenever he met her in the street. The dim, dusty room, with the busts staring down from the tall book-cases, the cosy chairs, the globes, and, best of all, the wilderness of books, in which she could wander where she liked, made the library a region of bliss to her. The moment Aunt March took her nap, or was busy with company, Jo hurried to this quiet place, and, curling herself up in the big chair, devoured poetry, romance, history, travels, and pictures, like a regular book-worm. But, like all happiness, it did not last long; for as sure as she had just reached the heart of the story, the sweetest verse of the song, or the most perilous adventure of her traveller, a shrill voice called, 'Josy-phine! Josy-phine!' and she had to leave her paradise to wind yarn, wash the poodle, or read Belsham's Essays, by the hour together.

Jo's ambition was to do something very splendid; what it was she had no idea, but left it for time to tell her; and, meanwhile, found her greatest affliction in the fact that she couldn't read, run, and ride as much as she liked. A quick temper, sharp tongue, and restless spirit were always getting her into scrapes, and her life was a series of ups and downs, which were both comic and pathetic. But the training she received at Aunt March's was just what she needed; and the thought that she was doing something to support herself made her happy, in spite of the perpetual 'Josy-phine!'

Beth was too bashful to go to school; it had been tried, but she suffered so much that it was given up, and she did her lessons at home, with her father. Even when he went away, and her mother was called to devote her skill and energy to Soldiers' Aid Societies, Beth went faithfully on by herself, and did the best she could. She was a housewifely little creature, and helped Hannah keep home neat and comfortable for the workers, never thinking of any reward but to be loved. Long, quiet days she spent, not lonely nor idle, for her little world was peopled with imaginary friends, and she was by nature a busy bee. There were six dolls to be taken up and dressed every morning, for Beth was a child still, and loved her pets as well as ever; not one whole or handsome one among them; all were outcasts till Beth took them in; for, when her sisters outgrew these idols, they passed to her, because Amy would have nothing old or ugly. Beth cherished them all the more tenderly for that very reason, and set up a hospital for infirm dolls. No pins were ever stuck into their cotton vitals; no harsh words or blows were ever given them; no neglect ever saddened the heart of the most repulsive, but all were fed and clothed, nursed and caressed, with an affection which never failed. One forlorn fragment of *dollanity* had belonged to Jo; and, having led a tempestuous life, was left a wreck in the rag-bag, from which dreary poorhouse it was rescued by Beth, and taken to her refuge. Having no top to its head, she tied on a neat little cap, and, as both arms and legs were gone, she hid these deficiencies by folding it in a blanket, and devoting her best bed to this chronic invalid. If any one had known the care lavished on that dolly, I think it would have touched their hearts, even while they laughed. She brought it bits of bouquets; she read to it, took it out to breathe the air, hidden under her coat; she sung it lullabys, and never went to bed without kissing its dirty face, and whispering tenderly, 'I hope you'll have a good night, my poor dear.'

Beth had her troubles as well as the others; and not being an angel, but a very human little girl, she often 'wept a little weep', as Jo said, because she couldn't take music lessons and have a fine piano. She loved music so dearly, tried so hard to learn, and practised away so patiently at the jingling old instrument, that it did seem as if some one (not to hint Aunt March) ought to help her. Nobody did, however, and nobody saw Beth wipe the tears off the yellow keys, that wouldn't keep in tune, when she was all alone. She sung like a little lark about her work, never was too tired to play for Marmee and the girls, and day after day said hopefully to herself, 'I know I'll get my music some time, if I'm good.'

There are many Beths in the world, shy and quiet, sitting in corners till needed, and living for others so cheerfully, that no one sees the sacrifices till the little cricket on the hearth stops chirping, and the sweet, sunshiny presence vanishes, leaving silence and shadow behind.

If anybody had asked Amy what the greatest trial of her life was, she would have answered at once, 'My nose.' When she was a baby, Jo had accidentally dropped her into the coal-hod, and Amy insisted that the fall had ruined her nose for-ever. It was not big, nor red, like poor 'Petrea's'; it was only rather flat, and all the pinching in the world could not give it an aristocratic point. No one minded it but herself, and it was doing its best to grow, but Amy felt deeply the want of a Grecian nose, and drew whole sheets of handsome ones to console herself.

'Little Raphael', as her sisters called her, had a decided tal-ent for drawing, and was never so happy as when copying flowers, designing fairies, or illustrating stories with queer specimens of art. Her teachers complained that instead of doing her sums, she covered her slate with animals; the blank pages of her atlas were used to copy maps on, and caricatures of the most ludicrous description came fluttering out of all her books at unlucky moments. She got through her lessons as well as she could, and managed to escape reprimands by being a model of deportment. She was a great favorite with her mates, being good-tempered, and possessing the happy art of pleasing without effort. Her little airs and graces were much admired, so were her accomplishments; for beside her drawing, she could play twelve tunes, crochet, and read French without mispronouncing more than two-thirds of the words. She had a plaintive way of saying, 'When papa was rich we did so-and-so,' which was very touching; and her long words were considered 'perfectly elegant' by the girls.

Amy was in a fair way to be spoilt; for every one petted her, and her small vanities and selfishnesses were growing nicely. One thing, however, rather quenched the vanities; she had to wear her cousin's clothes. Now Florence's mamma hadn't a particle of taste, and Amy suffered deeply at having to wear a red instead of a blue bonnet, unbecoming gowns, and fussy aprons that did not fit. Everything was good, well made, and little worn; but Amy's artistic eyes were much afflicted, especially this winter, when her school dress was a dull purple, with yellow dots, and no trimming.

'My only comfort,' she said to Meg, with tears in her eyes, 'is, that mother don't take tucks in my dresses whenever I'm naughty, as Maria Parks' mother does. My dear, it's really dreadful; for sometimes she is so bad, her frock is up to her knees, and she can't come to school. When I think of this *deggerredation*, I feel that I can bear even my flat nose and purple gown, with yellow sky-rockets on it.'

Meg was Amy's confidant and monitor, and, by some strange attraction of opposites, Jo was gentle Beth's. To Jo alone did the shy child tell her thoughts; and over her big, harum-scarum sister, Beth unconsciously exercised more influence than any one in the family. The two older girls were a great deal to each other, but both took one of the younger into their keeping, and watched over them in their own way; 'playing mother' they called it, and put their sisters in the places of discarded dolls, with the maternal instinct of little women.

'Has anybody got anything to tell? It's been such a dismal day I'm really dying for some amusement,' said Meg, as they sat sewing together that evening.

'I had a queer time with aunt to-day, and, as I got the best of it, I'll tell you about it,' began Jo, who dearly loved to tell stories. 'I was reading that everlasting Belsham, and droning away as I always do, for aunt soon drops off, and then I take out some nice book, and read like fury, till she wakes up. I actually made myself sleepy; and, before she began to nod, I gave such a gape that she asked me what I meant by opening my mouth wide enough to take the whole book in at once.

'"I wish I could, and be done with it," said I, trying not to be saucy.

'Then she gave me a long lecture on my sins, and told me to sit and think them over while she just "lost" herself for a moment. She never finds herself very soon; so the minute her cap began to bob, like a top-heavy dahlia, I whipped the *Vicar of Wakefield* out of my pocket, and read away, with one eye on him, and one on aunt. I'd just got to where they all tumbled into the water, when I forgot, and laughed out loud. Aunt woke up; and, being more good-natured after her nap, told me to read a bit, and show what frivolous work I preferred to the worthy and instructive Belsham. I did my very best, and she liked it, though she only said,—

' "I don't understand what it's all about; go back and begin it, child."

'Back I went, and made the Primroses as interesting as ever I could. Once I was wicked enough to stop in a thrilling place, and say meekly, "I'm afraid it tires you, ma'am; shan't I stop now?"

'She caught up her knitting which had dropped out of her hands, gave me a sharp look through her specs, and said, in her short way,—

'"Finish the chapter, and don't be impertinent, miss."'

'Did she own she liked it?' asked Meg.

'Oh, bless you, no! but she let old Belsham rest; and, when I ran back after my gloves this afternoon, there she was, so hard at the Vicar, that she didn't hear me laugh as I danced a jig in the hall, because of the good time coming. What a pleasant life she might have, if she only chose. I don't envy her much, in spite of her money, for after all rich people have about as many worries as poor ones, I guess,' added Jo.

'That reminds me,' said Meg, 'that I've got something to tell. It isn't funny, like Jo's story, but I thought about it a good deal as I came home. At the Kings' to-day I found everybody in a flurry, and one of the children said that her oldest brother had done something dreadful, and papa had sent him away. I heard Mrs King crying, and Mr King talking very loud, and Grace and Ellen turned away their faces when they passed me, so I shouldn't see how red their eyes were. I didn't ask any questions, of course; but I felt so sorry for them, and was rather glad I hadn't any wild brothers to do wicked things, and disgrace the family.'

'I think being disgraced in school is a great deal try*inger* than anything bad boys can do,' said Amy, shaking her head, as if her experience of life had been a deep one. 'Susie Perkins came to school to-day with a lovely red carnelian ring; I wanted it dreadfully, and wished I was her with all my might. Well, she drew a picture of Mr Davis, with a monstrous nose and a hump, and the words, "Young ladies, my eye is upon you!" coming out of his mouth in a balloon thing. We were laughing over it, when all of a sudden his eye *was* on us, and he ordered Susie to bring up her slate. She was *parry*lized with fright, but she went, and oh, what *do* you think he did? He took her by the ear, the ear! just fancy how horrid! and led her to the recitation platform, and made her stand there half an hour, holding that slate so every one could see.'

'Didn't the girls shout at the picture?' asked Jo, who relished the scrape.

'Laugh! not a one; they sat as still as mice, and Susie cried quarts, I know she did. I didn't envy her then, for I felt that millions of carnelian rings wouldn't have made me happy after that. I never, never should have got over such a agonizing mortification;' and Amy went on with her work, in the proud consciousness of virtue, and the successful utterance of two long words in a breath.

'I saw something that I liked this morning, and I meant to tell it at dinner, but I forgot,' said Beth, putting Jo's topsy-turvy basket in order as she talked. 'When I went to get some oysters for Hannah, Mr Laurence was in the fish shop, but he didn't see me, for I kept behind a barrel, and he was busy with Mr Cutter, the fish-man. A poor woman came in with a pail and a mop, and asked Mr Cutter if he would let her do some scrubbing for a bit of fish, because she hadn't any dinner for her children, and had been disappointed of a day's work. Mr Cutter was in a hurry, and said "No," rather crossly; so she was going away, looking hungry and sorry, when Mr Laurence hooked up a big fish with the crooked end of his cane, and held it out to her. She was so glad and surprised she took it right in her arms, and thanked him over and over. He told her to "go along and cook it", and she hurried off, so happy! wasn't it nice of him? Oh, she did look so funny, hugging the big, slippery fish, and hoping Mr Laurence's bed in heaven would be "aisy".'

When they had laughed at Beth's story, they asked their mother for one; and, after a moment's thought, she said soberly,—

'As I sat cutting out blue flannel jackets to-day, at the rooms, I felt very anxious about father, and thought how lonely and helpless we should be if anything happened to him. It was not a wise thing to do, but I kept on worrying, till an old man came in with an order for some things. He sat down near me, and I began to talk to him, for he looked poor, and tired, and anxious.

'"Have you sons in the army?" I asked, for the note he brought was not to me.

'"Yes, ma'am; I had four, but two were killed; one is a prisoner, and I'm going to the other, who is very sick in a Washington hospital," he answered, quietly.

'"You have done a great deal for your country, sir," I said, feeling respect now, instead of pity.

'"Not a mite more than I ought, ma'am. I'd go myself, if I was any use; as I ain't, I give my boys, and give 'em free."

'He spoke so cheerfully, looked so sincere, and seemed so glad to give his all, that I was ashamed of myself. I'd given one man, and thought it too much, while he gave four, without grudging them; I had all my girls to comfort me at home, and his last son was waiting, miles away, to say "good-by" to him, perhaps. I felt so rich, so happy, thinking of my blessings, that I made him a nice bundle, gave him some money, and thanked him heartily for the lesson he had taught me.'

'Tell another story, mother; one with a moral to it, like this. I like to think about them afterwards, if they are real, and not too preachy,' said Jo, after a minute's silence.

Mrs March smiled, and began at once; for she had told stories to this little audience for many years, and knew how to please them.

'Once upon a time there were four girls, who had enough to eat, and drink, and wear; a good many comforts and pleasures, kind friends and parents, who loved them dearly, and yet they were not contented.' (Here the listeners stole sly looks at one another, and began to sew diligently.) 'These girls were anxious to be good, and made many excellent resolutions, but somehow they did not keep them very well, and were constantly saying, "If we only had this," or "if we could only do that," quite forgetting how much they already had, and how many pleasant things they actually could do; so they asked an old woman what spell they could use to make them happy, and she said, "When you feel discontented, think over your blessings, and be grateful."' (Here Jo looked up quickly, as if about to speak, but changed her mind, seeing that the story was not done yet.)

'Being sensible girls, they decided to try her advice, and soon were surprised to see how well off they were. One discovered that money couldn't keep shame and sorrow out of rich people's houses; another that though she was poor, she was a great deal happier with her youth, health, and good spirits, than a certain fretful, feeble old lady, who couldn't enjoy her comforts; a third, that, disagreeable as it was to help get dinner, it was harder still to have to go begging for it; and the fourth, that even carnelian rings were not so valuable as good behavior. So they agreed to stop complaining, to enjoy the blessings already possessed, and try to deserve them, lest they should be taken away entirely, instead of increased; and I believe they were never disappointed, or sorry that they took the old woman's advice.'

'Now, Marmee, that is very cunning of you to turn our own stories against us, and give us a sermon instead of a "spin",' cried Meg.

'I like that kind of sermon; it's the sort father used to tell us,' said Beth, thoughtfully, putting the needles straight on Jo's cushion.

'I don't complain near as much as the others do, and I shall be more careful than ever now, for I've had warning from Susie's downfall,' said Amy, morally.

'We needed that lesson, and we won't forget it. If we do, you just say to us as Old Chloe did in *Uncle Tom,*—"Tink ob yer marcies, chillen, tink ob yer marcies."' added Jo, who could not for the life of her help getting a morsel of fun out of the little sermon, though she took it to heart as much as any of them.

CHAPTER FIVE

— • —

Being Neighborly

'What in the world are you going to do now, Jo?' asked Meg, one snowy afternoon, as her sister came clumping through the hall, in rubber boots, old sack and hood, with a broom in one hand and a shovel in the other.

'Going out for exercise,' answered Jo, with a mischievous twinkle in her eyes.

'I should think two long walks, this morning, would have been enough. It's cold and dull out, and I advise you to stay, warm and dry, by the fire, as I do,' said Meg, with a shiver.

'Never take advice; can't keep still all day, and not being a pussycat, I don't like to doze by the fire. I like adventures, and I'm going to find some.'

Meg went back to toast her feet, and read *Ivanhoe*, and Jo began to dig paths with great energy. The snow was light; and with her broom she soon swept a path all round the garden, for Beth to walk in when the sun came out; and the invalid dolls needed air. Now the garden separated the Marches' house from that of Mr Laurence; both stood in a suburb of the city, which was still country-like, with groves and lawns, large gardens, and quiet streets. A low hedge parted the two estates. On one side was an old brown house, looking rather bare and shabby, robbed of the vines that in summer covered its walls, and the flowers which then surrounded it. On the other side was a stately stone mansion, plainly betokening every sort of comfort and luxury, from the big coach-house and well-kept grounds to the conservatory, and the glimpses of lovely things one caught between the rich curtains. Yet it seemed a lonely, lifeless sort of house; for no children frolicked on the lawn, no motherly face ever smiled at the windows, and few people went in and out, except the old gentleman and his grandson.

To Jo's lively fancy this fine house seemed a kind of enchanted palace, full of splendors and delights, which no one enjoyed. She had long wanted to behold these hidden glories, and to know the 'Laurence boy', who looked as if he would like to be known, if he only knew how to begin. Since the party she had been more eager than ever, and had planned many ways of making friends with him; but he had not been lately seen, and Jo began to think he had gone away, when she one day spied a brown face at an upper window, looking wistfully down into their garden, where Beth and Amy were snow-balling one another.

'That boy is suffering for society and fun,' she said to herself. 'His grandpa don't know what's good for him, and keeps him shut up all alone. He needs a lot of jolly boys to play with, or somebody young and lively. I've great mind to go over and tell the old gentleman so.'

The idea amused Jo, who liked to do daring things, and was always scandalizing Meg by her queer performances. The plan of 'going over' was not forgotten; and, when the snowy afternoon came, Jo resolved to try what could be done. She saw Mr Laurence drive off, and then sallied out to dig her way down to the hedge, where she paused, and took a survey. All quiet; curtains down at the lower windows; servants out of sight, and nothing human visible but a curly black head leaning on a thin hand, at the upper window.

'There he is,' thought Jo; 'poor boy! all alone, and sick, this dismal day! It's a shame! I'll toss up a snow-ball, and make him look out, and then say a kind word to him.'

Up went a handful of soft snow, and the head turned at once, showing a face which lost its listless look in a minute, as the big eyes brightened, and the mouth began to smile. Jo nodded, and laughed, and flourished her broom as she called out,—

'How do you do? Are you sick?'

Laurie opened the window and croaked out as hoarsely as a raven,—

'Better, thank you, I've had a horrid cold, and been shut up a week.'

'I'm sorry. What do you amuse yourself with?'

'Nothing; it's as dull as tombs up here.'

'Don't you read?'

'Not much; they won't let me.'

'Can't somebody read to you?'

'Grandpa does, sometimes; but my books don't interest him, and I hate to ask Brooke all the time.'

'Have some one come and see you, then.'

'There isn't any one I'd like to see. Boys make such a row, and my head is weak.'

'Isn't there some nice girl who'd read and amuse you? Girls are quiet, and like to play nurse.'

'Don't know any.'

'You know me,' began Jo, then laughed, and stopped.

'So I do! Will you come, please?' cried Laurie.

'I'm not quiet and nice; but I'll come, if mother will let me. I'll go ask her. Shut that window, like a good boy, and wait till I come.'

With that, Jo shouldered her broom and marched into the house, wondering what they would all say to her. Laurie was in a little flutter of excitement at the idea of having company, and flew about to get ready; for, as Mrs March said, he was 'a little gentleman', and did honor to the coming guest by brushing his curly pate, putting on a fresh collar, and trying to tidy up the room, which, in spite of half a dozen servants, was anything but neat. Presently, there came a loud ring, then a decided voice, asking for 'Mr Laurie', and a surprised-looking servant came running up to announce a young lady.

'All right, show her up, it's Miss Jo,' said Laurie, going to the door of his little parlor to meet Jo, who appeared, looking rosy and kind, and quite at her ease, with a covered dish in one hand, and Beth's three kittens in the other.

'Here I am, bag and baggage,' she said, briskly. 'Mother sent her love, and was glad if I could do anything for you. Meg wanted me to bring some of her blanc-mange; she makes it very nice, and Beth thought her cats would be comforting. I knew you'd shout at them, but I couldn't refuse, she was so anxious to do something.'

It so happened that Beth's funny loan was just the thing; for, in laughing over the kits, Laurie forgot his bashfulness, and grew sociable at once.

'That looks too pretty to eat,' he said, smiling with pleasure, as Jo uncovered the dish, and showed the blanc-mange, surrounded by a garland of green leaves, and the scarlet flowers of Amy's pet geranium.

'It isn't anything, only they all felt kindly, and wanted to show it. Tell the girl to put it away for your tea; it's so simple, you can eat it; and, being soft, it will slip down without hurting your sore throat. What a cosy room this is.'

'It might be, if it was kept nice; but the maids are lazy, and I don't know how to make them mind. It worries me, though.'

'I'll right it up in two minutes; for it only needs to have the hearth brushed, so, –and the things stood straight on the mantelpiece, so,—and the books put here, and the bottles there, and your sofa turned from the light, and the pillows plumped up a bit. Now, then, you're fixed.'

And so he was; for, as she laughed and talked, Jo had whisked things into place, and given quite a different air to the room. Laurie watched her in respectful silence; and, when she beckoned him to his sofa, he sat down with a sign of satisfaction, saying, gratefully,—

'How kind you are! Yes, that's what it wanted. Now please take the big chair, and let me do something to amuse my company.'

'No; I came to amuse you. Shall I read aloud?' and Jo looked affectionately toward some inviting books near by.

'Thank you; I've read all those, and if you don't mind, I'd rather talk,' answered Laurie.

'Not a bit; I'll talk all day if you'll only set me going. Beth says I never know when to stop.'

'Is Beth the rosy one, who stays at home a good deal, and sometimes goes out with a little basket?' asked Laurie, with interest.

'Yes, that's Beth; she's my girl, and a regular good one she is, too.'

'The pretty one is Meg, and the curly-haired one is Amy, I believe?'

'How did you find that out?'

Laurie colored up, but answered frankly, 'Why, you see, I often hear you calling to one another, and when I'm alone up here, I can't help looking over at your house, you always seem to be having such good times. I beg your pardon for being so rude, but sometimes you forget to put down the curtain at the window where the flowers are; and, when the lamps are lighted, it's like looking at a picture to see the fire, and you all round the table with your mother; her face is right opposite, and it looks so sweet behind the flowers, I can't help watching it. I haven't got any mother, you know;' and Laurie poked the fire to hide a little twitching of the lips that he could not control.

The solitary, hungry look in his eyes went straight to Jo's warm heart. She had been so simply taught that there was no nonsense in her head, and at fifteen she was as innocent and frank as any child. Laurie was sick and lonely; and, feeling how rich she was in home-love and happiness, she gladly tried to share it with him. Her brown face was very friendly, and her sharp voice unusually gentle, as she said,—

'We'll never draw that curtain any more, and I give you leave to look as much as you like. I just wish, though, instead of peeping, you'd come over and see us. Mother is so splendid, she'd do you heaps of good, and Beth would sing to you if *I* begged her to, and Amy would dance; Meg and I would make you laugh over our funny stage properties, and we'd have jolly times. Wouldn't your grandpa let you?'

'I think he would, if your mother asked him. He's very kind, though he don't look it; and he lets me do what I like, pretty much, only he's afraid I might be a bother to strangers,' began Laurie, brightening more and more.

'We ain't strangers, we are neighbors, and you needn't think you'd be a bother. We *want* to know you, and I've been trying to do it this ever so long. We haven't been here a great while, you know, but we have got acquainted with all our neighbors but you.'

'You see grandpa lives among his books, and don't mind much what happens outside. Mr Brooke, my tutor, don't stay here, you know, and I have no one to go round with me, so I just stop at home and get on as I can.'

'That's bad; you ought to make a dive, and go visiting everywhere you are asked; then you'll have lots of friends, and pleasant places to go to. Never mind being bashful, it won't last long if you keep going.'

Laurie turned red again, but wasn't offended at being accused of bashfulness; for there was so much good-will in Jo, it was impossible not to take her blunt speeches as kindly as they were meant.

'Do you like your school?' asked the boy, changing the subject, after a little pause, during which he stared at the fire, and Jo looked about her well pleased.

'Don't go to school; I'm a business man—girl, I mean. I go

65

to wait on my aunt, and a dear, cross old soul she is, too,'
answered Jo.

Laurie opened his mouth to ask another question; but remembering just in time that it wasn't manners to make too
many inquiries into people's affairs, he shut it again, and
looked uncomfortable. Jo liked his good breeding, and didn't
mind having a laugh at Aunt March, so she gave him a lively
description of the fidgety old lady, her fat poodle, the parrot
that talked Spanish, and the library where she revelled. Laurie
enjoyed that immensely; and when she told about the prim
old gentleman who came once to woo Aunt March, and, in
the middle of a fine speech, how Poll had tweaked his wig off
to his great dismay, the boy lay back and laughed till the tears
ran down his cheeks, and a maid popped her head in to see
what was the matter.

'Oh! that does me lots of good; tell on, please,' he said,
taking his face out of the sofa-cushion, red and shining with
merriment.

Much elated with her success, Jo did 'tell on', all about
their plays and plans, their hopes and fears for father, and the
most interesting events of the little world in which the sisters
lived. Then they got to talking about books; and to Jo's delight
she found that Laurie loved them as well as she did, and had
read even more than herself.

'If you like them so much, come down and see ours. Grandpa
is out, so you needn't be afraid,' said Laurie, getting up.

'I'm not afraid of anything,' returned Jo, with a toss of the
head.

'I don't believe you are!' exclaimed the boy, looking at her
with much admiration, though he privately thought she

would have good reason to be a trifle afraid of the old gentleman, if she met him in some of his moods.

The atmosphere of the whole house being summer-like, Laurie led the way from room to room, letting Jo stop to examine whatever struck her fancy; and so at last they came to the library, where she clapped her hands, and pranced, as she always did when especially delighted. It was lined with books, and there were pictures and statues, and distracting little cabinets full of coins and curiosities, and Sleepy-Hollow chairs, and queer tables, and bronzes; and, best of all, a great, open fireplace, with quaint tiles all around it.

'What richness!' sighed Jo, sinking into the depths of a velvet chair, and gazing about her with an air of intense satisfaction. 'Theodore Laurence, you ought to be the happiest boy in the world,' she added, impressively.

'A fellow can't live on books,' said Laurie, shaking his head, as he perched on a table opposite.

Before he could say more, a bell rung, and Jo flew up, exclaiming with alarm, 'Mercy me! it's your grandpa!'

'Well, what if it is? You are not afraid of anything, you know,' returned the boy, looking wicked.

'I think I am a little bit afraid of him, but I don't know why I should be. Marmee said I might come, and I don't think you're any the worse for it,' said Jo, composing herself, though she kept her eyes on the door.

'I'm a great deal better for it, and ever so much obliged. I'm only afraid you are very tired talking to me; it was *so* pleasant, I couldn't bear to stop,' said Laurie, gratefully.

'The doctor to see you, sir,' and the maid beckoned as she spoke.

'Would you mind if I left you for a minute? I suppose I must see him,' said Laurie.

'Don't mind me. I'm as happy as a cricket here,' answered Jo.

Laurie went away, and his guest amused herself in her own way. She was standing before a fine portrait of the old gentleman, when the door opened again, and, without turning, she said decidedly, 'I'm sure now that I shouldn't be afraid of him, for he's got kind eyes, though his mouth is grim, and he looks as if he had a tremendous will of his own. He isn't as handsome as *my* grandfather, but I like him.'

'Thank you, ma'am,' said a gruff voice behind her; and there, to her great dismay, stood old Mr Laurence.

Poor Jo blushed till she couldn't blush any redder, and her heart began to beat uncomfortably fast as she thought what she had said. For a minute a wild desire to run away possessed her; but that was cowardly, and the girls would laugh at her; so she resolved to stay, and get out of the scrape as she could. A second look showed her that the living eyes, under the bushy gray eyebrows, were kinder even than the painted ones; and there was a sly twinkle in them, which lessened her fear a good deal. The gruff voice was gruffer than ever, as the old gentleman said abruptly, after that dreadful pause, 'So, you're not afraid of me, hey?'

'Not much, sir.'

'And you don't think me as handsome as your grandfather?'

'Not quite, sir.'

'And I've got a tremendous will, have I?'

'I only said I thought so.'

'But you like me, in spite of it?'

'Yes, I do, sir.'

That answer pleased the old gentleman; he gave a short laugh, shook hands with her, and putting his finger under her chin, turned up her face, examined it gravely, and let it go, saying, with a nod, 'You've got your grandfather's spirit, if you haven't his face. He *was* a fine man, my dear; but, what is better, he was a brave and an honest one, and I was proud to be his friend.'

'Thank you, sir;' and Jo was quite comfortable after that, for it suited her exactly.

'What have you been doing to this boy of mine, hey?' was the next question, sharply put.

'Only trying to be neighborly, sir;' and Jo told how her visit came about.

'You think he needs cheering up a bit, do you?'

'Yes, sir; he seems a little lonely, and young folks would do him good, perhaps. We are only girls, but we should be glad to help if we could, for we don't forget the splendid Christmas present you sent us,' said Jo, eagerly.

'Tut, tut, tut; that was the boy's affair. How is the poor woman?'

'Doing nicely, sir;' and off went Jo, talking very fast, as she told all about the Hummels, in whom her mother had interested richer friends than they were.

'Just her father's way of doing good. I shall come and see your mother some fine day. Tell her so. There's the tea-bell; we have it early, on the boy's account. Come down, and go on being neighborly.'

'If you'd like to have me, sir.'

'Shouldn't ask you, if I didn't;' and Mr Laurence offered her his arm with old-fashioned courtesy.

'What *would* Meg say to this?' thought Jo, as she was marched away, while her eyes danced with fun as she imagined herself telling the story at home.

'Hey! why, what the dickens has come to the fellow?' said the old gentleman, as Laurie came running down stairs, and brought up with a start of surprise at the astonishing sight of Jo arm in arm with his redoubtable grandfather.

'I didn't know you'd come, sir,' he began, as Jo gave him a triumphant little glance.

'That's evident, by the way you racket down stairs. Come to your tea, sir, and behave like a gentleman;' and having pulled the boy's hair by way of a caress, Mr Laurence walked on, while Laurie went through a series of comic evolutions behind their backs, which nearly produced an explosion of laughter from Jo.

The old gentleman did not say much as he drank his four cups of tea, but he watched the young people, who soon chatted away like old friends, and the change in his grandson did not escape him. There was color, light and life in the boy's face now, vivacity in his manner, and genuine merriment in his laugh.

'She's right; the lad *is* lonely. I'll see what these little girls can do for him,' thought Mr Laurence, as he looked and listened. He liked Jo, for her odd, blunt ways suited him; and she seemed to understand the boy almost as well as if she had been one herself.

If the Laurences had been what Jo called 'prim and poky', she would not have got on at all, for such people always made her shy and awkward; but finding them free and easy, she was so herself, and made a good impression. When they rose she proposed to go, but Laurie said he had something more to show her, and took her away to the conservatory, which had been lighted for her benefit. It seemed quite fairy-like to Jo, as she went up and down the walks, enjoying the blooming walls on either side,—the soft light, the damp, sweet air, and the wonderful vines and trees that hung above her,—while her new friend cut the finest flowers till his hands were full; then he tied them up, saying, with the happy look Jo liked to see, 'Please give these to your mother, and tell her I like the medicine she sent me very much.'

They found Mr Laurence standing before the fire in the great drawing-room, but Jo's attention was entirely absorbed by a grand piano which stood open.

'Do you play?' she asked, turning to Laurie with a respectful expression.

'Sometimes,' he answered, modestly.

'Please do now; I want to hear it, so I can tell Beth.'

'Won't you first?'

'Don't know how; too stupid to learn, but I love music dearly.'

So Laurie played, and Jo listened, with her nose luxuriously buried in heliotrope and tea roses. Her respect and regard for the 'Laurence boy' increased very much, for he played remarkably well, and didn't put on any airs. She wished Beth could hear him, but she did not say so; only praised him till he was quite abashed, and his grandfather came to the rescue. 'That will do, that will do, young lady; too many sugar-plums are not good for him. His music isn't bad, but I hope he will do as well in more important things. Going? Well, I'm much obliged to you, and I hope you'll come again. My respects to your mother; good-night, Doctor Jo.'

He shook hands kindly, but looked as if something did not please him. When they got into the hall, Jo asked Laurie if she had said anything amiss; he shook his head.

'No, it was me; he don't like to hear me play.'

'Why not?'

'I'll tell you some day. John is going home with you, as I can't.'

'No need of that; I ain't a young lady, and it's only a step. Take care of yourself, won't you?'

'Yes, but you will come again, I hope?'

'If you promise to come and see us after you are well.'

'I will.'

'Good-night, Laurie.'

'Good-night, Jo, good-night.'

When all the afternoon's adventures had been told, the family felt inclined to go visiting in a body, for each found something very attractive in the big house on the other side of the hedge. Mrs March wanted to talk of her father with the old man who had not forgotten him; Meg longed to walk in the conservatory; Beth sighed for the grand piano, and Amy was eager to see the fine pictures and statues.

'Mother, why didn't Mr Laurence like to have Laurie play?' asked Jo, who was of an inquiring disposition.

'I'm not sure, but I think it was because his son, Laurie's father, married an Italian lady, a musician, which displeased the old man, who is very proud. The lady was good and lovely and accomplished, but he did not like her, and never saw his son after he married. They both died when Laurie was a little child, and then his grandfather took him home. I fancy the boy, who was born in Italy, is not very strong, and the old man is afraid of losing him, which makes him so careful. Laurie comes naturally by his love of music, for he is like his mother, and I dare say his "grandfather" fears that he may want to be a musician; at any rate, his skill reminds him of the woman he did not like, and so he "glowered", as Jo said.'

'Dear me, how romantic!' exclaimed Meg.

'How silly,' said Jo; 'let him be a musician, if he wants to, and not plague his life out sending him to college, when he hates to go.'

'That's why he has such handsome black eyes and pretty manners, I suppose; Italians are always nice,' said Meg, who was a little sentimental.

'What do you know about his eyes and his manners? you never spoke to him, hardly;' cried Jo, who was *not* sentimental.

'I saw him at the party, and what you tell shows that he knows how to behave. That was a nice little speech about the medicine mother sent him.'

'He meant the blanc-mange, I suppose.'

'How stupid you are, child; he meant you, of course.'

'Did he?' and Jo opened her eyes as if it had never occurred to her before.

'I never saw such a girl! You don't know a compliment when you get it,' said Meg, with the air of a young lady who knew all about the matter.

'I think they are great nonsense, and I'll thank you not to be silly, and spoil my fun. Laurie's a nice boy, and I like him, and I won't have any sentimental stuff about compliments and such rubbish. We'll all be good to him, because he hasn't got any mother, and he *may* come over and see us, mayn't he, Marmee?'

'Yes, Jo, your little friend is very welcome, and I hope Meg will remember that children should be children as long as they can.'

'I don't call myself a child, and I'm not in my teens yet,' observed Amy. 'What do you say, Beth?'

'I was thinking about our "Pilgrim's Progress",' answered Beth, who had not heard a word. 'How we got out of the Slough and through the Wicket Gate by resolving to be good, and up the steep hill, by trying; and that maybe the house over there, full of splendid things, is going to be our Palace Beautiful.'

'We have got to get by the lions, first,' said Jo, as if she rather liked the prospect.

CHAPTER SIX

Beth Finds the Palace Beautiful

The big house did prove a Palace Beautiful, though it took some time for all to get in, and Beth found it very hard to pass the lions. Old Mr Laurence was the biggest one; but, after he had called, said something funny or kind to each one of the girls, and talked over old times with their mother, nobody felt much afraid of him, except timid Beth. The other lion was the fact that they were poor and Laurie rich; for this made them shy of accepting favors which they could not return. But after a while they found that he considered them the benefactors, and could not do enough to show how grateful he was for Mrs March's motherly welcome, their cheerful society, and the comfort he took in that humble home of theirs; so they soon forgot their pride, and interchanged kindnesses without stopping to think which was the greater.

All sorts of pleasant things happened about that time, for the new friendship flourished like grass in spring. Every one liked Laurie, and he privately informed his tutor that 'the Marches were regularly splendid girls'. With the delightful enthusiasm of youth, they took the solitary boy into their midst, and made much of him, and he found something very charming in the innocent companionship of these simple-hearted girls. Never having known mother or sisters, he was quick to feel the influences they brought about him; and their busy, lively ways made him ashamed of the indolent life he led. He was tired of books, and found people so interesting now, that Mr Brooke was obliged to make very unsatisfactory reports; for Laurie was always playing truant, and running over to the Marches.

'Never mind, let him take a holiday, and make it up afterward,' said the old gentleman. 'The good lady next door says he is studying too hard, and needs young society, amusement, and exercise. I suspect she is right, and that I've been coddling the fellow as if I'd been his grandmother. Let him do what he likes, as long as he is happy; he can't get into mischief in that little nunnery over there, and Mrs March is doing more for him than we can.'

What good times they had, to be sure! Such plays and tableaux; such sleigh-rides and skating frolics; such pleasant evenings in the old parlor, and now and then such gay little parties at the great house. Meg could walk in the conservatory whenever she liked, and revel in bouquets; Jo browsed over the new library voraciously, and convulsed the old gentleman with her criticisms; Amy copied pictures and enjoyed beauty to her heart's content, and Laurie played lord of the manor in the most delightful style.

But Beth, though yearning for the grand piano, could not

pluck up courage to go to the 'mansion of bliss', as Meg called it. She went once with Jo, but the old gentleman, not being aware of her infirmity, stared at her so hard from under his heavy eyebrows, and said 'hey!' so loud, that he frightened her so much her 'feet chattered on the floor', she told her mother; and she ran away, declaring she would never go there any more, not even for the dear piano. No persuasions or entice-ments could overcome her fear, till the fact coming to Mr Laurence's ear in some mysterious way, he set about mending matters. During one of the brief calls he made, he artfully led the conversation to music, and talked away about great singers whom he had seen, fine organs he had heard, and told such charming anecdotes, that Beth found it impossible to stay in her distant corner, but crept nearer and nearer, as if fascinated. At the back of his chair she stopped, and stood listening with her great eyes wide open, and her cheeks red with the excite-ment of this unusual performance. Taking no more notice of her than if she had been a fly, Mr Laurence talked on about Laurie's lessons and teachers; and presently, as if the idea had just occurred to him, he said to Mrs March,—

'The boy neglects his music now, and I'm glad of it, for he was getting too fond of it. But the piano suffers for want of use; wouldn't some of your girls like to run over, and practice on it now and then, just to keep it in tune, you know, ma'am?'

Beth took a step forward, and pressed her hands tightly together, to keep from clapping them, for this was an irre-sistible temptation; and the thought of practising on that splendid instrument quite took her breath away. Before Mrs March could reply, Mr Laurence went on with an odd little nod and smile,—

'They needn't see or speak to any one, but run in at any time, for I'm shut up in my study at the other end of the house. Laurie is out a great deal, and the servants are never near the drawing-room after nine o'clock.' Here he rose, as if going, and Beth made up her mind to speak, for that last arrangement left nothing to be desired. 'Please tell the young ladies what I say, and if they don't care to come, why, never mind;' here a little hand slipped into his, and Beth looked up at him with a face full of gratitude, as she said, in her earnest, yet timid way,—

'Oh, sir! they do care, very, very much!'

'Are you the musical girl?' he asked, without any startling 'hey!' as he looked down at her very kindly.

'I'm Beth; I love it dearly, and I'll come if you are quite sure nobody will hear me—and be disturbed,' she added, fearing to be rude, and trembling at her own boldness as she spoke.

'Not a soul, my dear; the house is empty half the day, so come and drum away as much as you like, and I shall be obliged to you.'

'How kind you are, sir.'

Beth blushed like a rose under the friendly look he wore, but she was not frightened now, and gave the big hand a grateful squeeze, because she had no words to thank him for the precious gift he had given her. The old gentleman softly stroked the hair off her forehead, and, stooping down, he kissed her, saying, in a tone few people ever heard,—

'I had a little girl once with eyes like these; God bless you, my dear; good-day, madam,' and away he went, in a great hurry.

Beth had a rapture with her mother, and then rushed up to impart the glorious news to her family of invalids, as the girls were not at home. How blithely she sung that evening, and how they all laughed at her, because she woke Amy in the night, by playing the piano on her face in her sleep. Next day, having seen both the old and young gentleman out of the house, Beth, after two or three retreats, fairly got in at the side-door, and made her way as noiselessly as any mouse to the drawing-room, where her idol stood. Quite by accident, of course, some pretty, easy music lay on the piano; and, with trembling fingers, and frequent stops to listen and look about, Beth at last touched the great instrument, and straightway forgot her fear, herself, and everything else but the unspeakable delight which the music gave her, for it was like the voice of a beloved friend.

She stayed till Hannah came to take her home to dinner; but she had no appetite, and could only sit and smile upon every one in a general state of beatitude.

After that, the little brown hood slipped through the hedge nearly every day, and the great drawing-room was haunted by a tuneful spirit that came and went unseen. She never knew that Mr Laurence often opened his study door to hear the old-fashioned airs he liked; she never saw Laurie mount guard in the hall, to warn the servants away; she never suspected that the exercise-books and new songs which she found in the rack were put there for her especial benefit; and when he talked to her about music at home, she only thought how kind he was to tell things that helped her so much. So she enjoyed herself heartily, and found, what isn't always the case, that her granted wish was all she had hoped. Perhaps it was because she was so grateful for this blessing that a greater was given her; at any rate, she deserved both.

'Mother, I'm going to work Mr Laurence a pair of slippers. He is so kind to me I must thank him, and I don't know any other way. Can I do it?' asked Beth, a few weeks after that eventful call of his.

'Yes, dear; it will please him very much, and be a nice way of thanking him. The girls will help you about them, and I will pay for the making up,' replied Mrs March, who took peculiar pleasure in granting Beth's requests, because she so seldom asked anything for herself.

After many serious discussions with Meg and Jo, the pattern was chosen, the materials bought, and the slippers begun. A cluster of grave yet cheerful pansies, on a deeper purple ground, was pronounced very appropriate and pretty, and Beth worked away early and late, with occasional lifts over hard parts. She was a nimble little needle-woman, and they were finished before any one got tired of them. Then she wrote a very short, simple note, and, with Laurie's help, got them smuggled on to the study-table one morning before the old gentleman was up.

When this excitement was over, Beth waited to see what would happen. All that day passed, and a part of the next, before any acknowledgment arrived, and she was beginning to fear she had offended her crotchety friend. On the afternoon of the second day she went out to do an errand, and give poor Joanna, the invalid doll, her daily exercise. As she came up the street on her return she saw three—yes, four heads popping in and out of the parlor windows; and the moment they saw her several hands were waved, and several joyful voices screamed,—

'Here's a letter from the old gentleman; come quick, and read it!'

'Oh, Beth! he's sent you—' began Amy, gesticulating with unseemly energy; but she got no further, for Jo quenched her by slamming down the window.

Beth hurried on in a twitter of suspense; at the door her sisters seized and bore her to the parlor in a triumphal procession, all pointing, and all saying at once, 'Look there! look there!' Beth did look, and turned pale with delight and surprise; for there stood a little cabinet piano, with a letter lying on the glossy lid, directed like a sign-board, to 'Miss Elizabeth March'.

'For me?' gasped Beth, holding on to Jo, and feeling as if she should tumble down, it was such an overwhelming thing altogether.

'Yes; all for you, my precious! Isn't it splendid of him? Don't you think he's the dearest old man in the world? Here's the key in the letter; we didn't open it, but we are dying to know what he says,' cried Jo, hugging her sister, and offering the note.

'You read it; I can't, I feel so queer. Oh, it is too lovely!' and Beth hid her face in Jo's apron, quite upset by her present.

Jo opened the paper, and began to laugh, for the first words she saw were:—

'Miss March:
'*Dear Madam*—'

'How nice it sounds! I wish someone would write to me so!' said Amy, who thought the old-fashioned address very elegant.

'"I have had many pairs of slippers in my life, but I never had any that suited me so well as yours,"'

continued Jo.

'"Heart's-ease is my favorite flower, and these will always remind me of the gentle giver. I like to pay my debts, so I know you will allow 'the old gentleman' to send you something which once belonged to the little granddaughter he lost. With hearty thanks, and best wishes, I remain,

'"Your grateful friend and humble servant,

'"James Laurence."'

'There, Beth, that's an honor to be proud of, I'm sure! Laurie told me how fond Mr Laurence used to be of the child who died, and how he kept all her little things carefully. Just think; he's given you her piano! That comes of having big blue eyes and loving music,' said Jo, trying to soothe Beth, who trembled, and looked more excited than she had ever been before.

'See the cunning brackets to hold candles, and the nice green silk, puckered up with a gold rose in the middle, and the pretty rack and stool, all complete,' added Meg, opening the instrument, and displaying its beauties.

' "Your humble servant, James Laurence"; only think of his writing that to you. I'll tell the girls; they'll think it's killing,' said Amy, much impressed by the note.

'Try it, honey; let's hear the sound of the baby pianny,' said Hannah, who always took a share in the family joys and sorrows.

So Beth tried it, and every one pronounced it the most remarkable piano ever heard. It had evidently been newly tuned, and put in apple-pie order; but, perfect as it was, I think the real charm of it lay in the happiest of all happy faces which leaned over it, as Beth lovingly touched the beautiful black and white keys, and pressed the shiny pedals.

'You'll have to go and thank him,' said Jo, by way of a joke; for the idea of the child's really going, never entered her head.

'Yes, I mean to; I guess I'll go now, before I get frightened thinking about it;' and, to the utter amazement of the assembled family, Beth walked deliberately down the garden, through the hedge, and in at the Laurences' door.

'Well, I wish I may die, if it ain't the queerest thing I ever see! The pianny has turned her head; she'd never have gone, in her right mind,' cried Hannah, staring after her, while the girls were rendered quite speechless by the miracle.

They would have been still more amazed, if they had seen what Beth did afterward. If you will believe me, she went and knocked at the study door, before she gave herself time to think; and when a gruff voice called out, 'Come in!' she did go in, right up to Mr Laurence, who looked quite taken aback, and held out her hand, saying, with only a small quaver in her voice, 'I came to thank you, sir, for—' but she didn't finish, for he looked so friendly that she forgot her speech; and, only remembering that he had lost the little girl he loved, she put both arms round his neck, and kissed him.

If the roof of the house had suddenly flown off, the old gentleman wouldn't have been more astonished; but he liked it—oh dear, yes! he liked it amazingly; and was so touched and pleased by that confiding little kiss, that all his crustiness vanished; and he just set her on his knee, and laid his wrinkled cheek against her rosy one, feeling as if he had got his own little granddaughter back again. Beth ceased to fear him from that moment, and sat there talking to him as cosily as if she had known him all her life; for love casts out fear, and gratitude can conquer pride. When she went home, he walked with her to her own gate, shook hands cordially, and touched his hat as he marched back again, looking very stately and erect, like a handsome, soldierly old gentleman, as he was.

When the girls saw that performance, Jo began to dance a jig, by way of expressing her satisfaction; Amy nearly fell out of the window in her surprise, and Meg exclaimed, with up-lifted hands, 'Well, I do believe the world is coming to an end!'

CHAPTER SEVEN

Amy's Valley of Humiliation

'That boy is a perfect Cyclops, isn't he?' said Amy, one day, as Laurie clattered by on horseback, with a flourish of his whip as he passed.

'How dare you say so, when he's got both his eyes? and very handsome ones they are, too;' cried Jo, who resented any slighting remarks about her friend.

'I didn't say anything about his eyes, and I don't see why you need fire up when I admire his riding.'

'Oh, my goodness! that little goose means a centaur, and she called him a Cyclops,' exclaimed Jo, with a burst of laughter.

'You needn't be so rude, it's only a "lapse of lingy", as Mr Davis says,' retorted Amy, finishing Jo with her Latin. 'I just wish I had a little of the money Laurie spends on that horse,' she added, as if to herself, yet hoping her sisters would hear.

'Why?' asked Meg, kindly, for Jo had gone off in another laugh at Amy's second blunder.

'I need it so much; I'm dreadfully in debt, and it won't be my turn to have the rag-money for a month.'

'In debt, Amy; what do you mean?' and Meg looked sober.

'Why, I owe at least a dozen pickled limes, and I can't pay them, you know, till I have money, for Marmee forbid my having anything charged at the shop.'

'Tell me all about it. Are limes the fashion now? It used to be pricking bits of rubber to make balls;' and Meg tried to keep her countenance, Amy looked so grave and important.

'Why, you see, the girls are always buying them, and unless you want to be thought mean, you must do it, too. It's nothing but limes now, for every one is sucking them in their desks in school-time, and trading them off for pencils, bead-rings, paper dolls, or something else, at recess. If one girl likes another, she gives her a lime; if she's mad with her, she eats one before her face, and don't offer even a suck. They treat by turns; and I've had ever so many, but haven't returned them, and I ought, for they are debts of honor, you know.'

'How much will pay them off, and restore your credit?' asked Meg, taking out her purse.

'A quarter would more than do it, and leave a few cents over for a treat for you. Don't you like limes?'

'Not much; you may have my share. Here's the money,— make it last as long as you can, for it isn't very plenty, you know.'

'Oh, thank you! it must be so nice to have pocket-money. I'll have a grand feast, for I haven't tasted a lime this week. I felt delicate about taking any, as I couldn't return them, and I'm actually suffering for one.'

Next day Amy was rather late at school; but could not resist the temptation of displaying, with pardonable pride, a moist brown paper parcel, before she consigned it to the in-most recesses of her desk. During the next few minutes the rumor that Amy March had got twenty-four delicious limes (she ate one on the way), and was going to treat, circulated through her 'set', and the attentions of her friends became quite overwhelming. Katy Brown invited her to her next party on the spot; Mary Kingsley insisted on lending her watch till recess, and Jenny Snow, a satirical young lady who had basely twitted Amy upon her limeless state, promptly buried the hatchet, and offered to furnish answers to certain appalling sums. But Amy had not forgotten Miss Snow's cutting re-marks about 'some persons whose noses were not too flat to smell other people's limes, and stuck-up people, who were not too proud to ask for them'; and she instantly crushed 'that Snow girl's' hopes by the withering telegram, 'You needn't be so polite all of a sudden, for you won't get any.'

A distinguished personage happened to visit the school that morning, and Amy's beautifully drawn maps received praise, which honor to her foe rankled in the soul of Miss Snow, and caused Miss March to assume the airs of a studious young peacock. But, alas, alas! pride goes before a fall, and the revengeful Snow turned the tables with disastrous success. No sooner had the guest paid the usual stale compliments, and bowed himself out, than Jenny, under pretence of asking an important question, informed Mr Davis, the teacher, that Amy March had pickled limes in her desk.

Now Mr Davis had declared limes a contraband article, and solemnly vowed to publicly ferule the first person who was found breaking the law. This much-enduring man had succeeded in banishing gum after a long and stormy war, had made a bonfire of the confiscated novels and newspapers, had suppressed a private post-office, had forbidden distortions of the face, nicknames, and caricatures, and done all that one man could do to keep half a hundred rebellious girls in order. Boys are trying enough to human patience, goodness knows! but girls are infinitely more so, especially to nervous gentlemen with tyrannical tempers and no more talent for teaching than 'Dr Blimber'. Mr Davis knew any quantity of Greek, Latin, Algebra, and ologies of all sorts, so he was called a fine teacher; and manners, morals, feelings, and examples were not considered of any particular importance. It was a most unfortunate moment for denouncing Amy, and Jenny knew it. Mr Davis had evidently taken his coffee too strong that morning; there was an east wind, which always affected his neuralgia, and his pupils had not done him the credit which he felt he deserved; therefore, to use the expressive, if not elegant, language of a school-girl, 'he was as nervous as a witch and as cross as a bear.' The word 'limes' was like fire to powder; his yellow face flushed, and he rapped on his desk with an energy which made Jenny skip to her seat with unusual rapidity.

'Young ladies, attention, if you please!'

At the stern order the buzz ceased, and fifty pairs of blue, black, gray, and brown eyes were obediently fixed upon his awful countenance.

'Miss March, come to the desk.'

Amy rose to comply, with outward composure, but a secret fear oppressed her, for the limes weighed upon her conscience.

'Bring with you the limes you have in your desk,' was the unexpected command which arrested her before she got out of her seat.

'Don't take all,' whispered her neighbor, a young lady of great presence of mind.

Amy hastily shook out half a dozen, and laid the rest down before Mr Davis, feeling that any man possessing a human heart would relent when that delicious perfume met his nose. Unfortunately, Mr Davis particularly detested the odor of the fashionable pickle, and disgust added to his wrath.

'Is that all?'

'Not quite,' stammered Amy.

'Bring the rest, immediately.'

With a despairing glance at her set she obeyed.

'You are sure there are no more?'

'I never lie, sir.'

'So I see. Now take these disgusting things, two by two, and throw them out of the window.'

There was a simultaneous sigh, which created quite a little gust as the last hope fled, and the treat was ravished from their longing lips. Scarlet with shame and anger, Amy went to and fro twelve mortal times; and as each doomed couple, looking, oh, so plump and juicy! fell from her reluctant hands, a shout from the street completed the anguish of the girls, for it told them that their feast was being exulted over by the little Irish children, who were their sworn foes. This—this was too much; all flashed indignant or appealing glances at the inexorable Davis, and one passionate lime-lover burst into tears.

As Amy returned from her last trip, Mr Davis gave a portentous 'hem', and said, in his most impressive manner,—

'Young ladies, you remember what I said to you a week ago. I am sorry this has happened; but I never allow my rules to be infringed, and I *never* break my word. Miss March, hold out your hand.'

Amy started, and put both hands behind her, turning on him an imploring look, which pleaded for her better than the words she could not utter. She was rather a favorite with 'old Davis', as, of course, he was called, and it's my private belief that he *would* have broken his word if the indignation of one irrepressible young lady had not found vent in a hiss. That hiss, faint as it was, irritated the irascible gentleman, and sealed the culprit's fate.

'Your hand, Miss March!' was the only answer her mute appeal received; and, too proud to cry or beseech, Amy set her teeth, threw back her head defiantly, and bore without flinching several tingling blows on her little palm. They were neither many nor heavy, but that made no difference to her. For the first time in her life she had been struck; and the disgrace, in her eyes, was as deep as if he had knocked her down.

'You will now stand on the platform till recess,' said Mr Davis, resolved to do the thing thoroughly, since he had begun.

That was dreadful; it would have been bad enough to go to her seat and see the pitying faces of her friends, or the satisfied ones of her few enemies; but to face the whole school, with that shame fresh upon her, seemed impossible, and for a second she felt as if she could only drop down where she stood, and break her heart with crying. A bitter sense of wrong, and the thought of Jenny Snow, helped her to bear it; and, taking the ignominious place, she fixed her eyes on the stove-funnel above what now seemed a sea of faces, and stood there so motionless and white, that the girls found it very hard to study, with the pathetic little figure before them.

During the fifteen minutes that followed, the proud and sensitive little girl suffered a shame and pain which she never forgot. To others it might seem a ludicrous or trivial affair, but to her it was a hard experience; for during the twelve years of her life she had been governed by love alone, and a blow of that sort had never touched her before. The smart of her hand, and the ache of her heart, were forgotten in the sting of the thought,—

'I shall have to tell at home, and they will be so disappointed in me!'

The fifteen minutes seemed an hour; but they came to an end at last, and the word 'recess!' had never seemed so welcome to her before.

'You can go, Miss March,' said Mr Davis, looking, as he felt, uncomfortable.

He did not soon forget the reproachful look Amy gave him, as she went, without a word to any one, straight into the anteroom, snatched her things, and left the place 'forever', as she passionately declared to herself. She was in a sad state when she got home; and when the older girls arrived, some time later, an indignation meeting was held at once. Mrs March did not say much, but looked disturbed, and comforted her afflicted little daughter in her tenderest manner. Meg bathed the insulted hand with glycerine and tears; Beth felt that even her beloved kittens would fail as a balm for griefs like this, and Jo wrathfully proposed that Mr Davis be arrested without delay, while Hannah shook her fist at the 'villain', and pounded potatoes for dinner as if she had him under her pestle.

No notice was taken of Amy's flight, except by her mates; but the sharp-eyed demoiselles discovered that Mr Davis was quite benignant in the afternoon, also unusually nervous. Just before school closed, Jo appeared, wearing a grim expression, as she stalked up to the desk, and delivered a letter from her mother; then collected Amy's property, and departed, carefully scraping the mud from her boots on the door-mat, as if she shook the dust of the place off her feet.

'Yes, you can have a vacation from school, but I want you to study a little every day, with Beth,' said Mrs March, that evening. 'I don't approve of corporal punishment, especially for girls. I dislike Mr Davis' manner of teaching, and don't think the girls you associate with are doing you any good, so I shall ask your father's advice before I send you anywhere else.'

'That's good! I wish all the girls would leave, and spoil his old school. It's perfectly maddening to think of those lovely limes,' sighed Amy, with the air of a martyr.

'I am not sorry you lost them, for you broke the rules, and deserved some punishment for disobedience,' was the severe reply, which rather disappointed the young lady, who expected nothing but sympathy.

'Do you mean you are glad I was disgraced before the whole school?' cried Amy.

'I should not have chosen that way of mending a fault,' replied her mother; 'but I'm not sure that it won't do you more good than a milder method. You are getting to be altogether too conceited and important, my dear, and it is quite time you set about correcting it. You have a good many little gifts and virtues, but there is no need of parading them, for conceit spoils the finest genius. There is not much danger that real talent or goodness will be overlooked long; even if it is, the consciousness of possessing and using it well should satisfy one, and the great charm of all power is modesty.'

'So it is,' cried Laurie, who was playing chess in a corner with Jo. 'I knew a girl, once, who had a really remarkable talent for music, and she didn't know it; never guessed what sweet little things she composed when she was alone, and wouldn't have believed it if any one had told her.'

'I wish I'd known that nice girl, maybe she would have helped me, I'm so stupid,' said Beth, who stood beside him, listening eagerly.

'You do know her, and she helps you better than any one else could,' answered Laurie, looking at her with such mischievous meaning in his merry black eyes, that Beth suddenly turned very red, and hid her face in the sofa-cushion, quite overcome by such an unexpected discovery.

Jo let Laurie win the game, to pay for that praise of her Beth, who could not be prevailed upon to play for them after her compliment. So Laurie did his best, and sung delightfully, being in a particularly lively humor, for to the Marches he seldom showed the moody side of his character. When he was gone, Amy, who had been pensive all the evening, said, suddenly, as if busy over some new idea,—

'Is Laurie an accomplished boy?'

'Yes; he has had an excellent education, and has much talent; he will make a fine man, if not spoilt by petting,' replied her mother.

'And he isn't conceited, is he?' asked Amy.

'Not in the least; that is why he is so charming, and we all like him so much.'

'I see; it's nice to have accomplishments, and be elegant; but not to show off, or get perked up,' said Amy, thoughtfully.

'These things are always seen and felt in a person's manner and conversation, if modestly used; but it is not necessary to display them,' said Mrs March.

'Any more than it's proper to wear all your bonnets, and gowns, and ribbons, at once, that folks may know you've got 'em,' added Jo; and the lecture ended in a laugh.

CHAPTER EIGHT

◄●●►

Jo Meets Apollyon

'Girls, where are you going?' asked Amy, coming into their room one Saturday afternoon, and finding them getting ready to go out, with an air of secrecy which excited her curiosity.

'Never mind; little girls shouldn't ask questions,' returned Jo, sharply.

Now if there is anything mortifying to our feelings, when we are young, it is to be told that; and to be bidden to 'run away, dear', is still more trying to us. Amy bridled up at this insult, and determined to find out the secret, if she teased for an hour. Turning to Meg, who never refused her anything very long, she said, coaxingly, 'Do tell me! I should think you might let me go, too; for Beth is fussing over her dolls, and I haven't got anything to do, and am *so* lonely.'

'I can't, dear, because you aren't invited,' began Meg; but Jo broke in impatiently, 'Now, Meg, be quiet, or you will spoil it all. You can't go, Amy; so don't be a baby, and whine about it.'

'You are going somewhere with Laurie, I know you are; you were whispering and laughing together, on the sofa, last night, and you stopped when I came in. Aren't you going with him?'

'Yes, we are; now do be still, and stop bothering.'

Amy held her tongue, but used her eyes, and saw Meg slip a fan into her pocket.

'I know! I know! you're going to the theatre to see the *Seven Castles*!' she cried; adding, resolutely, 'and I *shall* go, for mother said I might see it; and I've got my rag-money, and it was mean not to tell me in time.'

'Just listen to me a minute, and be a good child,' said Meg, soothingly. 'Mother doesn't wish you to go this week, because your eyes are not well enough yet to bear the light of this fairy piece. Next week you can go with Beth and Hannah, and have a nice time.'

'I don't like that half as well as going with you and Laurie. Please let me; I've been sick with this cold so long, and shut up, I'm dying for some fun. Do, Meg! I'll be ever so good,' pleaded Amy, looking as pathetic as she could.

'Suppose we take her. I don't believe mother would mind, if we bundle her up well,' began Meg.

'If *she* goes *I* shan't; and if I don't, Laurie won't like it; and it will be very rude, after he invited only us, to go and drag in Amy. I should think she'd hate to poke herself where she isn't wanted,' said Jo, crossly, for she disliked the trouble of overseeing a fidgety child, when she wanted to enjoy herself.

Her tone and manner angered Amy, who began to put her boots on, saying, in her most aggravating way, 'I *shall* go; Meg says I may; and if I pay for myself, Laurie hasn't anything to do with it.'

'You can't sit with us, for our seats are reserved, and you mustn't sit alone; so Laurie will give you his place, and that will spoil our pleasure; or he'll get another seat for you, and that isn't proper, when you weren't asked. You shan't stir a step; so you may just stay where you are,' scolded Jo, crosser than ever, having just pricked her finger in her hurry.

Sitting on the floor, with one boot on, Amy began to cry, and Meg to reason with her, when Laurie called from below, and the two girls hurried down, leaving their sister wailing; for now and then she forgot her grown-up ways, and acted like a spoilt child. Just as the party was setting out, Amy called over the banisters, in a threatening tone, 'You'll be sorry for this, Jo March! see if you ain't.'

'Fiddlesticks!' returned Jo, slamming the door.

They had a charming time, for *The Seven Castles of the Diamond Lake* were as brilliant and wonderful as a heart could wish. But, in spite of the comical red imps, sparkling elves, and gorgeous princes and princesses, Jo's pleasure had a drop of bitterness in it; the fairy queen's yellow curls reminded her of Amy; and between the acts she amused herself with wondering what her sister would do to make her 'sorry for it'. She and Amy had had many lively skirmishes in the course of their lives, for both had quick tempers, and were apt to be violent when fairly roused. Amy teased Jo, and Jo irritated Amy, and semi-occasional explosions occurred, of which both were much ashamed afterward. Although the oldest, Jo had the least self-control, and had hard times trying to curb the fiery spirit which was continually getting her into trouble;

her anger never lasted long, and, having humbly confessed her fault, she sincerely repented, and tried to do better. Her sisters used to say, that they rather liked to get Jo into a fury, because she was such an angel afterward. Poor Jo tried desperately to be good, but her bosom enemy was always ready to flame up and defeat her; and it took years of patient effort to subdue it.

When they got home, they found Amy reading in the parlor. She assumed an injured air as they came in; never lifted her eyes from her book, or asked a single question. Perhaps curiosity might have conquered resentment, if Beth had not been there to inquire, and receive a glowing description of the play. On going up to put away her best hat, Jo's first look was toward the bureau; for, in their last quarrel, Amy had soothed her feelings by turning Jo's top drawer upside down, on the floor. Everything was in its place, however; and after a hasty glance into her various closets, bags and boxes, Jo decided that Amy had forgiven and forgotten her wrongs.

There Jo was mistaken; for next day she made a discovery which produced a tempest. Meg, Beth and Amy were sitting together, late in the afternoon, when Jo burst into the room, looking excited, and demanding, breathlessly, 'Has any one taken my story?'

Meg and Beth said 'No,' at once, and looked surprised; Amy poked the fire, and said nothing. Jo saw her color rise, and was down upon her in a minute.

'Amy, you've got it!'

'No, I haven't.'

'You know where it is, then!'

'No, I don't.'

'That's a fib!' cried Jo, taking her by the shoulders, and looking fierce enough to frighten a much braver child than Amy.

'It isn't. I haven't got it, don't know where it is now, and don't care.'

'You know something about it, and you'd better tell at once, or I'll make you,' and Jo gave her a slight shake.

'Scold as much as you like, you'll never get your silly old story again,' cried Amy, getting excited in her turn.

'Why not?'

'I burnt it up.'

'What! my little book I was so fond of, and worked over, and meant to finish before father got home? Have you really burnt it?' said Jo, turning very pale, while her eyes kindled and her hands clutched Amy nervously.

'Yes, I did! I told you I'd make you pay for being so cross yesterday, and I have, so—'

Amy got no farther, for Jo's hot temper mastered her, and she shook Amy till her teeth chattered in her head; crying, in a passion of grief and anger,—

'You wicked, wicked girl! I never can write it again, and I'll never forgive you as long as I live.'

Meg flew to rescue Amy, and Beth to pacify Jo, but Jo was quite beside herself; and, with a parting box on her sister's ear, she rushed out of the room up to the old sofa in the garret, and finished her fight alone.

The storm cleared up below, for Mrs March came home, and, having heard the story, soon brought Amy to a sense of the wrong she had done her sister. Jo's book was the pride of her heart, and was regarded by her family as a literary sprout of great promise. It was only half a dozen little fairy tales, but Jo had worked over them patiently, putting her whole heart into her work, hoping to make something good enough to print. She had just copied them with great care, and had destroyed the old manuscript, so that Amy's bonfire had consumed the loving work of several years. It seemed a small loss to others, but to Jo it was a dreadful calamity, and she felt that it never could be made up to her. Beth mourned as for a departed kitten, and Meg refused to defend her pet; Mrs March looked grave and grieved, and Amy felt that no one would love her till she had asked pardon for the act which she now regretted more than any of them.

When the tea-bell rung, Jo appeared, looking so grim and unapproachable, that it took all Amy's courage to say, meekly,—

'Please forgive me, Jo; I'm very, very sorry.'

'I never shall forgive you,' was Jo's stern answer; and, from that moment, she ignored Amy entirely.

No one spoke of the great trouble,—not even Mrs March,—for all had learned by experience that when Jo was in that mood words were wasted; and the wisest course was to wait till some little accident, or her own generous nature, softened Jo's resentment, and healed the breach. It was not a happy evening; for, though they sewed as usual, while their mother read aloud from Bremer, Scott, or Edgeworth, something was wanting, and the sweet home-peace was disturbed. They felt this most when singing-time came; for Beth could only play, Jo stood dumb as a stone, and Amy broke down, so Meg and mother sung alone. But, in spite of their efforts to be as cheery as larks, the flute-like voices did not seem to chord as well as usual, and all felt out of tune.

As Jo received her good-night kiss, Mrs March whispered, gently,—

'My dear, don't let the sun go down upon your anger; forgive each other, help each other, and begin again to-morrow.'

Jo wanted to lay her head down on that motherly bosom, and cry her grief and anger all away; but tears were an unmanly weakness, and she felt so deeply injured that she really *couldn't* quite forgive yet. So she winked hard, shook her head, and said, gruffly, because Amy was listening,—

'It was an abominable thing, and she don't deserve to be forgiven.'

With that she marched off to bed, and there was no merry or confidential gossip that night.

Amy was much offended that her overtures of peace had been repulsed, and began to wish she had not humbled herself, to feel more injured than ever, and to plume herself on her superior virtue in a way which was particularly exasperating. Jo still looked like a thunder-cloud, and nothing went well all day. It was bitter cold in the morning; she dropped her precious turn-over in the gutter, Aunt March had an attack of fidgets, Meg was pensive, Beth *would* look grieved and wistful when she got home, and Amy kept making remarks about people who were always talking about being good, and yet wouldn't try, when other people set them a virtuous example.

'Everybody is so hateful, I'll ask Laurie to go skating. He is always kind and jolly, and will put me to rights, I know,' said Jo to herself, and off she went.

Amy heard the clash of skates, and looked out with an impatient exclamation,—

'There! she promised I should go next time, for this is the last ice we shall have. But it's no use to ask such a cross patch to take me.'

'Don't say that; you *were* very naughty, and it is hard to forgive the loss of her precious little book; but I think she might do it now, and I guess she will, if you try her at the right minute,' said Meg. 'Go after them; don't say anything till Jo has got good-natured with Laurie, then take a quiet minute, and just kiss her, or do some kind thing, and I'm sure she'll be friends again, with all her heart.'

'I'll try,' said Amy, for the advice suited her; and, after a flurry to get ready, she ran after the friends, who were just disappearing over the hill.

It was not far to the river, but both were ready before Amy reached them. Jo saw her coming, and turned her back; Laurie did not see, for he was carefully skating along the shore, sounding the ice, for a warm spell had preceded the cold snap.

'I'll go on to the first bend, and see if it's all right, before we begin to race,' Amy heard him say, as he shot away, looking like a young Russian, in his fur-trimmed coat and cap.

Jo heard Amy panting after her run, stamping her feet, and blowing her fingers, as she tried to put her skates on; but Jo never turned, and went slowly zigzagging down the river, taking a bitter, unhappy sort of satisfaction in her sister's troubles. She had cherished her anger till it grew strong, and took possession of her, as evil thoughts and feelings always do, unless cast out at once. As Laurie turned the bend, he shouted back,—

'Keep near the shore; it isn't safe in the middle.'

Jo heard, but Amy was just struggling to her feet, and did not catch a word. Jo glanced over her shoulder, and the little demon she was harboring said in her ear,—

'No matter whether she heard or not, let her take care of herself.'

Laurie had vanished round the bend; Jo was just at the turn, and Amy, far behind, striking out toward the smoother ice in the middle of the river. For a minute Jo stood still, with a strange feeling at her heart; then she resolved to go on, but something held and turned her round, just in time to see Amy throw up her hands and go down, with the sudden crash of rotten ice, the splash of water, and a cry that made Jo's heart stand still with fear. She tried to call Laurie, but her voice was gone; she tried to rush forward, but her feet seemed to have no strength in them; and, for a second, she could only stand motionless, staring, with a terror-stricken face, at the little blue hood above the black water. Something rushed swiftly by her, and Laurie's voice cried out,—

'Bring a rail; quick, quick!'

How she did it, she never knew; but for the next few minutes she worked as if possessed, blindly obeying Laurie, who was quite self-possessed; and, lying flat, held Amy up by his arm and hockey, till Jo dragged a rail from the fence, and together they got the child out, more frightened than hurt.

'Now then, we must walk her home as fast as we can; pile our things on her, while I get off these confounded skates,' cried Laurie, wrapping his coat round Amy, and tugging away at the straps, which never seemed so intricate before.

Shivering, dripping, and crying, they got Amy home; and, after an exciting time of it, she fell asleep, rolled in blankets, before a hot fire. During the bustle Jo had scarcely spoken; but flown about, looking pale and wild, with her things half off, her dress torn, and her hands cut and bruised by ice and rails, and refractory buckles. When Amy was comfortably asleep, the house quiet, and Mrs March sitting by the bed, she called Jo to her, and began to bind up the hurt hands.

'Are you sure she is safe?' whispered Jo, looking remorsefully at the golden head, which might have been swept away from her sight forever, under the treacherous ice.

'Quite safe, dear; she is not hurt, and won't even take cold, I think, you were so sensible in covering and getting her home quickly,' replied her mother, cheerfully.

'Laurie did it all; I only let her go. Mother, if she *should* die, it would be my fault;' and Jo dropped down beside the bed, in a passion of penitent tears, telling all that had happened, bitterly condemning her hardness of heart, and sobbing out her gratitude for being spared the heavy punishment which might have come upon her.

'It's my dreadful temper! I try to cure it; I think I have, and then it breaks out worse than ever. Oh, mother! what shall I do! what shall I do?' cried poor Jo, in despair.

'Watch and pray, dear; never get tired of trying; and never think it is impossible to conquer your fault,' said Mrs March, drawing the blowzy head to her shoulder, and kissing the wet cheek so tenderly, that Jo cried harder than ever.

'You don't know; you can't guess how bad it is! It seems as if I could do anything when I'm in a passion; I get so savage, I could hurt any one, and enjoy it. I'm afraid I *shall* do something dreadful some day, and spoil my life, and make everybody hate me. Oh, mother! help me, do help me!'

'I will, my child; I will. Don't cry so bitterly, but remember this day, and resolve, with all your soul, that you will never know another like it. Jo, dear, we all have our temptations, some far greater than yours, and it often takes us all our lives to conquer them. You think your temper is the worst in the world; but mine used to be just like it.'

'Yours, mother? Why, you are never angry!' and, for the moment, Jo forgot remorse in surprise.

'I've been trying to cure it for forty years, and have only succeeded in controlling it. I am angry nearly every day of my life, Jo; but I have learned not to show it; and I still hope to learn not to feel it, though it may take me another forty years to do so.'

The patience and the humility of the face she loved so well, was a better lesson to Jo than the wisest lecture, the sharpest reproof. She felt comforted at once by the sympathy and confidence given her; the knowledge that her mother had a fault like hers, and tried to mend it, made her own easier to bear, and strengthened her resolution to cure it; though forty years seemed rather a long time to watch and pray, to a girl of fifteen.

'Mother, are you angry when you fold your lips tight together, and go out of the room sometimes, when Aunt March scolds, or people worry you?' asked Jo, feeling nearer and dearer to her mother than ever before.

'Yes, I've learned to check the hasty words that rise to my lips; and when I feel that they mean to break out against my will, I just go away a minute, and give myself a little shake, for being so weak and wicked,' answered Mrs March, with a sigh and a smile, as she smoothed and fastened up Jo's dishevelled hair.

'How did you learn to keep still? That is what troubles me—for the sharp words fly out before I know what I'm about; and the more I say the worse I get, till it's a pleasure to hurt people's feelings, and say dreadful things. Tell me how you do it, Marmee dear.'

'My good mother used to help me—'

'As you do us—' interrupted Jo, with a grateful kiss.

'But I lost her when I was a little older than you are, and for years had to struggle on alone, for I was too proud to confess my weakness to any one else. I had a hard time, Jo, and shed a good many bitter tears over my failures; for, in spite of my efforts, I never seemed to get on. Then your father came, and I was so happy that I found it easy to be good. But by and by, when I had four little daughters round me, and we were poor, then the old trouble began again; for I am not patient by nature, and it tried me very much to see my children wanting anything.'

'Poor mother! what helped you then?'

'Your father, Jo. He never loses patience,—never doubts or complains,—but always hopes, and works and waits so cheerfully, that one is ashamed to do otherwise before him. He helped and comforted me, and showed me that I must try to practise all the virtues I would have my little girls possess, for I was their example. It was easier to try for your sakes than for my own; a startled or surprised look from one of you, when I spoke sharply, rebuked me more than any words could have done; and the love, respect, and confidence of my children was the sweetest reward I could receive for my efforts to be the woman I would have them copy.'

'Oh, mother! if I'm ever half as good as you, I shall be satisfied,' cried Jo, much touched.

'I hope you will be a great deal better, dear; but you must keep watch over your "bosom enemy", as father calls it, or it may sadden, if not spoil, your life. You have had a warning; remember it, and try with heart and soul to master this quick temper, before it brings you greater sorrow and regret than you have known today.'

'I will try, mother; I truly will. But you must help me, remind me, and keep me from flying out. I used to see father sometimes put his finger on his lips, and look at you with a very kind, but sober face; and you always folded your lips tight, or went away; was he reminding you then?' asked Jo, softly.

'Yes, I asked him to help me so, and he never forgot it, but saved me from many a sharp word by that little gesture and kind look.'

Jo saw that her mother's eyes filled, and her lips trembled, as she spoke; and, fearing that she had said too much, she whispered anxiously, 'Was it wrong to watch you, and to speak of it? I didn't mean to be rude, but it's so comfortable to say all I think to you, and feel so safe and happy here.'

'My Jo, you may say anything to your mother, for it is my greatest happiness and pride to feel that my girls confide in me, and know how much I love them.'

'I thought I'd grieved you.'

'No, dear; but speaking of father reminded me how much I miss him, how much I owe him, and how faithfully I should watch and work to keep his little daughters safe and good for him.'

'Yet you told him to go, mother, and didn't cry when he went, and never complain now, or seem as if you needed any help,' said Jo, wondering.

'I gave my best to the country I love, and kept my tears till he was gone. Why should I complain, when we both have merely done our duty, and will surely be the happier for it in the end? If I don't seem to need help, it is because I have a better friend, even than father, to comfort and sustain me. My child, the troubles and temptations of your life are beginning, and may be many; but you can overcome and outlive them all, if you learn to feel the strength and tenderness of your Heavenly Father as you do that of your earthly one. The more you love and trust Him, the nearer you will feel to Him, and the less you will depend on human power and wisdom. His love and care never tire or change, can never be taken from you, but may become the source of lifelong peace, happiness, and strength. Believe this heartily, and go to God with all your little cares, and hopes, and sins, and sorrows, as freely and confidingly as you come to your mother.'

Jo's only answer was to hold her mother close, and, in the silence which followed, the sincerest prayer she had ever prayed left her heart, without words; for in that sad, yet happy hour, she had learned not only the bitterness of remorse and despair, but the sweetness of self-denial and self-control; and, led by her mother's hand, she had drawn nearer to the Friend who welcomes every child with a love stronger than that of any father, tenderer than that of any mother.

Amy stirred, and sighed in her sleep; and, as if eager to begin at once to mend her fault, Jo looked up with an expression on her face which it had never worn before.

'I let the sun go down on my anger; I wouldn't forgive her, and today, if it hadn't been for Laurie, it might have been too late! How could I be so wicked?' said Jo, half aloud, as she leaned over her sister, softly stroking the wet hair scattered on the pillow.

As if she heard, Amy opened her eyes, and held out her arms, with a smile that went straight to Jo's heart. Neither said a word, but they hugged one another close, in spite of the blankets, and everything was forgiven and forgotten in one hearty kiss.

CHAPTER NINE

---●---

Meg Goes to Vanity Fair

'I do think it was the most fortunate thing in the world, that those children should have the measles just now,' said Meg, one April day, as she stood packing the 'go abroady' trunk in her room, surrounded by her sisters.

'And so nice of Annie Moffat, not to forget her promise. A whole fortnight of fun will be regularly splendid,' replied Jo, looking like a windmill, as she folded skirts with her long arms.

'And such lovely weather; I'm so glad of that,' added Beth, tidily sorting neck and hair ribbons in her best box, lent for the great occasion.

'I wish I was going to have a fine time, and wear all these nice things,' said Amy, with her mouth full of pins, as she artistically replenished her sister's cushion.

'I wish you were all going; but, as you can't, I shall keep my adventures to tell you when I come back. I'm sure it's the least I can do, when you have been so kind, lending me things, and helping me get ready,' said Meg, glancing round the room at the very simple outfit, which seemed nearly perfect in their eyes.

'What did mother give you out of the treasure-box?' asked Amy, who had not been present at the opening of a certain cedar chest, in which Mrs March kept a few relics of past splendor, as gifts for her girls when the proper time came.

'A pair of silk stockings, that pretty carved fan, and a lovely blue sash. I wanted the violet silk; but there isn't time to make it over, so I must be contented with my old tarleton.'

'It will look nicely over my new muslin skirt, and the sash will set it off beautifully. I wish I hadn't smashed my coral bracelet, for you might have had it,' said Jo, who loved to give and lend, but whose possessions were usually too dilapidated to be of much use.

'There is a lovely old-fashioned pearl set in the treasure-box; but mother said real flowers were the prettiest ornament for a young girl, and Laurie promised to send me all I want,' replied Meg. 'Now, let me see; there's my new gray walking-suit,—just curl up the feather in my hat, Beth,—then my poplin, for Sunday, and the small party,—it looks heavy for spring, don't it? the violet silk would be so nice; oh, dear!'

'Never mind; you've got the tarleton for the big party, and you always look like an angel in white,' said Amy, brooding over the little store of finery in which her soul delighted.

'It isn't low-necked, and it don't sweep enough, but it will have to do. My blue house-dress looks so well, turned and freshly trimmed, that I feel as if I'd got a new one. My silk sacque isn't a bit the fashion, and my bonnet don't look like Sallie's; I didn't like to say anything, but I was dreadfully disappointed in my umbrella. I told mother black, with a white handle, but she forgot, and bought a green one, with an ugly yellowish handle. It's strong and neat, so I ought not to complain, but I know I shall feel ashamed of it beside Annie's silk one, with a gold top,' sighed Meg, surveying the little umbrella with great disfavor.

'Change it,' advised Jo.

'I won't be so silly, or hurt Marmee's feelings, when she took so much pains to get my things. It's a nonsensical notion of mine, and I'm not going to give up to it. My silk stockings and two pairs of spandy gloves are my comfort. You are a dear, to lend me yours, Jo; I feel so rich, and sort of elegant, with two new pairs, and the old ones cleaned up for common;' and Meg took a refreshing peep at her glove-box.

'Annie Moffat has blue and pink bows on her night-caps; would you put some on mine?' she asked, as Beth brought up a pile of snowy muslins, fresh from Hannah's hands.

'No, I wouldn't; for the smart caps won't match the plain gowns, without any trimming on them. Poor folks shouldn't rig,' said Jo, decidedly.

'I wonder if I shall *ever* be happy enough to have real lace on my clothes, and bows on my caps?' said Meg, impatiently.

'You said the other day that you'd be perfectly happy if you could only go to Annie Moffat's,' observed Beth, in her quiet way.

'So I did! Well, I *am* happy, and I *won't* fret; but it does seem as if the more one gets the more one wants, don't it? There, now, the trays are ready, and everything in but my ball-dress, which I shall leave for mother,' said Meg, cheering up, as she glanced from the half-filled trunk to the many-times

pressed and mended white tarleton, which she called her
'ball-dress', with an important air.

The next day was fine, and Meg departed, in style, for a
fortnight of novelty and pleasure. Mrs March had consented
to the visit rather reluctantly, fearing that Margaret would
come back more discontented than she went. But she had
begged so hard, and Sallie had promised to take good care of
her, and a little pleasure seemed so delightful after a winter of
hard work, that the mother yielded, and the daughter went to
take her first taste of fashionable life.

The Moffats *were* very fashionable, and simple Meg was
rather daunted, at first, by the splendor of the house, and
the elegance of its occupants. But they were kindly people,
in spite of the frivolous life they led, and soon put their
guest at her ease. Perhaps Meg felt, without understanding
why, that they were not particularly cultivated or intelligent
people, and that all their gilding could not quite conceal the
ordinary material of which they were made. It certainly was
agreeable to fare sumptuously, drive in a fine carriage, wear
her best frock every day, and do nothing but enjoy herself.
It suited her exactly; and soon she began to imitate the
manners and conversation of those about her; to put on little airs and graces, use French phrases, crimp her hair, take
in her dresses, and talk about the fashions, as well as she
could. The more she saw of Annie Moffat's pretty things,
the more she envied her, and sighed to be rich. Home now
looked bare and dismal as she thought of it, work grew
harder than ever, and she felt that she was a very destitute
and much injured girl, in spite of the new gloves and silk
stockings.

She had not much time for repining, however, for the three young girls were busily employed in 'having a good time'. They shopped, walked, rode, and called all day; went to theatres and operas, or frolicked at home in the evening; for Annie had many friends, and knew how to entertain them. Her older sisters were very fine young ladies, and one was engaged, which was extremely interesting and romantic, Meg thought. Mr Moffat was a fat, jolly old gentleman, who knew her father; and Mrs Moffat, a fat, jolly old lady, who took as great a fancy to Meg as her daughter had done. Every one petted her; and 'Daisy', as they called her, was in a fair way to have her head turned.

When the evening for the 'small party' came, she found that the poplin wouldn't do at all, for the other girls were putting on thin dresses, and making themselves very fine indeed; so out came the tarleton, looking older, limper, and shabbier than ever, beside Sallie's crisp new one. Meg saw the girls glance at it, and then at one another, and her cheeks began to burn; for, with all her gentleness, she was very proud. No one said a word about it, but Sallie offered to do her hair, and Annie to tie her sash, and Belle, the engaged sister, praised her white arms; but, in their kindness, Meg saw only pity for her poverty, and her heart felt very heavy as she stood by herself, while the others laughed and chattered, prinked, and flew about like gauzy butterflies. The hard, bitter feeling was getting pretty bad, when the maid brought in a box of flowers. Before she could speak, Annie had the cover off, and all were exclaiming at the lovely roses, heath, and ferns within.

'It's for Belle, of course; George always sends her some, but these are altogether ravishing,' cried Annie, with a great sniff.

'They are for Miss March,' the man said. 'And here's a note,' put in the maid, holding it to Meg.

'What fun! Who are they from? Didn't know you had a lover,' cried the girls, fluttering about Meg in a high state of curiosity and surprise.

'The note is from mother, and the flowers from Laurie,' said Meg, simply, yet much gratified that he had not forgotten her.

'Oh, indeed!' said Annie, with a funny look, as Meg slipped the note into her pocket, as a sort of talisman against envy, vanity, and false pride; for the few loving words had done her good, and the flowers cheered her up by their beauty.

Feeling almost happy again, she laid by a few ferns and roses for herself, and quickly made up the rest in dainty bouquets for the breasts, hair, or skirts of her friends, offering them so prettily, that Clara, the elder sister, told her she was 'the sweetest little thing she ever saw'; and they looked quite charmed with her small attention. Somehow the kind act finished her despondency; and, when all the rest went to show themselves to Mrs Moffat, she saw a happy, bright-eyed face in the mirror, as she laid her ferns against her rippling hair, and fastened the roses in the dress that didn't strike her as so *very* shabby now.

She enjoyed herself very much that evening, for she danced to her heart's content; every one was very kind, and she had three compliments. Annie made her sing, and some one said she had a remarkably fine voice; Major Lincoln asked who 'the fresh little girl, with the beautiful eyes, was'; and Mr Moffat insisted on dancing with her, because she 'didn't dawdle, but had some spring in her', as he gracefully expressed it.

So, altogether, she had a very nice time, till she overheard a bit of a conversation, which disturbed her extremely. She was sitting just inside the conservatory, waiting for her partner to bring her an ice, when she heard a voice ask, on the other side of the flowery wall,—

'How old is he?'

'Sixteen or seventeen, I should say,' replied another voice.

'It would be a grand thing for one of those girls, wouldn't it? Sallie says they are very intimate now, and the old man quite dotes on them.'

'Mrs M. has laid her plans, I dare say, and will play her cards well, early as it is. The girl evidently doesn't think of it yet,' said Mrs Moffat.

'She told that fib about her mamma, as if she did know, and colored up when the flowers came, quite prettily. Poor thing! she'd be so nice if she was only got up in style. Do you think she'd be offended if we offered to lend her a dress for Thursday?' asked another voice.

'She's proud, but I don't believe she'd mind, for that dowdy tarleton is all she has got. She may tear it to-night, and that will be a good excuse for offering a decent one.'

'We'll see; I shall ask that Laurence, as a compliment to her, and we'll have fun about it afterward.'

Here Meg's partner appeared, to find her looking much flushed, and rather agitated. She was proud, and her pride was useful just then, for it helped her hide her mortification, anger, and disgust, at what she had just heard; for, innocent and unsuspicious as she was, she could not help understanding the gossip of her friends. She tried to forget it, but could not, and kept repeating to herself, 'Mrs M. has her plans', 'that

117

fib about her mamma', and 'dowdy tarleton', till she was ready to cry, and rush home to tell her troubles, and ask for advice. As that was impossible, she did her best to seem gay; and, being rather excited, she succeeded so well, that no one dreamed what an effort she was making. She was very glad when it was all over and she was quiet in her bed, where she could think and wonder and fume till her head ached, and her hot cheeks were cooled by a few natural tears. Those foolish, yet well-meant, words had opened a new world to Meg, and much disturbed the peace of the old one, in which, till now, she had lived as happily as a child. Her innocent friendship with Laurie was spoilt by the silly speeches she had over-heard; her faith in her mother was a little shaken by the worldly plans attributed to her by Mrs Moffat, who judged others by herself; and the sensible resolution to be con-tented with the simple wardrobe which suited a poor man's daughter, was weakened by the unnecessary pity of girls, who thought a shabby dress one of the greatest calamities under heaven.

Poor Meg had a restless night, and got up heavy-eyed, un-happy, half resentful toward her friends, and half ashamed of herself for not speaking out frankly, and setting everything right. Everybody dawdled that morning, and it was noon be-fore the girls found energy enough even to take up their worsted work. Something in the manner of her friends struck Meg at once; they treated her with more respect, she thought; took quite a tender interest in what she said, and looked at her with eyes that plainly betrayed curiosity. All this surprised and flattered her, though she did not understand it till Miss Belle looked up from her writing, and said, with a sentimental air,—

'Daisy, dear, I've sent an invitation to your friend, Mr Laurence, for Thursday. We should like to know him, and it's only a proper compliment to you.'

Meg colored, but a mischievous fancy to tease the girls made her reply, demurely,—

'You are very kind, but I'm afraid he won't come.'

'Why not, chérie?' asked Miss Belle.

'He's too old.'

'My child, what do you mean? What is his age, I beg to know!' cried Miss Clara.

'Nearly seventy, I believe,' answered Meg, counting stitches, to hide the merriment in her eyes.

'You sly creature! of course, we meant the young man,' exclaimed Miss Belle, laughing.

'There isn't any; Laurie is only a little boy,' and Meg laughed also at the queer look which the sisters exchanged, as she thus described her supposed lover.

'About your age,' Nan said.

'Nearer my sister Jo's; *I* am seventeen in August,' returned Meg, tossing her head.

'It's very nice of him to send you flowers, isn't it?' said Annie, looking wise about nothing.

'Yes, he often does, to all of us; for their house is full, and we are so fond of them. My mother and old Mr Laurence are friends, you know, so it is quite natural that we children should play together;' and Meg hoped they would say no more.

'It's evident Daisy isn't out yet,' said Miss Clara to Belle, with a nod.

'Quite a pastoral state of innocence all round,' returned Miss Belle, with a shrug.

'I'm going out to get some little matters for my girls; can I do anything for you, young ladies?' asked Mrs Moffat, lumbering in, like an elephant, in silk and lace.

'No, thank you, ma'am,' replied Sallie; 'I've got my new pink silk for Thursday, and I don't want a thing.'

'Nor I—' began Meg, but stopped, because it occurred to her that she *did* want several things, and could not have them.

'What shall you wear?' asked Sallie.

'My old white one again, if I can mend it fit to be seen; it got sadly torn last night,' said Meg, trying to speak quite easily, but feeling very uncomfortable.

'Why don't you send home for another?' said Sallie, who was not an observing young lady.

'I haven't got any other.' It cost Meg an effort to say that, but Sallie did not see it, and exclaimed, in amiable surprise,—

'Only that? how funny—' She did not finish her speech, for Belle shook her head at her, and broke in, saying, kindly,—

'Not at all; where is the use of having a lot of dresses when she isn't out? There's no need of sending home, Daisy, even if you had a dozen, for I've got a sweet blue silk laid away, which I've outgrown, and you shall wear it, to please me; won't you, dear?'

'You are very kind, but I don't mind my old dress, if you don't; it does well enough for a little girl like me,' said Meg.

'Now do let me please myself by dressing you up in style. I admire to do it, and you'd be a regular little beauty, with a touch here and there. I shan't let any one see you till you are done, and then we'll burst upon them like Cinderella and her godmother, going to the ball,' said Belle, in her persuasive tone.

Meg couldn't refuse the offer so kindly made, for a desire to see if she would be 'a little beauty' after touching up caused her to accept, and forget all her former uncomfortable feelings towards the Moffats.

On the Thursday evening, Belle shut herself up with her maid; and, between them, they turned Meg into a fine lady. They crimped and curled her hair, they polished her neck and arms with some fragrant powder, touched her lips with coralline salve, to make them redder, and Hortense would have added 'a *soupçon* of rouge', if Meg had not rebelled. They laced her into a sky-blue dress, which was so tight she could hardly breathe, and so low in the neck that modest Meg blushed at herself in the mirror. A set of silver filagree was added, bracelets, necklace, brooch, and even ear-rings, for Hortense tied them on, with a bit of pink silk, which did not show. A cluster of tea rose-buds at the bosom, and a *ruche*, reconciled Meg to the display of her pretty white shoulders, and a pair of high-heeled blue silk boots satisfied the last wish of her heart. A laced handkerchief, a plumy fan, and a bouquet in a silver holder, finished her off; and Miss Belle surveyed her with the satisfaction of a little girl with a newly dressed doll.

'Mademoiselle is charmante, très jolie, is she not?' cried Hortense, clasping her hands in an affected rapture.

'Come and show yourself,' said Miss Belle, leading the way to the room where the others were waiting.

As Meg went rustling after, with her long skirts trailing, her earrings tinkling, her curls waving, and her heart beating, she felt as if her 'fun' had really begun at last, for the mirror had plainly told her that she *was* 'a little beauty'. Her friends repeated the pleasing phrase enthusiastically; and, for several minutes, she stood, like the jackdaw in the fable, enjoying her borrowed plumes, while the rest chattered like a party of magpies.

'While I dress, do you drill her, Nan, in the management of her skirt, and those French heels, or she will trip herself up. Put your silver butterfly in the middle of that white barbe, and catch up that long curl on the left side of her head, Clara, and don't any of you disturb the charming work of my hands,' said Belle, as she hurried away, looking well pleased with her success.

'I'm afraid to go down, I feel so queer and stiff, and half-dressed,' said Meg to Sallie, as the bell rang, and Mrs Moffat sent to ask the young ladies to appear at once.

'You don't look a bit like yourself, but you are very nice. I'm nowhere beside you, for Belle has heaps of taste, and you're quite French, I assure you. Let your flowers hang; don't be so careful of them, and be sure you don't trip,' returned Sallie, trying not to care that Meg was prettier than herself.

Keeping that warning carefully in mind, Margaret got safely down stairs, and sailed into the drawing-rooms, where the Moffats and a few early guests were assembled. She very soon discovered that there is a charm about fine clothes which attracts a certain class of people, and secures their respect. Several young ladies, who had taken no notice of her before, were very affectionate all of a sudden; several young gentlemen, who had only stared at her at the other party, now not only stared, but asked to be introduced, and said all manner of foolish but agreeable things to her; and several old ladies, who sat on sofas, and criticized the rest of the party, inquired who she was, with an air of interest. She heard Mrs Moffat reply to one of them,—

'Daisy March—father a colonel in the army—one of our first families, but reverses of fortune, you know; intimate friends of the Laurences; sweet creature, I assure you; my Ned is quite wild about her.'

'Dear me!' said the old lady, putting up her glass for another observation of Meg, who tried to look as if she had not heard, and been rather shocked at Mrs Moffat's fibs.

The 'queer feeling' did not pass away, but she imagined herself acting the new part of fine lady, and so got on pretty well, though the tight dress gave her a side-ache, the train kept getting under her feet, and she was in constant fear lest her ear-rings should fly off, and get lost or broken. She was flirting her fan, and laughing at the feeble jokes of a young gentleman who tried to be witty, when she suddenly stopped laughing, and looked confused; for, just opposite, she saw Laurie. He was staring at her with undisguised surprise, and disapproval also, she thought; for, though he bowed and smiled, yet something in his honest eyes made her blush, and wish she had her old dress on. To complete her confusion, she saw Belle nudge Annie, and both glance from her to Laurie, who, she was happy to see, looked unusually boyish and shy.

'Silly creatures, to put such thoughts into my head! I won't care for it, or let it change me a bit,' thought Meg, and rustled across the room to shake hands with her friend.

'I'm glad you came, for I was afraid you wouldn't,' she said, with her most grown-up air.

'Jo wanted me to come, and tell her how you looked, so I did;' answered Laurie, without turning his eyes upon her, though he half smiled at her maternal tone.

'What shall you tell her?' asked Meg, full of curiosity to know his opinion of her, yet feeling ill at ease with him, for the first time.

'I shall say I didn't know you; for you look so grown-up, and unlike yourself, I'm quite afraid of you,' he said, fumbling at his glove-button.

'How absurd of you! the girls dressed me up for fun, and I rather like it. Wouldn't Jo stare if she saw me?' said Meg, bent on making him say whether he thought her improved or not.

'Yes, I think she would,' returned Laurie, gravely.

'Don't you like me so?' asked Meg.

'No, I don't,' was the blunt reply.

'Why not?' in an anxious tone.

He glanced at her frizzled head, bare shoulders, and fantastically trimmed dress, with an expression that abashed her more than his answer, which had not a particle of his usual politeness about it.

'I don't like fuss and feathers.'

That was altogether too much from a lad younger than herself; and Meg walked away, saying, petulantly,—

'You are the rudest boy I ever saw.'

Feeling very much ruffled, she went and stood at a quiet window, to cool her cheeks, for the tight dress gave her an uncomfortably brilliant color. As she stood there, Major Lincoln passed by; and, a minute after, she heard him saying to his mother,—

'They are making a fool of that little girl; I wanted you to see her, but they have spoilt her entirely; she's nothing but a doll, to-night.'

'Oh, dear!' sighed Meg; 'I wish I'd been sensible, and worn my own things; then I should not have disgusted other people, or felt so uncomfortable and ashamed myself.'

She leaned her forehead on the cool pane, and stood half hidden by the curtains, never minding that her favorite waltz had begun, till some one touched her; and, turning, she saw Laurie looking penitent, as he said, with his very best bow, and his hand out,—

'Please forgive my rudeness, and come and dance with me.'

'I'm afraid it will be too disagreeable to you,' said Meg, trying to look offended, and failing entirely.

'Not a bit of it; I'm dying to do it. Come, I'll be good; I don't like your gown, but I do think you are—just splendid;' and he waved his hands, as if words failed to express his admiration.

Meg smiled, and relented, and whispered, as they stood waiting to catch the time.

'Take care my skirt don't trip you up; it's the plague of my life, and I was a goose to wear it.'

'Pin it round your neck, and then it will be useful,' said Laurie, looking down at the little blue boots, which he evidently approved of.

Away they went, fleetly and gracefully; for, having practised at home, they were well matched, and the blithe young couple were a pleasant sight to see, as they twirled merrily round and round, feeling more friendly than ever after their small tiff.

'Laurie, I want you to do me a favor; will you?' said Meg, as he stood fanning her, when her breath gave out, which it did, very soon, though she would not own why.

'Won't I!' said Laurie, with alacrity.

'Please don't tell them at home about my dress to-night. They won't understand the joke, and it will worry mother.'

'Then why did you do it?' said Laurie's eyes, so plainly, that Meg hastily added,—

'I shall tell them, myself, all about it, and "'fess" to mother how silly I've been. But I'd rather do it myself; so you'll not tell, will you?'

'I give you my word I won't; only what shall I say when they ask me?'

'Just say I looked nice, and was having a good time.'

'I'll say the first, with all my heart; but how about the other? You don't look as if you were having a good time; are you?' and Laurie looked at her with an expression which made her answer, in a whisper,—-

'No; not just now. Don't think I'm horrid; I only wanted a little fun, but this sort don't pay, I find, and I'm getting tired of it.'

'Here comes Ned Moffat; what does he want?' said Laurie, knitting his black brows, as if he did not regard his young host in the light of a pleasant addition to the party.

'He put his name down for three dances, and I suppose he's coming for them; what a bore!' said Meg, assuming a languid air, which amused Laurie immensely.

He did not speak to her again till supper-time, when he saw her drinking champagne with Ned, and his friend Fisher, who were behaving 'like a pair of fools', as Laurie said to himself, for he felt a brotherly sort of right to watch over the Marches, and fight their battles, whenever a defender was needed.

'You'll have a splitting headache to-morrow, if you drink much of that. I wouldn't, Meg; your mother don't like it, you know,' he whispered, leaning over her chair, as Ned turned to refill her glass, and Fisher stooped to pick up her fan.

'I'm not Meg, to-night; I'm "a doll", who does all sorts of crazy things. To-morrow I shall put away my "fuss and feathers", and be desperately good again,' she answered, with an affected little laugh.

'Wish to-morrow was here, then,' muttered Laurie, walking off, ill-pleased at the change he saw in her.

Meg danced and flirted, chattered and giggled, as the other girls did; after supper she undertook the German, and blundered through it, nearly upsetting her partner with her long skirt, and romping in a way that scandalized Laurie, who looked on and meditated a lecture. But he got no chance to deliver it, for Meg kept away from him till he came to say good-night.

'Remember!' she said, trying to smile, for the splitting headache had already begun.

'Silence à la mort,' replied Laurie, with a melodramatic flourish, as he went away.

This little bit of by-play excited Annie's curiosity; but Meg was too tired for gossip, and went to bed, feeling as if she had been to a masquerade, and hadn't enjoyed herself as much as she expected. She was sick all the next day, and on Saturday went home, quite used up with her fortnight's fun, and feeling that she had sat in the lap of luxury long enough.

'It does seem pleasant to be quiet, and not have company manners on all the time. Home *is* a nice place, though it isn't splendid,' said Meg, looking about her with a restful expression, as she sat with her mother and Jo on the Sunday evening.

'I'm glad to hear you say so, dear, for I was afraid home would seem dull and poor to you, after your fine quarters,' replied her mother, who had given her many anxious looks that day; for motherly eyes are quick to see any change in children's faces.

Meg had told her adventures gaily, and said over and over what a charming time she had had; but something still seemed to weigh upon her spirits, and, when the younger girls were gone to bed, she sat thoughtfully staring at the fire, saying little, and looking worried. As the clock struck nine, and Jo proposed bed, Meg suddenly left her chair, and, taking Beth's stool, leaned her elbows on her mother's knee, saying, bravely,—

'Marmee, I want to "'fess".'

'I thought so; what is it, dear?'

'Shall I go away?' asked Jo discreetly.

'Of course not; don't I always tell you everything? I was ashamed to speak of it before the children, but I want you to know all the dreadful things I did at the Moffats'.'

'We are prepared,' said Mrs March, smiling, but looking a little anxious.

'I told you they rigged me up, but I didn't tell you that they powdered, and squeezed, and frizzled, and made me look like a fashion-plate. Laurie thought I wasn't proper; I know he did, though he didn't say so, and one man called me "a doll". I knew it was silly, but they flattered me, and said I was a beauty, and quantities of nonsense, so I let them make a fool of me.'

'Is that all?' asked Jo, as Mrs March looked silently at the downcast face of her pretty daughter, and could not find it in her heart to blame her little follies.

'No; I drank champagne, and romped, and tried to flirt, and was, altogether, abominable,' said Meg, self-reproachfully.

'There is something more, I think;' and Mrs March smoothed the soft cheek, which suddenly grew rosy, as Meg answered, slowly,—

'Yes; it's very silly, but I want to tell it, because I hate to have people say and think such things about us and Laurie.'

Then she told the various bits of gossip she had heard at the Moffats'; and, as she spoke, Jo saw her mother fold her lips tightly, as if ill pleased that such ideas should be put into Meg's innocent mind.

'Well, if that isn't the greatest rubbish I ever heard,' cried Jo, indignantly. 'Why didn't you pop out and tell them so, on the spot?'

'I couldn't, it was so embarrassing for me. I couldn't help hearing, at first, and then I was so angry and ashamed, I didn't remember that I ought to go away.'

'Just wait till *I* see Annie Moffat, and I'll show you how to settle such ridiculous stuff. The idea of having "plans", and be-ing kind to Laurie, because he's rich, and may marry us by and by! Won't he shout, when I tell him what those silly things say about us poor children?' and Jo laughed, as if, on second thoughts, the thing struck her as a good joke.

'If you tell Laurie, I'll never forgive you! She mustn't, must she, mother?' said Meg, looking distressed.

'No; never repeat that foolish gossip, and forget it as soon as you can,' said Mrs March, gravely. 'I was very unwise to let you go among people of whom I know so little; kind, I dare say, but worldly, ill-bred, and full of these vulgar ideas about young people. I am more sorry than I can express, for the mischief this visit may have done you, Meg.'

'Don't be sorry, I won't let it hurt me; I'll forget all the bad, and remember only the good; for I did enjoy a great deal, and thank you very much for letting me go. I'll not be sentimental or dissatisfied, mother; I know I'm a silly little girl, and I'll stay with you till I'm fit to take care of myself. But it *is* nice to be praised and admired, and I can't help saying I like it,' said Meg, looking half ashamed of the confession.

'That is perfectly natural, and quite harmless, if the liking does not become a passion, and lead one to do foolish or unmaidenly things. Learn to know and value the praise which is worth having, and to excite the admiration of excellent people, by being modest as well as pretty, Meg.'

Margaret sat thinking a moment, while Jo stood with her hands behind her, looking both interested and a little perplexed; for it was a new thing to see Meg blushing and talking about admiration, lovers, and things of that sort, and Jo felt as if during that fortnight her sister had grown up amazingly, and was drifting away from her into a world where she could not follow.

'Mother, do you have "plans", as Mrs Moffat said?' asked Meg, bashfully.

'Yes, my dear, I have a great many; all mothers do, but mine differ somewhat from Mrs Moffat's, I suspect. I will tell you some of them, for the time has come when a word may set this romantic little head and heart of yours right, on a very serious subject. You are young, Meg; but not too young to understand me, and mothers' lips are the fittest to speak of such things to girls like you. Jo, your turn will come in time, perhaps, so listen to my "plans", and help me carry them out, if they are good.'

Jo went and sat on one arm of the chair, looking as if she thought they were about to join in some very solemn affair. Holding a hand of each, and watching the two young faces wistfully, Mrs March said, in her serious yet cheery way,—

'I want my daughters to be beautiful, accomplished, and good; to be admired, loved, and respected, to have a happy youth, to be well and wisely married, and to lead useful, pleasant lives, with as little care and sorrow to try them as God sees fit to send. To be loved and chosen by a good man is the best and sweetest thing which can happen to a woman; and I sincerely hope my girls may know this beautiful experience. It is natural to think of it, Meg; right to hope and wait for it, and wise to prepare for it; so that, when the happy time comes, you may feel ready for the duties, and worthy of the joy. My dear girls, I *am* ambitious for you, but not to have you make a dash in the world,—marry rich men merely because they are rich, or have splendid houses, which are not homes, because love is wanting. Money is a needful and precious thing,—and, when well used, a noble thing,—but I never want you to think it is the first or only prize to strive for. I'd rather see you poor men's wives, if you were happy, beloved, contented, than queens on thrones, without self-respect and peace.'

'Poor girls don't stand any chance, Belle says, unless they put themselves forward,' sighed Meg.

'Then we'll be old maids,' said Jo, stoutly.

'Right, Jo; better be happy old maids than unhappy wives, or unmaidenly girls, running about to find husbands,' said Mrs March, decidedly. 'Don't be troubled, Meg; poverty seldom daunts a sincere lover. Some of the best and most honored women I know were poor girls, but so love-worthy that they were not allowed to be old maids. Leave these things to time; make this home happy, so that you may be fit for homes of your own, if they are offered you, and contented here if they are not. One thing remember, my girls, mother is always ready to be your confidant, father to be your friend; and both of us trust and hope that our daughters, whether married or single, will be the pride and comfort of our lives.'

'We will, Marmee, we will!' cried both, with all their hearts, as she bade them good-night.

CHAPTER TEN

The P. C. and P. O.

As spring came on, a new set of amusements became the fashion, and the lengthening days gave long afternoons for work and play of all sorts. The garden had to be put in order, and each sister had a quarter of the little plot to do what she liked with. Hannah used to say, 'I'd know which each of them gardings belonged to, ef I see 'em in Chiny;' and so she might, for the girls' tastes differed as much as their characters. Meg's had roses and heliotrope, myrtle, and a little orange-tree in it. Jo's bed was never alike two seasons, for she was always trying experiments; this year it was to be a plantation of sunflowers, the seeds of which cheerful and aspiring plant were to feed 'Aunt Cockle-top' and her family of chicks. Beth had old-fashioned, fragrant flowers in her garden; sweet peas and mignonette, larkspur, pinks, pansies, and southernwood, with chickweed for the bird and catnip for the pussies. Amy had a bower in hers,— rather small and earwiggy, but very pretty to look at,—with honeysuckles and morning-glories hanging their colored horns and bells in graceful wreaths all over it; tall white lilies, delicate ferns, and as many brilliant, picturesque plants as would consent to blossom there.

Gardening, walks, rows on the river, and flower-hunts employed the fine days; and for rainy ones, they had house diversions,—some old, some new,—all more or less original. One of these was the 'P. C.'; for, as secret societies were the fashion, it was thought proper to have one; and, as all of the girls admired Dickens, they called themselves the Pickwick Club. With a few interruptions, they had kept this up for a year, and met every Saturday evening in the big garret, on which occasions the ceremonies were as follows: Three chairs were arranged in a row before a table, on which was a lamp, also four white badges, with a big 'P. C.' in different colors on each, and the weekly newspaper, called 'The Pickwick Portfolio', to which all contributed something; while Jo, who revelled in pens and ink, was the editor. At seven o'clock, the four members ascended to the clubroom, tied their badges round their heads, and took their seats with great solemnity. Meg, as the eldest, was Samuel Pickwick; Jo, being of a literary turn, Augustus Snodgrass; Beth, because she was round and rosy, Tracy Tupman; and Amy, who was always trying to do what she couldn't, was Nathaniel Winkle. Pickwick, the President, read the paper, which was filled with original tales, poetry, local news, funny advertisements, and hints, in which they good-naturedly reminded each other of their faults and shortcomings. On one occasion, Mr Pickwick put on a pair of spectacles without any glasses, rapped upon the table, hemmed, and, having stared hard at Mr Snodgrass, who was tilting back in his chair, till he arranged himself properly, began to read,—

'The Pickwick Portfolio.'

MAY 20, 18—.

Poet's Corner.

ANNIVERSARY ODE.

Again we meet to celebrate
  With badge and solemn rite,
Our fifty-second anniversary,
  In Pickwick Hall, to-night.

We all are here in perfect health,
  None gone from our small band;
Again we see each well-known
    face,
  And press each friendly hand.

Our Pickwick, always at his
    post,
  With reverence we greet,
As, spectacles on nose, he reads
  Our well-filled weekly sheet.

Although he suffers from a cold,
  We joy to hear him speak,
For words of wisdom from him
    fall,
  In spite of croak or squeak.

Old six-foot Snodgrass looms on
    high,
  With elephantine grace,
And beams upon the company,
  With brown and jovial face.

Poetic fire lights up his eye,
  He struggles 'gainst his lot;
Behold ambition on his brow,
  And on his nose a blot!

Next our peaceful Tupman comes,
  So rosy, plump and sweet.
Who chokes with laughter at the
    puns,
  And tumbles off his seat.

Prim little Winkle too is here,
  With every hair in place,
A model of propriety,
  Though he hates to wash his
    face.

The year is gone, we still unite
  To joke and laugh and read,

And tread the path of literature
　That doth to glory lead.

Long may our paper prosper well.
　Our club unbroken be,
And coming years their blessings
　　pour
On the useful, gay 'P. C.'
　　　　　　　A. SNODGRASS.

THE MASKED MARRIAGE.
A TALE OF VENICE.

Gondola after gondola swept up to the marble steps, and left its lovely load to swell the brilliant throng that filled the stately halls of Count de Adelon. Knights and ladies, elves and pages, monks and flower-girls, all mingled gaily in the dance. Sweet voices and rich melody filled the air; and so with mirth and music the masquerade went on.

'Has your Highness seen the Lady Viola to-night?' asked a gallant troubadour of the fairy queen who floated down the hall upon his arm.

'Yes; is she not lovely, though so sad! Her dress is well chosen, too, for in a week she weds Count Antonio, whom she passionately hates.'

'By my faith I envy him. Yonder he comes, arrayed like a bridegroom, except the black mask. When that is off we shall see how he regards the fair maid whose heart he cannot win, though her stern father bestows her hand,' returned the troubadour.

' 'Tis whispered that she loves the young English artist who haunts her steps, and is spurned by the old count,' said the lady, as they joined the dance.

The revel was at its height when a priest appeared, and, withdrawing the young pair to an alcove hung with purple velvet, he motioned them to kneel. Instant silence fell upon the gay throng; and not a sound, but the dash of fountains or the rustle of orange groves sleeping in the moonlight, broke the hush, as Count de Adelon spoke thus:—

'My lords and ladies; pardon the ruse by which I have gathered you here to witness the marriage of my daughter. Father, we wait your services.'

All eyes turned toward the bridal party, and a low murmur of amazement went through the throng, for neither bride nor groom removed their masks. Curiosity and wonder possessed all hearts, but respect restrained all tongues till the holy rite was over. Then the eager spectators gathered round the count, demanding an explanation.

'Gladly would I give it if I could; but I only know that it was the whim of my timid Viola, and I yielded to it. Now, my children, let the play end. Unmask, and receive my blessing.'

But neither bent the knee; for the young bridegroom replied, in a tone that startled all listeners, as the mask fell, disclosing the noble face of Ferdinand Devereux, the artist lover, and, leaning on the breast where now flashed the star of an English earl, was the lovely Viola, radiant with joy and beauty.

'My lord, you scornfully bade me claim your daughter when I could boast as high a name and vast a fortune as the Count Antonio. I can do more; for even your ambitious soul cannot refuse the Earl of Devereux and De Vere, when he gives his ancient name and boundless wealth in return for the beloved hand of this fair lady, now my wife.'

The count stood like one changed to stone; and, turning to the bewildered crowd, Ferdinand added, with a gay smile of triumph, 'To you, my gallant friends, I can only wish that your wooing may prosper as mine has done; and that you may all win as fair a bride as I have, by this masked marriage.'

S. PICKWICK.

———

Why is the P. C. like the Tower of Babel? It is full of unruly members.

———

THE HISTORY OF A SQUASH.

Once upon a time a farmer planted a little seed in his garden, and after a while it sprouted and became a vine, and bore many squashes. One day in October, when they were ripe, he picked one and took it to market. A grocer man bought and put it in his shop. That same morning, a little girl, in a brown hat and blue dress, with a round face and snubby nose, went and bought it for her mother. She lugged it home, cut it up, and boiled it in the big pot; mashed some of it, with salt and butter, for dinner; and to the rest she added a pint of milk, two eggs, four spoons of sugar, nutmeg, and some crackers; put it in a deep dish, and baked it till it was brown and nice; and next day it was eaten by a family named March.

T. TUPMAN.

––––––––––

Mr PICKWICK, *Sir:*

I address you upon the subject of sin the sinner I mean is a man named Winkle who makes trouble in his club by laughing and sometimes won't write his piece in this fine paper I hope you will pardon his badness and let him send a French fable because he can't write out of his head as he has so many lessons to do and no brains in future I will try to take time by the fetlock and prepare some work which will be all *commy la fo* that means all right I am in haste as it is nearly school time.

Yours respectably N. WINKLE.

[*The above is a manly and handsome acknowledgment of past misdemeanors. If our young friend studied punctuation, it would be well.*]

––––––––––

A SAD ACCIDENT.

On Friday last, we were startled by a violent shock in our basement, followed by cries of distress. On rushing, in a body, to the cellar, we discovered our beloved President prostrate upon the floor, having tripped and fallen while getting wood for domestic purposes. A perfect scene of ruin met our eyes; for in his fall Mr Pickwick had plunged his head and shoulders into a tub of water, upset a keg of soft soap upon his manly form, and torn his garments badly. On being removed from this perilous situation, it was discovered that he had suffered no injury but several bruises; and, we are happy to add, is now doing well.

ED.

THE PUBLIC BEREAVEMENT.

It is our painful duty to record the sudden and mysterious disappearance of our cherished friend, Mrs Snowball Pat Paw. This lovely and beloved cat was the pet of a large circle of warm and admiring friends; for her beauty attracted all eyes, her graces and virtues endeared her to all hearts, and her loss is deeply felt by the whole community.

When last seen, she was sitting at the gate, watching the butcher's cart; and it is feared that some villain, tempted by her charms, basely stole her. Weeks have passed, but no trace of her has been discovered; and we relinquish all hope, tie a black ribbon to her basket, set aside her dish, and weep for her as one lost to us forever.

A sympathizing friend sends the following gem: —

A LAMENT
FOR S. B. PAT PAW.

We mourn the loss of our little
    pet,
  And sigh o'er her hapless fate,
For never more by the fire she'll
    sit,
  Nor play by the old green gate.

The little grave where her infant
    sleeps,
  Is 'neath the chestnut tree;
But o'er *her* grave we may not
    weep,
  We know not where it may be.

Her empty bed, her idle ball,
  Will never see her more;
No gentle tap, no loving purr
  Is heard at the parlor door.

Another cat comes after her mice,
  A cat with a dirty face;
But she does not hunt as our
    darling did,
  Nor play with her airy grace.

Her stealthy paws tread the very
    hall
  Where Snowball used to play,
But she only spits at the dogs
    our pet
  So gallantly drove away.

She is useful and mild, and does
    her best,
  But she is not fair to see;
And we cannot give her your
    place, dear,
  Nor worship her as we worship
    thee.

A. S.

ADVERTISEMENTS.

MISS ORANTHY BLUGGAGE, the accomplished Strong-Minded Lecturer, will deliver her famous Lecture on 'WOMAN AND HER POSITION,' at Pickwick Hall, next Saturday Evening, after the usual performances.

A WEEKLY MEETING will be held at Kitchen Place, to teach young ladies how to cook. Hannah Brown will preside; and all are invited to attend.

THE DUSTPAN SOCIETY will meet on Wednesday next, and parade in the upper story of the Club House. All members to appear in uniform and shoulder their brooms at nine precisely.

MRS BETH BOUNCER will open her new assortment of Doll's Millinery next week. The latest Paris Fashions have arrived, and orders are respectfully solicited.

A NEW PLAY will appear at the Barnville Theatre, in the course of a few weeks, which will surpass anything ever seen on the American stage. 'THE GREEK SLAVE, or Constantine the Avenger' is the name of this thrilling drama!!!

HINTS.

If S. P. didn't use so much soap on his hands, he wouldn't always be

late at breakfast. A. S. is requested	WEEKLY REPORT.
not to whistle in the street. T. T.	Meg—Good.
please don't forget Amy's napkin.	Jo—Bad.
N. W. must not fret because his	Beth—Very good.
dress has not nine tucks.	Amy—Middling.

As the President finished reading the paper (which I beg leave to assure my readers is a *bona fide* copy of one written by *bona fide* girls once upon a time), a round of applause followed, and then Mr Snodgrass rose to make a proposition.

'Mr President and gentlemen,' he began, assuming a parliamentary attitude and tone, 'I wish to propose the admission of a new member; one who highly deserves the honor, would be deeply grateful for it, and would add immensely to the spirit of the club, the literary value of the paper, and be no end jolly and nice. I propose Mr Theodore Laurence as an honorary member of the P. C. Come now, do have him.'

Jo's sudden change of tone made the girls laugh; but all looked rather anxious, and no one said a word, as Snodgrass took his seat.

'We'll put it to vote,' said the President. 'All in favor of this motion please to manifest it by saying "Aye".'

A loud response from Snodgrass, followed, to everybody's surprise, by a timid one from Beth.

'Contrary minded say "no".'

Meg and Amy were contrary minded; and Mr Winkle rose to say, with great elegance, 'We don't wish any boys; they only joke and bounce about. This is a ladies' club, and we wish to be private and proper.'

'I'm afraid he'll laugh at our paper, and make fun of us afterward,' observed Pickwick, pulling the little curl on her forehead, as she always did when doubtful.

Up bounced Snodgrass, very much in earnest. 'Sir! I give you my word as a gentleman, Laurie won't do anything of the sort. He likes to write, and he'll give a tone to our contributions, and keep us from being sentimental, don't you see? We can do so little for him, and he does so much for us, I think the least we can do is to offer him a place here, and make him welcome, if he comes.'

This artful allusion to benefits conferred, brought Tupman to his feet, looking as if he had quite made up his mind.

'Yes; we ought to do it, even if we *are* afraid. I say he may come, and his grandpa too, if he likes.'

This spirited burst from Beth electrified the club, and Jo left her seat to shake hands approvingly. 'Now then, vote again. Everybody remember it's our Laurie, and say "Aye"!' cried Snodgrass, excitedly.

'Aye! aye! aye!' replied three voices at once.

'Good! bless you! now, as there's nothing like "taking time by the *fetlock*", as Winkle characteristically observes, allow me to present the new member;' and, to the dismay of the rest of the club, Jo threw open the door of the closet, and displayed Laurie sitting on a rag-bag, flushed and twinkling with suppressed laughter.

'You rogue! you traitor! Jo, how could you?' cried the three girls, as Snodgrass led her friend triumphantly forth; and, producing both a chair and a badge, installed him in a jiffy.

'The coolness of you two rascals is amazing,' began Mr Pickwick, trying to get up an awful frown, and only succeeding in producing an amiable smile. But the new member was equal to the occasion; and, rising with a grateful salutation to the Chair, said, in the most engaging manner,—'Mr President and ladies,—I beg pardon, gentlemen,—allow me to introduce myself as Sam Weller, the very humble servant of the club.'

'Good, good!' cried Jo, pounding with the handle of the old warming-pan on which she leaned.

'My faithful friend and noble patron,' continued Laurie, with a wave of the hand, 'who has so flatteringly presented me, is not to be blamed for the base stratagem of to-night. I planned it, and she only gave in after lots of teasing.'

'Come now, don't lay it all on yourself; you know I proposed the cupboard,' broke in Snodgrass, who was enjoying the joke amazingly.

'Never you mind what she says. I'm the wretch that did it, sir,' said the new member, with a Welleresque nod to Mr Pickwick. 'But on my honor, I never will do so again, and henceforth *dewote* myself to the interest of this immortal club.'

'Hear! hear!' cried Jo, clashing the lid of the warming-pan like a cymbal.

'Go on, go on!' added Winkle and Tupman, while the President bowed benignly.

'I merely wish to say, that as a slight token of my gratitude for the honor done me, and as a means of promoting friendly relations between adjoining nations, I have set up a post-office in the hedge in the lower corner of the garden; a fine, spacious building, with padlocks on the doors, and every convenience for the mails,—also the females, if I may be allowed the expression. It's the old martin-house; but I've stopped up the door, and made the roof open, so it will hold all sorts of things, and save our valuable time. Letters, manuscripts, books and bundles can be passed in there; and, as each nation has a key, it will be uncommonly nice, I fancy. Allow me to present the club key; and, with many thanks for your favor, take my seat.'

Great applause as Mr Weller deposited a little key on the table, and subsided; the warming-pan clashed and waved wildly, and it was some time before order could be restored. A long discussion followed, and every one came out surprising, for every one did her best; so it was an unusually lively meeting, and did not adjourn till a late hour, when it broke up with three shrill cheers for the new member.

No one ever regretted the admittance of Sam Weller, for a more devoted, well-behaved, and jovial member no club could have. He certainly did add 'spirit' to the meetings, and 'a tone' to the paper; for his orations convulsed his hearers, and his contributions were excellent, being patriotic, classical, comical, or dramatic, but never sentimental. Jo regarded them as worthy of Bacon, Milton, or Shakespeare; and remodelled her own works with good effect, she thought.

The P. O. was a capital little institution, and flourished wonderfully, for nearly as many queer things passed through it as through the real office. Tragedies and cravats, poetry and pickles, garden seeds and long letters, music and gingerbread, rubbers, invitations, scoldings and puppies. The old gentleman liked the fun, and amused himself by sending odd bundles, mysterious messages, and funny telegrams; and his gardener, who was smitten with Hannah's charms, actually sent a love-letter to Jo's care. How they laughed when the secret came out, never dreaming how many love-letters that little post-office would hold in the years to come!

CHAPTER ELEVEN

---•●•---

Experiments

'The first of June; the Kings are off to the seashore to-morrow, and I'm free! Three months' vacation! how I shall enjoy it!' exclaimed Meg, coming home one warm day to find Jo laid upon the sofa in an unusual state of exhaustion, while Beth took off her dusty boots, and Amy made lemonade for the refreshment of the whole party.

'Aunt March went to-day, for which, oh be joyful!' said Jo. 'I was mortally afraid she'd ask me to go with her; if she had, I should have felt as if I ought to do it; but Plumfield is about as festive as a churchyard, you know, and I'd rather be excused. We had a flurry getting the old lady off, and I had a scare every time she spoke to me, for I was in such a hurry to be through that I was uncommonly helpful and sweet, and feared she'd find it impossible to part from me. I quaked till she was fairly in the carriage, and had a final fright, for, as it drove off, she popped out her head, saying, "Josyphine, won't you—?" I didn't hear any more, for I basely turned and fled; I did actually run, and whisked round the corner, where I felt safe.'

'Poor old Jo! she came in looking as if bears were after her,' said Beth, as she cuddled her sister's feet with a motherly air.

'Aunt March is a regular samphire, is she not?' observed Amy, tasting her mixture critically.

'She means *vampire*, not sea-weed; but it don't matter; it's too warm to be particular about one's parts of speech,' murmured Jo.

'What shall you do all your vacation?' asked Amy, changing the subject, with tact.

'I shall lie abed late, and do nothing,' replied Meg, from the depths of the rocking-chair. 'I've been routed up early all winter, and had to spend my days working for other people; so now I'm going to rest and revel to my heart's content.'

'Hum!' said Jo; 'that dozy way wouldn't suit me. I've laid in a heap of books, and I'm going to improve my shining hours reading on my perch in the old apple-tree, when I'm not having l—'

'Don't say "larks"!' implored Amy, as a return snub for the 'samphire' correction.

'I'll say "nightingales", then, with Laurie; that's proper and appropriate, since he's a warbler.'

'Don't let us do any lessons, Beth, for a while, but play all the time, and rest, as the girls mean to,' proposed Amy.

'Well, I will, if mother don't mind. I want to learn some new songs, and my children need fixing up for the summer; they are dreadfully out of order, and really suffering for clothes.'

'May we, mother?' asked Meg, turning to Mrs March, who sat sewing, in what they called 'Marmee's corner'.

'You may try your experiment for a week, and see how you like it. I think by Saturday night you will find that all play, and no work, is as bad as all work, and no play.'

'Oh, dear, no! it will be delicious, I'm sure,' said Meg, complacently.

'I now propose a toast, as my "friend and pardner, Sairy Gamp", says. Fun forever, and no grubbage,' cried Jo, rising, glass in hand, as the lemonade went round.

They all drank it merrily, and began the experiment by lounging for the rest of the day. Next morning, Meg did not appear till ten o'clock; her solitary breakfast did not taste good, and the room seemed lonely and untidy, for Jo had not filled the vases, Beth had not dusted, and Amy's books lay scattered about. Nothing was neat and pleasant but 'Marmee's corner', which looked as usual; and there she sat, to 'rest and read', which meant yawn, and imagine what pretty summer dresses she would get with her salary. Jo spent the morning on the river, with Laurie, and the afternoon reading and crying over *The Wide, Wide World* up in the apple-tree. Beth began by rummaging everything out of the big closet, where her family resided; but, getting tired before half done, she left her establishment topsy-turvy, and went to her music, rejoicing that she had no dishes to wash. Amy arranged her bower, put on her best white frock, smoothed her curls, and sat down to draw, under the honeysuckles, hoping some one would see and inquire who the young artist was. As no one appeared but an inquisitive daddy-long-legs, who examined her work with interest, she went to walk, got caught in a shower, and came home dripping.

At tea-time they compared notes, and all agreed that it had been a delightful, though unusually long, day. Meg, who went shopping in the afternoon, and got a 'sweet blue muslin', had discovered, after she had cut the breadths off, that it wouldn't wash, which mishap made her slightly cross. Jo had burnt the skin off her nose boating, and got a raging headache by reading too long. Beth was worried by the confusion of her closet, and the difficulty of learning three or four songs at once; and Amy deeply regretted the damage done her frock, for Katy Brown's party was to be the next day; and now, like Flora McFlimsy, she had 'nothing to wear'. But these were mere trifles; and they assured their mother that the experiment was working finely. She smiled, said nothing, and, with Hannah's help, did their neglected work, keeping home pleasant, and the domestic machinery running smoothly. It was astonishing what a peculiar and uncomfortable state of things was produced by the 'resting and revelling' process. The days kept getting longer and longer; the weather was unusually variable, and so were tempers; an unsettled feeling possessed every one, and Satan found plenty of mischief for the idle hands to do. As the height of luxury, Meg put out some of her sewing, and then found time hang so heavily, that she fell to snipping and spoiling her clothes, in her attempts to furbish them up, à la Moffat. Jo read till her eyes gave out, and she was sick of books; got so fidgety that even good-natured Laurie had a quarrel with her, and so reduced in spirits that she desperately wished she had gone with Aunt March. Beth got on pretty well, for she was constantly forgetting that it was to be *all play, and no work*, and fell back into her old ways, now and then; but something in the air affected her, and, more than once, her tranquillity was much disturbed; so much so, that, on one occasion, she actually shook poor dear Joanna, and told her she was 'a fright'. Amy fared worst of all, for her resources were small; and, when her sisters left her to amuse and care for herself, she soon found that accomplished and important little self a great burden. She didn't like dolls; fairy tales were childish, and one couldn't draw all the time. Tea-parties didn't amount to much, neither did picnics, unless very well conducted. 'If one could have a fine house, full of nice girls, or go travelling, the summer would be delightful; but to stay at home with three selfish sisters, and a grown-up boy, was enough to try the patience of a Boaz,' complained Miss Malaprop, after several days devoted to pleasure, fretting, and *ennui*.

No one would own that they were tired of the experiment; but, by Friday night, each acknowledged to herself that they were glad the week was nearly done. Hoping to impress the lesson more deeply, Mrs March, who had a good deal of humor, resolved to finish off the trial in an appropriate manner; so she gave Hannah a holiday, and let the girls enjoy the full effect of the play system.

When they got up on Saturday morning, there was no fire in the kitchen, no breakfast in the dining-room, and no mother anywhere to be seen.

'Mercy on us! what *has* happened?' cried Jo, staring about her in dismay.

Meg ran upstairs, and soon came back again, looking relieved, but rather bewildered, and a little ashamed.

'Mother isn't sick, only very tired, and she says she is going to stay quietly in her room all day, and let us do the best we can. It's a very queer thing for her to do, she don't act a bit like herself; but she says it *has* been a hard week for her, so we mustn't grumble, but take care of ourselves.'

'That's easy enough, and I like the idea; I'm aching for something to do—that is, some new amusement, you know,' added Jo, quickly.

In fact it *was* an immense relief to them all to have a little work, and they took hold with a will, but soon realized the truth of Hannah's saying, 'Housekeeping ain't no joke.' There was plenty of food in the larder, and while Beth and Amy set the table, Meg and Jo got breakfast; wondering, as they did so, why servants ever talked about hard work.

'I shall take some up to mother, though she said we were not to think of her, for she'd take care of herself,' said Meg, who presided, and felt quite matronly behind the teapot.

So a tray was fitted out before any one began, and taken up, with the cook's compliments. The boiled tea was very bitter, the omelette scorched, and the biscuits speckled with saleratus; but Mrs March received her repast with thanks, and laughed heartily over it after Jo was gone.

'Poor little souls, they will have a hard time, I'm afraid; but they won't suffer, and it will do them good,' she said, producing the more palatable viands with which she had provided herself, and disposing of the bad breakfast, so that their feelings might not be hurt;—a motherly little deception, for which they were grateful.

Many were the complaints below, and great the chagrin of the head cook, at her failures. 'Never mind, I'll get the dinner, and be servant; you be missis, keep your hands nice, see company, and give orders,' said Jo, who knew still less than Meg about culinary affairs.

This obliging offer was gladly accepted and Margaret retired to the parlor, which she hastily put in order by whisking
the litter under the sofa, and shutting the blinds, to save the
trouble of dusting. Jo, with perfect faith in her own powers,
and a friendly desire to make up the quarrel, immediately put
a note in the office, inviting Laurie to dinner.

'You'd better see what you have got before you think of
having company,' said Meg, when informed of the hospitable,
but rash act.

'Oh, there's corned beef, and plenty of potatoes; and I shall
get some asparagus, and a lobster, "for a relish", as Hannah
says. We'll have lettuce, and make a salad; I don't know how,
but the book tells. I'll have blanc-mange and strawberries for
dessert; and coffee, too, if you want to be elegant.'

'Don't try too many messes, Jo, for you can't make
anything but gingerbread and molasses candy, fit to eat. I wash
my hands of the dinner-party; and, since you have asked
Laurie on your own responsibility, you may just take care
of him.'

'I don't want you to do anything but be clever to him, and
help to the pudding. You'll give me your advice if I get stuck,
won't you?' asked Jo, rather hurt.

'Yes; but I don't know much, except about bread, and a
few trifles. You had better ask mother's leave, before you
order anything,' returned Meg, prudently.

'Of course I shall; I ain't a fool,' and Jo went off in a huff
at the doubts expressed of her powers.

'Get what you like, and don't disturb me; I'm going out to
dinner, and can't worry about things at home,' said Mrs
March, when Jo spoke to her. 'I never enjoyed housekeeping,

and I'm going to take a vacation today, and read, write, go visiting and amuse myself.'

The unusual spectacle of her busy mother rocking comfortably, and reading early in the morning, made Jo feel as if some natural phenomenon had occurred; for an eclipse, an earthquake, or a volcanic eruption would hardly have seemed stranger.

'Everything is out of sorts, somehow,' she said to herself, going down stairs. 'There's Beth crying; that's a sure sign that something is wrong with this family. If Amy is bothering, I'll shake her.'

Feeling very much out of sorts herself, Jo hurried into the parlor to find Beth sobbing over Pip, the canary, who lay dead in the cage, with his little claws pathetically extended, as if imploring the food, for want of which he had died.

'It's all my fault—I forgot him—there isn't a seed or drop left—oh, Pip! oh, Pip! how could I be so cruel to you?' cried Beth, taking the poor thing in her hands, and trying to restore him.

Jo peeped into his half-open eye, felt his little heart, and finding him stiff and cold, shook her head, and offered her domino-box for a coffin.

'Put him in the oven, and maybe he will get warm, and revive,' said Amy, hopefully.

'He's been starved, and he shan't be baked, now he's dead. I'll make him a shroud, and he shall be buried in the grave; and I'll never have another bird, never, my Pip! for I am too bad to own one,' murmured Beth, sitting on the floor with her pet folded in her hands.

'The funeral shall be this afternoon, and we will all go.

Now, don't cry, Bethy; it's a pity, but nothing goes right this week, and Pip has had the worst of the experiment. Make the shroud, and lay him in my box; and, after the dinner-party, we'll have a nice little funeral,' said Jo, beginning to feel as if she had undertaken a good deal.

Leaving the others to console Beth, she departed to the kitchen, which was in a most discouraging state of confusion. Putting on a big apron, she fell to work, and got the dishes piled up ready for washing, when she discovered that the fire was out.

'Here's a sweet prospect!' muttered Jo, slamming the stove door open, and poking vigorously among the cinders.

Having rekindled it, she thought she would go to market while the water heated. The walk revived her spirits; and, flattering herself that she had made good bargains, she trudged home again, after buying a very young lobster, some very old asparagus, and two boxes of acid strawberries. By the time she got cleared up, the dinner arrived, and the stove was red-hot. Hannah had left a pan of bread to rise, Meg had worked it up early, set it on the hearth for a second rising, and forgotten it. Meg was entertaining Sallie Gardiner, in the parlor, when the door flew open, and a floury, crocky, flushed and dishevelled figure appeared, demanding, tartly,—

'I say, isn't bread "riz" enough when it runs over the pans?'

Sallie began to laugh; but Meg nodded, and lifted her eyebrows as high as they would go, which caused the apparition to vanish, and put the sour bread into the oven without further delay. Mrs March went out, after peeping here and there to see how matters went, also saying a word of comfort to Beth, who sat making a winding-sheet, while the dear departed lay in state in the domino-box. A strange sense of helplessness fell upon the girls as the gray bonnet vanished round the corner; and despair seized them, when, a few minutes later, Miss Crocker appeared, and said she'd come to dinner. Now this lady was a thin, yellow spinster, with a sharp nose, and inquisitive eyes, who saw everything, and gossiped about all she saw. They disliked her, but had been taught to be kind to her, simply because she was old and poor, and had few friends. So Meg gave her the easy-chair, and tried to entertain her, while she asked questions, criticized everything, and told stories of the people whom she knew.

Language cannot describe the anxieties, experiences, and exertions which Jo underwent that morning; and the dinner she served up became a standing joke. Fearing to ask any more advice, she did her best alone, and discovered that something more than energy and good-will is necessary to make a cook. She boiled the asparagus hard for an hour, and was grieved to find the heads cooked off, and the stalks harder than ever. The bread burnt black; for the salad dressing so aggravated her, that she let everything else go, till she had convinced herself that she could not make it fit to eat. The lobster was a scarlet mystery to her, but she hammered and poked, till it was unshelled, and its meagre proportions concealed in a grove of lettuce-leaves. The potatoes had to be hurried, not to keep the asparagus waiting, and were not done at last. The blanc-mange was lumpy, and the strawberries not as ripe as they looked, having been skillfully 'deaconed'.

'Well, they can eat beef, and bread and butter, if they are hungry; only it's mortifying to have to spend your whole morning for nothing,' thought Jo, as she rang the bell half an hour later than usual, and stood hot, tired, and dispirited, surveying the feast spread for Laurie, accustomed to all sorts of elegance, and Miss Crocker, whose curious eyes would mark all failures, and whose tattling tongue would report them far and wide.

Poor Jo would gladly have gone under the table, as one thing after another was tasted and left; while Amy giggled, Meg looked distressed, Miss Crocker pursed up her lips, and Laurie talked and laughed with all his might, to give a cheerful tone to the festive scene. Jo's one strong point was the fruit, for she had sugared it well, and had a pitcher of rich cream to eat with it. Her hot cheeks cooled a trifle, and she drew a long breath, as the pretty glass plates went round, and every one looked graciously at the little rosy islands floating in a sea of cream. Miss Crocker tasted first, made a wry face, and drank some water hastily. Jo, who had refused, thinking there might not be enough, for they dwindled sadly after the picking over, glanced at Laurie, but he was eating away manfully, though there was a slight pucker about his mouth, and he kept his eye fixed on his plate. Amy, who was fond of delicate fare, took a heaping spoonful, choked, hid her face in her napkin, and left the table precipitately.

'Oh, what is it?' exclaimed Jo, trembling.

'Salt instead of sugar, and the cream is sour,' replied Meg, with a tragic gesture.

Jo uttered a groan, and fell back in her chair; remembering that she had given a last hasty powdering to the berries out of one of the two boxes on the kitchen table, and had neglected to put the milk in the refrigerator. She turned scarlet, and was on the verge of crying, when she met Laurie's eyes, which *would* look merry in spite of his heroic efforts; the comical side of the affair suddenly struck her, and she laughed till the tears ran down her cheeks. So did every one else, even 'Croaker', as the girls called the old lady; and the unfortunate dinner ended gaily, with bread and butter, olives and fun.

'I haven't strength of mind enough to clear up now, so we will sober ourselves with a funeral,' said Jo, as they rose; and Miss Crocker made ready to go, being eager to tell the new story at another friend's dinner-table.

They did sober themselves, for Beth's sake; Laurie dug a grave under the ferns in the grove, little Pip was laid in, with many tears, by his tender-hearted mistress, and covered with moss, while a wreath of violets and chickweed was hung on the stone which bore his epitaph, composed by Jo, while she struggled with the dinner:—

> *'Here lies Pip March,*
> *Who died the 7th of June;*
> *Loved and lamented sore,*
> *And not forgotten soon.'*

At the conclusion of the ceremonies, Beth retired to her room, overcome with emotion and lobster; but there was no place of repose, for the beds were not made, and she found her grief much assuaged by beating up pillows and putting things in order. Meg helped Jo clear away the remains of the feast, which took half the afternoon, and left them so tired that they agreed to be contented with tea and toast for supper. Laurie took Amy to drive, which was a deed of charity, for the sour cream seemed to have had a bad effect upon her temper. Mrs March came home to find the three older girls hard at work in the middle of the afternoon; and a glance at the closet gave her an idea of the success of one part of the experiment.

Before the housewives could rest, several people called, and there was a scramble to get ready to see them; then tea must be got, errands done; and one or two bits of sewing were necessary, but neglected till the last minute. As twilight fell, dewy and still, one by one they gathered in the porch where the June roses were budding beautifully, and each groaned or sighed as she sat down, as if tired or troubled.

'What a dreadful day this has been!' began Jo, usually the first to speak.

'It has seemed shorter than usual, but *so* uncomfortable,' said Meg.

'Not a bit like home,' added Amy.

'It can't seem so without Marmee and little Pip,' sighed Beth, glancing, with full eyes, at the empty cage above her head.

'Here's mother, dear, and you shall have another bird to-morrow, if you want it.'

As she spoke, Mrs March came and took her place among them, looking as if her holiday had not been much pleasanter than theirs.

'Are you satisfied with your experiment, girls, or do you want another week of it?' she asked, as Beth nestled up to her, and the rest turned toward her with brightening faces, as flowers turn toward the sun.

'I don't!' cried Jo, decidedly.

'Nor I,' echoed the others.

'You think, then, that it is better to have a few duties, and live a little for others, do you?'

'Lounging and larking don't pay,' observed Jo, shaking her head. 'I'm tired of it, and mean to go to work at something right off.'

'Suppose you learn plain cooking; that's a useful accomplishment, which no woman should be without,' said Mrs March, laughing audibly at the recollection of Jo's dinnerparty; for she had met Miss Crocker, and heard her account of it.

'Mother! did you go away and let everything be, just to see how we'd get on?' cried Meg, who had had suspicions all day.

'Yes; I wanted you to see how the comfort of all depends on each doing their share faithfully. While Hannah and I did your work, you got on pretty well, though I don't think you were very happy or amiable; so I thought, as a little lesson, I would show you what happens when every one thinks only of herself. Don't you feel that it is pleasanter to help one another, to have daily duties which make leisure sweet when it comes, and to bear or forbear, that home may be comfortable and lovely to us all?'

'We do, mother, we do!' cried the girls.

'Then let me advise you to take up your little burdens again; for though they seem heavy sometimes, they are good for us, and lighten as we learn to carry them. Work is wholesome, and there is plenty for every one; it keeps us from *ennui* and mischief; is good for health and spirits, and gives us a sense of power and independence better than money or fashion.'

'We'll work like bees, and love it too; see if we don't!' said

Jo. 'I'll learn plain cooking for my holiday task; and the next dinner-party I have shall be a success.'

'I'll make the set of shirts for father, instead of letting you do it, Marmee. I can and I will, though I'm not fond of sewing; that will be better than fussing over my own things, which are plenty nice enough as they are,' said Meg.

'I'll do my lessons every day, and not spend so much time with my music and dolls. I am a stupid thing, and ought to be studying, not playing,' was Beth's resolution; while Amy followed their example, by heroically declaring, 'I shall learn to make buttonholes, and attend to my parts of speech.'

'Very good! then I am quite satisfied with the experiment, and fancy that we shall not have to repeat it; only don't go to the other extreme, and delve like slaves. Have regular hours for work and play; make each day both useful and pleasant, and prove that you understand the worth of time by employing it well. Then youth will be delightful, old age will bring few regrets, and life become a beautiful success, in spite of poverty.'

'We'll remember, mother!' and they did.

CHAPTER TWELVE

Camp Laurence

Beth was post-mistress, for, being most at home, she could attend to it regularly, and dearly liked the daily task of unlocking the little door and distributing the mail. One July day she came in with her hands full, and went about the house leaving letters and parcels, like the penny post.

'Here's your posy, mother! Laurie never forgets that,' she said, putting the fresh nosegay in the vase that stood in 'Marmee's corner', and was kept supplied by the affectionate boy.

'Miss Meg March, one letter, and a glove,' continued Beth, delivering the articles to her sister, who sat near her mother, stitching wristbands.

'Why, I left a pair over there, and here is only one,' said Meg, looking at the gray cotton glove.

'Didn't you drop the other in the garden?'

'No, I'm sure I didn't; for there was only one in the office.'

'I hate to have odd gloves! Never mind, the other may be found. My letter is only a translation of the German song I wanted; I guess Mr Brooke did it, for this isn't Laurie's writing.'

Mrs March glanced at Meg, who was looking very pretty in her gingham morning-gown, with the little curls blowing about her forehead, and very womanly, as she sat sewing at her little work-table, full of tidy white rolls; so, unconscious of the thought in her mother's mind, she sewed and sung while her fingers flew, and her mind was busied with girlish fancies as innocent and fresh as the pansies in her belt, that Mrs March smiled, and was satisfied.

'Two letters for Doctor Jo, a book, and a funny old hat, which covered the whole post-office, stuck outside,' said Beth, laughing, as she went into the study, where Jo sat writing.

'What a sly fellow Laurie is! I said I wished bigger hats were the fashion, because I burn my face every hot day. He said, "Why mind the fashion? wear a big hat, and be comfortable!" I said I would, if I had one, and he has sent me this, to try me; I'll wear it, for fun, and show him I *don't* care for the fashion;' and, hanging the antique broad-brim on a bust of Plato, Jo read her letters.

One from her mother made her cheeks glow, and her eyes fill, for it said to her,—

'My dear:
'I write a little word to tell you with how much satisfaction I watch your efforts to control your temper. You say nothing about your trials, failures, or successes, and think, perhaps, that no one sees them but the Friend whose help you daily ask, if I may trust the well-worn cover of your guidebook,

I, too, have seen them all, and heartily believe in the sincerity of your resolution, since it begins to bear fruit. Go on, dear, patiently and bravely, and always believe that no one sympathizes more tenderly with you than your loving

Mother.'

'That does me good! that's worth millions of money, and pecks of praise. Oh, Marmee, I do try! I will keep on trying, and not get tired, since I have you to help me.'

Laying her head on her arms, Jo wet her little romance with a few happy tears, for she *had* thought that no one saw and appreciated her efforts to be good, and this assurance was doubly precious, doubly encouraging, because unexpected, and from the person whose commendation she most valued. Feeling stronger than ever to meet and subdue her Apollyon, she pinned the note inside her frock, as a shield and a reminder, lest she be taken unaware, and proceeded to open her other letter, quite ready for either good or bad news. In a big, dashing hand, Laurie wrote,—

'Dear Jo,
What ho!

Some English girls and boys are coming to see me to-morrow, and I want to have a jolly time. If it's fine, I'm going to pitch my tent in Longmeadow, and row up the whole crew to lunch and croquet;—have a fire, make messes, gipsey fashion, and all sorts of larks. They are nice people, and like such things. Brooke will go, to keep us boys steady, and Kate Vaughn will play propriety for the girls. I want you all to come; can't let Beth off, at any price, and noboby shall worry her. Don't

bother about rations,—I'll see to that, and everything else,—
only do come, there's a good fellow!

'In a tearing hurry,
Yours ever, Laurie.'

'Here's richness!' cried Jo, flying in to tell the news to Meg.
'Of course we can go, mother! it will be such a help to Laurie,
for I can row, and Meg see to the lunch, and the children be
useful some way.'

'I hope the Vaughns are not fine, grown-up people. Do you
know anything about them, Jo?' asked Meg.

'Only that there are four of them. Kate is older than you,
Fred and Frank (twins) about my age, and a little girl (Grace),
who is nine or ten. Laurie knew them abroad, and liked the
boys; I fancied, from the way he primmed up his mouth in
speaking of her, that he didn't admire Kate much.'

'I'm so glad my French print is clean, it's just the thing, and
so becoming!' observed Meg, complacently. 'Have you anything decent, Jo?'

'Scarlet and gray boating suit, good enough for me; I shall
row and tramp about, so I don't want any starch to think of.
You'll come, Betty?'

'If you won't let any of the boys talk to me.'

'Not a boy!'

'I like to please Laurie; and I'm not afraid of Mr Brooke, he
is so kind; but I don't want to play, or sing, or say anything. I'll
work hard, and not trouble any one; and you'll take care of
me, Jo, so I'll go.'

'That's my good girl; you do try to fight off your shyness,
and I love you for it; fighting faults isn't easy, as I know; and a

cheery word kind of gives a lift. Thank you, mother,' and Jo gave the thin cheek a grateful kiss, more precious to Mrs March than if it had given her back the rosy roundness of her youth.

'I had a box of chocolate drops, and the picture I wanted to copy,' said Amy, showing her mail.

'And I got a note from Mr Laurence, asking me to come over and play to him to-night, before the lamps are lighted, and I shall go,' added Beth, whose friendship with the old gentleman prospered finely.

'Now let's fly round, and do double duty today, so that we can play to-morrow with free minds,' said Jo, preparing to re-place her pen with a broom.

When the sun peeped into the girls' room early next morning, to promise them a fine day, he saw a comical sight. Each had made such preparation for the fête as seemed necessary and proper. Meg had an extra row of little curl pa-pers across her forehead, Jo had copiously anointed her af-flicted face with cold cream, Beth had taken Joanna to bed with her to atone for the approaching separation, and Amy had capped the climax by putting a clothes-pin on her nose, to uplift the offending feature. It was one of the kind artists use to hold the paper on their drawing-boards; therefore, quite appropriate and effective for the purpose to which it was now put. This funny spectacle appeared to amuse the sun, for he burst out with such radiance that Jo woke up, and roused all her sisters by a hearty laugh at Amy's ornament.

Sunshine and laughter were good omens for a pleasure party, and soon a lively bustle began in both houses. Beth, who was ready first, kept reporting what went on next door, and enlivened her sisters' toilets by frequent telegrams from the window.

'There goes the man with the tent! I see Mrs Barker doing up the lunch, in a hamper, and a great basket. Now Mr Laurence is looking up at the sky, and the weathercock; I wish he would go, too! There's Laurie looking like a sailor,— nice boy! Oh, mercy me! here's a carriage full of people—a tall lady, a little girl, and two dreadful boys. One is lame; poor thing, he's got a crutch! Laurie didn't tell us that. Be quick, girls! it's getting late. Why, there is Ned Moffat, I do declare. Look, Meg! isn't that the man who bowed to you one day, when we were shopping?'

'So it is; how queer that he should come! I thought he was at the Mountains. There is Sallie; I'm glad she got back in time. Am I all right, Jo?' cried Meg, in a flutter.

'A regular daisy; hold up your dress, and put your hat straight; it looks sentimental tipped that way, and will fly off at the first puff. Now, then, come on!'

'Oh, oh, Jo! you ain't going to wear that awful hat? It's too absurd! You shall *not* make a guy of yourself,' remonstrated Meg, as Jo tied down, with a red ribbon, the broad-brimmed, old-fashioned Leghorn Laurie had sent for a joke.

'I just will, though! it's capital; so shady, light, and big. It will make fun; and I don't mind being a guy, if I'm comfortable.' With that Jo marched straight away, and the rest followed; a bright little band of sisters, all looking their best, in summer suits, with happy faces, under the jaunty hat-brims.

Laurie ran to meet, and present them to his friends, in the most cordial manner. The lawn was the reception room, and for several minutes a lively scene was enacted there. Meg was grateful to see that Miss Kate, though twenty, was dressed with a simplicity which American girls would do well to imitate; and she was much flattered by Mr Ned's assurances that he came especially to see her. Jo understood why Laurie 'primmed up his mouth' when speaking of Kate, for that young lady had a stand-off-don't-touch-me air, which contrasted strongly with the free and easy demeanor of the other girls. Beth took an observation of the new boys, and decided that the lame one was not 'dreadful', but gentle and feeble, and she would be kind to him, on that account. Amy found Grace a well-mannered, merry little person; and, after staring dumbly at one another for a few minutes, they suddenly became very good friends.

Tents, lunch, and croquet utensils having been sent on beforehand, the party was soon embarked, and the two boats pushed off together, leaving Mr Laurence waving his hat on the shore. Laurie and Jo rowed one boat; Mr Brooke and Ned the other; while Fred Vaughn, the riotous twin, did his best to upset both, by paddling about in a wherry, like a disturbed waterbug. Jo's funny hat deserved a vote of thanks, for it was of general utility; it broke the ice in the beginning, by producing a laugh; it created quite a refreshing breeze, flapping to and fro, as she rowed, and would make an excellent umbrella for the whole party, if a shower came up, she said. Kate looked rather amazed at Jo's proceedings, especially as she exclaimed 'Christopher Columbus!' when she lost her oar; and Laurie said, 'My dear fellow, did I hurt you?' when he tripped over her feet in taking his place. But after putting up her glass to examine the queer girl several times, Miss Kate decided that she was 'odd, but rather clever', and smiled upon her from afar.

Meg, in the other boat, was delightfully situated, face to face with the rowers, who both admired the prospect, and feathered their oars with uncommon 'skill and dexterity'. Mr Brooke was a grave, silent young man, with handsome brown eyes, and a pleasant voice. Meg liked his quiet manners, and considered him a walking encyclopædia of useful knowledge. He never talked to her much; but he looked at her a good deal, and she felt sure that he did not regard her with aversion. Ned being in college, of course put on all the airs which Freshmen think it their bounden duty to assume; he was not very wise, but very good-natured and merry, and, altogether, an excellent person to carry on a picnic. Sallie Gardiner was absorbed in keeping her white piqué dress clean, and chattering with the ubiquitous Fred, who kept Beth in constant terror by his pranks.

It was not far to Longmeadow; but the tent was pitched, and the wickets down, by the time they arrived. A pleasant green field, with three wide-spreading oaks in the middle, and a smooth strip of turf for croquet.

'Welcome to Camp Laurence!' said the young host, as they landed, with exclamations of delight. 'Brooke is commander-in-chief; I am commissary-general; the other fellows are staff-officers; and you, ladies, are company. The tent is for your especial benefit, and that oak is your drawing-room; this is the mess-room, and the third is the camp kitchen. Now let's have a game before it gets hot, and then we'll see about dinner.'

Frank, Beth, Amy, and Grace, sat down to watch the game played by the other eight. Mr Brooke chose Meg, Kate, and Fred; Laurie took Sallie, Jo, and Ned. The Englishers played well; but the Americans played better, and contested every inch of the ground as strongly as if the spirit of '76 inspired them. Jo and Fred had several skirmishes, and once narrowly escaped high words. Jo was through the last wicket, and had missed the stroke, which failure ruffled her a good deal. Fred was close behind her, and his turn came before hers; he gave a stroke, his ball hit the wicket, and stopped an inch on the wrong side. No one was very near; and, running up to examine, he gave it a sly nudge with his toe, which put it just an inch on the right side.

'I'm through! now, Miss Jo, I'll settle you, and get in first,' cried the young gentleman, swinging his mallet for another blow.

'You pushed it; I saw you; it's my turn now,' said Jo, sharply.

'Upon my word I didn't move it! it rolled a bit, perhaps, but that is allowed; so stand off, please, and let me have a go at the stake.'

'We don't cheat in America; but *you* can, if you choose,' said Jo, angrily.

'Yankees are a deal the most tricky, everybody knows. There you go,' returned Fred, croqueting her ball far away.

Jo opened her lips to say something rude; but checked herself in time, colored up to her forehead, and stood a minute, hammering down a wicket with all her might, while Fred hit the stake, and declared himself out, with much exultation. She went off to get her ball, and was a long time finding it, among the bushes; but she came back, looking cool and quiet, and waited her turn patiently. It took several strokes to regain the place she had lost; and, when she got there, the other side had nearly won, for Kate's ball was the last but one, and lay near the stake.

'By George, it's all up with us! Good-by, Kate; Miss Jo owes me one, so you are finished,' cried Fred, excitedly, as they all drew near to see the finish.

'Yankees have a trick of being generous to their enemies,' said Jo, with a look that made the lad redden, 'especially when they beat them,' she added, as, leaving Kate's ball untouched, she won the game by a clever stroke.

Laurie threw up his hat; then remembered that it wouldn't do to exult over the defeat of his guests, and stopped in the middle of a cheer to whisper to his friend,—

'Good for you, Jo! he did cheat, I saw him; we can't tell him so, but he won't do it again, take my word for it.'

Meg drew her aside, under pretence of pinning up a loose braid, and said, approvingly,—

'It was dreadfully provoking; but you kept your temper, and I'm so glad, Jo.'

'Don't praise me, Meg, for I could box his ears this minute. I should certainly have boiled over, if I hadn't stayed among the nettles till I got my rage under enough to hole my tongue. It's simmering now, so I hope he'll keep out of my way,' returned Jo, biting her lips, as she glowered at Fred from under her big hat.

'Time for lunch,' said Mr Brooke, looking at his watch. 'Commissary-general, will you make the fire, and get water, while Miss March, Miss Sallie, and I spread the table. Who can make good coffee?'

'Jo can,' said Meg, glad to recommend her sister. So Jo, feeling that her late lessons in cookery were to do her honor, went to preside over the coffee-pot, while the children collected dry sticks, and the boys made a fire, and got water from a spring near by. Miss Kate sketched, and Frank talked to Beth, who was making little mats of braided rushes, to serve as plates.

The commander-in-chief and his aides soon spread the tablecloth with an inviting array of eatables and drinkables, prettily decorated with green leaves. Jo announced that the coffee was ready, and every one settled themselves to a hearty meal; for youth is seldom dyspeptic, and exercise develops wholesome appetites. A very merry lunch it was; for everything seemed fresh and funny, and frequent peals of laughter startled a venerable horse, who fed near by. There was a pleasing inequality in the table, which produced many mishaps to cups and plates; acorns dropped into the milk, little black ants partook of the refreshments without being invited, and fuzzy caterpillars swung down from the tree, to see what was going on. Three white-headed children peeped over the fence, and an objectionable dog barked at them from the other side of the river, with all his might and main.

'There's salt, here, if you prefer it,' said Laurie, as he handed Jo a saucer of berries.

'Thank you; I prefer spiders,' she replied, fishing up two unwary little ones, who had gone to a creamy death. 'How dare you remind me of that horrid dinner-party, when yours is so nice in every way?' added Jo, as they both laughed, and ate out of one plate, the china having run short.

'I had an uncommonly good time that day, and haven't got over it yet. This is no credit to me, you know; I don't do anything; it's you, and Meg, and Brooke, who make it go, and I'm no end obliged to you. What shall we do when we can't eat any more?' asked Laurie, feeling that his trump card had been played when lunch was over.

'Have games, till it's cooler. I brought "Authors", and I dare say Miss Kate knows something new and nice. Go and ask her; she's company, and you ought to stay with her more.'

'Aren't you company, too? I thought she'd suit Brooke; but he keeps talking to Meg, and Kate just stares at them through that ridiculous glass of hers. I'm going, so you needn't try to preach propriety, for you can't do it, Jo.'

Miss Kate did know several new games; and as the girls would not, and the boys could not, eat any more, they all adjourned to the drawing-room, to play 'Rigmarole'.

'One person begins a story, any nonsense you like, and tells as long as they please, only taking care to stop short at some exciting point, when the next takes it up, and does the same. It's very funny, when well done, and makes a perfect jumble of tragical comical stuff to laugh over. Please start it, Mr Brooke,' said Kate, with a commanding gesture, which surprised Meg, who treated the tutor with as much respect as any other gentleman.

Lying on the grass, at the feet of the two young ladies, Mr Brooke obediently began the story, with the handsome brown eyes steadily fixed upon the sun-shiny river.

'Once on a time, a knight went out into the world to seek his fortune, for he had nothing but his sword and his shield. He travelled a long while, nearly eight-and-twenty years, and had a hard time of it, till he came to the palace of a good old king, who had offered a reward to any one who would tame and train a fine, but unbroken colt, of which he was very fond. The knight agreed to try, and got on slowly, but surely; for the colt was a gallant fellow, and soon learned to love his new master, though he was freakish and wild. Every day, when he gave his lessons to this pet of the king's, the knight rode him through the city; and, as he rode, he looked everywhere for a certain beautiful face, which he had seen many times in his dreams, but never found. One day, as he went prancing down a quiet street, he saw at the window of a ruinous castle the lovely face. He was delighted, inquired who lived in this old castle, and was told that several captive princesses were kept there by a spell, and spun all day to lay up money to buy their liberty. The knight wished intensely that he could free them; but he was poor, and could only go by each day, watching for the sweet face, and longing to see it out in the sunshine. At last, he resolved to get into the castle, and ask how he could help them. He went and knocked; the great door flew open, and he beheld—'

'A ravishingly lovely lady, who exclaimed, with a cry of rapture, "At last! at last!"' continued Kate, who had read French novels, and admired the style. '"'Tis she!" cried Count Gustave, and fell at her feet in an ecstasy of joy. "Oh, rise!" she said, extending a hand of marble fairness. "Never! till you tell me how I may rescue you," swore the knight, still kneeling. "Alas, my cruel fate condemns me to remain here till my tyrant is destroyed." "Where is the villain?" "In the mauve salon; go, brave heart, and save me from despair." "I obey, and return victorious or dead!" With these thrilling words he rushed away, and, flinging open the door of the mauve salon, was about to enter, when he received—'

'A stunning blow from the big Greek lexicon, which an old fellow in a black gown fired at him,' said Ned. 'Instantly Sir What's-his-name recovered himself, pitched the tyrant out of the window, and turned to join the lady, victorious, but with a bump on his brow; found the door locked, tore up the curtains, made a rope ladder, got half-way down when ladder broke, and he went head first into the moat, sixty feet below. Could swim like a duck, paddled round the castle till he came to a little door guarded by two stout fellows; knocked their heads together till they cracked like a couple of nuts, then, by a trifling exertion of his prodigious strength, he smashed in the door, went up a pair of stone steps covered with dust a foot thick, toads as big as your fist, and spiders that would frighten you into hysterics, Miss March. At the top of these steps he came plump upon a sight that took his breath away and chilled his blood—'

'A tall figure, all in white, with a veil over its face, and a lamp in its wasted hand,' went on Meg. 'It beckoned, gliding noiselessly before him down a corridor as dark and cold as any tomb. Shadowy effigies in armor stood on either side, a dead silence reigned, the lamp burned blue, and the ghostly figure ever and anon turned its face toward him, showing the glitter of awful eyes through its white veil. They reached a curtained door, behind which sounded lovely music; he sprang forward to enter, but the spectre plucked him back, and waved, threateningly, before him a—'

'Snuff-box,' said Jo, in a sepulchral tone, which convulsed the audience. ' "Thankee," said the knight, politely, as he took a pinch, and sneezed seven times so violently that his head fell off. "Ha! ha!" laughed the ghost; and, having peeped through the keyhole at the princesses spinning away for dear life, the evil spirit picked up her victim and put him in a large tin box, where there were eleven other knights packed together without their heads, like sardines, who all rose and began to—'

'Dance a hornpipe,' cut in Fred, as Jo paused for breath; 'and, as they danced, the rubbishy old castle turned to a man-of-war in full sail. "Up with the jib, reef the tops'l halliards, helm hard a lee, and man the guns," roared the captain, as a Portuguese pirate hove in sight, with a flag black as ink flying from her foremast. "Go in and win, my hearties," says the captain; and a tremendous fight begun. Of course the British beat—they always do; and, having taken the pirate captain prisoner, sailed slap over the schooner, whose decks were piled with dead, and whose lee-scuppers ran blood, for the order had been "Cutlasses, and die hard." "Bosen's mate, take a bight of the flying jib sheet, and start this villain if he don't confess his sins double quick," said the British captain. The Portuguese held his tongue like a brick, and walked the plank, while the jolly tars cheered like mad. But the sly dog dived, came up under the man-of-war, scuttled her, and down she went, with all sail set, "To the bottom of the sea, sea, sea," where—'

'Oh, gracious! what *shall* I say?' cried Sallie, as Fred ended his rigmarole, in which he had jumbled together, pell-mell, nautical phrases and facts, out of one of his favorite books. 'Well, they went to the bottom, and a nice mermaid welcomed them, but was much grieved on finding the box of headless knights, and kindly pickled them in brine, hoping to discover the mystery about them; for, being a woman, she was curious. By and by a diver came down, and the mermaid said, "I'll give you this box of pearls if you can take it up;" for she wanted to restore the poor things to life, and couldn't raise the heavy load herself. So the diver hoisted it up, and was much disappointed, on opening it, to find no pearls. He left it in a great lonely field, where it was found by a—'

'Little goose-girl, who kept a hundred fat geese in the field,' said Amy, when Sallie's invention gave out. 'The little girl was sorry for them, and asked an old woman what she should do to help them. "Your geese will tell you, they know everything," said the old woman. So she asked what she should use for new heads, since the old ones were lost, and all the geese opened their hundred mouths, and screamed—'

'"Cabbages!" continued Laurie, promptly. "Just the thing," said the girl, and ran to get twelve fine ones from her garden. She put them on, the knights revived at once, thanked her, and went on their way rejoicing, never knowing the difference, for there were so many other heads like them in the world, that no one thought anything of it. The knight in whom I'm interested went back to find the pretty face, and learned that the princesses had spun themselves free, and all gone to be married, but one. He was in a great state of mind at that; and, mounting the colt, who stood by him through thick and thin, rushed to the castle to see which was left. Peeping over the hedge, he saw the queen of his affections picking flowers in her garden. "Will you give me a rose?" said he. "You must come and get it; I can't come to you; it isn't proper," said she, as sweet as honey. He tried to climb over the hedge, but it seemed to grow higher and higher; then he tried to push through, but it grew thicker and thicker, and he was in despair. So he patiently broke twig after twig, till he had made a little hole, through which he peeped, saying, imploringly, "Let me in! let me in!" But the pretty princess did not seem to understand, for she picked her roses quietly, and left him to fight his way in. Whether he did or not, Frank will tell you.'

'I can't; I'm not playing, I never do,' said Frank, dismayed at the sentimental predicament out of which he was to rescue the absurd couple. Beth had disappeared behind Jo, and Grace was asleep.

'So the poor knight is to be left sticking in the hedge, is he?' asked Mr Brooke, still watching the river, and playing with the wild rose in his button-hole.

'I guess the princess gave him a posy, and opened the gate, after awhile,' said Laurie, smiling to himself, as he threw acorns at his tutor.

'What a piece of nonsense we have made! With practice we might do something quite clever. Do you know "Truth"?' asked Sallie, after they had laughed over their story.

'I hope so,' said Meg, soberly.

'The game, I mean?'

'What is it?' said Fred.

'Why, you pile up your hands, choose a number, and draw out in turn, and the person who draws out the number has to answer truly any questions put by the rest. It's great fun.'

'Let's try it,' said Jo, who liked new experiments.

Miss Kate and Mr Brooke, Meg and Ned, declined; but Fred, Sallie, Jo and Laurie piled and drew; and the lot fell to Laurie.

'Who are your heroes?' asked Jo.

'Grandfather and Napoleon.'

'What lady do you think prettiest?' said Sallie.

'Margaret.'

'Which do you like best?' from Fred.

'Jo, of course.'

'What silly questions you ask!' and Jo gave a disdainful shrug as the rest laughed at Laurie's matter-of-fact tone.

'Try again; Truth isn't a bad game,' said Fred.

'It's a very good one for you,' retorted Jo, in a low voice.

Her turn came next.

'What is your greatest fault?' asked Fred, by way of testing in her the virtue he lacked himself.

'A quick temper.'

'What do you most wish for?' said Laurie.

'A pair of boot-lacings,' returned Jo, guessing and defeating his purpose.

'Not a true answer; you must say what you really do want most.'

'Genius; don't you wish you could give it to me, Laurie?' and she slyly smiled in his disappointed face.

'What virtues do you most admire in a man?' asked Sallie.

'Courage and honesty.'

'Now my turn,' said Fred, as his hand came last.

'Let's give it to him,' whispered Laurie to Jo, who nodded, and asked at once,—

'Didn't you cheat at croquet?'

'Well, yes, a little bit.'

'Good! Didn't you take your story out of "The Sea Lion"?' said Laurie.

'Rather.'

'Don't you think the English nation perfect in every respect?' asked Sallie.

'I should be ashamed of myself if I didn't.'

'He's a true John Bull. Now, Miss Sallie, you shall have a chance without waiting to draw. I'll harrow up your feelings first by asking if you don't think you are something of a flirt,' said Laurie, as Jo nodded to Fred, as a sign that peace was declared.

'You impertinent boy! of course I'm not,' exclaimed Sallie, with an air that proved the contrary.

'What do you hate most?' asked Fred.

'Spiders and rice pudding.'

'What do you like best?' asked Jo.

'Dancing and French gloves.'

'Well, *I* think Truth is a very silly play; let's have a sensible game of Authors, to refresh our minds,' proposed Jo.

Ned, Frank, and the little girls joined in this, and, while it went on, the three elders sat apart, talking. Miss Kate took out her sketch again, and Margaret watched her, while Mr Brooke lay on the grass, with a book, which he did not read.

'How beautifully you do it; I wish I could draw,' said Meg, with mingled admiration and regret in her voice.

'Why don't you learn? I should think you had taste and talent for it,' replied Miss Kate, graciously.

'I haven't time.'

'Your mamma prefers other accomplishments, I fancy. So did mine; but I proved to her that I had talent, by taking a few lessons privately, and then she was quite willing I should go on. Can't you do the same with your governess?'

'I have none.'

'I forgot; young ladies in America go to school more than with us. Very fine schools they are, too, papa says. You go to a private one, I suppose?'

'I don't go at all; I am a governess myself.'

'Oh, indeed!' said Miss Kate; but she might as well have said, 'Dear me, how dreadful!' for her tone implied it, and something in her face made Meg color, and wish she had not been so frank.

Mr Brooke looked up, and said, quickly, 'Young ladies in America love independence as much as their ancestors did, and are admired and respected for supporting themselves.'

'Oh, yes; of course! it's very nice and proper in them to do so. We have many most respectable and worthy young women, who do the same; and are employed by the nobility, because, being the daughters of gentlemen, they are both well-bred and accomplished, you know,' said Miss Kate, in a patronizing tone, that hurt Meg's pride, and made her work seem not only more distasteful, but degrading.

'Did the German song suit, Miss March?' inquired Mr Brooke, breaking an awkward pause.

'Oh, yes! it was very sweet, and I'm much obliged to who-ever translated it for me;' and Meg's downcast face brightened as she spoke.

'Don't you read German?' asked Miss Kate, with a look of surprise.

'Not very well. My father, who taught me, is away, and I don't get on very fast alone, for I've no one to correct my pronunciation.'

'Try a little now; here is Schiller's *Mary Stuart*, and a tutor who loves to teach,' and Mr Brooke laid his book on her lap, with an inviting smile.

'It's so hard, I'm afraid to try,' said Meg, grateful, but bash-ful in the presence of the accomplished young lady beside her.

'I'll read a bit, to encourage you;' and Miss Kate read one of the most beautiful passages, in a perfectly correct, but per-fectly expressionless, manner.

Mr Brooke made no comment, as she returned the book to Meg, who said, innocently,—

'I thought it was poetry.'

'Some of it is; try this passage.'

There was a queer smile about Mr Brooke's mouth, as he opened at poor Mary's lament.

Meg, obediently following the long grass-blade which her new tutor used to point with, read, slowly and timidly, unconsciously making poetry of the hard words, by the soft intonation of her musical voice. Down the page went the green guide, and presently, forgetting her listener in the beauty of the sad scene, Meg read as if alone, giving a little touch of tragedy to the words of the unhappy queen. If she had seen the brown eyes then, she would have stopped short; but she never looked up, and the lesson was not spoilt for her.

'Very well, indeed!' said Mr Brooke, as she paused, quite ignoring her many mistakes, and looking as if he did, indeed, 'love to teach'.

Miss Kate put up her glass, and, having taken a survey of the little tableau before her, shut her sketchbook, saying, with condescension,—

'You've a nice accent, and, in time, will be a clever reader. I advise you to learn, for German is a valuable accomplishment to teachers. I must look after Grace, she is romping;' and Miss Kate strolled away, adding to herself, with a shrug, 'I didn't come to chaperone a governess, though she *is* young and pretty. What odd people these Yankees are! I'm afraid Laurie will be quite spoilt among them.'

'I forgot that English people rather turn up their noses at governesses, and don't treat them as we do,' said Meg, looking after the retreating figure with an annoyed expression.

'Tutors, also, have rather a hard time of it there, as I know to my sorrow. There's no place like America for us workers, Miss Margaret,' and Mr Brooke looked so contented and cheerful, that Meg was ashamed to lament her hard lot.

'I'm glad I live in it, then. I don't like my work, but I get a good deal of satisfaction out of it, after all, so I won't complain; I only wish I liked teaching as you do.'

'I think you would, if you had Laurie for a pupil. I shall be very sorry to lose him next year,' said Mr Brooke, busily punching holes in the turf.

'Going to college, I suppose?' Meg's lips asked that question, but her eyes added, 'And what becomes of you?'

'Yes; it's high time he went, for he is nearly ready, and as soon as he is off I shall turn soldier.'

'I'm glad of that!' exclaimed Meg; 'I should think every young man would want to go; though it is hard for the mothers and sisters, who stay at home,' she added, sorrowfully.

'I have neither, and very few friends, to care whether I live or die,' said Mr Brooke, rather bitterly, as he absently put the dead rose in the hole he had made, and covered it up, like a little grave.

'Laurie and his grandfather would care a great deal, and we should all be very sorry to have any harm happen to you,' said Meg, heartily.

'Thank you; that sounds pleasant,' began Mr Brooke, looking cheerful again; but, before he could finish his speech, Ned, mounted on the old horse, came lumbering up, to display his equestrian skill before the young ladies, and there was no more quiet that day.

'Don't you love to ride?' asked Grace of Amy, as they stood resting, after a race round the field with the others, led by Ned.

'I dote upon it; my sister Meg used to ride, when papa was rich, but we don't keep any horses now,—except Ellen Tree,' added Amy, laughing.

'Tell me about Ellen Tree; is it a donkey?' asked Grace, curiously.

'Why, you see, Jo is crazy about horses, and so am I, but we've only got an old side-saddle, and no horse. Out in our garden is an apple-tree, that has a nice low branch; so I put the saddle on it, fixed some reins on the part that turns up, and we bounce away on Ellen Tree whenever we like.'

'How funny!' laughed Grace. 'I have a pony at home, and ride nearly every day in the park, with Fred and Kate; it's very nice, for my friends go too, and the Row is full of ladies and gentlemen.'

'Dear, how charming! I hope I shall go abroad, some day; but I'd rather go to Rome than the Row,' said Amy, who had not the remotest idea what the Row was, and wouldn't have asked for the world.

Frank, sitting just behind the little girls, heard what they were saying, and pushed his crutch away from him with an impatient gesture, as he watched the active lads going through all sorts of comical gymnastics. Beth, who was collecting the scattered Authorcards, looked up and said, in her shy yet friendly way,—

'I'm afraid you are tired; can I do anything for you?'

'Talk to me, please; it's dull, sitting by myself,' answered Frank, who had evidently been used to being made much of at home.

If he had asked her to deliver a Latin oration, it would not have seemed a more impossible task to bashful Beth; but there

183

was no place to run to, no Jo to hide behind now, and the poor boy looked so wistfully at her, that she bravely resolved to try.

'What do you like to talk about?' she asked, fumbling over the cards, and dropping half as she tried to tie them up.

'Well, I like to hear about cricket, and boating, and hunting,' said Frank, who had not yet learned to suit his amusements to his strength.

'My heart! whatever shall I do! I don't know anything about them,' thought Beth; and, forgetting the boy's misfortune in her flurry, she said, hoping to make him talk, 'I never saw any hunting, but I suppose you know all about it.'

'I did once; but I'll never hunt again, for I got hurt leaping a confounded five-barred gate; so there's no more horses and hounds for me,' said Frank, with a sigh that made Beth hate herself for her innocent blunder.

'Your deer are much prettier than our ugly buffaloes,' she said, turning to the prairies for help, and feeling glad that she had read one of the boys' books in which Jo delighted.

Buffaloes proved soothing and satisfactory; and, in her eagerness to amuse another, Beth forgot herself, and was quite unconscious of her sister's surprise and delight at the unusual spectacle of Beth talking away to one of the dreadful boys, against whom she had begged protection.

'Bless her heart! She pities him, so she is good to him,' said Jo, beaming at her from the croquet-ground.

'I always said she was a little saint,' added Meg, as if there could be no further doubt of it.

'I haven't heard Frank laugh so much for ever so long,' said Grace to Amy, as they sat discussing dolls, and making tea-sets out of the acorn-cups.

'My sister Beth is a very fastidious girl, when she likes to be,' said Amy, well pleased at Beth's success. She meant 'fascinating', but, as Grace didn't know the exact meaning of either word, 'fastidious' sounded well, and made a good impression.

An impromptu circus, fox and geese, and an amicable game of croquet finished the afternoon. At sunset the tent was struck, hampers packed, wickets pulled up, boats loaded, and the whole party floated down the river, singing at the tops of their voices. Ned, getting sentimental, warbled a serenade with the pensive refrain,—

> 'Alone, alone, ah! woe, alone,'

and at the lines—

> 'We each are young, we each have a heart,
> Oh, why should we stand thus coldly apart?'

he looked at Meg with such a lackadaisical expression, that she laughed outright, and spoilt his song.

'How can you be so cruel to me?' he whispered, under cover of a lively chorus; 'you've kept close to that starched-up English woman all day, and now you snub me.'

'I didn't mean to; but you looked so funny I really couldn't help it,' replied Meg, passing over the first part of his reproach; for it was quite true that she *had* shunned him, remembering the Moffat party and the talk after it.

Ned was offended, and turned to Sallie for consolation, saying to her, rather pettishly, 'There isn't a bit of flirt in that girl, is there?'

'Not a particle; but she's a dear,' returned Sallie, defending her friend even while confessing her shortcomings.

'She's not a stricken deer, any-way,' said Ned, trying to be witty, and succeeding as well as very young gentlemen usually do.

On the lawn where it had gathered, the little party separated with cordial good-nights and good-byes, for the Vaughns were going to Canada. As the four sisters went home through the garden, Miss Kate looked after them, saying, without the patronizing tone in her voice, 'In spite of their demonstrative manners, American girls are very nice when one knows them.'

'I quite agree with you,' said Mr Brooke.

CHAPTER THIRTEEN

———◆———

Castles in the Air

Laurie lay luxuriously swinging to and fro in his hammock, one warm September afternoon, wondering what his neighbors were about, but too lazy to go and find out. He was in one of his moods; for the day had been both unprofitable and unsatisfactory, and he was wishing he could live it over again. The hot weather made him indolent; and he had shirked his studies, tried Mr Brooke's patience to the utmost, displeased his grandfather by practising half the afternoon, frightened the maid-servants half out of their wits, by mischievously hinting that one of his dogs was going mad, and, after high words with the stableman about some fancied neglect of his horse, he had flung himself into his hammock, to fume over the stupidity of the world in general, till the peace of the lovely day quieted him in spite of himself. Staring up into the green gloom of the horse-chestnut trees above him, he dreamed dreams of all sorts, and was just imagining himself tossing on the ocean, in a voyage round the world, when the sound of voices brought him ashore in a flash. Peeping through the meshes of the hammock, he saw the Marches coming out, as if bound on some expedition.

'What in the world are those girls about now?' thought Laurie, opening his sleepy eyes to take a good look, for there was something rather peculiar in the appearance of his neighbors. Each wore a large, flapping hat, a brown linen pouch slung over one shoulder, and carried a long staff; Meg had a cushion, Jo a book, Beth a dipper, and Amy a portfolio. All walked quietly through the garden, out at the little back gate, and began to climb the hill that lay between the house and river.

'Well, that's cool!' said Laurie to himself, 'to have a picnic and never ask me. They can't be going in the boat, for they haven't got the key. Perhaps they forgot it; I'll take it to them, and see what's going on.'

Though possessed of half a dozen hats, it took him some time to find one; then there was a hunt for the key, which was at last discovered in his pocket, so that the girls were quite out of sight when he leaped the fence and ran after them. Taking the shortest way to the boat-house, he waited for them to appear; but no one came, and he went up the hill to take an observation. A grove of pines covered one part of it, and from the heart of this green spot came a clearer sound than the soft sigh of the pines, or the drowsy chirp of the crickets.

'Here's a landscape!' thought Laurie, peeping through the bushes, and looking wide awake and good-natured already.

It *was* rather a pretty little picture; for the sisters sat together in the shady nook, with sun and shadow flickering over them,—the aromatic wind lifting their hair and cooling their hot cheeks,—and all the little wood-people going on with their affairs as if these were no strangers, but old friends. Meg sat upon her cushion, sewing daintily with her white hands, and looking as fresh and sweet as a rose, in her pink dress, among the green. Beth was sorting the cones that lay thick under the hemlock near by, for she made pretty things of them. Amy was sketching a group of ferns, and Jo was knitting as she read aloud. A shadow passed over the boy's face as he watched them, feeling that he ought to go, because uninvited; yet lingering, because home seemed very lonely, and this quiet party in the woods most attractive to his restless spirit. He stood so still, that a squirrel, busy with its harvesting, ran down a pine close beside him, saw him suddenly, and skipped back, scolding so shrilly that Beth looked up, espied the wistful face behind the birches, and beckoned with a reassuring smile.

'May I come in, please? or shall I be a bother?' he asked, advancing slowly.

Meg lifted her eyebrows, but Jo scowled at her defiantly, and said, at once, 'Of course you may. We should have asked you before, only we thought you wouldn't care for such a girl's game as this.'

'I always like your games; but if Meg don't want me, I'll go away.'

'I've no objection, if you do something; it's against the rule to be idle here,' replied Meg, gravely, but graciously.

'Much obliged; I'll do anything if you'll let me stop a bit, for it's as dull as the desert of Sahara down there. Shall I sew, read, cone, draw, or do all at once? Bring on your bears; I'm ready,' and Laurie sat down with a submissive expression delightful to behold.

'Finish this story while I set my heel,' said Jo, handing him the book.

'Yes'm,' was the meek answer, as he began, doing his best to prove his gratitude for the favor of an admission into the 'Busy Bee Society'.

The story was not a long one, and, when it was finished, he ventured to ask a few questions as a reward of merit.

'Please, mum, could I inquire if this highly instructive and charming institution is a new one?'

'Would you tell him?' asked Meg of her sisters.

'He'll laugh,' said Amy, warningly.

'Who cares?' said Jo.

'I guess he'll like it,' added Beth.

'Of course I shall! I give you my word I won't laugh. Tell away, Jo, and don't be afraid.'

'The idea of being afraid of you! Well, you see we used to play "Pilgrim's Progress", and we have been going on with it in earnest, all winter and summer.'

'Yes, I know,' said Laurie, nodding wisely.

'Who told you?' demanded Jo.

'Spirits.'

'No, it was me; I wanted to amuse him one night when you were all away, and he was rather dismal. He did like it, so don't scold, Jo,' said Beth, meekly.

'You can't keep a secret. Never mind; it saves trouble now.'

'Go on, please,' said Laurie, as Jo became absorbed in her work, looking a trifle displeased.

'Oh, didn't she tell you about this new plan of ours? Well, we have tried not to waste our holiday, but each has had a task, and worked at it with a will. The vacation is nearly over, the stints are all done, and we are ever so glad that we didn't dawdle.'

'Yes, I should think so;' and Laurie thought regretfully of his own idle days.

'Mother likes to have us out of doors as much as possible; so we bring our work here, and have nice times. For the fun of it we bring our things in these bags, wear the old hats, use poles to climb the hill, and play pilgrims, as we used to do years ago. We call this hill the "Delectable Mountain", for we can look far away and see the country where we hope to live some time.'

Jo pointed, and Laurie sat up to examine; for through an opening in the wood one could look across the wide, blue river,—the meadows on the other side,— far over the outskirts of the great city, to the green hills that rose to meet the sky. The sun was low, and the heavens glowed with the splendor of an autumn sunset. Gold and purple clouds lay on the hill-tops; and rising high into the ruddy light were silvery white peaks, that shone like the airy spires of some Celestial City.

'How beautiful that is!' said Laurie, softly, for he was quick to see and feel beauty of any kind.

'It's often so; and we like to watch it, for it is never the same, but always splendid,' replied Amy, wishing she could paint it.

'Jo talks about the country where we hope to live some time; the real country, she means, with pigs and chickens, and haymaking. It would be nice, but I wish the beautiful country up there was real, and we could ever go to it,' said Beth, musingly.

'There is a lovelier country even than that, where we *shall* go, by and by, when we are good enough,' answered Meg, with her sweet voice.

'It seems so long to wait, so hard to do; I want to fly away at once, as those swallows fly, and go in at that splendid gate.'

'You'll get there, Beth, sooner or later; no fear of that,' said Jo; 'I'm the one that will have to fight and work, and climb and wait, and maybe never get in after all.'

'You'll have me for company, if that's any comfort. I shall have to do a deal of travelling before I come in sight of your Celestial City. If I arrive late, you'll say a good word for me, won't you, Beth?'

Something in the boy's face troubled his little friend; but she said cheerfully, with her quiet eyes on the changing clouds, 'If people really want to go, and really try all their lives, I think they will get in; for I don't believe there are any locks on that door, or any guards at the gate. I always imagine it is as it is in the picture, where the shining ones stretch out their hands to welcome poor Christian as he comes up from the river.'

'Wouldn't it be fun if all the castles in the air which we make could come true, and we could live in them?' said Jo, after a little pause.

'I've made such quantities it would be hard to choose which I'd have,' said Laurie, lying flat, and throwing cones at the squirrel who had betrayed him.

'You'd have to take your favorite one. What is it?' asked Meg.

'If I tell mine, will you tell yours?'

'Yes, if the girls will too.'

'We will. Now, Laurie!'

'After I'd seen as much of the world as I want to, I'd like to settle in Germany, and have just as much music as I choose. I'm to be a famous musician myself, and all creation is to rush to hear me; and I'm never to be bothered about money or business, but just enjoy myself, and live for what I like. That's my favorite castle. What's yours, Meg?'

Margaret seemed to find it a little hard to tell hers, and moved a brake before her face, as if to disperse imaginary gnats, while she said, slowly, 'I should like a lovely house, full of all sorts of luxurious things; nice food, pretty clothes, handsome furniture, pleasant people, and heaps of money. I am to be mistress of it, and manage it as I like, with plenty of servants, so I never need work a bit. How I should enjoy it! for I wouldn't be idle, but do good, and make every one love me dearly.'

'Wouldn't you have a master for your castle in the air?' asked Laurie, slyly.

'I said "pleasant people", you know;' and Meg carefully tied up her shoe as she spoke, so that no one saw her face.

'Why don't you say you'd have a splendid, wise, good husband, and some angelic little children? you know your castle wouldn't be perfect without,' said blunt Jo, who had no tender fancies yet, and rather scorned romance, except in books.

'You'd have nothing but horses, inkstands, and novels in yours,' answered Meg, petulantly.

'Wouldn't I, though! I'd have a stable full of Arabian steeds, rooms piled with books, and I'd write out of a magic inkstand, so that my works should be as famous as Laurie's music. I want to do something splendid before I go into my

193

castle,—something heroic, or wonderful,—that won't be forgotten after I'm dead. I don't know what, but I'm on the watch for it, and mean to astonish you all, some day. I think I shall write books, and get rich and famous; that would suit me, so that is *my* favorite dream.'

'Mine is to stay at home safe with father and mother, and help take care of the family,' said Beth, contentedly.

'Don't you wish for anything else?' asked Laurie.

'Since I had my little piano I am perfectly satisfied. I only wish we may all keep well, and be together; nothing else.'

'I have lots of wishes; but the pet one is to be an artist, and go to Rome, and do fine pictures, and be the best artist in the whole world,' was Amy's modest desire.

'We're an ambitious set, aren't we? Every one of us, but Beth, wants to be rich and famous, and gorgeous in every respect. I do wonder if any of us will ever get our wishes,' said Laurie, chewing grass, like a meditative calf.

'I've got the key to my castle in the air; but whether I can unlock the door, remains to be seen,' observed Jo, mysteriously.

'I've got the key to mine, but I'm not allowed to try it. Hang college!' muttered Laurie, with an impatient sigh.

'Here's mine!' and Amy waved her pencil.

'I haven't got any,' said Meg, forlornly.

'Yes you have,' said Laurie, at once.

'Where?'

'In your face.'

'Nonsense; that's of no use.'

'Wait and see if it doesn't bring you something worth having,' replied the boy, laughing at the thought of a charming little secret which he fancied he knew.

Meg colored behind the brake, but asked no questions, and looked across the river with the same expectant expression which Mr Brooke had worn when he told the story of the knight.

'If we are all alive ten years hence, let's meet, and see how many of us have got our wishes, or how much nearer we are them than now,' said Jo, always ready with a plan.

'Bless me! how old I shall be,—twenty-seven!' exclaimed Meg, who felt grown up already, having just reached seventeen.

'You and I shall be twenty-six, Teddy; Beth twenty-four, and Amy twenty-two; what a venerable party!' said Jo.

'I hope I shall have done something to be proud of by that time; but I'm such a lazy dog, I'm afraid I shall "dawdle", Jo.'

'You need a motive, mother says; and when you get it, she is sure you'll work splendidly.'

'Is she? By Jupiter I will, if I only get the chance!' cried Laurie, sitting up with sudden energy. 'I ought to be satisfied to please grandfather, and I do try, but it's working against the grain, you see, and comes hard. He wants me to be an India merchant, as he was, and I'd rather be shot; I hate tea, and silk, and spices, and every sort of rubbish his old ships bring, and I don't care how soon they go to the bottom when I own them. Going to college ought to satisfy him, for if I give him four years he ought to let me off from the business; but he's set, and I've got to do just as he did, unless I break away and please myself, as my father did. If there was any one left to stay with the old gentleman, I'd do it to-morrow.'

Laurie spoke excitedly, and looked ready to carry his threat into execution on the slightest provocation; for he was growing up very fast, and, in spite of his indolent ways, had a young man's hatred of subjection,—a young man's restless longing to try the world for himself.

'I advise you to sail away in one of your ships, and never come home again till you have tried your own way,' said Jo, whose imagination was fired by the thought of such a daring exploit, and whose sympathy was excited by what she called 'Teddy's wrongs'.

'That's not right, Jo; you mustn't talk in that way, and Laurie mustn't take your bad advice. You should do just what your grandfather wishes, my dear boy,' said Meg, in her most maternal tone. 'Do your best at college, and, when he sees that you try to please him, I'm sure he won't be hard or unjust to you. As you say, there is no one else to stay with and love him, and you'd never forgive yourself if you left him without his permission. Don't be dismal, or fret, but do your duty; and you'll get your reward, as good Mr Brooke has, by being respected and loved.'

'What do you know about him?' asked Laurie, grateful for the good advice, but objecting to the lecture, and glad to turn the conversation from himself, after his unusual outbreak.

'Only what your grandpa told mother about him; how he took good care of his own mother till she died, and wouldn't go abroad as tutor to some nice person, because he wouldn't leave her; and how he provides now for an old woman who nursed his mother; and never tells any one, but is just as generous, and patient, and good as he can be.'

'So he is, dear old fellow!' said Laurie, heartily, as Meg paused, looking flushed and earnest, with her story. 'It's like grandpa to find out all about him, without letting him know, and to tell all his goodness to others, so that they might like him. Brooke couldn't understand why your mother was so kind to him, asking him over with me, and treating him in her beautiful, friendly way. He thought she was just perfect, and talked about it for days and days, and went on about you all, in flaming style. If ever I do get my wish, you see what I'll do for Brooke.'

'Begin to do something now, by not plaguing his life out,' said Meg, sharply.

'How do you know I do, miss?'

'I can always tell by his face, when he goes away. If you have been good, he looks satisfied, and walks briskly; if you have plagued him, he's sober, and walks slowly, as if he wanted to go back and do his work better.'

'Well, I like that! So you keep an account of my good and bad marks in Brooke's face, do you? I see him bow and smile as he passes your window, but I didn't know you'd got up a telegraph.'

'We haven't; don't be angry, and oh, don't tell him I said anything! It was only to show that I cared how you get on, and what is said here is said in confidence, you know,' cried Meg, much alarmed at the thought of what might follow from her careless speech.

'I don't tell tales,' replied Laurie, with his 'high and mighty' air, as Jo called a certain expression which he occasionally wore. 'Only if Brooke is going to be a thermometer, I must mind and have fair weather for him to report.'

'Please don't be offended; I didn't mean to preach or tell tales, or be silly; I only thought Jo was encouraging you in a feeling which you'd be sorry for, by and by. You are so kind to us, we feel as if you were our brother, and say just what we think; forgive me, I meant it kindly!' and Meg offered her hand with a gesture both affectionate and timid.

Ashamed of his momentary pique, Laurie squeezed the kind little hand, and said, frankly, 'I'm the one to be forgiven; I'm cross, and have been out of sorts all day. I like to have you tell me my faults, and be sisterly; so don't mind if I am grumpy sometimes; I thank you all the same.'

Bent on showing that he was not offended, he made himself as agreeable as possible; wound cotton for Meg, recited poetry to please Jo, shook down cones for Beth, and helped Amy with her ferns,—proving himself a fit person to belong to the 'Busy Bee Society'. In the midst of an animated discussion on the domestic habits of turtles (one of which amiable creatures having strolled up from the river), the faint sound of a bell warned them that Hannah had put the tea 'to draw', and they would just have time to get home to supper.

'May I come again?' asked Laurie.

'Yes, if you are good, and love your book, as the boys in the primer are told to do,' said Meg, smiling.

'I'll try.'

'Then you may come, and I'll teach you to knit as the Scotchmen do; there's a demand for socks just now,' added Jo, waving hers, like a big blue worsted banner, as they parted at the gate.

That night, when Beth played to Mr Laurence in the twilight, Laurie, standing in the shadow of the curtain, listened to the little David, whose simple music always quieted his moody spirit, and watched the old man, who sat with his gray head on his hand, thinking tender thoughts of the dead child he had loved so much. Remembering the conversation of the afternoon, the boy said to himself, with the resolve to make the sacrifice cheerfully, 'I'll let my castle go, and stay with the dear old gentleman while he needs me, for I am all he has.'

CHAPTER FOURTEEN

Secrets

Jo was very busy up in the garret, for the October days began to grow chilly, and the afternoons were short. For two or three hours the sun lay warmly in at the high window, showing Jo seated on the old sofa writing busily, with her papers spread out upon a trunk before her, while Scrabble, the pet rat, promenaded the beams overhead, accompanied by his oldest son, a fine young fellow, who was evidently very proud of his whiskers. Quite absorbed in her work, Jo scribbled away till the last page was filled, when she signed her name with a flourish, and threw down her pen, exclaiming,—

'There, I've done my best! If this don't suit I shall have to wait till I can do better.'

Lying back on the sofa, she read the manuscript carefully through, making dashes here and there, and putting in many exclamation points, which looked like little balloons; then she tied it up with a smart red ribbon, and sat a minute looking at it with a sober, wistful expression, which plainly showed how earnest her work had been. Jo's desk up here was an old tin kitchen, which hung against the wall. In it she kept her papers, and a few books, safely shut away from Scrabble, who, being likewise of a literary turn, was fond of making a circulating library of such books as were left in his way, by eating the leaves. From this tin receptacle Jo produced another manuscript; and, putting both in her pocket, crept quietly down stairs, leaving her friends to nibble her pens and taste her ink.

She put on her hat and jacket as noiselessly as possible, and, going to the back entry window, got out upon the roof of a low porch, swung herself down to the grassy bank, and took a round-about way to the road. Once there she composed herself, hailed a passing omnibus, and rolled away to town, looking very merry and mysterious.

If any one had been watching her, he would have thought her movements decidedly peculiar; for, on alighting, she went off at a great pace till she reached a certain number in a certain busy street; having found the place with some difficulty, she went into the door-way, looked up the dirty stairs, and, after standing stock still a minute, suddenly dived into the street, and walked away as rapidly as she came. This manœuvre she repeated several times, to the great amusement of a black-eyed young gentleman lounging in the window of a building opposite. On returning for the third time, Jo gave herself a shake, pulled her hat over her eyes, and walked up the stairs, looking as if she was going to have all her teeth out.

There was a dentist's sign, among others, which adorned the entrance, and, after staring a moment at the pair of artificial jaws which slowly opened and shut to draw attention to a fine set of teeth, the young gentleman put on his coat, took

his hat, and went down to post himself in the opposite door-
way, saying, with a smile and a shiver,—

'It's like her to come alone, but if she has a bad time she'll
need some one to help her home.'

In ten minutes Jo came running down stairs with a very
red face, and the general appearance of a person who had just
passed through a trying ordeal of some sort. When she saw
the young gentleman she looked anything but pleased, and
passed him with a nod; but he followed, asking with an air of
sympathy,—

'Did you have a bad time?'

'Not very.'

'You got through quick.'

'Yes, thank goodness!'

'Why did you go alone?'

'Didn't want any one to know.'

'You're the oddest fellow I ever saw. How many did you
have out?'

Jo looked at her friend as if she did not understand him;
then began to laugh, as if mightily amused at something.

'There are two which I want to have come out, but I must
wait a week.'

'What are you laughing at? You are up to some mischief,
Jo,' said Laurie, looking mystified.

'So are you. What were you doing, sir, up in that billiard
saloon?'

'Begging your pardon, ma'am, it wasn't a billiard saloon,
but a gymnasium, and I was taking a lesson in fencing.'

'I'm glad of that!'

'Why?'

'You can teach me; and then, when we play *Hamlet*, you can be Laertes, and we'll make a fine thing of the fencing scene.'

Laurie burst out with a hearty boy's laugh, which made several passers-by smile in spite of themselves.

'I'll teach you, whether we play *Hamlet* or not; it's grand fun, and will straighten you up capitally. But I don't believe that was your only reason for saying "I'm glad", in that decided way; was it, now?'

'No, I was glad you were not in the saloon, because I hope you never go to such places. Do you?'

'Not often.'

'I wish you wouldn't.'

'It's no harm, Jo, I have billiards at home, but it's no fun unless you have good players; so, as I'm fond of it, I come sometimes and have a game with Ned Moffat or some of the other fellows.'

'Oh dear, I'm so sorry, for you'll get to liking it better and better, and will waste time and money, and grow like those dreadful boys. I did hope you'd stay respectable, and be a satisfaction to your friends,' said Jo, shaking her head.

'Can't a fellow take a little innocent amusement now and then without losing his respectability?' asked Laurie, looking nettled.

'That depends upon how and where he takes it. I don't like Ned and his set, and wish you'd keep out of it. Mother won't let us have him at our house, though he wants to come, and if you grow like him she won't be willing to have us frolic together as we do now.'

'Won't she?' asked Laurie, anxiously.

'No, she can't bear fashionable young men, and she'd shut us all up in bandboxes rather than have us associate with them.'

'Well, she needn't get out her bandboxes yet; I'm not a fashionable party, and don't mean to be; but I do like harmless larks now and then, don't you?'

'Yes, nobody minds them, so lark away, but don't get wild, will you? or there will be an end of all our good times.'

'I'll be a double distilled saint.'

'I can't bear saints; just be a simple, honest, respectable boy, and we'll never desert you. I don't know what I *should* do if you acted like Mr King's son; he had plenty of money, but didn't know how to spend it, and got tipsey, and gambled, and ran away, and forged his father's name, I believe, and was altogether horrid.'

'You think I'm likely to do the same? Much obliged.'

'No I don't—oh, *dear*, no!—but I hear people talking about money being such a temptation, and I sometimes wish you were poor; I shouldn't worry then.'

'Do you worry about me, Jo?'

'A little, when you look moody or discontented, as you sometimes do, for you've got such a strong will if you once get started wrong, I'm afraid it would be hard to stop you.'

Laurie walked in silence a few minutes, and Jo watched him, wishing she had held her tongue, for his eyes looked angry, though his lips still smiled as if at her warnings.

'Are you going to deliver lectures all the way home?' he asked, presently.

'Of course not; why?'

'Because if you are, I'll take a 'bus; if you are not, I'd like to walk with you, and tell you something very interesting.'

'I won't preach any more, and I'd like to hear the news immensely.'

'Very well, then; come on. It's a secret, and if I tell you, you must tell me yours.'

'I haven't got any,' began Jo, but stopped suddenly, remembering that she had.

'You know you have; you can't hide anything, so up and 'fess, or I won't tell,' cried Laurie.

'Is your secret a nice one?'

'Oh, isn't it! all about people you know, and such fun! You ought to hear it, and I've been aching to tell this long time. Come! you begin.'

'You'll not say anything about it at home, will you?'

'Not a word.'

'And you won't tease me in private?'

'I never tease.'

'Yes, you do; you get everything you want out of people. I don't know how you do it, but you are a born wheedler.'

'Thank you; fire away!'

'Well, I've left two stories with a newspaper man, and he's to give his answer next week,' whispered Jo, in her confidant's ear.

'Hurrah for Miss March, the celebrated American authoress!' cried Laurie, throwing up his hat and catching it again, to the great delight of two ducks, four cats, five hens, and half a dozen Irish children; for they were out of the city now.

'Hush! it won't come to anything, I dare say; but I couldn't rest till I had tried, and I said nothing about it, because I don't want any one else to be disappointed.'

'It won't fail! Why, Jo, your stories are works of Shakespeare compared to half the rubbish that's published every day. Won't it be fun to see them in print; and shan't we feel proud of our authoress?'

Jo's eyes sparkled, for it's always pleasant to be believed in; and a friend's praise is always sweeter than a dozen newspaper puffs.

'Where's *your* secret? Play fair, Teddy, or I'll never believe you again,' she said, trying to extinguish the brilliant hopes that blazed up at a word of encouragement.

'I may get into a scrape for telling; but I didn't promise not to, so I will, for I never feel easy in my mind till I've told you any plummy bit of news I get. I know where Meg's glove is.'

'Is that all?' said Jo, looking disappointed, as Laurie nodded and twinkled, with a face full of mysterious intelligence.

'It's quite enough for the present, as you'll agree when I tell you where it is.'

'Tell, then.'

Laurie bent and whispered three words in Jo's ear, which produced a comical change. She stood and stared at him for a minute, looking both surprised and displeased, then walked on, saying sharply, 'How do you know?'

'Saw it.'

'Where?'

'Pocket.'

'All this time?'

'Yes; isn't that romantic?'

'No, it's horrid.'

'Don't you like it?'

'Of course I don't; it's ridiculous; it won't be allowed. My patience! what would Meg say?'

'You are not to tell any one; mind that.'

'I didn't promise.'

'That was understood, and I trusted you.'

'Well, I won't for the present, anyway; but I'm disgusted, and wish you hadn't told me.'

'I thought you'd be pleased.'

'At the idea of anybody coming to take Meg away? No, thank you.'

'You'll feel better about it when somebody comes to take you away.'

'I'd like to see any one try it,' cried Jo, fiercely.

'So should I!' and Laurie chuckled at the idea.

'I don't think secrets agree with me; I feel rumpled up in my mind since you told me that,' said Jo, rather ungratefully.

'Race down this hill with me, and you'll be all right,' suggested Laurie.

No one was in sight; the smooth road sloped invitingly before her, and, finding the temptation irresistible, Jo darted away, soon leaving hat and comb behind her, and scattering hair-pins as she ran. Laurie reached the goal first, and was quite satisfied with the success of his treatment; for his Atlanta came panting up with flying hair, bright eyes, ruddy cheeks, and no signs of dissatisfaction in her face.

'I wish I was a horse; then I could run for miles in this splendid air, and not lose my breath. It was capital; but see what a guy it's made me. Go, pick up my things, like a cherub as you are,' said Jo, dropping down under a maple tree, which was carpeting the bank with crimson leaves.

Laurie leisurely departed to recover the lost property, and Jo bundled up her braids, hoping no one would pass by till she was tidy again. But some one did pass, and who should it be but Meg, looking particularly lady-like in her state and festival suit, for she had been making calls.

'What in the world are you doing here?' she asked, regarding her dishevelled sister with well-bred surprise.

'Getting leaves,' meekly answered Jo, sorting the rosy handful she had just swept up.

'And hair-pins,' added Laurie, throwing half a dozen into Jo's lap. 'They grow on this road, Meg; so do combs and brown straw hats.'

'You have been running, Jo; how could you? When *will* you stop such romping ways?' said Meg, reprovingly, as she settled her cuffs and smoothed her hair, with which the wind had taken liberties.

'Never till I'm stiff and old, and have to use a crutch. Don't try to make me grow up before my time, Meg; it's hard enough to have you change all of a sudden; let me be a little girl as long as I can.'

As she spoke, Jo bent over her work to hide the trembling of her lips; for lately she had felt that Margaret was fast getting to be a woman, and Laurie's secret made her dread the separation which must surely come some time, and now seemed very near. He saw the trouble in her face, and drew Meg's attention from it by asking, quickly, 'Where have you been calling, all so fine?'

'At the Gardiners; and Sallie has been telling me all about Belle Moffat's wedding. It was very splendid, and they have gone to spend the winter in Paris; just think how delightful that must be!'

'Do you envy her, Meg?' said Laurie.

'I'm afraid I do.'

'I'm glad of it!' muttered Jo, tying on her hat with a jerk.

'Why?' asked Meg, looking surprised.

'Because, if you care much about riches, you will never go and marry a poor man,' said Jo, frowning at Laurie, who was mutely warning her to mind what she said.

'I shall never "*go* and marry" any one,' observed Meg, walking on with great dignity, while the others followed, laughing, whispering, skipping stones, and 'behaving like children', as Meg said to herself, though she might have been tempted to join them if she had not had her best dress on.

For a week or two Jo behaved so queerly, that her sisters got quite bewildered. She rushed to the door when the postman rang; was rude to Mr Brooke whenever they met; would sit looking at Meg with a woe-begone face, occasionally jumping up to shake, and then to kiss her, in a very mysterious manner; Laurie and she were always making signs to one another, and talking about 'Spread Eagles', till the girls declared they had both lost their wits. On the second Saturday after Jo got out of the window, Meg, as she sat sewing at her window, was scandalized by the sight of Laurie chasing Jo all over the garden, and finally capturing her in Amy's bower. What went on there, Meg could not see, but shrieks of laughter were heard, followed by the murmur of voices, and a great flapping of newspapers.

'What shall we do with that girl? She never *will* behave like a young lady,' sighed Meg, as she watched the race with a disapproving face.

'I hope she won't; she is so funny and dear as she is,' said Beth, who had never betrayed that she was a little hurt at Jo's having secrets with any one but her.

'It's very trying, but we never can make her *comme la fo*,' added Amy, who sat making some new frills for herself, with her curls tied up in a very becoming way,—two agreeable things, which made her feel unusually elegant and lady-like.

In a few minutes Jo bounced in, laid herself on the sofa, and affected to read.

'Have you anything interesting there?' asked Meg, with condescension.

'Nothing but a story; don't amount to much, I guess,' returned Jo, carefully keeping the name of the paper out of sight.

'You'd better read it loud; that will amuse us, and keep you out of mischief,' said Amy, in her most grown-up tone.

'What's the name?' asked Beth, wondering why Jo kept her face behind the sheet.

'*The Rival Painters*.'

'That sounds well; read it,' said Meg.

With a loud 'hem!' and a long breath, Jo began to read very fast. The girls listened with interest, for the tale was romantic, and somewhat pathetic, as most of the characters died in the end.

'I like that about the splendid picture,' was Amy's approving remark, as Jo paused.

'I prefer the lovering part. Viola and Angelo are two of our favorite names; isn't that queer?' said Meg, wiping her eyes, for the 'lovering part' was tragical.

'Who wrote it?' asked Beth, who had caught a glimpse of Jo's face.

The reader suddenly sat up, cast away the paper, displayed a flushed countenance, and, with a funny mixture of solemnity and excitement, replied in a loud voice, 'Your sister!'

211

'You?' cried Meg, dropping her work.

'It's very good,' said Amy, critically.

'I knew it! I knew it! oh, my Jo, I *am* so proud!' and Beth ran to hug her sister and exult over this splendid success.

Dear me, how delighted they all were, to be sure; how Meg wouldn't believe it till she saw the words, 'Miss Josephine March', actually printed in the paper; how graciously Amy criticized the artistic parts of the story, and offered hints for a sequel, which unfortunately couldn't be carried out, as the hero and heroine were dead; how Beth got excited, and skipped and sung with joy; how Hannah came in to exclaim, 'Sakes alive, well I never!' in great astonishment at 'that Jo's doin's'; how proud Mrs March was when she knew it; how Jo laughed, with tears in her eyes, as she declared she might as well be a peacock and done with it; and how the 'Spread Eagle' might be said to flap his wings triumphantly over the house of March, as the paper passed from hand to hand.

'Tell us about it,' 'When did it come?' 'How much did you get for it?' 'What *will* father say?' 'Won't Laurie laugh?' cried the family, all in one breath, as they clustered about Jo; for these foolish, affectionate people made a jubilee of every little household joy.

'Stop jabbering, girls, and I'll tell you everything,' said Jo, wondering if Miss Burney felt any grander over her *Evelina* than she did over her *Rival Painters*. Having told how she disposed of her tales, Jo added,—'And when I went to get my answer the man said he liked them both, but didn't pay beginners, only let them print in his paper, and noticed the stories. It was good practice, he said; and, when the beginners improved, any one would pay. So I let him have the two stories,

212

and today this was sent to me, and Laurie caught me with it, and insisted on seeing it, so I let him; and he said it was good, and I shall write more, and he's going to get the next paid for, and oh—I *am* so happy, for in time I may be able to support myself and help the girls.'

Jo's breath gave out here; and, wrapping her head in the paper, she bedewed her little story with a few natural tears; for to be independent, and earn the praise of those she loved, were the dearest wishes of her heart, and this seemed to be the first step toward that happy end.

CHAPTER FIFTEEN

A Telegram

'November is the most disagreeable month in the whole year,' said Margaret, standing at the window one dull afternoon, looking out at the frost-bitten garden.

'That's the reason I was born in it,' observed Jo, pensively, quite unconscious of the blot on her nose.

'If something very pleasant should happen now, we should think it a delightful month,' said Beth, who took a hopeful view of everything, even November.

'I dare say; but nothing pleasant ever *does* happen in this family,' said Meg, who was out of sorts. 'We go grubbing along day after day, without a bit of change, and very little fun. We might as well be in a tread-mill.'

'My patience, how blue we are!' cried Jo. 'I don't much wonder, poor dear, for you see other girls having splendid times, while you grind, grind, year in and year out. Oh, don't I wish I could fix things for you as I do for my heroines! you're pretty enough and good enough already, so I'd have some rich relation leave you a fortune unexpectedly; then you'd dash out as an heiress, scorn every one who has slighted you, go abroad, and come home my Lady Something, in a blaze of splendor and elegance.'

'People don't have fortunes left them in that style now-a-days; men have to work, and women to marry for money. It's a dreadfully unjust world,' said Meg, bitterly.

'Jo and I are going to make fortunes for you all; just wait ten years, and see if we don't,' said Amy, who sat in a corner making 'mud pies', as Hannah called her little clay models of birds, fruit and faces.

'Can't wait, and I'm afraid I haven't much faith in ink and dirt, though I'm grateful for your good intentions.'

Meg sighed, and turned to the frost-bitten garden again; Jo groaned, and leaned both elbows on the table in a despondent attitude, but Amy spatted away energetically; and Beth, who sat at the other window, said, smiling, 'Two pleasant things are going to happen right away; Marmee is coming down the street, and Laurie is tramping through the garden as if he had something nice to tell.'

In they both came, Mrs March with her usual question, 'Any letter from father, girls?' and Laurie to say, in his persuasive way, 'Won't some of you come for a drive? I've been pegging away at mathematics till my head is in a muddle, and I'm going to freshen my wits by a brisk turn. It's a dull day, but the air isn't bad, and I'm going to take Brooke home, so it will be gay inside, if it isn't out. Come, Jo, you and Beth will go, won't you?'

'Of course we will.'

'Much obliged, but I'm busy;' and Meg whisked out her workbasket, for she had agreed with her mother that it was best, for her at least, not to drive often with the young gentleman.

'Can I do anything for you, Madam Mother?' asked Laurie, leaning over Mrs March's chair, with the affectionate look and tone he always gave her.

'No, thank you, except call at the office, if you'll be so kind, dear. It's our day for a letter, and the penny postman hasn't been. Father is as regular as the sun, but there's some delay on the way, perhaps.'

A sharp ring interrupted her, and a minute after Hannah came in with a letter.

'It's one of them horrid telegraph things, mum,' she said, handling it as if she was afraid it would explode, and do some damage.

At the word 'telegraph', Mrs March snatched it, read the two lines it contained, and dropped back into her chair as white as if the little paper had sent a bullet to her heart. Laurie dashed down stairs for water, while Meg and Hannah supported her, and Jo read aloud, in a frightened voice,—

'Mrs March:
'Your husband is very ill. Come at once.

'S. Hale,
'Blank Hospital, Washington'

How still the room was as they listened breathlessly! how strangely the day darkened outside! and how suddenly the whole world seemed to change, as the girls gathered about

217

their mother, feeling as if all the happiness and support of their lives was about to be taken from them. Mrs March was herself again directly; read the message over, and stretched out her arms to her daughters, saying, in a tone they never forgot, 'I shall go at once, but it may be too late; oh, children, children! help me to bear it!'

For several minutes there was nothing but the sound of sobbing in the room, mingled with broken words of comfort, tender assurances of help, and hopeful whispers, that died away in tears. Poor Hannah was the first to recover, and with unconscious wisdom she set all the rest a good example; for, with her, work was the panacea for most afflictions.

'The Lord keep the dear man! I won't waste no time a cryin', but git your things ready right away, mum,' she said, heartily, as she wiped her face on her apron, gave her mistress a warm shake of the hand with her own hard one, and went away to work, like three women in one.

'She's right; there's no time for tears now. Be calm, girls, and let me think.'

They tried to be calm, poor things, as their mother sat up, looking pale, but steady, and put away her grief to think and plan for them.

'Where's Laurie?' she asked presently, when she had collected her thoughts, and decided on the first duties to be done.

'Here, ma'am; oh, let me do something!' cried the boy, hurrying from the next room, whither he had withdrawn, feeling that their first sorrow was too sacred for even his friendly eyes to see.

'Send a telegram saying I will come at once. The next train goes early in the morning; I'll take that.'

'What else? The horses are ready; I can go anywhere,—do anything,' he said, looking ready to fly to the ends of the earth.

'Leave a note at Aunt March's. Jo, give me that pen and paper.'

Tearing off the blank side of one of her newly-copied pages, Jo drew the table before her mother, well knowing that money for the long, sad journey, must be borrowed, and feeling as if she could do anything to add a little to the sum for her father.

'Now go, dear; but don't kill yourself driving at a desperate pace; there is no need of that.'

Mrs March's warning was evidently thrown away; for five minutes later Laurie tore by the window, on his own fleet horse, riding as if for his life.

'Jo, run to the rooms, and tell Mrs King that I can't come. On the way get these things. I'll put them down; they'll be needed, and I must go prepared for nursing. Hospital stores are not always good. Beth, go and ask Mr Laurence for a couple of bottles of old wine; I'm not too proud to beg for father; he shall have the best of everything. Amy, tell Hannah to get down the black trunk; and Meg, come and help me find my things, for I'm half bewildered.'

Writing, thinking, and directing all at once, might well bewilder the poor lady, and Meg begged her to sit quietly in her room for a little while, and let them work. Every one scattered, like leaves before a gust of wind; and the quiet, happy household was broken up as suddenly as if the paper had been an evil spell.

Mr Laurence came hurrying back with Beth, bringing every comfort the kind old gentleman could think of for the invalid, and friendliest promises of protection for the girls, during the mother's absence, which comforted her very much. There was nothing he didn't offer, from his own dressing-gown to himself as escort. But that last was impossible. Mrs March would not hear of the old gentleman's undertaking the long journey; yet an expression of relief was visible when he spoke of it, for anxiety ill fits one for travelling. He saw the look, knit his heavy eyebrows, rubbed his hands, and marched abruptly away, saying he'd be back directly. No one had time to think of him again till, as Meg ran through the entry, with a pair of rubbers in one hand and a cup of tea in the other, she came suddenly upon Mr Brooke.

'I'm very sorry to hear of this, Miss March,' he said, in the kind, quiet tone which sounded very pleasantly to her perturbed spirit. 'I came to offer myself as escort to your mother. Mr Laurence has commissions for me in Washington, and it will give me real satisfaction to be of service to her there.'

Down dropped the rubbers, and the tea was very near following, as Meg put out her hand, with a face so full of gratitude, that Mr Brooke would have felt repaid for a much greater sacrifice than the trifling one of time and comfort, which he was about to make.

'How kind you all are! Mother will accept, I'm sure; and it will be such a relief to know that she has some one to take care of her. Thank you very, very much!'

Meg spoke earnestly, and forgot herself entirely till something in the brown eyes looking down at her made her remember the cooling tea, and lead the way into the parlor, saying she would call her mother.

Everything was arranged by the time Laurie returned with

a note from Aunt March, enclosing the desired sum, and a few lines repeating what she had often said before, that she had always told them it was absurd for March to go into the army, always predicted that no good would come of it, and she hoped they would take her advice next time. Mrs March put the note in the fire, the money in her purse, and went on with her preparations, with her lips folded tightly, in a way which Jo would have understood if she had been there.

The short afternoon wore away; all the other errands were done, and Meg and her mother busy at some necessary needlework, while Beth and Amy got tea, and Hannah finished her ironing with what she called a 'slap and a bang', but still Jo did not come. They began to get anxious; and Laurie went off to find her, for no one ever knew what freak Jo might take into her head. He missed her, however, and she came walking in with a very queer expression of countenance, for there was a mixture of fun and fear, satisfaction and regret in it, which puzzled the family as much as did the roll of bills she laid before her mother, saying, with a little choke in her voice, 'That's my contribution towards making father comfortable, and bringing him home!'

'My dear, where did you get it! Twenty-five dollars! Jo, I hope you haven't done anything rash?'

'No, it's mine honestly; I didn't beg, borrow, nor steal it. I earned it; and I don't think you'll blame me, for I only sold what was my own.'

As she spoke, Jo took off her bonnet, and a general outcry arose, for all her abundant hair was cut short.

'Your hair! Your beautiful hair!' 'Oh, Jo, how could you? Your one beauty.' 'My dear girl, there was no need of this.'

'She don't look like my Jo any more, but I love her dearly for it!'

As every one exclaimed, and Beth hugged the cropped head tenderly, Jo assumed an indifferent air, which did not deceive any one a particle, and said, rumpling up the brown bush, and trying to look as if she liked it, 'It doesn't affect the fate of the nation, so don't wail, Beth. It will be good for my vanity; I was getting too proud of my wig. It will do my brains good to have that mop taken off; my head feels deliciously light and cool, and the barber said I could soon have a curly crop, which will be boyish, becoming, and easy to keep in order. I'm satisfied; so please take the money, and let's have supper.'

'Tell me all about it, Jo; *I* am not quite satisfied, but I can't blame you, for I know how willingly you sacrificed your vanity, as you call it, to your love. But, my dear, it was not necessary, and I'm afraid you will regret it, one of these days,' said Mrs March.

'No I won't!' returned Jo, stoutly, feeling much relieved that her prank was not entirely condemned.

'What made you do it?' asked Amy, who would as soon have thought of cutting off her head as her pretty hair.

'Well, I was wild to do something for father,' replied Jo, as they gathered about the table, for healthy young people can eat even in the midst of trouble. 'I hate to borrow as much as mother does, and I knew Aunt March would croak; she always does, if you ask for a ninepence. Meg gave all her quarterly salary toward the rent, and I only got some clothes with mine, so I felt wicked, and was bound to have some money, if I sold the nose off my face to get it.'

'You needn't feel wicked, my child, you had no winter things, and got the simplest, with your own hard earnings,' said Mrs March, with a look that warmed Jo's heart.

'I hadn't the least idea of selling my hair at first, but as I went along I kept thinking *what* I could do, and feeling as if I'd like to dive into some of the rich stores and help myself. In a barber's window I saw tails of hair with the prices marked; and one black tail, longer, but not so thick as mine, was forty dollars. It came over me all of a sudden that I had one thing to make money out of, and, without stopping to think, I walked in, asked if they bought hair, and what they would give for mine.'

'I don't see how you dared to do it,' said Beth, in a tone of awe.

'Oh, he was a little man who looked as if he merely lived to oil his hair. He rather stared, at first, as if he wasn't used to having girls bounce into his shop and ask him to buy their hair. He said he didn't care about mine, it wasn't the fashionable color, and he never paid much for it in the first place; the work put into it made it dear, and so on. It was getting late, and I was afraid, if it wasn't done right away, that I shouldn't have it done at all, and you know, when I start to do a thing, I hate to give it up; so I begged him to take it, and told him why I was in such a hurry. It was silly, I dare say, but it changed his mind, for I got rather excited, and told the story in my topsy-turvy way, and his wife heard, and said so kindly,—

'"Take it, Thomas, and oblige the young lady; I'd do as much for our Jimmy any day if I had a spire of hair worth selling."'

'Who was Jimmy?' asked Amy, who liked to have things explained as they went along.

'Her son, she said, who is in the army. How friendly such things make strangers feel, don't they? She talked away all the time the man clipped, and diverted my mind nicely.'

'Didn't you feel dreadfully when the first cut came?' asked Meg, with a shiver.

'I took a last look at my hair while the man got his things, and that was the end of it. I never snivel over trifles like that; I will confess, though, I felt queer when I saw the dear old hair laid out on the table, and felt only the short, rough ends on my head. It almost seemed as if I'd an arm or a leg off. The woman saw me look at it, and picked out a long lock for me to keep. I'll give it to you, Marmee, just to remember past glories by; for a crop is so comfortable I don't think I shall ever have a mane again.'

Mrs March folded the wavy, chestnut lock, and laid it away with a short gray one in her desk. She only said 'Thank you, deary,' but something in her face made the girls change the subject, and talk as cheerfully as they could about Mr Brooke's kindness, the prospect of a fine day to-morrow, and the happy times they would have when father came home to be nursed.

No one wanted to go to bed, when, at ten o'clock, Mrs March put by the last finished job, and said, 'Come, girls.' Beth went to the piano and played the father's favorite hymn; all began bravely, but broke down one by one till Beth was left alone, singing with all her heart, for to her music was always a sweet consoler.

'Go to bed, and don't talk, for we must be up early, and shall need all the sleep we can get. Good-night, my darlings,' said Mrs March, as the hymn ended, for no one cared to try another.

They kissed her quietly, and went to bed as silently as if the dear invalid lay in the next room. Beth and Amy soon fell asleep in spite of the great trouble, but Meg lay awake thinking the most serious thoughts she had ever known in her short life. Jo lay motionless, and her sister fancied that she was asleep, till a stifled sob made her exclaim, as she touched a wet cheek,—

'Jo, dear, what is it? Are you crying about father?'

'No, not now.'

'What then?'

'My—my hair,' burst out poor Jo, trying vainly to smother her emotion in the pillow.

It did not sound at all comical to Meg, who kissed and caressed the afflicted heroine in the tenderest manner.

'I'm not sorry,' protested Jo, with a choke. 'I'd do it again tomorrow, if I could. It's only the vain, selfish part of me that goes and cries in this silly way. Don't tell any one, it's all over now. I thought you were asleep, so I just made a little private moan for my one beauty. How came you to be awake?'

'I can't sleep, I'm so anxious,' said Meg.

'Think about something pleasant and you'll soon drop off.'

'I tried it, but felt wider awake than ever.'

'What did you think of?'

'Handsome faces; eyes particularly,' answered Meg smilingly, to herself, in the dark.

'What color do you like best?'

'Brown—that is sometimes—blue are lovely.'

Jo laughed, and Meg sharply ordered her not to talk, then amiably promised to make her hair curl, and fell asleep to dream of living in her castle in the air.

The clocks were striking midnight, and the rooms were very still, as a figure glided quietly from bed to bed, smoothing a coverlid here, setting a pillow there, and pausing to look long and tenderly at each unconscious face, to kiss each with lips that mutely blessed, and to pray the fervent prayers which only mothers utter. As she lifted the curtain to look out into the dreary night, the moon broke suddenly from behind the clouds, and shone upon her like a bright benignant face, which seemed to whisper in the silence, 'Be comforted, dear heart! there is always light behind the clouds.'

CHAPTER SIXTEEN

—•—

Letters

In the cold gray dawn the sisters lit their lamp, and read
their chapter with an earnestness never felt before, for
now the shadow of a real trouble had come, showing
them how rich in sunshine their lives had been. The little
books were full of help and comfort; and, as they dressed, they
agreed to say good-by cheerfully, hopefully, and send their
mother on her anxious journey unsaddened by tears or complaints from them. Everything seemed very strange when they
went down; so dim and still outside, so full of light and bustle
within. Breakfast at that early hour seemed odd, and even
Hannah's familiar face looked unnatural as she flew about her
kitchen with her night cap on. The big trunk stood ready in
the hall, mother's cloak and bonnet lay on the sofa, and
mother herself sat trying to eat, but looking so pale and worn
with sleeplessness and anxiety, that the girls found it very hard
to keep their resolution. Meg's eyes kept filling in spite of herself; Jo was obliged to hide her face in the kitchen roller more

than once, and the little girls' young faces wore a grave, troubled expression, as if sorrow was a new experience to them.

Nobody talked much, but, as the time drew very near, and they sat waiting for the carriage, Mrs March said to the girls, who were all busied about her, one folding her shawl, another smoothing out the strings of her bonnet, a third putting on her over-shoes, and a fourth fastening up her travelling bag,—

'Children, I leave you to Hannah's care, and Mr Laurence's protection; Hannah is faithfulness itself, and our good neighbor will guard you as if you were his own. I have no fears for you, yet I am anxious that you should take this trouble rightly. Don't grieve and fret when I am gone, or think that you can comfort yourselves by being idle, and trying to forget. So on with your work as usual, for work is a blessed solace. Hope, and keep busy; and, whatever happens, remember that you never can be fatherless.'

'Yes, mother.'

'Meg dear, be prudent, watch over your sisters, consult Hannah, and, in any perplexity, go to Mr Laurence. Be patient, Jo, don't get despondent, or do rash things; write to me often, and be my brave girl, ready to help and cheer us all. Beth, comfort yourself with your music, and be faithful to the little home duties; and you, Amy, help all you can, be obedient, and keep happy safe at home.'

'We will, mother! we will!'

The rattle of an approaching carriage made them all start and listen. That was the hard minute, but the girls stood it well; no one cried, no one ran away, or uttered a lamentation, though their hearts were very heavy as they sent loving messages to father, remembering, as they spoke, that it might be too late to deliver them. They kissed their mother quietly, clung about her tenderly, and tried to wave their hands cheerfully, when she drove away.

Laurie and his grandfather came over to see her off, and Mr Brooke looked so strong, and sensible, and kind, that the girls christened him 'Mr Greatheart' on the spot.

'Good-by, my darlings! God bless and keep us all,' whispered Mrs March, as she kissed one dear little face after the other, and hurried into the carriage.

As she rolled away, the sun came out, and, looking back, she saw it shining on the group at the gate, like a good omen. They saw it also, and smiled and waved their hands; and the last thing she beheld, as she turned the corner, was the four bright faces, and behind them, like a body-guard, old Mr Laurence, faithful Hannah, and devoted Laurie.

'How kind every one is to us,' she said, turning to find fresh proof of it in the respectful sympathy of the young man's face.

'I don't see how they can help it,' returned Mr Brooke, laughing so infectiously that Mrs March could not help smiling; and so the long journey began with the good omens of sunshine, smiles, and cheerful words.

'I feel as if there had been an earthquake,' said Jo, as their neighbors went home to breakfast, leaving them to rest and refresh themselves.

'It seems as if half the house was gone,' added Meg, forlornly.

Beth opened her lips to say something, but could only point to the pile of nicely-mended hose which lay on mother's table, showing that even in her last hurried moments she had thought and worked for them. It was a little thing, but it went straight to their hearts; and, in spite of their brave resolutions, they all broke down, and cried bitterly.

Hannah wisely allowed them to relieve their feelings; and, when the shower showed signs of clearing up, she came to the rescue, armed with a coffee-pot.

'Now, my dear young ladies, remember what your ma said, and don't fret; come and have a cup of coffee all round, and then let's fall to work, and be a credit to the family.'

Coffee was a treat, and Hannah showed great tact in making it that morning. No one could resist her persuasive nods, or the fragrant invitation issuing from the nose of the coffee-pot. They drew up to the table, exchanged their handkerchiefs for napkins, and, in ten minutes, were all right again.

' "Hope and keep busy"; that's the motto for us, so let's see who will remember it best. I shall go to Aunt March, as usual; oh, won't she lecture, though!' said Jo, as she sipped, with returning spirit.

'I shall go to my Kings, though I'd much rather stay at home and attend to things here,' said Meg, wishing she hadn't made her eyes so red.

'No need of that; Beth and I can keep house perfectly well,' put in Amy, with an important air.

'Hannah will tell us what to do; and we'll have everything nice when you come home,' added Beth, getting out her mop and dishtub without delay.

'I think anxiety is very interesting,' observed Amy, eating sugar, pensively.

The girls couldn't help laughing, and felt better for it, though Meg shook her head at the young lady who could find consolation in a sugar-bowl.

The sight of the turn-overs made Jo sober again; and, when the two went out to their daily tasks, they looked sorrowfully back at the window where they were accustomed to see their mother's face. It was gone; but Beth had remembered the little household ceremony, and there she was, nodding away at them like a rosy-faced mandarin.

'That's so like my Beth!' said Jo, waving her hat, with a grateful face. 'Good-by, Meggy; I hope the Kings won't train to-day. Don't fret about father, dear,' she added, as they parted.

'And I hope Aunt March won't croak. Your hair *is* becoming, and it looks very boyish and nice,' returned Meg, trying not to smile at the curly head, which looked comically small on her tall sister's shoulders.

'That's my only comfort;' and, touching her hat à la Laurie, away went Jo, feeling like a shorn sheep on a wintry day.

News from their father comforted the girls very much; for, though dangerously ill, the presence of the best and tenderest of nurses had already done him good. Mr Brooke sent a bulletin every day, and, as the head of the family, Meg insisted on reading the despatches, which grew more and more cheering as the week passed. At first, every one was eager to write, and plump envelopes were carefully poked into the letter-box, by one or other of the sisters, who felt rather important with their Washington correspondence. As one of these packets contained characteristic notes from the party, we will rob an imaginary mail, and read them:—

'My Dearest Mother,—
'It is impossible to tell you how happy your last letter made us, for the news was so good we couldn't help laughing and

231

LITTLE WOMEN

crying over it. How very kind Mr Brooke is, and how fortunate that Mr Laurence's business detains him near you so long, since he is so useful to you and father. The girls are all as good as gold. Jo helps me with the sewing, and insists on doing all sorts of hard jobs. I should be afraid she might overdo, if I didn't know that her "moral fit" wouldn't last long. Beth is as regular about her tasks as a clock, and never forgets what you told her. She grieves about father, and looks sober, except when she is at her little piano. Amy minds me nicely, and I take great care of her. She does her own hair, and I am teaching her to make button-holes, and mend her stockings. She tries very hard, and I know you will be pleased with her improvement when you come. Mr Laurence watches over us like a motherly old hen, as Jo says; and Laurie is very kind and neighborly. He and Jo keep us merry, for we get pretty blue sometimes, and feel like orphans, with you so far away. Hannah is a perfect saint; she does not scold at all, and always calls me "Miss Margaret", which is quite proper, you know, and treats me with respect. We are all well and busy; but we long, day and night, to have you back. Give my dearest love to father, and believe me, ever your own

Meg.'

This note, prettily written on scented paper, was a great contrast to the next, which was scribbled on a big sheet of thin, foreign paper, ornamented with blots, and all manner of flourishes and curly-tailed letters:—

'My Precious Marmee,—

'Three cheers for dear old father! Brooke was a trump to telegraph right off, and let us know the minute he was better. I rushed up garret when the letter came, and tried to thank God for being so good to us; but I could only cry, and say, "I'm glad! I'm glad!" Didn't that do as well as a regular prayer? for I felt a great many in my heart. We have such funny times; and now I can enjoy 'em, for every one is so desperately good, it's like living in a nest of turtle-doves. You'd laugh to see Meg head the table, and try to be motherish. She gets prettier every day, and I'm in love with her sometimes. The children are regular archangels, and I—well, I'm Jo, and never shall be anything else. Oh, I must tell you that I came near having a quarrel with Laurie. I freed my mind about a silly little thing, and he was offended. I was right, but didn't speak as I ought, and he marched home, saying he wouldn't come again till I begged pardon. I declared I wouldn't, and got mad. It lasted all day; I felt bad, and wanted you very much. Laurie and I are both so proud, it's hard to beg pardon; but I thought he'd come to it, for I *was* in the right. He didn't come; and just at night I remembered what you said when Amy fell into the river. I read my little book, felt better, resolved not to let the sun set on *my* anger, and ran over to tell Laurie I was sorry. I met him at the gate, coming for the same thing. We both laughed, begged each other's pardon, and felt all good and comfortable again.

'I made a "pome" yesterday, when I was helping Hannah wash; and, as father likes my silly little things, I put it in to amuse him. Give him the lovingest hug that ever was, and kiss yourself a dozen times, for your

'Topsy-Turvy Jo.

'A SONG FROM THE SUDS.

'Queen of my tub, I merrily sing,
While the white foam rises high;

233

And sturdily wash, and rinse, and wring,
*   And fasten the clothes to dry;*
Then out in the free fresh air they swing,
*   Under the sunny sky.*
'I wish we could wash from our hearts and souls
*   The stains of the week away,*
And let water and air by their magic make
*   Ourselves as pure as they;*
Then on the earth there would be indeed
*   A glorious washing-day!*

'Along the path of a useful life,
*   Will heart's-ease ever bloom;*
The busy mind has no time to think
*   Of sorrow, or care, or gloom;*
And anxious thoughts may be swept away,
*   As we busily wield a broom.*

'I am glad a task to me is given,
*   To labor at day by day;*
For it brings me health, and strength, and hope,
*   And I cheerfully learn to say,—*
"Head you may think, Heart you may feel,
*   But Hand you shall work alway!"'*

'Dear Mother:

'There is only room for me to send my love, and some pressed pansies from the root I have been keeping safe in the house, for father to see. I read every morning, try to be good all day, and sing myself to sleep with father's tune. I can't

234

sing "Land of the Leal" now; it makes me cry. Every one is very kind, and we are as happy as we can be without you. Amy wants the rest of the page, so I must stop. I didn't forget to cover the holders, and I wind the clock and air the rooms every day.

'Kiss dear father on the cheek he calls mine. Oh, do come soon to your loving

'Little Beth.'

'Ma Chere Mamma:

'We are all well I do my lessons always and never corroberate the girls—Meg says I mean contradick so I put in both words and you can take the properest. Meg is a great comfort to me and lets me have jelly every night at tea its so good for me Jo says because it keeps me sweet tempered. Laurie is not as respeckful as he ought to be now I am almost in my teens, he calls me Chick and hurts my feelings by talking French to me very fast when I say Merci or Bon jour as Hattie King does. The sleeves of my blue dress were all worn out and Meg put in new ones but the full front came wrong and they are more blue than the dress. I felt bad but did not fret I bear my troubles well but I do wish Hannah would put more starch in my aprons and have buck wheats every day. Can't she? Didn't I make that interrigation point nice. Meg says my punchtuation and spelling are disgraceful and I am mortyfied but dear me I have so many things to do I can't stop. Adieu, I send heaps of love to Papa.

'Your affectionate daughter,

'Amy Curtis March.'

'Dear Mis March:

'I jes drop a line to say we git on fust rate. The girls is clever and fly round right smart. Miss Meg is goin to make a proper good housekeeper; she hes the liking for it, and gits the hang of things surprisin quick. Jo doos beat all for goin ahead, but she don't stop to cal'k'late fust, and you never know where she's like to bring up. She done out a tub of clothes on Monday, but she starched em afore they was wrenched, and blued a pink calico dress till I thought I should a died a laughin. Beth is the best of little creeters, and a sight of help to me, bein so forehanded and dependable. She tries to learn everything, and really goes to market beyond her years; likewise keeps accounts, with my help, quite wonderful. We have got on very economical so fur; I don't let the girls hev coffee only once a week, accordin to your wish, and keep em on plain wholesome vittles. Amy does well about frettin, wearin her best clothes and eatin sweet stuff. Mr Laurie is as full of didoes as usual, and turns the house upside down frequent; but he heartens up the girls, and so I let em hev full swing. The old man sends heaps of things, and is rather wearin, but means wal, and it aint my place to say nothin. My bread is riz, so no more at this time. I send my duty to Mr March, and hope he's seen the last of his Pewmonia.

'Yours respectful,

'Hannah Mullet'

'Head Nurse of Ward II:

'All serene on the Rappahannock, troops in fine condition, commissary department well conducted, the Home Guard under Colonel Teddy always on duty, Commander-in-chief General Laurence reviews the army daily, Quartermaster Mullet keeps order in camp, and Major Lion does picket duty at night. A salute of twenty-four guns was fired on receipt of good news from Washington, and a dress parade took place at headquarters. Commander-in-chief sends best wishes, in which he is heartily joined by

Colonel Teddy.

'Dear Madam:

'The little girls are all well; Beth and my boy report daily; Hannah is a model servant, guards pretty Meg like a dragon. Glad the fine weather holds; pray make Brooke useful, and draw on me for funds if expenses exceed your estimate. Don't let your husband want anything. Thank God he is mending.

'Your sincere friend and servant,

'James Laurence.'

CHAPTER SEVENTEEN

———•———

Little Faithful

For a week the amount of virtue in the old house would have supplied the neighborhood. It was really amazing, for every one seemed in a heavenly frame of mind, and self-denial was all the fashion. Relieved of their first anxiety about their father, the girls insensibly relaxed their praiseworthy efforts a little, and began to fall back into the old ways. They did not forget their motto, but hoping and keeping busy seemed to grow easier; and, after such tremendous exertions, they felt that Endeavor deserved a holiday, and gave it a good many.

Jo caught a bad cold through neglecting to cover the shorn head enough, and was ordered to stay at home till she was better, for Aunt March didn't like to hear people read with colds in their heads. Jo liked this, and after an energetic rummage from garret to cellar, subsided on to the sofa to nurse her cold with arsenicum and books. Amy found that house-work and art did not go well together, and returned to her mud pies.

LITTLE WOMEN

Meg went daily to her kingdom, and sewed, or thought she did, at home, but much time was spent in writing long letters to her mother, or reading the Washington despatches over and over. Beth kept on with only slight relapses into idleness or grieving. All the little duties were faithfully done each day, and many of her sisters' also, for they were forgetful, and the house seemed like a clock, whose pendulum was gone a-visiting. When her heart got heavy with longings for mother, or fears for father, she went away into a certain closet, hid her face in the folds of a certain dear old gown, and made her little moan, and prayed her little prayer quietly by herself. Nobody knew what cheered her up after a sober fit, but every one felt how sweet and helpful Beth was, and fell into a way of going to her for comfort or advice in their small affairs.

All were unconscious that this experience was a test of character; and, when the first excitement was over, felt that they had done well, and deserved praise. So they did; but their mistake was in ceasing to do well, and they learned this lesson through much anxiety and regret.

'Meg, I wish you'd go and see the Hummels; you know mother told us not to forget them,' said Beth, ten days after Mrs March's departure.

'I'm too tired to go this afternoon,' replied Meg, rocking comfortably, as she sewed.

'Can't you, Jo?' asked Beth.

'Too stormy for me, with my cold.'

'I thought it was most well.'

'It's well enough for me to go out with Laurie, but not well enough to go to the Hummels,' said Jo, laughing, but looking a little ashamed of her inconsistency.

'Why don't you go yourself?' asked Meg.

'I *have* been every day, but the baby is sick, and I don't know what to do for it. Mrs Hummel goes away to work, and Lottchen takes care of it; but it gets sicker and sicker, and I think you or Hannah ought to go.'

Beth spoke earnestly, and Meg promised she would go to-morrow.

'Ask Hannah for some nice little mess, and take it round, Beth, the air will do you good;' said Jo, adding apologetically, 'I'd go, but I want to finish my story.'

'My head aches, and I'm tired, so I thought maybe some of you would go,' said Beth.

'Amy will be in presently, and she will run down for us,' suggested Meg.

'Well, I'll rest a little, and wait for her.'

So Beth lay down on the sofa, the others returned to their work, and the Hummels were forgotten. An hour passed, Amy did not come; Meg went to her room to try on a new dress; Jo was absorbed in her story, and Hannah was sound asleep before the kitchen fire, when Beth quietly put on her hood, filled her basket with odds and ends for the poor children, and went out into the chilly air with a heavy head, and a grieved look in her patient eyes. It was late when she came back, and no one saw her creep upstairs and shut herself into her mother's room. Half an hour after, Jo went to 'mother's closet' for something, and there found Beth sitting on the medicine chest, looking very grave, with red eyes, and a camphor bottle in her hand.

'Christopher Columbus! what's the matter?' cried Jo, as Beth put out her hand as if to warn her off, and asked quickly,—

'You've had scarlet fever, haven't you?'

'Years ago, when Meg did. Why?'

'Then I'll tell you—oh, Jo, the baby's dead!'

'What baby?'

'Mrs Hummel's; it died in my lap before she got home,' cried Beth, with a sob.

'My poor dear, how dreadful for you! I ought to have gone,' said Jo, taking her sister in her lap as she sat down in her mother's big chair, with a remorseful face.

'It wasn't dreadful, Jo, only so sad! I saw in a minute that it was sicker, but Lottchen said her mother had gone for a doctor, so I took baby and let Lotty rest. It seemed asleep, but all of a sudden it gave a little cry, and trembled, and then lay very still. I tried to warm its feet, and Lotty gave it some milk, but it didn't stir, and I knew it was dead.'

'Don't cry, dear! what did you do?'

'I just sat and held it softly till Mrs Hummel came with the doctor. He said it was dead, and looked at Heinrich and Minna, who have got sore throats. "Scarlet fever, ma'am; ought to have called me before," he said, crossly. Mrs Hummel told him she was poor, and had tried to cure baby herself, but now it was too late, and she could only ask him to help the others, and trust to charity for his pay. He smiled then, and was kinder, but it was very sad, and I cried with them till he turned round all of a sudden, and told me to go home and take belladonna right away, or I'd have the fever.'

'No you won't!' cried Jo, hugging her close, with a frightened look. 'Oh, Beth, if you should be sick I never could forgive myself! What *shall* we do?'

'Don't be frightened, I guess I shan't have it badly; I looked in mother's book, and saw that it begins with headache, sore throat, and queer feelings like mine, so I did take some bella-donna, and I feel better,' said Beth, laying her cold hands on her hot forehead, and trying to look well.

'If mother was only at home!' exclaimed Jo, seizing the book, and feeling that Washington was an immense way off. She read a page, looked at Beth, felt her head, peeped into her throat, and then said, gravely, 'You've been over the baby every day for more than a week, and among the others who are going to have it, so I'm afraid you're going to have it, Beth. I'll call Hannah; she knows all about sickness.'

'Don't let Amy come; she never had it, and I should hate to give it to her. Can't you and Meg have it over again?' asked Beth, anxiously.

'I guess not; don't care if I do; serve me right, selfish pig, to let you go, and stay writing rubbish myself!' muttered Jo, as she went to consult Hannah.

The good soul was wide awake in a minute, and took the lead at once, assuring Jo that there was no need to worry; every one had scarlet fever, and, if rightly treated, nobody died; all of which Jo believed, and felt much relieved as they went up to call Meg.

'Now I'll tell you what we'll do,' said Hannah, when she had examined and questioned Beth; 'we will have Dr Bangs, just to take a look at you, dear, and see that we start right; then we'll send Amy off to Aunt March's, for a spell, to keep her out of harm's way, and one of you girls can stay at home and amuse Beth for a day or two.'

'I shall stay, of course, I'm oldest;' began Meg, looking anxious and self-reproachful.

'*I* shall, because it's my fault she is sick; I told mother I'd do the errands, and I haven't,' said Jo, decidedly.

'Which will you have, Beth? there ain't no need of but one,' said Hannah.

'Jo, please;' and Beth leaned her head against her sister, with a contented look, which effectually settled that point.

'I'll go and tell Amy,' said Meg, feeling a little hurt, yet rather relieved, on the whole, for she did not like nursing, and Jo did.

Amy rebelled outright, and passionately declared that she had rather have the fever than go to Aunt March. Meg reasoned, pleaded, and commanded, all in vain. Amy protested that she would *not* go; and Meg left her in despair, to ask Hannah what should be done. Before she came back, Laurie walked into the parlor to find Amy sobbing, with her head in the sofa cushions. She told her story, expecting to be consoled; but Laurie only put his hands in his pockets and walked about the room, whistling softly, as he knit his brows in deep thought. Presently he sat down beside her, and said, in his most wheedlesome tone, 'Now be a sensible little woman, and do as they say. No, don't cry, but hear what a jolly plan I've got. You go to Aunt March's, and I'll come and take you out every day, driving or walking, and we'll have capital times. Won't that be better than moping here?'

'I don't wish to be sent off as if I was in the way,' began Amy, in an injured voice.

'Bless your heart, child! it's to keep you well. You don't want to be sick, do you?'

'No, I'm sure I don't; but I dare say I shall be, for I've been with Beth all this time.'

'That's the very reason you ought to go away at once, so that you may escape it. Change of air and care will keep you well, I dare say; or, if it don't entirely, you will have the fever more lightly. I advise you to be off as soon as you can, for scarlet fever is no joke, miss.'

'But it's dull at Aunt March's, and she is so cross,' said Amy, looking rather frightened.

'It won't be dull with me popping in every day to tell you how Beth is, and take you out gallivanting. The old lady likes me, and I'll be as clever as possible to her, so she won't peck at us, whatever we do.'

'Will you take me out in the trotting wagon with Puck?'

'On my honor as a gentleman.'

'And come every single day?'

'See if I don't.'

'And bring me back the minute Beth is well?'

'The identical minute.'

'And go to the theatre, truly?'

'A dozen theatres, if we may.'

'Well—I guess—I will,' said Amy, slowly.

'Good girl! Sing out for Meg, and tell her you'll give in,' said Laurie, with an approving pat, which annoyed Amy more than the 'giving in'.

Meg and Jo came running down to behold the miracle which had been wrought; and Amy, feeling very precious and self-sacrificing, promised to go, if the doctor said Beth was going to be ill.

'How is the little dear?' asked Laurie; for Beth was his especial pet, and he felt more anxious about her than he liked to show.

'She is lying down on mother's bed, and feels better. The baby's death troubled her, but I dare say she has only got cold. Hannah *says* she thinks so; but she *looks* worried, and that makes me fidgety,' answered Meg.

'What a trying world it is!' said Jo, rumpling up her hair in a fretful sort of way. 'No sooner do we get out of one trouble than down comes another. There don't seem to be anything to hold on to when mother's gone; so I'm all at sea.'

'Well, don't make a porcupine of yourself, it isn't becoming. Settle your wig, Jo, and tell me if I shall telegraph to your mother, or do anything?' asked Laurie, who never had been reconciled to the loss of his friend's one beauty.

'That is what troubles me,' said Meg. 'I think we ought to tell her if Beth is really ill, but Hannah says we mustn't, for mother can't leave father, and it will only make them anxious. Beth won't be sick long, and Hannah knows just what to do, and mother said we were to mind her, so I suppose we must, but it don't seem quite right to me.'

'Hum, well, I can't say; suppose you ask grandfather, after the doctor has been.'

'We will; Jo, go and get Dr Bangs at once,' commanded Meg; 'we can't decide anything till he has been.'

'Stay where you are, Jo; I'm errand boy to this establishment,' said Laurie, taking up his cap.

'I'm afraid you are busy,' began Meg.

'No, I've done my lessons for the day.'

'Do you study in vacation time?' asked Jo.

'I follow the good example my neighbors set me,' was Laurie's answer, as he swung himself out of the room.

'I have great hopes of my boy,' observed Jo, watching him fly over the fence with an approving smile.

'He does very well—for a boy,' was Meg's somewhat ungracious answer, for the subject did not interest her.

Dr Bangs came, said Beth had symptoms of the fever, but thought she would have it lightly, though he looked sober over the Hummel story. Amy was ordered off at once, and provided with something to ward off danger; she departed in great state, with Jo and Laurie as escort.

Aunt March received them with her usual hospitality.

'What do you want now?' she asked, looking sharply over her spectacles, while the parrot, sitting on the back of her chair, called out,—

'Go away; no boys allowed here.'

Laurie retired to the window, and Jo told her story.

'No more than I expected, if you are allowed to go poking about among poor folks. Amy can stay and make herself useful if she isn't sick, which I've no doubt she will be,—looks like it now. Don't cry, child, it worries me to hear people sniff.'

Amy *was* on the point of crying, but Laurie slyly pulled the parrot's tail, which caused Polly to utter an astonished croak, and call out,—

'Bless my boots!' in such a funny way, that she laughed instead.

'What do you hear from your mother?' asked the old lady, gruffly.

'Father is much better,' replied Jo, trying to keep sober.

'Oh, is he? Well, that won't last long, I fancy; March never had any stamina,' was the cheerful reply.

'Ha, ha! never say die, take a pinch of snuff, good-by,

good-by!' squalled Polly, dancing on her perch, and clawing at the old lady's cap as Laurie tweaked him in the rear.

'Hold your tongue, you disrespectful old bird! and, Jo, you'd better go at once; it isn't proper to be gadding about so late with a rattle-pated boy like—'

'Hold your tongue, you disrespectful old bird!' cried Polly, tumbling off the chair with a bounce, and running to peck the 'rattle-pated' boy, who was shaking with laughter at the last speech.

'I don't think I *can* bear it, but I'll try,' thought Amy, as she was left alone with Aunt March.

'Get along, you're a fright!' screamed Polly, and at that rude speech Amy could not restrain a sniff.

CHAPTER EIGHTEEN

———•●•———

Dark Days

Beth did have the fever, and was much sicker than any one but Hannah and the doctor suspected. The girls knew nothing about illness, and Mr Laurence was not allowed to see her, so Hannah had everything all her own way, and busy Dr Bangs did his best, but left a good deal to the excellent nurse. Meg stayed at home, lest she should infect the Kings, and kept house, feeling very anxious, and a little guilty, when she wrote letters in which no mention was made of Beth's illness. She could not think it right to deceive her mother, but she had been bidden to mind Hannah, and Hannah wouldn't hear of 'Mrs March bein' told, and worried just for sech a trifle.' Jo devoted herself to Beth day and night; not a hard task, for Beth was very patient, and bore her pain uncomplainingly as long as she could control herself. But there came a time when during the fever fits she began to talk in a hoarse, broken voice, to play on the coverlet, as if on her beloved little piano, and try to sing with a throat so swollen,

that there was no music left; a time when she did not know
the familiar faces round her, but addressed them by wrong
names, and called imploringly for her mother. Then Jo grew
frightened, Meg begged to be allowed to write the truth, and
even Hannah said she 'would think of it, though there was no
danger *yet*'. A letter from Washington added to their trouble,
for Mr March had had a relapse, and could not think of coming home for a long while.

How dark the days seemed now, how sad and lonely the
house, and how heavy were the hearts of the sisters as they
worked and waited, while the shadow of death hovered over
the once happy home! Then it was that Margaret, sitting alone
with tears dropping often on her work, felt how rich she had
been in things more precious than any luxuries money could
buy; in love, protection, peace and health, the real blessings of
life. Then it was that Jo, living in the darkened room with that
suffering little sister always before her eyes, and that pathetic
voice sounding in her ears, learned to see the beauty and the
sweetness of Beth's nature, to feel how deep and tender a
place she filled in all hearts, and to acknowledge the worth of
Beth's unselfish ambition, to live for others, and make home
happy by the exercise of those simple virtues which all may
possess, and which all should love and value more than talent,
wealth or beauty. And Amy, in her exile, longed eagerly to be
at home, that she might work for Beth, feeling now that no
service would be hard or irksome, and remembering, with re-
gretful grief, how many neglected tasks those willing hands
had done for her. Laurie haunted the house like a restless
ghost, and Mr Laurence locked the grand piano, because he
could not bear to be reminded of the young neighbor who

used to make the twilight pleasant for him. Every one missed Beth. The milk-man, baker, grocer and butcher inquired how she did; poor Mrs Hummel came to beg pardon for her thoughtlessness, and to get a shroud for Minna; the neighbors sent all sorts of comforts and good wishes, and even those who knew her best were surprised to find how many friends shy little Beth had made.

Meanwhile she lay on her bed with old Joanna at her side, for even in her wanderings she did not forget her forlorn *protégé*. She longed for her cats, but would not have them brought, lest they should get sick; and, in her quiet hours, she was full of anxiety about Jo. She sent loving messages to Amy, bade them tell her mother that she would write soon; and often begged for pencil and paper to try to say a word, that father might not think she had neglected him. But soon even these intervals of consciousness ended, and she lay hour after hour tossing to and fro with incoherent words on her lips, or sank into a heavy sleep which brought her no refreshment. Dr Bangs came twice a day, Hannah sat up at night, Meg kept a telegram in her desk all ready to send off at any minute, and Jo never stirred from Beth's side.

The first of December was a wintry day indeed to them, for a bitter wind blew, snow fell fast, and the year seemed getting ready for its death. When Dr Bangs came that morning, he looked long at Beth, held the hot hand in both his own a minute, and laid it gently down, saying, in a low tone, to Hannah,—

'If Mrs March *can* leave her husband, she'd better be sent for.'

Hannah nodded without speaking, for her lips twitched nervously; Meg dropped down into a chair as the strength seemed to go out of her limbs at the sound of those words, and Jo, after standing with a pale face for a minute, ran to the parlor, snatched up the telegram, and, throwing on her things, rushed out into the storm. She was soon back, and, while noiselessly taking off her cloak, Laurie came in with a letter, saying that Mr March was mending again. Jo read it thankfully, but the heavy weight did not seem lifted off her heart, and her face was so full of misery that Laurie asked, quickly,—

'What is it? is Beth worse?'

'I've sent for mother,' said Jo, tugging at her rubber boots with a tragical expression.

'Good for you, Jo! Did you do it on your own responsibility?' asked Laurie, as he seated her in the hall chair and took off the rebellious boots, seeing how her hands shook.

'No, the doctor told us to.'

'Oh, Jo, it's not so bad as that?' cried Laurie, with a startled face.

'Yes, it is; she don't know us, she don't even talk about the flocks of green doves, as she calls the vine leaves on the wall; she don't look like my Beth, and there's nobody to help us bear it; mother and father both gone, and God seems so far away I can't find Him.'

As the tears streamed fast down poor Jo's cheeks, she stretched out her hand in a helpless sort of way, as if groping in the dark, and Laurie took it in his, whispering, as well as he could, with a lump in his throat,—

'I'm here, hold on to me, Jo, dear!'

She could not speak, but she did 'hold on', and the warm grasp of the friendly human hand comforted her sore heart, and seemed to lead her nearer to the Divine arm which alone could uphold her in her trouble. Laurie longed to say something tender and comfortable, but no fitting words came to him, so he stood silent, gently stroking her bent head as her mother used to do. It was the best thing he could have done; far more soothing than the most eloquent words, for Jo felt the unspoken sympathy, and, in the silence, learned the sweet solace which affection administers to sorrow. Soon she dried the tears which had relieved her, and looked up with a grateful face.

'Thank you, Teddy, I'm better now; I don't feel so forlorn, and will try to bear it if it comes.'

'Keep hoping for the best; that will help you lots, Jo. Soon your mother will be here, and then everything will be right.'

'I'm so glad father is better; now she won't feel so bad about leaving him. Oh, me! it does seem as if all the troubles came in a heap, and I got the heaviest part on my shoulders,' sighed Jo, spreading her wet handkerchief over her knees, to dry.

'Don't Meg pull fair?' asked Laurie, looking indignant.

'Oh, yes; she tries to, but she don't love Bethy as I do; and she won't miss her as I shall. Beth is my conscience, and I *can't* give her up; I can't! I can't!'

Down went Jo's face into the wet handkerchief, and she cried despairingly; for she had kept up bravely till now, and never shed a tear. Laurie drew his hand across his eyes, but could not speak till he had subdued the choky feeling in his throat, and steadied his lips. It might be unmanly, but he couldn't help it, and I am glad of it. Presently, as Jo's sobs quieted, he said, hopefully, 'I don't think she will die; she's so good, and we all love her so much, I don't believe God will take her away yet.'

'The good and dear people always do die,' groaned Jo, but she stopped crying, for her friend's words cheered her up, in spite of her own doubts and fears.

'Poor girl! you're worn out. It isn't like you to be forlorn. Stop a bit; I'll hearten you up in a jiffy.'

Laurie went off two stairs at a time, and Jo laid her wearied head down on Beth's little brown hood, which no one had thought of moving from the table where she left it. It must have possessed some magic, for the submissive spirit of its gentle owner seemed to enter into Jo; and, when Laurie came running down with a glass of wine, she took it with a smile, and said, bravely, 'I drink—Health to my Beth! You are a good doctor, Teddy, and *such* a comfortable friend; how can I ever pay you?' she added, as the wine refreshed her body, as the kind words had done her troubled mind.

'I'll send in my bill, by and by; and to-night I'll give you something that will warm the cockles of your heart better than quarts of wine,' said Laurie, beaming at her with a face of suppressed satisfaction at something.

'What is it?' cried Jo, forgetting her woes for a minute, in her wonder.

'I telegraphed to your mother yesterday, and Brooke answered she'd come at once, and she'll be here to-night, and everything will be all right. Aren't you glad I did it?'

Laurie spoke very fast, and turned red and excited all in a minute, for he had kept his plot a secret, for fear of disappointing the girls or harming Beth. Jo grew quite white, flew out of her chair, and the moment he stopped speaking she electrified him by throwing her arms round his neck, and crying out, with a joyful cry, 'Oh, Laurie! oh, mother! I *am* so glad!' She did not weep again, but laughed hysterically, and trembled and clung to her friend as if she was a little bewildered by the sudden news. Laurie, though decidedly amazed, behaved with great presence of mind; he patted her back soothingly, and, finding that she was recovering, followed it up by a bashful kiss or two, which brought Jo round at once. Holding on to the banisters, she put him gently away, saying, breathless, 'Oh, don't! I didn't mean to; it was dreadful of me; but you were such a dear to go and do it in spite of Hannah, that I couldn't help flying at you. Tell me all about it, and don't give me wine again; it makes me act so.'

'I don't mind!' laughed Laurie, as he settled his tie. 'Why, you see I got fidgety, and so did grandpa. We thought Hannah was overdoing the authority business, and your mother ought to know. She'd never forgive us if Beth,—well, if anything happened, you know. So I got grandpa to say it was high time we did something, and off I pelted to the office yesterday, for the doctor looked sober, and Hannah most took my head off when I proposed a telegram. I never *can* bear to be "marmed over"; so that settled my mind, and I did it. Your mother will come, I know, and the late train is in at two, A.M. I shall go for her; and you've only got to bottle up your rapture, and keep Beth quiet, till that blessed lady gets here.'

'Laurie, you're an angel! How shall I ever thank you?'

'Fly at me again; I rather like it,' said Laurie, looking mischievous,—a thing he had not done for a fortnight.

'No, thank you. I'll do it by proxy, when your grandpa comes. Don't tease, but go home and rest, for you'll be up half the night. Bless you, Teddy; bless you!'

Jo had backed into a corner; and, as she finished her

speech, she vanished precipitately into the kitchen, where she sat down upon a dresser, and told the assembled cats that she was 'happy, oh, *so* happy!' while Laurie departed, feeling that he had made rather a neat thing of it.

'That's the interferingest chap I ever see; but I forgive him, and do hope Mrs March is coming on right away,' said Hannah, with an air of relief, when Jo told the good news.

Meg had a quiet rapture, and then brooded over the letter, while Jo set the sick room in order, and Hannah 'knocked up a couple of pies in case of company unexpected'. A breath of fresh air seemed to blow through the house, and something better than sunshine brightened the quiet rooms; everything appeared to feel the hopeful change; Beth's bird began to chirp again, and a half-blown rose was discovered on Amy's bush in the window; the fires seemed to burn with unusual cheeriness, and every time the girls met their pale faces broke into smiles as they hugged one another, whispering, encouragingly, 'Mother's coming, dear! mother's coming!' Every one rejoiced but Beth; she lay in that heavy stupor, alike unconscious of hope and joy, doubt and danger. It was a piteous sight,—the once rosy face so changed and vacant,—the once busy hands so weak and wasted,—the once smiling lips quite dumb,—and the once pretty, well-kept hair scattered rough and tangled on the pillow. All day she lay so, only rousing now and then to mutter, 'Water!' with lips so parched they could hardly shape the word; all day Jo and Meg hovered over her, watching, waiting, hoping, and trusting in God and mother; and all day the snow fell, the bitter wind raged, and the hours dragged slowly by. But night came at last; and every time the clock struck the sisters, still sitting on either side the bed, looked at each other with brightening eyes, for each hour brought help nearer. The doctor had been in to say that some change for better or worse would probably take place about midnight, at which time he would return.

Hannah, quite worn out, lay down on the sofa at the bed's foot, and fell fast asleep; Mr Laurence marched to and fro in the parlor, feeling that he would rather face a rebel battery than Mrs March's anxious countenance as she entered; Laurie lay on the rug, pretending to rest, but staring into the fire with the thoughtful look which made his black eyes beautifully soft and clear.

The girls never forgot that night, for no sleep came to them as they kept their watch, with that dreadful sense of powerlessness which comes to us in hours like those.

'If God spares Beth I never will complain again,' whispered Meg, earnestly.

'If God spares Beth I'll try to love and serve Him all my life,' answered Jo, with equal fervor.

'I wish I had no heart, it aches so,' sighed Meg, after a pause.

'If life is often as hard as this, I don't see how we ever shall get through it,' added her sister, despondently.

Here the clock struck twelve, and both forgot themselves in watching Beth, for they fancied a change passed over her wan face. The house was still as death, and nothing but the wailing of the wind broke the deep hush. Weary Hannah slept on, and no one but the sisters saw the pale shadow which seemed to fall upon the little bed. An hour went by, and nothing happened except Laurie's quiet departure for the station. Another hour,—still no one came; and anxious fears of delay in the storm, or accidents by the way, or, worst of all, a great grief at Washington, haunted the poor girls.

It was past two, when Jo, who stood at the window thinking how dreary the world looked in its winding-sheet of snow, heard a movement by the bed, and, turning quickly, saw Meg kneeling before their mother's easy-chair, with her face hidden. A dreadful fear passed coldly over Jo, as she thought, 'Beth is dead, and Meg is afraid to tell me.'

She was back at her post in an instant, and to her excited eyes a great change seemed to have taken place. The fever flush, and the look of pain, were gone, and the beloved little face looked so pale and peaceful in its utter repose, that Jo felt no desire to weep or lament. Leaning low over this dearest of her sisters, she kissed the damp forehead with her heart on her lips, and softly whispered, 'Good-by, my Beth; good-by!'

As if waked by the stir, Hannah started out of her sleep, hurried to the bed, looked at Beth, felt her hands, listened at her lips, and then, throwing her apron over her head, sat down to rock to and fro, exclaiming, under her breath, 'The fever's turned; she's sleepin' nat'ral; her skin's damp, and she breathes easy. Praise be given! Oh, my goodness me!'

Before the girls could believe the happy truth, the doctor came to confirm it. He was a homely man, but they thought his face quite heavenly when he smiled, and said, with a fatherly look at them, 'Yes, my dears; I think the little girl will pull through this time. Keep the house quiet; let her sleep, and when she wakes, give her—'

What they were to give, neither heard; for both crept into the dark hall, and, sitting on the stairs, held each other close, rejoicing with hearts too full for words. When they went back to be kissed and cuddled by faithful Hannah, they found Beth lying, as she used to do, with her cheek pillowed on her hand, the dreadful pallor gone, and breathing quietly, as if just fallen asleep.

'If mother would only come now!' said Jo, as the winter night began to wane.

'See,' said Meg, coming up with a white, half-opened rose, 'I thought this would hardly be ready to lay in Beth's hand to-morrow if she—went away from us. But it has blossomed in the night, and now I mean to put it in my vase here, so that when the darling wakes, the first thing she sees will be the little rose, and mother's face.'

Never had the sun risen so beautifully, and never had the world seemed so lovely, as it did to the heavy eyes of Meg and Jo, as they looked out in the early morning, when their long, sad vigil was done.

'It looks like a fairy world,' said Meg, smiling to herself, as she stood behind the curtain watching the dazzling sight.

'Hark!' cried Jo, starting to her feet.

Yes, there was a sound of bells at the door below, a cry from Hannah, and then Laurie's voice, saying, in a joyful whisper, 'Girls! she's come! she's come!'

CHAPTER NINETEEN

———•———

Amy's Will

While these things were happening at home, Amy was having hard times at Aunt March's. She felt her exile deeply, and, for the first time in her life, realized how much she was beloved and petted at home. Aunt March never petted any one; she did not approve of it; but she meant to be kind, for the well-behaved little girl pleased her very much, and Aunt March had a soft place in her old heart for her nephew's children, though she didn't think proper to confess it. She really did her best to make Amy happy, but, dear me, what mistakes she made! Some old people keep young at heart in spite of wrinkles and gray hairs, can sympathize with children's little cares and joys, make them feel at home, and can hide wise lessons under pleasant plays, giving and receiving friendship in the sweetest way. But Aunt March had not this gift, and she worried Amy most to death with her rules and orders, her prim ways, and long, prosy talks. Finding the child more docile and amiable than her sister, the old lady felt it her duty to try and counteract, as far as possible, the bad effects of home freedom and indulgence. So she took Amy in hand, and taught her as she herself had been taught sixty years ago; a process which carried dismay to Amy's soul, and made her feel like a fly in the web of a very strict spider.

She had to wash the cups every morning, and polish up the old-fashioned spoons, the fat silver teapot, and the glasses, till they shone. Then she must dust the room, and what a trying job that was! Not a speck escaped Aunt March's eye, and all the furniture had claw legs, and much carving, which was never dusted to suit. Then Polly must be fed, the lap-dog combed, and a dozen trips upstairs and down, to get things or deliver orders, for the old lady was very lame, and seldom left her big chair. After these tiresome labors she must do her lessons, which was a daily trial of every virtue she possessed. Then she was allowed one hour for exercise or play, and didn't she enjoy it? Laurie came every day, and wheedled Aunt March till Amy was allowed to go out with him, when they walked and rode, and had capital times. After dinner she had to read aloud, and sit still while the old lady slept, which she usually did for an hour, as she dropped off over the first page. Then patchwork or towels appeared, and Amy sewed with outward meekness and inward rebellion till dusk, when she was allowed to amuse herself as she liked, till tea-time. The evenings were the worst of all, for Aunt March fell to telling long stories about her youth, which were so unutterably dull, that Amy was always ready to go to bed, intending to cry over her hard fate, but usually going to sleep before she had squeezed out more than a tear or two.

If it had not been for Laurie and old Esther, the maid, she

felt that she never could have got through that dreadful time. The parrot alone was enough to drive her distracted, for he soon felt that she did not admire him, and revenged himself by being as mischievous as possible. He pulled her hair whenever she came near him, upset his bread and milk to plague her when she had newly cleaned his cage, made Mop bark by pecking at him while Madame dozed; called her names before company, and behaved in all respects like a reprehensible old bird. Then she could not endure the dog, a fat, cross beast, who snarled and yelped at her when she made his toilet, and who laid on his back with all his legs in the air, and a most idiotic expression of countenance, when he wanted something to eat, which was about a dozen times a day. The cook was bad tempered, the old coachman deaf, and Esther the only one who ever took any notice of the young lady.

Esther was a French woman, who had lived with 'Madame', as she called her mistress, for many years, and who rather tyrannized over the old lady, who could not get along without her. Her real name was Estelle; but Aunt March ordered her to change it, and she obeyed, on condition that she was never asked to change her religion. She took a fancy to Mademoiselle, and amused her very much, with odd stories of her life in France, when Amy sat with her while she got up Madame's laces. She also allowed her to roam about the great house, and examine the curious and pretty things stored away in the big wardrobes and the ancient chests; for Aunt March hoarded like a magpie. Amy's chief delight was an Indian cabinet full of queer drawers, little pigeon-holes, and secret places in which were kept all sorts of ornaments, some precious, some merely curious, all more or less antique. To examine and arrange these things gave Amy great satisfaction, especially the jewel cases; in which, on velvet cushions, reposed the ornaments which had adorned a belle forty years ago. There was the garnet set which Aunt March wore when she came out, the pearls her father gave her on her wedding day, her lover's diamonds, the jet mourning rings and pins, the queer lockets, with portraits of dead friends, and weeping willows made of hair inside, the baby bracelets her one little daughter had worn; Uncle March's big watch, with the red seal so many childish hands had played with, and in a box, all by itself, lay Aunt March's wedding ring, too small now for her fat finger, but put carefully away, like the most precious jewel of them all.

'Which would Mademoiselle choose if she had her will?' asked Esther, who always sat near to watch over and lock up the valuables.

'I like the diamonds best, but there is no necklace among them, and I'm fond of necklaces, they are so becoming. I should choose this if I might,' replied Amy, looking with great admiration at a string of gold and ebony beads, from which hung a heavy cross of the same.

'I, too, covet that, but not as a necklace; ah, no! to me it is a rosary, and as such I should use it like a good Catholic,' said Esther, eyeing the handsome thing wistfully.

'Is it meant to use as you use the string of good-smelling wooden beads hanging over your glass?' asked Amy.

'Truly, yes, to pray with. It would be pleasing to the saints if one used so fine a rosary as this, instead of wearing it as a vain bijou.'

'You seem to take a deal of comfort in your prayers, Esther, and always come down looking quiet and satisfied. I wish I could.'

'If Mademoiselle was a Catholic, she would find true comfort; but, as that is not to be, it would be well if you went apart each day to meditate, and pray, as did the good mistress whom I served before Madame. She had a little chapel, and in it found solacement for much trouble.'

'Would it be right for me to do so too?' asked Amy, who, in her loneliness, felt the need of help of some sort, and found that she was apt to forget her little book, now that Beth was not there to remind her of it.

'It would be excellent and charming; and I shall gladly arrange the little dressing-room for you, if you like it. Say nothing to Madame, but when she sleeps go you and sit alone a while to think good thoughts, and ask the dear God to preserve your sister.'

Esther was truly pious, and quite sincere in her advice; for she had an affectionate heart, and felt much for the sisters in their anxiety. Amy liked the idea, and gave her leave to arrange the light closet next her room, hoping it would do her good.

'I wish I knew where all these pretty things would go when Aunt March dies,' she said, as she slowly replaced the shining rosary, and shut the jewel cases one by one.

'To you and your sisters. I know it; Madame confides in me; I witnessed her will, and it is to be so,' whispered Esther, smiling.

'How nice! but I wish she'd let us have them now. Procrastination is not agreeable,' observed Amy, taking a last look at the diamonds.

'It is too soon yet for the young ladies to wear these things. The first one who is affianced will have the pearls—Madame has said it; and I have a fancy that the little turquoise ring will be given to you when you go, for Madame approves your good behavior and charming manners.'

'Do you think so? Oh, I'll be a lamb, if I can only have that lovely ring! It's ever so much prettier than Kitty Bryant's. I do like Aunt March, after all;' and Amy tried on the blue ring with a delighted face, and a firm resolve to earn it.

From that day she was a model of obedience, and the old lady complacently admired the success of her training. Esther fitted up the closet with a little table, placed a footstool before it, and over it a picture, taken from one of the shut-up rooms. She thought it was of no great value, but, being appropriate, she borrowed it, well knowing that Madame would never know it, nor care if she did. It was, however, a very valuable copy of one of the famous pictures of the world, and Amy's beauty-loving eyes were never tired of looking up at the sweet face of the divine mother, while tender thoughts of her own were busy at her heart. On the table she laid her little Testament and hymn-book, kept a vase always full of the best flowers Laurie brought her, and came every day to 'sit alone, thinking good thoughts, and praying the dear God to preserve her sister'. Esther had given her a rosary of black beads, with a silver cross, but Amy hung it up, and did not use it, feeling doubtful as to its fitness for Protestant prayers.

The little girl was very sincere in all this, for, being left alone outside the safe home-nest, she felt the need of some kind hand to hold by so sorely, that she instinctively turned to the strong and tender Friend, whose fatherly love most closely surrounds His little children. She missed her mother's help to understand and rule herself, but having been taught where to look, she did her best to find the way, and walk in it confidingly. But Amy was a young pilgrim, and just now her burden seemed very heavy. She tried to forget herself, to keep cheerful, and be satisfied with doing right, though no one saw or praised her for it. In her first effort at being very, very good, she decided to make her will, as Aunt March had done; so that if she *did* fall ill and die, her possessions might be justly and generously divided. It cost her a pang even to think of giving up the little treasures which in her eyes were as precious as the old lady's jewels.

During one of her play hours she wrote out the important document as well as she could, with some help from Esther as to certain legal terms; and, when the good-natured French woman had signed her name, Amy felt relieved, and laid it by to show Laurie, whom she wanted as a second witness. As it was a rainy day, she went upstairs to amuse herself in one of the large chambers, and took Polly with her for company. In this room there was a wardrobe full of old-fashioned costumes, with which Esther allowed her to play, and it was her favorite amusement to array herself in the faded brocades, and parade up and down before the long mirror, making stately courtesies, and sweeping her train about, with a rustle which delighted her ears. So busy was she on this day, that she did not hear Laurie's ring, nor see his face peeping in at her, as she gravely promenaded to and fro, flirting her fan and tossing her head, on which she wore a great pink turban, contrasting oddly with her blue brocade dress and yellow quilted petticoat. She was obliged to walk carefully, for she had on high-heeled shoes, and, as Laurie told Jo afterward, it was a comical sight to see her mince along in her gay suit, with Polly sidling and bridling just behind her, imitating her as well as he could, and occasionally stopping to laugh, or exclaim, 'Ain't we fine? Get along you fright! Hold your tongue! Kiss me, dear; ha! ha!'

Having with difficulty restrained an explosion of merriment, lest it should offend her majesty, Laurie tapped, and was graciously received.

'Sit down and rest while I put these things away; then I want to consult you about a very serious matter,' said Amy, when she had shown her splendor, and driven Polly into a corner. 'That bird is the trial of my life,' she continued, removing the pink mountain from her head, while Laurie seated himself astride of a chair. 'Yesterday, when aunt was asleep, and I was trying to be as still as a mouse, Polly began to squall and flap about in his cage; so I went to let him out, and found a big spider there. I poked it out, and it ran under the book-case; Polly marched straight after it, stooped down and peeped under the book-case, saying, in his funny way, with a cock of his eye, "Come out and take a walk, my dear." I *couldn't* help laughing, which made Poll swear, and aunt woke up and scolded us both.'

'Did the spider accept the old fellow's invitation?' asked Laurie, yawning.

'Yes; out it came, and away ran Polly, frightened to death, and scrambled up on aunt's chair, calling out, "Catch her! catch her! catch her!" as I chased the spider.'

'That's a lie! Oh lor!' cried the parrot, pecking at Laurie's toes.

'I'd wring your neck if you were mine, you old torment,' cried Laurie, shaking his fist at the bird; who put his head on one side, and gravely croaked, 'Allyluyer! bless your buttons, dear!'

'Now I'm ready,' said Amy, shutting the wardrobe, and taking a paper out of her pocket. 'I want you to read that, please, and tell me if it is legal and right. I felt that I ought to do it, for life is uncertain, and I don't want any ill-feeling over my tomb.'

Laurie bit his lips, and turning a little from the pensive speaker, read the following document, with praiseworthy gravity, considering the spelling:—

'MY LAST WILL AND TESTIMENT.

'I, Amy Curtis March, being in my sane mind, do give and bequeethe all my earthly property—viz. to wit:—namely

'To my father, my best pictures, sketches, maps, and works of art, including frames. Also my $100, to do what he likes with.

'To my mother, all my clothes, except the blue apron with pockets,—also my likeness, and my medal, with much love.

'To my dear sister Margaret, I give my turkquoise ring (if I get it), also my green box with the doves on it, also my piece of real lace for her neck, and my sketch of her as a memorial of her "little girl".

'To Jo I leave my breast-pin, the one mended with sealing wax, also my bronze inkstand—she lost the cover,—and my most precious plaster rabbit, because I am sorry I burnt up her story.

'To Beth (if she lives after me) I give my dolls and the little bureau, my fan, my linen collars and my new slippers if she can wear them being thin when she gets well. And I herewith also leave her my regret that I ever made fun of old Joanna.

'To my friend and neighbor Theodore Laurence I bequeethe my paper marshay portfolio, my clay model of a horse though he did say it hadn't any neck. Also in return for his great kindness in the hour of affliction any one of my artistic works he likes, Noter Dame is the best.

'To our venerable benefactor Mr Laurence I leave my purple box with a looking glass in the cover which will be nice for his pens and remind him of the departed girl who thanks him for his favors to her family, specially Beth.

'I wish my favorite playmate Kitty Bryant to have the blue silk apron and my gold-bead ring with a kiss.

'To Hannah I give the band-box she wanted and all the patch work I leave hoping she "will remember me, when it you see".

'And now having disposed of my most valuable property I hope all will be satisfied and not blame the dead. I forgive every one, and trust we may all meet when the trump shall sound. Amen.

'To this will and testiment I set my hand and seal on this 20th day of Nov. Anni Domino 1861.

'Amy Curtis March.

'*Witnesses:* Estelle Valnor, Theodore Laurence.'

The last name was written in pencil, and Amy explained that he was to rewrite it in ink, and seal it up for her properly.

'What put it into your head? Did any one tell you about Beth's giving away her things?' asked Laurie, soberly, as Amy laid a bit of red tape, with sealing-wax, a taper, and a standish before him.

She explained; and then asked, anxiously, 'What about Beth?'

'I'm sorry I spoke; but as I did, I'll tell you. She felt so ill one day, that she told Jo she wanted to give her piano to Meg, her bird to you, and the poor old doll to Jo, who would love it for her sake. She was sorry she had so little to give, and left locks of hair to the rest of us, and her best love to grandpa. *She* never thought of a will.'

Laurie was signing and sealing as he spoke, and did not look up till a great tear dropped on the paper. Amy's face was full of trouble; but she only said, 'Don't people put sort of postscrips to their wills, sometimes.'

'Yes; "codicils", they call them.'

'Put one in mine then—that I wish *all* my curls cut off, and given round to my friends. I forgot it; but I want it done, though it will spoil my looks.'

Laurie added it, smiling at Amy's last and greatest sacrifice. Then he amused her for an hour, and was much interested in all her trials. But when he came to go, Amy held him back to whisper, with trembling lips, 'Is there really any danger about Beth?'

'I'm afraid there is; but we must hope for the best, so don't cry, dear;' and Laurie put his arm about her with a brotherly gesture, which was very comforting.

When he had gone, she went to her little chapel, and, sitting in the twilight, prayed for Beth with streaming tears and an aching heart, feeling that a million turquoise rings would not console her for the loss of her gentle little sister.

CHAPTER TWENTY

Confidential

I don't think I have any words in which to tell the meeting of the mother and daughters; such hours are beautiful to live, but very hard to describe, so I will leave it to the imagination of my readers; merely saying that the house was full of genuine happiness, and that Meg's tender hope was realized; for when Beth woke from that long, healing sleep, the first objects on which her eyes fell *were* the little rose and mother's face. Too weak to wonder at anything, she only smiled, and nestled close into the loving arms about her, feeling that the hungry longing was satisfied at last. Then she slept again, and the girls waited upon their mother, for she would not unclasp the thin hand which clung to hers, even in sleep. Hannah had 'dished up' an astonishing breakfast for the traveller, finding it impossible to vent her excitement in any other way; and Meg and Jo fed their mother like dutiful young storks, while they listened to her whispered account of father's state, Mr Brooke's promise to stay and nurse him, the

273

delays which the storm occasioned on the homeward journey, and the unspeakable comfort Laurie's hopeful face had given her when she arrived, worn out with fatigue, anxiety and cold.

What a strange, yet pleasant day that was! so brilliant and gay without, for all the world seemed abroad to welcome the first snow; so quiet and reposeful within, for every one slept, spent with watching, and a Sabbath stillness reigned through the house, while nodding Hannah mounted guard at the door. With a blissful sense of burdens lifted off, Meg and Jo closed their weary eyes, and lay at rest like storm-beaten boats, safe at anchor in a quiet harbor. Mrs March would not leave Beth's side, but rested in the big chair, waking often to look at, touch, and brood over her child, like a miser over some recovered treasure.

Laurie, meanwhile, posted off to comfort Amy, and told his story so well that Aunt March actually 'sniffed' herself, and never once said, 'I told you so.' Amy came out so strong on this occasion, that I think the good thoughts in the little chapel really began to bear fruit. She dried her tears quickly, restrained her impatience to see her mother, and never even thought of the turquoise ring, when the old lady heartily agreed in Laurie's opinion, that she behaved 'like a capital little woman'. Even Polly seemed impressed, for he called her 'good girl', blessed her buttons, and begged her to 'come and take a walk, dear', in his most affable tone. She would very gladly have gone out to enjoy the bright wintry weather; but, discovering that Laurie was dropping with sleep in spite of manful efforts to conceal the fact, she persuaded him to rest on the sofa, while she wrote a note to her mother. She was a long time about it; and, when returned, he was stretched out with both arms under his head, sound asleep, while Aunt March had pulled down the curtains, and sat doing nothing in an unusual fit of benignity.

After a while, they began to think he was not going to wake till night, and I'm not sure that he would, had he not been effectually roused by Amy's cry of joy at sight of her mother. There probably were a good many happy little girls in and about the city that day, but it is my private opinion that Amy was the happiest of all, when she sat in her mother's lap and told her trials, receiving consolation and compensation in the shape of approving smiles and fond caresses. They were alone together in the chapel, to which her mother did not object when its purpose was explained to her.

'On the contrary, I like it very much, dear,' she said, looking from the dusty rosary to the well-worn little book, and the lovely picture with its garland of evergreen. 'It is an excellent plan to have some place where we can go to be quiet, when things vex or grieve us. There are a good many hard times in this life of ours, but we can always bear them if we ask help in the right way. I think my little girl is learning this?'

'Yes, mother; and when I go home I mean to have a corner in the big closet to put my books, and the copy of that picture which I've tried to make. The woman's face is not good, it's too beautiful for me to draw, but the baby is done better, and I love it very much. I like to think He was a little child once, for then I don't seem so far away, and that helps me.'

As Amy pointed to the smiling Christ-child on his mother's knee, Mrs March saw something on the lifted hand that made her smile. She said nothing, but Amy understood the look, and, after a minute's pause, she added, gravely,—

'I wanted to speak to you about this, but I forgot it. Aunt gave me the ring today; she called me to her and kissed me, and put it on my finger, and said I was a credit to her, and she'd like to keep me always. She gave that funny guard to keep the turquoise on, as it's too big. I'd like to wear them, mother; can I?'

'They are very pretty, but I think you're rather too young for such ornaments, Amy,' said Mrs March, looking at the plump little hand, with the band of sky-blue stones on the forefinger, and the quaint guard, formed of two tiny, golden hands clasped together.

'I'll try not to be vain,' said Amy; 'I don't think I like it, only because it's so pretty; but I want to wear it as the girl in the story wore her bracelet, to remind me of something.'

'Do you mean Aunt March?' asked her mother, laughing.

'No, to remind me not to be selfish.' Amy looked so earnest and sincere about it, that her mother stopped laughing, and listened respectfully to the little plan.

'I've thought a great deal lately about "my bundle of naughties", and being selfish is the largest one in it; so I'm going to try hard to cure it, if I can. Beth isn't selfish, and that's the reason every one loves her, and feels so bad at the thoughts of losing her. People wouldn't feel half so bad about me if I was sick, and I don't deserve to have them; but I'd like to be loved and missed by a great many friends, so I'm going to try and be like Beth all I can. I'm apt to forget my resolutions; but, if I had something always about me to remind me, I guess I should do better. May I try this way?'

'Yes; but I have more faith in the corner of the big closet. Wear your ring, dear, and do your best; I think you will prosper, for the sincere wish to be good is half the battle. Now, I must go back to Beth. Keep up your heart, little daughter, and we will soon have you home again.'

That evening, while Meg was writing to her father, to report the traveller's safe arrival, Jo slipped upstairs into Beth's room, and, finding her mother in her usual place, stood a minute twisting her fingers in her hair, with a worried gesture and an undecided look.

'What is it, deary?' asked Mrs March, holding out her hand with a face which invited confidence.

'I want to tell you something, mother.'

'About Meg?'

'How quick you guessed! Yes, it's about her, and though it's a little thing, it fidgets me.'

'Beth is asleep; speak low, and tell me all about it. That Moffat hasn't been here, I hope?' asked Mrs March, rather sharply.

'No; I should have shut the door in his face if he had,' said Jo, settling herself on the floor at her mother's feet. 'Last summer Meg left a pair of gloves over at the Laurences, and only one was returned. We forgot all about it, till Teddy told me that Mr Brooke had it. He kept it in his waistcoat pocket, and once it fell out, and Teddy joked him about it, and Mr Brooke owned that he liked Meg, but didn't dare say so, she was so young and he so poor. Now isn't it a *dreadful* state of things?'

'Do you think Meg cares for him?' asked Mrs March, with an anxious look.

'Mercy me! I don't know anything about love, and such nonsense!' cried Jo, with a funny mixture of interest and contempt. 'In novels, the girls show it by starting and blushing, fainting away, growing thin, and acting like fools. Now Meg don't do anything of the sort; she eats and drinks, and sleeps, like a sensible creature; she looks straight in my face when I talk about that man, and only blushes a little bit when Teddy jokes about lovers. I forbid him to do it, but he don't mind me as he ought.'

'Then you fancy that Meg is *not* interested in John?'

'Who?' cried Jo, staring.

'Mr Brooke; I call him "John" now; we fell into the way of doing so at the hospital, and he likes it.'

'Oh, dear! I know you'll take his part; he's been good to father, and you won't send him away, but let Meg marry him, if she wants to. Mean thing! to go petting pa and truckling to you, just to wheedle you into liking him;' and Jo pulled her hair again with a wrathful tweak.

'My dear, don't get angry about it, and I will tell you how it happened. John went with me at Mr Laurence's request, and was so devoted to poor father, that we couldn't help getting fond of him. He was perfectly open and honorable about Meg, for he told us he loved her; but would earn a comfortable home before he asked her to marry him. He only wanted our leave to love her and work for her, and the right to make her love him if he could. He is a truly excellent young man, and we could not refuse to listen to him; but I will not consent to Meg's engaging herself so young.'

'Of course not; it would be idiotic! I knew there was mischief brewing; I felt it; and now it's worse than I imagined. I just wish I could marry Meg myself, and keep her safe in the family.'

This odd arrangement made Mrs March smile; but she

said, gravely, 'Jo, I confide in you, and don't wish you to say anything to Meg yet. When John comes back, and I see them together, I can judge better of her feelings toward him.'

'She'll see his in those handsome eyes that she talks about, and then it will be all up with her. She's got such a soft heart, it will melt like butter in the sun if any one looks sentimentally at her. She read the short reports he sent more than she did your letters, and pinched me when I spoke of it, and likes brown eyes, and don't think John an ugly name, and she'll go and fall in love, and there's an end of peace and fun, and cosy times, together. I see it all! they'll go lovering round the house, and we shall have to dodge; Meg will be absorbed, and no good to me any more; Brooke will scratch up a fortune somehow,—carry her off and make a hole in the family; and I shall break my heart, and everything will be abominably uncomfortable. Oh, deary me! why weren't we all boys? then there wouldn't be any bother!'

Jo leaned her chin on her knees, in a disconsolate attitude, and shook her fist at the reprehensible John. Mrs March sighed, and Jo looked up with an air of relief.

'You don't like it, mother? I'm glad of it; let's send him about his business, and not tell Meg a word of it, but all be jolly together as we always have been.'

'I did wrong to sigh, Jo. It is natural and right you should all go to homes of your own, in time; but I do want to keep my girls as long as I can; and I am sorry that this happened so soon, for Meg is only seventeen, and it will be some years before John can make a home for her. Your father and I have agreed that she shall not bind herself in any way, nor be married, before twenty. If she and John love one another, they can wait, and test the love by doing so. She is conscientious, and I have no fear of her treating him unkindly. My pretty, tender-hearted girl! I hope things will go happily with her.'

'Hadn't you rather have her marry a rich man?' asked Jo, as her mother's voice faltered a little over the last words.

'Money is a good and useful thing, Jo; and I hope my girls will never feel the need of it too bitterly, nor be tempted by too much. I should like to know that John was firmly established in some good business, which gave him an income large enough to keep free from debt, and make Meg comfortable. I'm not ambitious for a splendid fortune, a fashionable position, or a great name for my girls. If rank and money come with love and virtue, also, I should accept them gratefully, and enjoy your good fortune; but I know, by experience, how much genuine happiness can be had in a plain little house, where the daily bread is earned, and some privations give sweetness to the few pleasures; I am content to see Meg begin humbly, for, if I am not mistaken, she will be rich in the possession of a good man's heart, and that is better than a fortune.'

'I understand, mother, and quite agree; but I'm disappointed about Meg, for I'd planned to have her marry Teddy by and by, and sit in the lap of luxury all her days. Wouldn't it be nice?' asked Jo, looking up with a brighter face.

'He is younger than she, you know,' began Mrs March; but Jo broke in,—

'Oh, that don't matter; he's old for his age, and tall; and can be quite grown-up in his manners, if he likes. Then he's rich, and generous, and good, and loves us all; and I say it's a pity my plan is spoilt.'

'I'm afraid Laurie is hardly grown-up enough for Meg, and altogether too much of a weathercock, just now, for any one to depend on. Don't make plans, Jo; but let time and their own hearts mate your friends. We can't meddle safely in such matters, and had better not get "romantic rubbish", as you call it, into our heads, lest it spoil our friendship.'

'Well, I won't; but I hate to see things going all criss-cross, and getting snarled up, when a pull here, and a snip there, would straighten it out. I wish wearing flat-irons on our heads would keep us from growing up. But buds will be roses, and kittens, cats,—more's the pity!'

'What's that about flat-irons and cats?' asked Meg, as she crept into the room, with the finished letter in her hand.

'Only one of my stupid speeches. I'm going to bed; come on, Peggy,' said Jo, unfolding herself, like an animated puzzle.

'Quite right, and beautifully written. Please add that I send my love to John,' said Mrs March, as she glanced over the letter, and gave it back.

'Do you call him "John"?' asked Meg, smiling, with her innocent eyes looking down into her mother's.

'Yes; he has been like a son to us, and we are very fond of him,' replied Mrs March, returning the look with a keen one.

'I'm glad of that; he is so lonely. Good-night, mother, dear. It is so inexpressibly comfortable to have you here,' was Meg's quiet answer.

The kiss her mother gave her was a very tender one; and, as she went away, Mrs March said, with a mixture of satisfaction and regret, 'She does not love John yet, but will soon learn to.'

CHAPTER TWENTY-ONE

Laurie Makes Mischief, and Jo Makes Peace

Jo's face was a study next day, for the secret rather weighed upon her, and she found it hard not to look mysterious and important. Meg observed it, but did not trouble herself to make inquiries, for she had learned that the best way to manage Jo was by the law of contraries, so she felt sure of being told everything if she did not ask. She was rather surprised, therefore, when the silence remained unbroken, and Jo assumed a patronizing air, which decidedly aggravated Meg, who in her turn assumed an air of dignified reserve, and devoted herself to her mother. This left Jo to her own devices; for Mrs March had taken her place as nurse, and bid her rest, exercise, and amuse herself after her long confinement. Amy being gone, Laurie was her only refuge; and, much as she enjoyed his society, she rather dreaded him just then, for he was an incorrigible tease, and she feared he would coax her secret from her.

She was quite right; for the mischief-loving lad no sooner suspected a mystery, than he set himself to finding it out, and led Jo a trying life of it. He wheedled, bribed, ridiculed, threatened and scolded; affected indifference, that he might surprise the truth from her; declared he knew, then that he didn't care; and, at last, by dint of perseverance, he satisfied himself that it concerned Meg and Mr Brooke. Feeling indignant that he was not taken into his tutor's confidence, he set his wits to work to devise some proper retaliation for the slight.

Meg meanwhile had apparently forgotten the matter, and was absorbed in preparations for her father's return; but all of a sudden a change seemed to come over her, and, for a day or two, she was quite unlike herself. She started when spoken to, blushed when looked at, was very quiet, and sat over her sewing with a timid, troubled look on her face. To her mother's inquiries she answered that she was quite well, and Jo's she silenced by begging to be let alone.

'She feels it in the air—love, I mean—and she's going very fast. She's got most of the symptoms, is twittery and cross, don't eat, lies awake, and mopes in corners. I caught her singing that song about "the silver-voiced brook", and once she said "John", as you do, and then turned as red as a poppy. Whatever shall we do?' said Jo, looking ready for any measures, however violent.

'Nothing but wait. Let her alone, be kind and patient, and father's coming will settle everything,' replied her mother.

'Here's a note to you, Meg, all sealed up. How odd! Teddy never seals mine,' said Jo, next day, as she distributed the contents of the little post-office.

Mrs March and Jo were deep in their own affairs, when a sound from Meg made them look up to see her staring at her note, with a frightened face.

'My child, what is it?' cried her mother, running to her, while Jo tried to take the paper which had done the mischief.

'It's all a mistake—he didn't send it—oh, Jo, how could you do it?' and Meg hid her face in her hands, crying as if her heart was quite broken.

'Me! I've done nothing! What's she talking about?' cried Jo, bewildered.

Meg's mild eyes kindled with anger as she pulled a crumpled note from her pocket, and threw it at Jo, saying, reproachfully,—

'You wrote it, and that bad boy helped you. How could you be so rude, so mean, and cruel to us both?'

Jo hardly heard her, for she and her mother were reading the note, which was written in a peculiar hand.

'My Dearest Margaret,—
'I can no longer restrain my passion, and must know my fate before I return. I dare not tell your parents yet, but I think they would consent if they knew that we adored one another. Mr Laurence will help me to some good place, and then, my sweet girl, you will make me happy. I implore you to say nothing to your family yet, but to send one word of hope through Laurie to

'Your devoted
'John.'

'Oh, the little villain! that's the way he meant to pay me for keeping my word to mother. I'll give him a hearty scolding, and bring him over to beg pardon,' cried Jo, burning to execute immediate justice. But her mother held her back, saying, with a look she seldom wore,—

'Stop, Jo, you must clear yourself first. You have played so many pranks, that I am afraid you have had a hand in this.'

'On my word, mother, I haven't! I never saw that note before, and don't know anything about it, as true as I live!' said Jo, so earnestly, that they believed her. 'If I *had* taken a part in it I'd have done it better than this, and have written a sensible note. I should think you'd have known Mr Brooke wouldn't write such stuff as that,' she added, scornfully tossing down the paper.

'It's like his writing,' faltered Meg, comparing it with the note in her hand.

'Oh, Meg, you didn't answer it?' cried Mrs March, quickly.

'Yes, I did!' and Meg hid her face again, overcome with shame.

'Here's a scrape! *Do* let me bring that wicked boy over to explain, and be lectured. I can't rest till I get hold of him;' and Jo made for the door again.

'Hush! let me manage this, for it is worse than I thought. Margaret, tell me the whole story,' commanded Mrs March, sitting down by Meg, yet keeping hold of Jo, lest she should fly off.

'I received the first letter from Laurie, who didn't look as if he knew anything about it,' began Meg, without looking up. 'I was worried at first, and meant to tell you; then I remembered how you liked Mr Brooke, so I thought you wouldn't mind if I kept my little secret for a few days. I'm so silly that I liked to think no one knew; and, while I was deciding what to say, I felt like the girls in books, who have such things to do. Forgive me, mother, I'm paid for my silliness now; I never can look him in the face again.'

'What did you say to him?' asked Mrs March.

'I only said I was too young to do anything about it yet; that I didn't wish to have secrets from you, and he must speak to father. I was very grateful for his kindness, and would be his friend, but nothing more, for a long while.'

Mrs March smiled, as if well pleased, and Jo clapped her hands, exclaiming, with a laugh,—

'You are almost equal to Caroline Percy, who was a pattern of prudence! Tell on, Meg. What did he say to that?'

'He writes in a different way entirely; telling me that he never sent any love-letter at all, and is very sorry that my roguish sister, Jo, should take such liberties with our names. It's very kind and respectful, but think how dreadful for me!'

Meg leaned against her mother, looking the image of despair, and Jo tramped about the room, calling Laurie names. All of a sudden she stopped, caught up the two notes, and, after looking at them closely, said, decidedly, 'I don't believe Brooke ever saw either of these letters. Teddy wrote both, and keeps yours to crow over me with, because I wouldn't tell him my secret.'

'Don't have any secrets, Jo; tell it to mother, and keep out of trouble, as I should have done,' said Meg, warningly.

'Bless you, child! mother told me.'

'That will do, Jo. I'll comfort Meg while you go and get Laurie. I shall sift the matter to the bottom, and put a stop to such pranks at once.'

Away ran Jo, and Mrs March gently told Meg Mr Brooke's real feelings. 'Now, dear, what are your own? Do you love him enough to wait till he can make a home for you, or will you keep yourself quite free for the present?'

'I've been so scared and worried, I don't want to have anything to do with lovers for a long while,—perhaps never,' answered Meg, petulantly. 'If John *doesn't* know anything about this nonsense, don't tell him, and make Jo and Laurie hold their tongues. I won't be deceived and plagued, and made a fool of,—it's a shame!'

Seeing that Meg's usually gentle temper was roused, and her pride hurt by this mischievous joke, Mrs March soothed her by promises of entire silence, and great discretion for the future. The instant Laurie's step was heard in the hall, Meg fled into the study, and Mrs March received the culprit alone. Jo had not told him why he was wanted, fearing he wouldn't come; but he knew the minute he saw Mrs March's face, and stood twirling his hat with a guilty air, which convicted him at once. Jo was dismissed, but chose to march up and down the hall like a sentinel, having some fear that the prisoner might bolt. The sound of voices in the parlor rose and fell for half an hour; but what happened during that interview the girls never knew.

When they were called in, Laurie was standing by their mother with such a penitent face, that Jo forgave him on the spot, but did not think it wise to betray the fact. Meg received his humble apology, and was much comforted by the assurance that Brooke knew nothing of the joke.

'I'll never tell him to my dying day,—wild horses shan't drag it out of me; so you'll forgive me, Meg, and I'll do anything to show how out-and-out sorry I am,' he added, looking very much ashamed of himself.

'I'll try; but it was a very ungentlemanly thing to do. I didn't think you could be so sly and malicious, Laurie,' replied Meg, trying to hide her maidenly confusion under a gravely reproachful air.

'It was altogether abominable, and I don't deserve to be spoken to for a month; but you will, though, won't you?' and Laurie folded his hands together, with such an imploring gesture, and rolled up his eyes in such a meekly repentant way, as he spoke in his irresistibly persuasive tone, that it was impossible to frown upon him, in spite of his scandalous behavior. Meg pardoned him, and Mrs March's grave face relaxed, in spite of her efforts to keep sober, when she heard him declare that he would atone for his sins by all sorts of penances, and abase himself like a worm before the injured damsel.

Jo stood aloof, meanwhile, trying to harden her heart against him, and succeeding only in primming up her face into an expression of entire disapprobation. Laurie looked at her once or twice, but, as she showed no sign of relenting, he felt injured, and turned his back on her till the others were done with him, when he made her a low bow, and walked off without a word.

As soon as he had gone, she wished she had been more forgiving; and, when Meg and her mother went upstairs, she felt lonely, and longed for Teddy. After resisting for some time, she yielded to the impulse, and, armed with a book to return, went over to the big house.

'Is Mr Laurence in?' asked Jo, of a housemaid, who was coming down stairs.

'Yes, miss; but I don't believe he's seeable just yet.'

'Why not; is he ill?'

'La, no, miss! but he's had a scene with Mr Laurie, who is in one of his tantrums about something, which vexes the old gentleman, so I dursn't go nigh him.'

'Where is Laurie?'

'Shut up in his room, and he won't answer, though I've been a-tapping. I don't know what's to become of the dinner, for it's ready, and there's no one to eat it.'

'I'll go and see what the matter is. I'm not afraid of either of them.'

Up went Jo, and knocked smartly on the door of Laurie's little study.

'Stop that, or I'll open the door and make you!' called out the young gentleman, in a threatening tone.

Jo immediately pounded again; the door flew open, and in she bounced, before Laurie could recover from his surprise. Seeing that he really *was* out of temper, Jo, who knew how to manage him, assumed a contrite expression, and, going artistically down upon her knees, said, meekly, 'Please forgive me for being so cross. I came to make it up, and can't go away till I have.'

'It's all right; get up, and don't be a goose, Jo,' was the cavalier reply to her petition.

'Thank you; I will. Could I ask what's the matter? You don't look exactly easy in your mind.'

'I've been shaken, and I won't bear it!' growled Laurie, indignantly.

'Who did it?' demanded Jo.

'Grandfather; if it had been any one else I'd have—' and the injured youth finished his sentence by an energetic gesture of the right arm.

'That's nothing; I often shake you, and you don't mind,' said Jo, soothingly.

'Pooh! you're a girl, and it's fun; but I'll allow no man to shake *me*.'

'I don't think any one would care to try it, if you looked as much like a thunder-cloud as you do now. Why were you treated so?'

'Just because I wouldn't say what your mother wanted me for. I'd promised not to tell, and of course I wasn't going to break my word.'

'Couldn't you satisfy your grandpa in any other way?'

'No; he *would* have the truth, the whole truth, and nothing but the truth. I'd have told my part of the scrape, if I could, without bringing Meg in. As I couldn't, I held my tongue, and bore the scolding till the old gentleman collared me. Then I got angry, and bolted, for fear I should forget myself.'

'It wasn't nice, but he's sorry, I know; so go down and make up. I'll help you.'

'Hanged if I do! I'm not going to be lectured and pummelled by every one, just for a bit of a frolic. I *was* sorry about Meg, and begged pardon like a man; but I won't do it again, when I wasn't in the wrong.'

'He didn't know that.'

'He ought to trust me, and not act as if I was a baby. It's no use, Jo; he's got to learn that I'm able to take care of myself, and don't need any one's apron-string to hold on by.'

'What pepper-pots you are!' sighed Jo. 'How do you mean to settle this affair?'

'Well, he ought to beg pardon, and believe me when I say I can't tell him what the row's about.'

'Bless you! he won't do that.'

'I won't go down till he does.'

'Now, Teddy, be sensible; let it pass, and I'll explain what I can. You can't stay here, so what's the use of being melodramatic?'

'I don't intend to stay here long, any-way. I'll slip off and take a journey somewhere, and when grandpa misses me he'll come round fast enough.'

'I dare say; but you ought not to go and worry him.'

'Don't preach. I'll go to Washington and see Brooke; it's gay there, and I'll enjoy myself after the troubles.'

'What fun you'd have! I wish I could run off too!' said Jo, forgetting her part of Mentor in lively visions of martial life at the capital.

'Come on, then! Why not? You go and surprise your father, and I'll stir up old Brooke. It would be a glorious joke; let's do it, Jo! We'll leave a letter saying we are all right, and trot off at once. I've got money enough; it will do you good, and be no harm, as you go to your father.'

For a moment Jo looked as if she would agree; for, wild as the plan was, it just suited her. She was tired of care and confinement, longed for change, and thoughts of her father blended temptingly with the novel charms of camps and hospitals, liberty and fun. Her eyes kindled as they turned wistfully toward the window, but they fell on the old house opposite, and she shook her head with sorrowful decision.

'If I was a boy, we'd run away together, and have a capital time; but as I'm a miserable girl, I must be proper, and stop at home. Don't tempt me, Teddy, it's a crazy plan.'

That's the fun of it!' began Laurie, who had got a wilful fit on him, and was possessed to break out of bounds in some way.

'Hold your tongue!' cried Jo, covering her ears. '"Prunes and prisms" are my doom, and I may as well make up my mind to it. I came here to moralize, not to hear about things that make me skip to think of.'

'I knew Meg would wet-blanket such a proposal, but I thought you had more spirit,' began Laurie, insinuatingly.

'Bad boy, be quiet. Sit down and think of your own sins, don't go making me add to mine. If I get your grandpa to apologize for the shaking, will you give up running away?' asked Jo, seriously.

'Yes, but you won't do it,' answered Laurie, who wished to 'make up', but felt that his outraged dignity must be appeased first.

'If I can manage the young one I can the old one,' muttered Jo, as she walked away, leaving Laurie bent over a railroad map, with his head propped up on both hands.

'Come in!' and Mr Laurence's gruff voice sounded gruffer than ever, as Jo tapped at his door.

'It's only me, sir, come to return a book,' she said, blandly, as she entered.

'Want any more?' asked the old gentleman, looking grim and vexed, but trying not to show it.

'Yes, please, I like old Sam so well, I think I'll try the second volume,' returned Jo, hoping to propitiate him by accepting a second dose of Boswell's *Johnson*, as he had recommended that lively work.

The shaggy eyebrows unbent a little, as he rolled the steps toward the shelf where the Johnsonian literature was placed. Jo skipped up, and, sitting on the top step, affected to be searching for her book, but was really wondering how best to introduce the dangerous object of her visit. Mr Laurence seemed to suspect that something was brewing in her mind; for, after taking several brisk turns about the room, he faced round on her, speaking so abruptly, that *Rasselas* tumbled face downward on the floor.

'What has that boy been about? Don't try to shield him, now! I know he has been in mischief, by the way he acted when he came home. I can't get a word from him; and, when I threatened to shake the truth out of him, he bolted upstairs, and locked himself into his room.'

'He did do wrong, but we forgave him, and all promised not to say a word to any one,' began Jo, reluctantly.

'That won't do; he shall not shelter himself behind a promise from you soft-hearted girls. If he's done anything amiss, he shall confess, beg pardon, and be punished. Out with it, Jo! I won't be kept in the dark.'

Mr Laurence looked so alarming, and spoke so sharply, that Jo would have gladly run away, if she could, but she was perched aloft on the steps, and he stood at the foot, a lion in the path, so she had to stay and brave it out.

'Indeed, sir, I cannot tell, mother forbid it. Laurie has confessed, asked pardon, and been punished quite enough. We don't keep silence to shield him, but some one else, and it will make more trouble if you interfere. Please don't; it was partly my fault, but it's all right now, so let's forget it, and talk about the *Rambler*, or something pleasant.'

'Hang the *Rambler*! come down and give me your word that this harum-scarum boy of mine hasn't done anything ungrateful or impertinent. If he has, after all your kindness to him, I'll thrash him with my own hands.'

The threat sounded awful, but did not alarm Jo, for she knew the irascible old man would never lift a finger against his grandson, whatever he might say to the contrary. She obediently descended, and made as light of the prank as she could without betraying Meg, or forgetting the truth.

'Hum! ha! well, if the boy held his tongue because he'd promised, and not from obstinacy, I'll forgive him. He's a stubborn fellow, and hard to manage,' said Mr Laurence, rubbing up his hair till it looked as if he'd been out in a gale, and smoothing the frown from his brow with an air of relief.

'So am I; but a kind word will govern me when all the king's horses and all the king's men couldn't,' said Jo, trying to say a kind word for her friend, who seemed to get out of one scrape only to fall into another.

'You think I'm not kind to him, hey?' was the sharp answer.

'Oh, dear, no, sir; you are rather too kind sometimes, and then just a trifle hasty when he tries your patience. Don't you think you are?'

Jo was determined to have it out now, and tried to look quite placid, though she quaked a little after her bold speech. To her great relief and surprise, the old gentleman only threw his spectacles on to the table with a rattle, and exclaimed, frankly,—

'You're right, girl, I am! I love the boy, but he tries my patience past bearing, and I don't know how it will end, if we go on so.'

'I'll tell you,—he'll run away.' Jo was sorry for that speech the minute it was made; she meant to warn him that Laurie would not bear much restraint, and hoped he would be more forbearing with the lad.

Mr Laurence's ruddy face changed suddenly, and he sat down with a troubled glance at the picture of a handsome man, which hung over his table. It was Laurie's father, who *had* run away in his youth, and married against the imperious old man's will. Jo fancied he remembered and regretted the past, and she wished she had held her tongue.

'He won't do it, unless he is very much worried, and only threatens it sometimes, when he gets tired of studying. I often think I should like to, especially since my hair was cut; so, if you ever miss us, you may advertise for two boys, and look among the ships bound for India.'

She laughed as she spoke, and Mr Laurence looked relieved, evidently taking the whole as a joke.

'You hussy, how dare you talk in that way? where's your respect for me, and your proper bringing up? Bless the boys and girls! what torments they are; yet we can't do without them,' he said, pinching her cheeks good-humoredly.

'Go and bring that boy down to his dinner, tell him it's all right, and advise him not to put on tragedy airs with his grandfather; I won't bear it.'

'He won't come, sir; he feels badly because you didn't believe him when he said he couldn't tell. I think the shaking hurt his feelings very much.'

Jo tried to look pathetic, but must have failed, for Mr Laurence began to laugh, and she knew the day was won.

'I'm sorry for that, and ought to thank him for not shaking *me*, I suppose. What the dickens does the fellow expect?' and the old gentleman looked a trifle ashamed of his own testiness.

'If I was you, I'd write him an apology, sir. He says he won't come down till he has one; and talks about Washington, and goes on in an absurd way. A formal apology will make him see how foolish he is, and bring him down quite amiable. Try it; he likes fun, and this way is better than talking. I'll carry it up, and teach him his duty.'

Mr Laurence gave her a sharp look, and put on his spectacles, saying, slowly, 'You're a sly puss! but I don't mind being managed by you and Beth. Here, give me a bit of paper, and let us have done with this nonsense.'

The note was written in the terms which one gentleman would use to another after offering some deep insult. Jo dropped a kiss on the top of Mr Laurence's bald head, and ran up to slip the apology under Laurie's door, advising him, through the keyhole, to be submissive, decorous, and a few other agreeable impossibilities. Finding the door locked again, she left the note to do its work, and was going quietly away, when the young gentleman slid down the banisters, and waited for her at the bottom, saying, with his most virtuous expression of countenance, 'What a good fellow you are, Jo! Did you get blown up?' he added, laughing.

'No; he was pretty clever, on the whole.'

'Ah! I got it all around! even you cast me off over there, and I felt just ready to go to the deuce,' he began, apologetically.

'Don't talk in that way; turn over a new leaf and begin again, Teddy, my son.'

'I keep turning over new leaves, and spoiling them, as I used to spoil my copy-books; and I make so many beginnings there never will be an end,' he said, dolefully.

'Go and eat your dinner; you'll feel better after it. Men always croak when they are hungry,' and Jo whisked out at the front door after that.

'That's a "label" on my "sect",' answered Laurie, quoting Amy, as he went to partake of humble-pie dutifully with his grandfather, who was quite saintly in temper, and overwhelmingly respectful in manner, all the rest of the day.

Every one thought the matter ended, and the little cloud blown over; but the mischief was done, for, though others forgot it, Meg remembered. She never alluded to a certain person, but she thought of him a good deal, dreamed dreams more than ever; and, once, Jo, rummaging her sister's desk for stamps, found a bit of paper scribbled over with the words, 'Mrs John Brooke'; whereat she groaned tragically, and cast it into the fire, feeling that Laurie's prank had hastened the evil day for her.

CHAPTER TWENTY-TWO

Pleasant Meadows

L ike sunshine after storm were the peaceful weeks which
followed. The invalids improved rapidly, and Mr March
began to talk of returning early in the new year. Beth
was soon able to lie on the study sofa all day, amusing herself
with the well-beloved cats, at first, and, in time, with doll's
sewing, which had fallen sadly behindhand. Her once active
limbs were so stiff and feeble that Jo took her a daily airing
about the house, in her strong arms. Meg cheerfully blackened
and burnt her white hands cooking delicate messes for 'the
dear'; while Amy, a loyal slave of the ring, celebrated her
return by giving away as many of her treasures as she could
prevail on her sisters to accept.

As Christmas approached, the usual mysteries began to
haunt the house, and Jo frequently convulsed the family by
proposing utterly impossible, or magnificently absurd ceremonies, in honor of this unusually merry Christmas. Laurie
was equally impracticable, and would have had bonfires,

sky-rockets, and triumphal arches, if he had had his own way. After many skirmishes and snubbings, the ambitious pair were considered effectually quenched, and went about with forlorn faces, which were rather belied by explosions of laughter when the two got together.

Several days of unusually mild weather fitly ushered in a splendid Christmas-day. Hannah 'felt in her bones that it was going to be an uncommonly plummy day', and she proved herself a true prophetess, for everybody and everything seemed bound to produce a grand success. To begin with: Mr March wrote that he should soon be with them; then Beth felt uncommonly well that morning, and, being dressed in her mother's gift,—a soft crimson merino wrapper,—was borne in triumph to the window, to behold the offering of Jo and Laurie. The Unquenchables had done their best to be worthy of the name, for, like elves, they had worked by night, and conjured up a comical surprise. Out in the garden stood a stately snow-maiden, crowned with holly, bearing a basket of fruit and flowers in one hand, a great roll of new music in the other, a perfect rainbow of an Afghan round her chilly shoulders, and a Christmas carol issuing from her lips, on a pink paper streamer:—

'THE JUNGFRAU TO BETH.

'God bless you, dear Queen Bess!
  May nothing you dismay;
But health, and peace, and happiness,
  Be yours, this Christmas-day.

'Here's fruit to feed our busy bee,
  And flowers for her nose;

Here's music for her pianee,—
  An Afghan for her toes.

'A portrait of Joanna, see,
  By Raphael No. 2,
Who labored with great industry,
  To make it fair and true.

'Accept a ribbon red I beg,
  For Madam Purrer's tail;
And ice cream made by lovely Peg,—
  A Mont Blanc in a pail.

'Their dearest love my makers laid
  Within my breast of snow,
Accept it, and the Alpine maid,
  From Laurie and from Jo.'

How Beth laughed when she saw it! how Laurie ran up
and down to bring in the gifts, and what ridiculous speeches
Jo made as she presented them!

'I'm so full of happiness, that, if father was only here, I
couldn't hold one drop more,' said Beth, quite sighing with
contentment as Jo carried her off to the study to rest after the
excitement, and to refresh herself with some of the delicious
grapes the 'Jungfrau' had sent her.

'So am I,' added Jo, slapping the pocket wherein reposed
the long-desired *Undine and Sintram.*

'I'm sure I am,' echoed Amy, poring over the engraved
copy of the Madonna and Child, which her mother had given
her, in a pretty frame.

'Of course I am,' cried Meg, smoothing the silvery folds of
her first silk dress; for Mr Laurence had insisted on giving it.

'How can *I* be otherwise!' said Mrs March, gratefully, as her eyes went from her husband's letter to Beth's smiling face, and her hand caressed the brooch made of gray and golden, chestnut and dark brown hair, which the girls had just fastened on her breast.

Now and then, in this work-a-day world, things do happen in the delightful story-book fashion, and what a comfort that is. Half an hour after every one had said they were so happy they could only hold one drop more, the drop came. Laurie opened the parlor door, and popped his head in very quietly. He might just as well have turned a somersault, and uttered an Indian war-whoop; for his face was so full of suppressed excitement, and his voice so treacherously joyful, that every one jumped up, though he only said, in a queer, breathless voice, 'Here's another Christmas present for the March family.'

Before the words were well out of his mouth, he was whisked away somehow, and in his place appeared a tall man, muffled up to the eyes, leaning on the arm of another tall man, who tried to say something and couldn't. Of course there was a general stampede; and for several minutes everybody seemed to lose their wits, for the strangest things were done, and no one said a word. Mr March became invisible in the embrace of four pairs of loving arms; Jo disgraced herself by nearly fainting away, and had to be doctored by Laurie in the china closet; Mr Brooke kissed Meg entirely by mistake, as he somewhat incoherently explained; and Amy, the dignified, tumbled over a stool, and, never stopping to get up, hugged and cried over her father's boots in the most touching manner. Mrs March was the first to recover herself, and held up her hand with a warning, 'Hush! remember Beth!'

But it was too late; the study door flew open,—the little red wrapper appeared on the threshold,—joy put strength into the feeble limbs,—and Beth ran straight into her father's arms. Never mind what happened just after that; for the full hearts overflowed, washing away the bitterness of the past, and leaving only the sweetness of the present.

It was not at all romantic, but a hearty laugh set everybody straight again,—for Hannah was discovered behind the door, sobbing over the fat turkey, which she had forgotten to put down when she rushed up from the kitchen. As the laugh subsided, Mrs March began to thank Mr Brooke for his faithful care of her husband, at which Mr Brooke suddenly remembered that Mr March needed rest, and, seizing Laurie, he precipitately retired. Then the two invalids were ordered to repose, which they did, by both sitting in one big chair, and talking hard.

Mr March told how he had longed to surprise them, and how, when the fine weather came, he had been allowed by his doctor to take advantage of it; how devoted Brooke had been, and how he was altogether a most estimable and upright young man. Why Mr March paused a minute just there, and, after a glance at Meg, who was violently poking the fire, looked at his wife with an inquiring lift of the eyebrows, I leave you to imagine; also why Mrs March gently nodded her head, and asked, rather abruptly, if he wouldn't have something to eat. Jo saw and understood the look; and she stalked grimly away, to get wine and beef tea, muttering to herself, as she slammed the door, 'I hate estimable young men with brown eyes!'

There never *was* such a Christmas dinner as they had that day. The fat turkey was a sight to behold, when Hannah sent him up, stuffed, browned and decorated. So was the plum-pudding, which quite melted in one's mouth; likewise the jellies, in which Amy revelled like a fly in a honey-pot. Everything turned out well; which was a mercy, Hannah said, 'For my mind was that flustered, mum, that it's a merrycle I didn't roast the pudding and stuff the turkey with raisins, let alone bilin' of it in a cloth.'

Mr Laurence and his grandson dined with them; also Mr Brooke,—at whom Jo glowered darkly, to Laurie's infinite amusement. Two easy-chairs stood side by side at the head of the table, in which sat Beth and her father, feasting, modestly, on chicken and a little fruit. They drank healths, told stories, sung songs, 'reminisced', as the old folks say, and had a thoroughly good time. A sleigh-ride had been planned, but the girls would not leave their father; so the guests departed early, and, as twilight gathered, the happy family sat together round the fire.

'Just a year ago we were groaning over the dismal Christmas we expected to have. Do you remember?' asked Jo, breaking a short pause, which had followed a long conversation about many things.

'Rather a pleasant year on the whole!' said Meg, smiling at the fire, and congratulating herself on having treated Mr Brooke with dignity.

'I think it's been a pretty hard one,' observed Amy, watching the light shine on her ring, with thoughtful eyes.

'I'm glad it's over, because we've got you back,' whispered Beth, who sat on her father's knee.

'Rather a rough road for you to travel, my little pilgrims, especially the latter part of it. But you have got on bravely;

and I think the burdens are in a fair way to tumble off very soon,' said Mr March, looking, with fatherly satisfaction, at the four young faces gathered round him.

'How do you know? Did mother tell you?' asked Jo.

'Not much; straws show which way the wind blows; and I've made several discoveries today.'

'Oh, tell us what they are!' cried Meg, who sat beside him.

'Here is one!' and, taking up the hand which lay on the arm of his chair, he pointed to the roughened forefinger, a burn on the back, and two or three little hard spots on the palm. 'I remember a time when this hand was white and smooth, and your first care was to keep it so. It was very pretty then, but to me it is much prettier now,—for in these seeming blemishes I read a little history. A burnt offering has been made of vanity; this hardened palm has earned something better than blisters, and I'm sure the sewing done by these pricked fingers will last a long time, so much goodwill went into the stitches. Meg, my dear, I value the womanly skill which keeps home happy, more than white hands or fashionable accomplishments; I'm proud to shake this good, industrious little hand, and hope I shall not soon be asked to give it away.'

If Meg had wanted a reward for hours of patient labor, she received it in the hearty pressure of her father's hand, and the approving smile he gave her.

'What about Jo? Please say something nice; for she has tried so hard, and been so very, very good to me,' said Beth, in her father's ear.

He laughed, and looked across at the tall girl who sat opposite, with an unusually mild expression in her brown face.

'In spite of the curly crop, I don't see the "son Jo" whom I left a year ago,' said Mr March. 'I see a young lady who pins her collar straight, laces her boots neatly, and neither whistles, talks slang, nor lies on the rug, as she used to do. Her face is rather thin and pale, just now, with watching and anxiety; but I like to look at it, for it has grown gentler, and her voice is lower; she doesn't bounce, but moves quietly, and takes care of a certain little person in a motherly way, which delights me. I rather miss my wild girl; but if I get a strong, helpful, tender-hearted woman in her place, I shall feel quite satisfied. I don't know whether the shearing sobered our black sheep, but I do know that in all Washington I couldn't find anything beautiful enough to be bought with the five-and-twenty dollars which my good girl sent me.'

Jo's keen eyes were rather dim for a minute, and her thin face grew rosy in the firelight, as she received her father's praise, feeling that she did deserve a portion of it.

'Now Beth;' said Amy, longing for her turn, but ready to wait.

'There's so little of her I'm afraid to say much, for fear she will slip away altogether, though she is not so shy as she used to be,' began their father, cheerfully; but, recollecting how nearly he *had* lost her, he held her close, saying, tenderly, with her cheek against his own, 'I've got you safe, my Beth, and I'll keep you so, please God.'

After a minute's silence, he looked down at Amy, who sat on the cricket at his feet, and said, with a caress of the shining hair,—

'I observed that Amy took drumsticks at dinner, ran errands for her mother all the afternoon, gave Meg her place to-night, and has waited on every one with patience and good-humor. I also observe that she does not fret much, nor prink at the glass, and has not even mentioned a very pretty ring which she wears; so I conclude that she has learned to think of other people more, and of herself less, and has decided to try and mould her character as carefully as she moulds her little clay figures. I am glad of this; for though I should be very proud of a graceful statue made by her, I shall be infinitely prouder of a lovable daughter, with a talent for making life beautiful to herself and others.'

'What are you thinking of, Beth?' asked Jo, when Amy had thanked her father, and told about her ring.

'I read in *Pilgrim's Progress* today, how, after many troubles, Christian and Hopeful came to a pleasant green meadow, where lilies bloomed all the year round, and there they rested happily, as we do now, before they went on to their journey's end,' answered Beth; adding, as she slipped out of her father's arms, and went slowly to the instrument, 'It's singing time now, and I want to be in my old place. I'll try to sing the song of the shepherd boy which the Pilgrims heard. I made the music for father, because he likes the verses.'

So, sitting at the dear little piano, Beth softly touched the keys, and, in the sweet voice they had never thought to hear again, sung, to her own accompaniment, the quaint hymn, which was a singularly fitting song for her:—

> 'He that is down need fear no fall;
>   He that is low no pride;
> He that is humble ever shall
>   Have God to be his guide.

307

'I am content with what I have,
    Little be it or much;
And, Lord! contentment still I crave,
    Because Thou savest such.

'Fulness to them a burden is,
    That go on Pilgrimage;
Here little, and hereafter bliss,
    Is best from age to age!'

CHAPTER TWENTY-THREE

Aunt March Settles the Question

Like bees swarming after their queen, mother and daughters hovered about Mr March the next day, neglecting everything to look at, wait upon, and listen to, the new invalid, who was in a fair way to be killed by kindness. As he sat propped up in the big chair by Beth's sofa, with the other three close by, and Hannah popping in her head now and then, 'to peek at the dear man', nothing seemed needed to complete their happiness. But something *was* needed, and the elder ones felt it, though none confessed the fact. Mr and Mrs March looked at one another with an anxious expression, as their eyes followed Meg. Jo had sudden fits of sobriety, and was seen to shake her fist at Mr Brooke's umbrella, which had been left in the hall; Meg was absentminded, shy and silent, started when the bell rang, and colored when John's name was mentioned; Amy said, 'Every one seemed waiting for something, and couldn't settle down, which was queer, since father was safe at home,' and

Beth innocently wondered why their neighbors didn't run over as usual.

Laurie went by in the afternoon, and, seeing Meg at the window, seemed suddenly possessed with a melodramatic fit, for he fell down upon one knee in the snow, beat his breast, tore his hair, and clasped his hands imploringly, as if begging some boon; and when Meg told him to behave himself, and go away, he wrung imaginary tears out of his handkerchief, and staggered round the corner as if in utter despair.

'What does the goose mean?' said Meg, laughing, and trying to look unconscious.

'He's showing you how your John will go on by and by. Touching, isn't it?' answered Jo, scornfully.

'Don't say *my John*, it isn't proper or true;' but Meg's voice lingered over the words as if they sounded pleasant to her. 'Please don't plague me, Jo; I've told you I don't care *much* about him, and there isn't to be anything said, but we are all to be friendly, and go on as before.'

'We can't, for something *has* been said, and Laurie's mischief has spoilt you for me. I see it, and so does mother; you are not like your old self a bit, and seem ever so far away from me. I don't mean to plague you, and will bear it like a man, but I do wish it was all settled. I hate to wait; so if you mean ever to do it, make haste, and have it over quick,' said Jo, pettishly.

'*I* can't say or do anything till he speaks, and he won't, because father said I was too young,' began Meg, bending over her work with a queer little smile, which suggested that she did not quite agree with her father on that point.

'If he did speak, you wouldn't know what to say, but

would cry or blush, or let him have his own way, instead of giving a good, decided, No.'

'I'm not so silly and weak as you think. I know just what I should say, for I've planned it all, so I needn't be taken un-awares; there's no knowing what may happen, and I wished to be prepared.'

Jo couldn't help smiling at the important air which Meg had unconsciously assumed, and which was as becoming as the pretty color varying in her cheeks.

'Would you mind telling me what you'd say?' asked Jo, more respectfully.

'Not at all; you are sixteen now, quite old enough to be my confidant, and my experience will be useful to you by and by, perhaps, in your own affairs of this sort.'

'Don't mean to have any; it's fun to watch other people philander, but I should feel like a fool doing it myself,' said Jo, looking alarmed at the thought.

'I guess not, if you liked any one very much, and he liked you,' Meg spoke as if to herself, and glanced out at the lane where she had often seen lovers walking together in the summer twilight.

'I thought you were going to tell your speech to that man,' said Jo, rudely shortening her sister's little reverie.

'Oh, I should merely say, quite calmly and decidedly, "Thank you, Mr Brooke, you are very kind, but I agree with father, that I am too young to enter into any engagement at present; so please say no more, but let us be friends as we were."'

'Hum! that's stiff and cool enough. I don't believe you'll ever say it, and I know he won't be satisfied if you do. If he goes on like the rejected lovers in books, you'll give in, rather than hurt his feelings.'

'No I won't! I shall tell him I've made up my mind, and shall walk out of the room with dignity.'

Meg rose as she spoke, and was just going to rehearse the dignified exit, when a step in the hall made her fly into her seat, and begin to sew as if her life depended on finishing that particular seam in a given time. Jo smothered a laugh at the sudden change, and, when some one gave a modest tap, opened the door with a grim aspect, which was anything but hospitable.

'Good afternoon, I came to get my umbrella,—that is, to see how your father finds himself today,' said Mr Brooke, getting a trifle confused, as his eye went from one tell-tale face to the other.

'It's very well, he's in the rack, I'll get him, and tell it you are here,' and having jumbled her father and the umbrella well together in her reply, Jo slipped out of the room to give Meg a chance to make her speech, and air her dignity. But the instant she vanished, Meg began to sidle toward the door, murmuring,—

'Mother will like to see you, pray sit down, I'll call her.'

'Don't go; are you afraid of me, Margaret?' and Mr Brooke looked so hurt, that Meg thought she must have done something very rude. She blushed up to the little curls on her forehead, for he had never called her Margaret before, and she was surprised to find how natural and sweet it seemed to hear him say it. Anxious to appear friendly and at her ease, she put out her hand with a confiding gesture, and said, gratefully,—

'How can I be afraid when you have been so kind to father? I only wish I could thank you for it.'

'Shall I tell you how?' asked Mr Brooke, holding the small hand fast in both his big ones, and looking down at Meg with so much love in the brown eyes, that her heart began to flutter, and she both longed to run away and to stop and listen.

'Oh no, please don't—I'd rather not,' she said, trying to withdraw her hand, and looking frightened in spite of her denial.

'I won't trouble you, I only want to know if you care for me a little, Meg, I love you so much, dear,' added Mr Brooke, tenderly.

This was the moment for the calm, proper speech, but Meg didn't make it, she forgot every word of it, hung her head, and answered, 'I don't know,' so softly, that John had to stoop down to catch the foolish little reply.

He seemed to think it was worth the trouble, for he smiled to himself as if quite satisfied, pressed the plump hand grate-fully, and said, in his most persuasive tone, 'Will you try and find out? I want to know *so* much; for I can't go to work with any heart until I learn whether I am to have my reward in the end or not.'

'I'm too young,' faltered Meg, wondering why she was so fluttered, yet rather enjoying it.

'I'll wait; and, in the meantime, you could be learning to like me. Would it be a very hard lesson, dear?'

'Not if I chose to learn it, but—'

'Please choose to learn, Meg. I love to teach, and this is easier than German,' broke in John, getting possession of the other hand, so that she had no way of hiding her face, as he bent to look at it.

His tone was properly beseeching; but, stealing a shy look at him, Meg saw that his eyes were merry as well as tender, and that he wore the satisfied smile of one who had no doubt of his success. This nettled her; Annie Moffat's foolish lessons in coquetry came into her mind, and the love of power, which sleeps in the bosoms of the best of little women, woke up all of a sudden, and took possession of her. She felt excited and strange, and, not knowing what else to do, followed a capricious impulse, and, withdrawing her hands, said, petulantly, 'I *don't* choose; please go away, and let me be!'

Poor Mr Brooke looked as if his lovely castle in the air was tumbling about his ears, for he had never seen Meg in such a mood before, and it rather bewildered him.

'Do you really mean that?' he asked, anxiously, following her as she walked away.

'Yes, I do; I don't want to be worried about such things. Father says I needn't; it's too soon, and I'd rather not.'

'Mayn't I hope you'll change your mind by and by? I'll wait, and say nothing till you have had more time. Don't play with me, Meg. I didn't think that of you.'

'Don't think of me at all. I'd rather you wouldn't,' said Meg, taking a naughty satisfaction in trying her lover's patience and her own power.

He was grave and pale now, and looked decidedly more like the novel heroes whom she admired; but he neither slapped his forehead nor tramped about the room, as they did; he just stood looking at her so wistfully, so tenderly, that she found her heart relenting in spite of her. What would have happened next I cannot say, if Aunt March had not come hobbling in at this interesting minute.

The old lady couldn't resist her longing to see her nephew; for she had met Laurie as she took her airing, and, hearing of Mr March's arrival, drove straight out to see him. The family were all busy in the back part of the house, and she had made her way quietly in, hoping to surprise them. She did surprise two of them so much, that Meg started as if she had seen a ghost, and Mr Brooke vanished into the study.

'Bless me! what's all this?' cried the old lady, with a rap of her cane, as she glanced from the pale young gentleman to the scarlet young lady.

'It's father's friend. I'm *so* surprised to see you!' stammered Meg, feeling that she was in for a lecture now.

'That's evident,' returned Aunt March, sitting down. 'But what is father's friend saying, to make you look like a peony? There's mischief going on, and I insist upon knowing what it is!' with another rap.

'We were merely talking. Mr Brooke came for his umbrella,' began Meg, wishing that Mr Brooke and the umbrella were safely out of the house.

'Brooke? That boy's tutor? Ah! I understand now. I know all about it. Jo blundered into a wrong message in one of your pa's letters, and I made her tell me. You haven't gone and accepted him, child?' cried Aunt March, looking scandalized.

'Hush! he'll hear! Shan't I call mother?' said Meg, much troubled.

'Not yet. I've something to say to you, and I must free my

mind at once. Tell me, do you mean to marry this Cook? If you do, not one penny of my money ever goes to you. Remember that, and be a sensible girl,' said the old lady, impressively.

Now Aunt March possessed, in perfection, the art of rousing the spirit of opposition in the gentlest people, and enjoyed doing it. The best of us have a spice of perversity in us, especially when we are young, and in love. If Aunt March had begged Meg to accept John Brooke, she would probably have declared she couldn't think of it; but, as she was peremptorily ordered *not* to like him, she immediately made up her mind that she would. Inclination as well as perversity made the decision easy, and, being already much excited, Meg opposed the old lady with unusual spirit.

'I shall marry whom I please, Aunt March, and you can leave your money to any one you like,' she said, nodding her head with a resolute air.

'Highty tighty! Is that the way you take my advice, miss? You'll be sorry for it, by and by, when you've tried love in a cottage, and found it a failure.'

'It can't be a worse one than some people find in big houses,' retorted Meg.

Aunt March put on her glasses and took a look at the girl,—for she did not know her in this new mood. Meg hardly knew herself, she felt so brave and independent,—so glad to defend John, and assert her right to love him, if she liked. Aunt March saw that she had begun wrong, and, after a little pause, made a fresh start, saying, as mildly as she could, 'Now, Meg, my dear, be reasonable, and take my advice. I mean it kindly, and don't want you to spoil your whole life by making a mistake at the beginning. You ought to marry well, and help your family; it's your duty to make a rich match, and it ought to be impressed upon you.'

'Father and mother don't think so; they like John, though he *is* poor.'

'Your pa and ma, my dear, have no more worldly wisdom than two babies.'

'I'm glad of it,' cried Meg, stoutly.

Aunt March took no notice, but went on with her lecture. 'This Rook is poor, and hasn't got any rich relations, has he?'

'No; but he has many warm friends.'

'You can't live on friends; try it, and see how cool they'll grow. He hasn't any business, has he?'

'Not yet; Mr Laurence is going to help him.'

'That won't last long. James Laurence is a crotchety old fellow, and not to be depended on. So you intend to marry a man without money, position, or business, and go on working harder than you do now, when you might be comfortable all your days by minding me, and doing better? I thought you had more sense, Meg.'

'I couldn't do better if I waited half my life! John is good and wise; he's got heaps of talent; he's willing to work, and sure to get on, he's so energetic and brave. Every one likes and respects him, and I'm proud to think he cares for me, though I'm so poor, and young, and silly,' said Meg, looking prettier than ever in her earnestness.

'He knows *you* have got rich relations, child; that's the secret of his liking, I suspect.'

'Aunt March, how dare you say such a thing? John is above such meanness, and I won't listen to you a minute if you talk so,' cried Meg, indignantly, forgetting everything but the injustice of the old lady's suspicions. 'My John wouldn't marry for money, any more than I would. We are willing to work, and we mean to wait. I'm not afraid of being poor, for I've been happy so far, and I know I shall be with him, because he loves me, and I—'

Meg stopped there, remembering, all of a sudden, that she hadn't made up her mind; that she had told 'her John' to go away, and that he might be overhearing her inconsistent remarks.

Aunt March was very angry, for she had set her heart on having her pretty niece make a fine match, and something in the girl's happy young face made the lonely old woman feel both sad and sour.

'Well; I wash my hands of the whole affair! You are a wilful child, and you've lost more than you know by this piece of folly. No, I won't stop; I'm disappointed in you, and haven't spirits to see your pa now. Don't expect anything from me when you are married; your Mr Brooke's friends must take care of you. I'm done with you forever.'

And, slamming the door in Meg's face, Aunt March drove off in high dudgeon. She seemed to take all the girl's courage with her; for, when left alone, Meg stood a moment undecided whether to laugh or cry. Before she could make up her mind, she was taken possession of by Mr Brooke, who said, all in one breath, 'I couldn't help hearing, Meg. Thank you for defending me, and Aunt March for proving that you *do* care for me a little bit.'

'I didn't know how much, till she abused you,' began Meg.

'And I needn't go away, but may stay and be happy—may I, dear?'

Here was another fine chance to make the crushing speech and the stately exit, but Meg never thought of doing either, and disgraced herself forever in Jo's eyes, by meekly whispering, 'Yes, John,' and hiding her face on Mr Brooke's waistcoat.

Fifteen minutes after Aunt March's departure, Jo came softly down stairs, paused an instant at the parlor door, and, hearing no sound within, nodded and smiled, with a satisfied expression, saying to herself, 'She has sent him away as we planned, and that affair is settled. I'll go and hear the fun, and have a good laugh over it.'

But poor Jo never got her laugh, for she was transfixed upon the threshold by a spectacle which held her there, staring with her mouth nearly as wide open as her eyes. Going in to exult over a fallen enemy, and to praise a strong-minded sister for the banishment of an objectionable lover, it certainly *was* a shock to behold the aforesaid enemy serenely sitting on the sofa, with the strong-minded sister enthroned upon his knee, and wearing an expression of the most abject submission. Jo gave a sort of gasp, as if a cold shower-bath had suddenly fallen upon her,—for such an unexpected turning of the tables actually took her breath away. At the odd sound, the lovers turned and saw her. Meg jumped up, looking both proud and shy; but 'that man', as Jo called him, actually laughed, and said, coolly, as he kissed the astonished new comer, 'Sister Jo, congratulate us!'

That was adding insult to injury! it was altogether too much! and, making some wild demonstration with her hands, Jo vanished without a word. Rushing upstairs, she startled the invalids by exclaiming, tragically, as she burst into the room,

'Oh, *do* somebody go down quick! John Brooke is acting dreadfully, and Meg likes it!'

Mr and Mrs March left the room with speed; and, casting herself upon the bed, Jo cried and scolded tempestuously as she told the awful news to Beth and Amy. The little girls, however, considered it a most agreeable and interesting event, and Jo got little comfort from them; so she went up to her refuge in the garret, and confided her troubles to the rats.

Nobody ever knew what went on in the parlor that afternoon; but a great deal of talking was done, and quiet Mr Brooke astonished his friends by the eloquence and spirit with which he pleaded his suit, told his plans, and persuaded them to arrange everything just as he wanted it.

The tea-bell rang before he had finished describing the paradise which he meant to earn for Meg, and he proudly took her into supper, both looking so happy, that Jo hadn't the heart to be jealous or dismal. Amy was very much impressed by John's devotion and Meg's dignity. Beth beamed at them from a distance, while Mr and Mrs March surveyed the young couple with such tender satisfaction, that it was perfectly evident Aunt March was right in calling them as 'unworldly as a pair of babies'. No one ate much, but every one looked very happy, and the old room seemed to brighten up amazingly when the first romance of the family began there.

'You can't say "nothing pleasant ever happens now", can you, Meg?' said Amy, trying to decide how she would group the lovers in the sketch she was planning to make.

'No, I'm sure I can't. How much has happened since I said that! It seems a year ago,' answered Meg, who was in a blissful dream, lifted far above such common things as bread and butter.

'The joys come close upon the sorrows this time, and I rather think the changes have begun,' said Mrs March. 'In most families there comes, now and then, a year full of events; this has been such an one, but it ends well, after all.'

'Hope the next will end better,' muttered Jo, who found it very hard to see Meg absorbed in a stranger before her face; for Jo loved a few persons very dearly, and dreaded to have their affection lost or lessened in any way.

'I hope the third year from this *will* end better; I mean it shall, if I live to work out my plans,' said Mr Brooke, smiling at Meg, as if everything had become possible to him now.

'Doesn't it seem very long to wait?' asked Amy, who was in a hurry for the wedding.

'I've got so much to learn before I shall be ready, it seems a short time to me,' answered Meg, with a sweet gravity in her face, never seen there before.

'You have only to wait. *I* am to do the work,' said John, beginning his labors by picking up Meg's napkin, with an expression which caused Jo to shake her head, and then say to herself, with an air of relief, as the front door banged, 'Here comes Laurie; now we shall have a little sensible conversation.'

But Jo was mistaken; for Laurie came prancing in, overflowing with spirits, bearing a great bridal-looking bouquet for 'Mrs John Brooke', and evidently laboring under the delusion that the whole affair had been brought about by his excellent management.

'I knew Brooke would have it all his own way,—he always does; for when he makes up his mind to accomplish anything, it's done, though the sky falls,' said Laurie, when he had presented his offering and his congratulations.

'Much obliged for that recommendation. I take it as a good omen for the future, and invite you to my wedding on the spot,' answered Mr Brooke, who felt at peace with all mankind, even his mischievous pupil.

'I'll come if I'm at the ends of the earth; for the sight of Jo's face alone, on that occasion, would be worth a long journey. You don't look festive, ma'am; what's the matter?' asked Laurie, following her into a corner of the parlor, whither all had adjourned to greet Mr Laurence.

'I don't approve of the match, but I've made up my mind to bear it, and shall not say a word against it,' said Jo, solemnly. 'You can't know how hard it is for me to give up Meg,' she continued, with a little quiver in her voice.

'You don't give her up. You only go halves,' said Laurie, consolingly.

'It never can be the same again. I've lost my dearest friend,' sighed Jo.

'You've got me, anyhow. I'm not good for much, I know; but I'll stand by you, Jo, all the days of my life; upon my word I will!' and Laurie meant what he said.

'I know you will, and I'm ever so much obliged; you are always a great comfort to me, Teddy,' returned Jo, gratefully shaking hands.

'Well, now, don't be dismal, there's a good fellow. It's all right, you see. Meg is happy; Brooke will fly round and get settled immediately; grandpa will attend to him, and it will be very jolly to see Meg in her own little house. We'll have capital times after she is gone, for I shall be through college before long, and then we'll go abroad, or some nice trip or other. Wouldn't that console you?'

'I rather think it would; but there's no knowing what may happen in three years,' said Jo, thoughtfully.

'That's true! Don't you wish you could take a look forward, and see where we shall all be then? I do,' returned Laurie.

'I think not, for I might see something sad; and every one looks so happy now, I don't believe they could be much improved,' and Jo's eyes went slowly round the room, brightening as they looked, for the prospect was a pleasant one.

Father and mother sat together quietly re-living the first chapter of the romance which for them began some twenty years ago. Amy was drawing the lovers, who sat apart in a beautiful world of their own, the light of which touched their faces with a grace the little artist could not copy. Beth lay on her sofa talking cheerily with her old friend, who held her little hand as if he felt that it possessed the power to lead him along the peaceful ways she walked. Jo lounged in her favorite low seat, with the grave, quiet look which best became her; and Laurie, leaning on the back of her chair, his chin on a level with her curly head, smiled with his friendliest aspect, and nodded at her in the long glass which reflected them both.

So grouped the curtain falls upon Meg, Jo, Beth, and Amy. Whether it ever rises again, depends upon the reception given to the first act of the domestic drama, called 'LITTLE WOMEN'.

About the Author

LOUISA MAY ALCOTT was born in Pennsylvania, USA, in 1832. The Alcott family did not have much money and so when Louisa was in her teens she began to take various positions including teacher, seamstress, and servant. When the Civil War broke out she enlisted as a nurse and during this time contracted typhoid fever which would effect her health for the rest of her life. She had various stories published before being asked to write a children's book, the result of which was *Little Women*. The success of this book meant that she and her family were financially secure at last. Louisa died in 1888 and is buried in Sleepy Hollow Cemetery in Massachusetts.

CAPITAL FUNDS IN
UNDERDEVELOPED COUNTRIES

CAPITAL FUNDS IN UNDERDEVELOPED COUNTRIES

The Role of Financial Institutions

BY

EDWARD NEVIN
ECONOMIC RESEARCH INSTITUTE DUBLIN

LONDON
MACMILLAN & CO LTD
NEW YORK · ST MARTIN'S PRESS
1961

MACMILLAN AND COMPANY LIMITED
London Bombay Calcutta Madras Melbourne

THE MACMILLAN COMPANY OF CANADA LIMITED
Toronto

ST MARTIN'S PRESS INC
New York

PRINTED IN GREAT BRITAIN

Respectfully dedicated to the memory of

NOEL NETHERSOLE

*Good friend; tolerant master; faithful
servant of his people*

FOREWORD

My interest in the subject-matter of this essay was much stimulated by my experience during the years 1957 to 1959 when it was my privilege to serve the government of a territory within the British Commonwealth and to take a small part in the development of the financial system of its most beautiful and hospitable country. It is therefore considerably more than mere formality for me to emphasise upon the reader the wholly personal nature of the views expressed in the pages which follow. In no sense should they be taken as necessarily reflecting the opinion or policy of the present government of that country or of any of its predecessors.

The actual process of writing was completed while I was a member of the staff of the University College of Wales, Aberystwyth, and I have therefore to record (once again) my gratitude to the authorities of the College for placing at my disposal the facilities necessary for this task. I am also extremely grateful to Mr. W. T. Newlyn, of the University of Leeds, for reading through and commenting on the book in its typescript stage. Needless to say, he cannot be saddled with any of the responsibility for the imperfections which remain.

I should finally make clear that the opinions expressed in these pages must not be taken as necessarily representing the views of either the Executive Board or the staff of the Economic Research Institute, Dublin, in which it is my good fortune to be currently holding an appointment.

E. N.

DUBLIN
April 1961

CONTENTS

INTRODUCTION

THE development of economically backward countries is a subject which has very properly received a considerable amount of attention in recent years; no doubt it will continue to do so as long as the international maldistribution of wealth remains as marked as it is at the present time. The technical literature on the problem of stimulating growth in these countries is now of enormous magnitude, and its evolution has been distinguished by an increasing sub-division of the problem into its constituent parts. In the first flush of post-war interest in the topic, there was a clear tendency to over-simplify the problem so as to make it largely a matter of pumping sufficient capital into the territories concerned. Both the refinements of theoretical analysis and the shocks of practical experience have emphasised the superficiality and inadequacy of such a view. Capital, like patriotism, is not enough. Economic growth requires a great deal more than an outpouring of capital; it requires a minimum of natural endowments, a trained, healthy and mobile labour force, an adequate supply of entrepreneurs, engineers, teachers and administrators, the modification of social attitudes and organisation so as to make them conducive to, or at least not inconsistent with, increased production — in a word, it requires the conditioning of the whole environment so that it becomes one in which the initially delicate process of economic growth may flourish.

Yet the availability of capital lies ultimately at the root of many of these needs. Improvements in health and education imply the investment of capital in schools and hospitals and housing; the scarcity of personnel trained in science or sociology or administration can be overcome by the use of capital to buy them on the world market; the raising of standards of agricultural husbandry ultimately requires expenditure on equipment, materials and personnel from abroad or on their production at home. Capital alone will not solve the problem of under-development, but it provides access to the multiplicity of other ingredients whose intelligent combination can eventually bring the impoverished peoples of the world to a tolerable standard of living.

The supply of capital therefore remains one of the key factors in the solution of the problem. The world possesses something of a proliferation of international organisations intended to deal with this aspect of under-development, but, valuable though their contribution has been, their effectiveness has proved to be disappointingly limited. Statistics compiled by the United Nations indicate that during the two years 1958–9 the annual amount of international economic aid received by 45 under-developed countries — through bilateral assistance as well as through the international agencies — attained the ludicrous average of $1.9 per head of population.[1] The inadequacy of the capital flow to under-developed territories at the present time has perhaps been most strikingly emphasised by Professor Higgins' calculation that in order to attain the same rate of foreign investment (in real terms per head of its population) as was maintained by the United Kingdom during the nineteenth century in the under-developed territories of the time, the United States would need to carry out the entire European Recovery Programme twice a year.[2] Apart from the limited resources at their disposal, political difficulties (at both ends of the operation) have limited the role of the international agencies. So also has their general tendency to confine their investments to individual projects which hold definite promise of profit; thus, in discussing the role of the International Finance Corporation in economic development at the first annual meeting of its Board of Governors, the Corporation's President indicated that its operation required

> first, that we select projects which are well-conceived, well-executed, well-managed — with proper financial set-up and prospects of attractive profits related to the risks; and, second, that our investments be made on terms which promise returns greater than those available from more familiar, and generally safer, opportunities in the more developed countries.[3]

[1] *Statistical Yearbook 1960*, United Nations, New York, 1960, Table 157, p. 439. A group of experts estimated the amount of foreign capital needed by under-developed territories in 1949 to attain a growth of $2\frac{1}{2}$ per cent per annum in national income at about $14,000 million; the current inflow of capital to those territories in that year was estimated at little more than $1,000 million — *Measures for the economic development of under-developed countries*, United Nations, New York 1951 (1951. II. B2), Chap. XI, paras. 245–7, pp. 78–9. Another United Nations report of about the same vintage put the capital needs of under-developed countries over the following four years at about $66,000 million, of which about $16,000 million would need to come from external sources — *Methods of financing economic development in under-developed countries* (1949. II. B4), United Nations, New York 1949.
[2] B. Higgins, *Economic Development*, Norton, New York 1959, Chap. 10. p. 251.
[3] Address by Mr. Robert L. Garner to the first annual meeting of the Board of Governors of the International Finance Corporation, I.F.C. *First Annual Report, 1956–57*, Washington 1957.

This is no doubt a reasonable enough attitude from the standpoint of London or New York City, but it obviously leaves an immense gap to be filled of necessity by other means; the essential need in most under-developed economies is for the finance of general development programmes aimed at establishing a broad economic infrastructure, from which a predictable and high profit return is in the nature of the case absent.

Hence, with some air of disillusion, both developed and under-developed have come to lay increasing stress on the importance of an adequate flow of local, rather than external, funds for the finance of capital expenditure. The leading international lending agencies themselves emphasise that under-developed countries will need to finance the major part of their economic expansion from their own resources;[1] the United Nations Commission on Economic Development, for example, concluded that the financing of development must be based on the maximum exploitation of domestic sources of funds, and reported that

> it emphasises so much the role of domestic finance in economic development because it believes that it is the pre-requisite for enabling countries to implement the social, political and economic policies which they consider most suitable for the improvement of their standard of living. The role of foreign finance in economic development can therefore only be of a subordinate character.[2]

Private commentators have come to hold the same view. Professor Nurkse, for example, lays heavy stress on the importance of developing internal sources of development finance:

> External resources, even if they come in the most desirable forms, are not enough. . . . In my view, what needs to be stressed above all is that external sources can scarcely make a significant contribution to economic growth unless there is complementary action on the home front.[3]

Quite apart from these issues of the difficulty of obtaining foreign capital, and of properly integrating it into the local economy when it is obtained, there is the further problem of the balance of

[1] *Methods of financing economic development in under-developed countries,* United Nations, New York 1949, p. 3.
[2] Ibid., para 17, p. 94. A critical analysis of the role of foreign capital in contemporary economic development may also be found in A. H. Hanson, *Public enterprise and economic development,* Routledge & Kegan Paul, London 1959, Chap. II, pp. 24-35.
[3] R. Nurkse, *Problems of capital formation in under-developed countries,* Blackwell, Oxford 1953, Chap. VIII, pp. 140-1.

payments burden implicit in it. Most under-developed countries are dependent on the export of a limited number of primary products, and there are obvious dangers in the existence of a substantial fixed charge on the debit side of the external account when the credit side is prone to violent oscillations because of movements in international demand and world prices. Increasing anxiety has been felt in recent years about the danger to which many under-developed areas are now exposed on this account.[1] The crucial importance of internal flows of investible funds in the general struggle against economic under-development is thus beyond question.

Broadly speaking, internal supplies of capital funds can be mobilised through two main channels — those of fiscal and monetary measures. The former involves important and difficult problems concerning the relationship between taxation and incentives, the types of tax most suited to the administrative machinery of under-developed countries, the conflicts between equity and efficiency, and so on. It is with the latter, however, that this essay is concerned — the contribution which can be made to the finance of development by the reformation, or creation, of monetary arrangements and institutions. This is only one aspect of a topic which is in itself only one element in a highly complex problem. Nevertheless, a discussion of the broad issues underlying this single strand in the whole complicated fabric may make some small contribution to the solution of the problem as a whole.

One other point should be made at this stage. In much of what follows, the discussion will be related to the experience of those territories which are, or were until recently, British overseas dependencies. This is mainly because this group of countries possesses a certain homogeneity of financial and legal arrangements, arrangements which are furthermore of the kind with which the author is most familiar. This should not unduly limit the general application of any conclusions which may emerge. In the first place, the British Commonwealth area includes a substantial proportion of the under-developed territories of the world. Secondly, and more important, what is true of British colonies is to a large extent true, *mutatis mutandis*, of under-developed territories outside the Commonwealth. This is perhaps least true of currency

---

[1] See, for example, International Monetary Fund, *Annual Report 1959*, Washington 1959, Chap. III, p. 69.

arrangements, but even here it is possible that certain general principles can emerge which apply to most under-developed countries. In any case, no attempt is made in this essay to describe organisational arrangements, actual or proposed, in much detail. The aim is rather to discuss the broad issues involved, in the hope that light will be thrown on both the difficulties and the opportunities faced by all economically backward territories contemplating monetary reforms as part of a programme aimed at the attainment of a higher standard of living.

Chapter 1

THE CURRENCY SYSTEM

1. *Currency as a savings medium*

An important task facing under-developed countries is the mobilisation of all the financial resources available to them in order to allow the maximum possible rate of economic development; the stimulation of the growth and application of local supplies of investible funds is imperative.[1] The term 'savings medium' is commonly taken to mean institutions and assets of all kinds through which this can be done — through which, in other words, an income is earned as a reward for the sacrifice of current liquidity or consumption. In practice, however, a currency issue — especially in an under-developed country — is an important channel into which the savings of a substantial proportion of the public are directed. Although currency is by definition an asset on which no monetary income is earned, it is nevertheless a savings medium in the sense that the current consumption of goods and services is foregone in order to acquire it. Because it is a perfectly liquid asset, no interest is earned on holdings of currency; this should not be allowed to obscure the fact that the currency of a modern state, like its public debt in the usual sense of that term, is a collection of assets by means of which the monetary authorities obtain control over part of the current supply of goods and services available. Under any system, as one writer has observed, the public must give up other resources if it is to hold more currency.[2]

A more or less constant feature of economic development is that the shift from the most elementary forms of economic organisation to the sophisticated and complex financial organisations of the

[1] It is assumed, of course, that it is desired to avoid — or at least minimise — inflationary effects. It is now generally accepted that the disadvantages of 'development by inflation' are more than sufficient to offset its advantages. For an excellent discussion of this issue see W. A. Lewis, *The theory of economic growth*, Allen and Unwin, London 1955, Chap. V, pp. 213–25.

[2] A. Hazlewood, 'The economics of colonial monetary arrangements', *Social and Economic Studies*, Vol. 3, December 1954, Section VI.

I

industrialised world occurs in a series of stages. The first, and earliest, stage of development — the barter system — gradually gives way to exchange carried out through the medium of some form of currency, a process which is a necessary pre-requisite for the development of commercial banking. The shift away from the use of notes and coin and towards the more complex practice of financing transactions by means of bank deposits, and other types of credit, is a later one.[1] This trend towards the establishment of bank credit as the major means of exchange has already occurred in the developed economies of Western Europe and North America, but it is one which is still in its early stages in many of the less developed countries of the world. In assessing the facilities at the disposal of governments for the collection and deployment of savings, therefore, the use of the currency system is one which should not be underestimated in an under-developed economy; in such an economy the use of currency is frequently still increasing in importance, both absolutely and in relation to the national income.

The data shown in Table I illustrate in a broad and general sense this development of systems of monetary exchange from a primary dependence on currency in the poorer and economically backward economies of the world to the overwhelming dominance of bank credit in the richer and developed economies.[2] As will be seen from the table, there is a discernible tendency for the importance of currency in the total money supply of an economy to decrease steadily as the country concerned moves up the development scale. The trend is by no means invariable or unbroken, but as a general rule currency nowadays forms something of the order of a half to two-thirds of the total money supply in the relatively poor economies shown in the table, and only between 20 and 40

[1] On this see, for example, P. Cagan, 'The demand for currency relative to the total money supply', *Journal of Political Economy*, Vol. LXVI, No. 4, August 1958, pp. 303–28, and A. K. Cairncross, 'Banking in developing countries', *The future organisation of banking*, Institute of Bankers in Scotland, Blackwood, Edinburgh 1958, pp. 87–9.

[2] In order to illustrate the point correctly, of course, it would be necessary to allow for the different velocities of circulation of currency and bank deposits respectively, a correction which is unfortunately beyond the means of statistical possibility. There seems to be general agreement, however, that the velocity of circulation of bank deposits is certainly higher than that of currency. According to one observer, for example, the velocity of circulation of bank deposits in Malaya is phenomenally high even by Western standards, approaching a turnover rate of once a week.— T. H. Silcock, *The Commonwealth economy in Southeast Asia*, Cambridge University Press, London 1959, Chap. 3, p. 121.

per cent in most of the richer economies of Europe, America and Australia. What is more — although here the exceptions are even more frequent and the trend even less definite — the shift away from currency towards bank credit is visible over a period of time. It is by and large true to say that amongst the more backward

Table I: CURRENCY ELEMENT IN MONEY SUPPLIES
(Currency as % of total money supply)

	1913	1938	1953
A. UNDER-DEVELOPED COUNTRIES			
Bolivia - - - - - -	64	63	65
Brazil - - - - - -	65	30	31
Chile - - - - - -	46	34	34
Costa Rica - - - - -	62	47	48
Ecuador - - - - - -	73	56	50
Guatemala - - - - -	77	63	66
Honduras - - - - - -	62	57	58
India - - - - - -	47	55	67
Nicaragua - - - - - -	90	51	48
Venezuela - - - - -	52	49	44
B. DEVELOPED COUNTRIES			
France - - - - - -	51	58	50
Netherlands - - - - -	66	41	40
Switzerland - - - - -	22	20	39
United Kingdom - - - -	4	27	28
United States - - - - -	20	18	21

SOURCE: Based on U Tun Wai, 'Interest rates in the organised money markets of under-developed countries', *I.M.F. Staff Papers*, Vol. V, No. 2, August 1956, Table 1, p. 251.

economies included in the table the importance of currency has significantly decreased during the last forty years as the level of their income has risen, with a corresponding increase in the importance of bank credit. Of course, special factors are operating in many cases; in four of the five developed economies included in the table, for example, the volume of currency has either remained of constant importance or has actually increased in relative importance during the last forty years. Nevertheless, it remains generally true that, on the one hand, the supply of currency is of particular importance in under-developed countries and, on the other hand, that although the relative importance of currency can be expected to diminish ultimately, it is likely that the growth of the national income of many under-developed territories will be associated for many years with an increase in their currency issues, at least in absolute terms.[1]

In view of this, it would be inadvisable to neglect the significance of a currency issue, and of the reserves which lie behind it, as a possible contributor to the finance of economic development. If a substantial element in the total national income of presently under-developed countries is to be handed over to the monetary authorities by the general public in return for notes and coin, it is obvious that the resources thus coming within the control of the monetary authorities can play an important part in a general development programme. The extent to which a currency reserve can be employed as an instrument of finance for development, however, will vary from country to country and from time to time.

When currencies are fully convertible it is often necessary for the authorities to ensure that a substantial fraction of the resources handed over to them in return for currency is held in the form of gold, or of foreign exchange easily convertible into gold. Since convertibility has to be guaranteed, the authorities incur the obligation to exchange currency for gold, or some other currency, on demand and at any time. It therefore follows that the currency backing cannot be wholly employed in some form of long-term investment. Where a currency is not convertible, however, or where for any reason it is not anticipated that the right to convert is likely to be used to any considerable extent, the possibility of the employment of resources obtained from a currency issue in some form of relatively long-term investment clearly does arise. Even where the exercise of the right of convertibility is theoretically likely, there remains the possibility of the use of exchange control to prevent any sudden and widespread conversion of a currency into foreign exchange.

Obviously the use or threat of exchange control is not in itself particularly advantageous for an under-developed country seeking to obtain capital, either from within its own territory or, more especially, from abroad. At the same time, it is nowadays inevitable that due acknowledgement must be given to the fact that the maximum rate of economic development in a backward territory cannot be left wholly to market forces. Economies are under-developed precisely because the normal market mechanism of

---

[1] For one case-study, see E. K. Hawkins, 'The growth of a money economy in Nigeria and Ghana', *Oxford Economic Papers*, Vol. 10, No. 3, October 1958, pp. 350–4.

profit and loss is insufficiently strong to overcome the natural obstacles of geography, or history, or politics. Unless the development of a country is to proceed at only a slow pace and over a protracted period of time, therefore, the normal forces operating in the market may well require some degree of central guidance and control. The extent and nature of such control is essentially a political matter which can be decided only in the light of the peculiar circumstances of each individual territory. There can be little doubt, however, that if government intervention is to be adopted at all, the maintenance of at least rudimentary exchange control may have to take a high priority. The right to convert domestic currency freely into some foreign currency may be the sort of privilege which only well-established and relatively well-to-do countries can afford; it may be one which a desperately poor economy will find too expensive. Whether it is fully convertible or not, therefore, to some varying degree the reserves held as backing for the currency represent a potential source of finance for economic development.

2. *The sterling exchange standard*

In view of this conclusion, it is relevant to consider in some detail the possibilities of the use of currency reserves in development finance, especially in the particular circumstances of British colonies, or ex-colonies, almost all of which are served by the currency system generally known as the sterling exchange standard.[1]

[1] This is described at considerable length in I. Greaves, *Colonial monetary conditions*, Colonial Research Studies No. 10, H.M.S.O., London 1953. See also P. W. Bell, *The sterling area in the post-war world*, Oxford University Press, London 1956, H. A. Shannon, 'The modern colonial sterling exchange standard', *I.M.F. Staff Papers*, Vol. 2, No. 2, April 1952, pp. 319–62, and W. T. Newlyn, 'The colonial empire', *Banking in the British Commonwealth*, ed. R. S. Sayers, Oxford University Press, London 1952, Chap. 13, pp. 421–36. A considerable controversy over the precise mechanism and merits of the sterling exchange standard has developed in recent years — see I. Greaves, 'The sterling balances of colonial territories', *Economic Journal*, Vol. LXI, No. 242, June 1951; A. Hazlewood, 'Sterling balances and the colonial currency system', *Economic Journal*, Vol. LXII, No. 247, December 1952; 'Analyst', 'Currency and banking in Jamaica', *Social and Economic Studies*, Vol. I, No. 4, August 1953; A. Hazlewood, 'Colonial external finance since the war', *Review of Economic Studies*, 1953–4, Vol. XXI(1), No. 54; I. Greaves, 'Sterling balances and the colonial currency system: a comment', *Economic Journal*, Vol. LXIII, No. 252, December 1953; A. Hazlewood, 'Sterling balances and the colonial currency system: a reply', *Economic Journal*, Vol. LXIV, No. 255, September 1954; B. M. Niculescu, 'Sterling balances and the colonial currency system: a comment', *Economic Journal*, Vol. LXIV, No. 255, September 1954; I. Greaves, *The colonial sterling balances*, Essays in international finance, No. 20,

The consideration of this currency system is of relevance in a discussion of the general subject of the finance of economic development, partly because it is a currency system operating in a substantial number of the territories which could be generally described as under-developed, partly because other under-developed territories outside the British colonial or ex-colonial range operate currency systems which are similar in principle to the sterling exchange standard[1] and partly because a discussion of the sterling exchange standard involves broad principles which are common to all currency systems.

In its original form, the sterling exchange standard implied that the money supply issued in the overseas territories of the British Commonwealth was in effect the same as the currency circulating within the United Kingdom itself.[2] More often than not, the local currency takes a form which is physically distinct from the currency in use within the United Kingdom, but this difference of appearance is of no more practical significance than, for example, the issue of notes by certain banks in Scotland which require a 100 per cent backing by Bank of England notes; they are in no fundamental sense distinct from the Bank of England issue. The backing held against sterling exchange currencies is of course not Bank of England notes, but what is in principle the same thing — i.e. securities issued by the United Kingdom Government or by other governments within the British Commonwealth except that of the territory in which the currency is issued. In effect, therefore, the resources sacrificed by a community when

Princeton University Press, September 1954; A. Hazlewood, 'Memorandum on the sterling assets of the British colonies: a comment', *Review of Economic Studies*, 1954–5, Vol. XXII(1), No. 57; A. Hazlewood, 'The economics of colonial monetary arrangements', *Social and Economic Studies*, Vol. 3, December 1954; F. H. H. King, 'Sterling balances in the colonial monetary system', *Economic Journal*, Vol. LXV, No. 260, December 1955; I. Greaves, 'Colonial trade and payments', *Economica*, Vol. XXIV, No. 93, February 1957.

[1] Amongst them the currency system of many French overseas territories, or of independent countries such as Panama and Liberia; legal requirements involving a high foreign-currency backing have the same effect — Iraq and the Lebanon are examples. (See A. Ali, 'Banking in the Middle East', *I.M.F. Staff Papers*, Vol. VI, No. I, November 1957, p. 71.) For a discussion of the policies adopted in the Dominican Republic, which until 1948 possessed a 100 per cent dollar exchange standard, see N. A. D. Macrae, 'Experiments in central banking: a study of San Domingo's new bank', *The Banker*, October 1948, especially pp. 44–5.

[2] 'In effect, colonial currency is an incidental part of the branch banking system with its centre in London' (I. Greaves, *The colonial sterling balances*, p. 11); it made the colonies 'an extension of the British monetary system' (T. H. Silcock, op. cit., Chap. 2, p. 97).

it elects to hold part of its wealth in the form of currency are invested in the securities of — that is to say, lent to — the United Kingdom Government or other Commonwealth Governments.[1]

In recent years there has been some substantial degree of modification of the system, especially in connection with the

Table II: CURRENCY RESERVES OF BRITISH COLONIAL TERRITORIES [a]

End of year	Total currency in circulation [b]	Currency funds held in London [c]	(3) as % of (2)
	£ million	£ million	%
(1)	(2)	(3)	(4)
1954	316	263	83·2
1955	348	288	82·8
1956	324	309	95·4
1957	333	327	98·2
1958	337	327	97·0
1959	364	299	82·2

[a] Excludes Hong Kong, Falkland Islands, St. Helena, Seychelles and Western Pacific H.C. territories.
[b] Excludes a small and declining total of notes issued by commercial banks in various territories.   [c] Market values.

SOURCES: Col. (2) — The Colonial Territories, 1957–1958, Cmd. 451, H.M.S.O., London 1958, Table 28, p. 82; The Colonial Territories 1958–1959, Cmd. 780, H.M.S.O., London 1959, Table 27, p. 103; The Colonial Territories 1959–1960, Cmd. 1065, H.M.S.O., London 1960, Table 30, p. 98. Col. (3) — Quarterly Digest of Colonial Statistics, No. 45, H.M.S.O., London 1960, Table 55, p. 62.

extent to which currency authorities are permitted to invest the sterling proceeds of currency issues in securities issued by the governments of their own territories as well as those of other Commonwealth governments. From December 1954 arrangements were made for a limited proportion of the currency backing to be held in local issues, and advantage has been taken of this to varying degrees by many authorities.[2] As may be seen from Table II, however, this has not resulted in any really fundamental change in the nature of the currency system; even at current market valuations the London investments of the British colonial

[1] There were one or two minor exceptions to this rule — see King, op. cit., p. 719.
[2] The highest 'local' proportion for which approval has been granted appears to be that of Jamaica, the currency authorities of which may now hold about one-third of the total circulation in local assets — The Colonial Territories 1959–60, Cmd 1065, H.M.S.O., London 1960, para. 586, p. 97.

currency authorities at the end of 1959 still represented over 80 per cent of the total volume of currency in issue.[1] The modification of the sterling exchange standard during recent years, in other words, has been only a marginal one.

There is no reason to deny that this currency system has many virtues, and in many respects has served the colonial territories extremely well. Being a rigid and inflexible system, there could be no possibility of an over-issue of currency such as has occurred in many countries, usually with injurious effects. (This does not mean, of course, that the territories operating this system are thereby protected completely against inflation. The expansion of the money supply is by no means the only, or even the main, method by which inflation can be engineered; in fact, it would be generally agreed that expansion of the currency is frequently an effect, rather than a cause, of inflation.)[2] It provided colonies with a simple and inexpensive currency-issue mechanism. Above all, the sterling exchange standard gave a complete and absolute guarantee of full and free convertibility into the British pound sterling at a stable rate of exchange, and provided for the automatic conversion of local currencies into pounds sterling without the possibility of any official intervention in such free exchange.

In the circumstances of the 19th and early 20th centuries, when the movement of capital into the colonial territories was for all practical purposes left entirely to private initiative, this currency system was, as one writer has put it, 'ideally suited to a period of colonial expansion and capital migration'. Under it, there could be no risk of any exchange-rate depreciation in the value of assets purchased or constructed within those territories, or of the income and profits arising from them.[3] These advantages are not lightly to be foregone or under-rated; insofar as under-developed territories look for capital to overseas sources, it is necessary for them to ensure that these qualities of complete convertibility and

---

[1] A word of caution should be given in connection with this table. The official statistics which it embodies are subject to rather surprising revisions from year to year, and these appear to be due to modifications in the coverage of the published data which — to put it mildly — are not always made quite explicit.

[2] As one commentator ruefully observes, Libyan experience shows clearly that even a 100 per cent currency reserve is no infallible safeguard against inflation — A. G. Chandaruarkar, 'Central banking in Libya', *The Bankers' Magazine*, Vol. CLXXXIX, No. 1395, June 1960, p. 7.

[3] H. A. Gunasekera, 'The money supply and the balance of payments in Ceylon', *Review of the Banca Nazionale del Lavoro*, Vol. 7, No. 30, September 1954, p. 146.

guaranteed parity are secured either by the currency system itself, or, failing this, by some other means.[1]

Admitting these advantages of the sterling exchange standard — advantages which could scarcely be other than overwhelming in an era in which overseas capital development was left wholly to private initiative — it is equally clear that the maintenance of the system in its most rigid form in an era when development has become a matter of joint public and private action, if not for public action alone, would have been indefensible. The advantages of the system — its complete inflexibility and absence of scope for monetary management — have become its disadvantages. By definition, it prevents any exercise on the part of the authorities in an under-developed country of monetary policy with the aim of encouraging and facilitating internal economic development.[2] This is not to say that it is necessarily a serious disadvantage in such countries for the authorities to be unable to expand or contract the total money supply after the fashion of monetary authorities in highly developed economies. There can be no escaping the fact that in the majority of under-developed territories an overall expansion of credit will not in itself stimulate the rate of economic development, since development would be limited by the lack of resources in real, rather than monetary, terms; credit expansion would usually generate little other than a series of inflationary increases in money incomes and prices. As has been remarked in connection with Ceylon, 'This should serve as a warning to those who might hope that some of the policies growing out of Keynesian economics can be uncritically adapted to Ceylon'.[3]

[1] Hence it is surely inadequate to dismiss the sterling exchange standard with the sentence 'This type of system, therefore, has long been a mark of colonialism.' — J. Exter, *Report on the establishment of a central bank for Ceylon*, Sessional Paper XIV, Government Printer, Colombo, November 1949, p. 4.

[2] Exter, op. cit., p. 4. Even in purely technical matters concerning the currency issue there have been some grounds for dissatisfaction: 'In our own day', remarks one commentator, 'the remoter parts of certain British colonies have been very ill-provided because the currency authority has taken a narrower view of its duties than might have been taken by a central bank having wide and acknowledged responsibility for ensuring the smooth working of the monetary system.' (R. S. Sayers, 'Central Banking in under-developed territories', *Central banking after Bagehot*, Oxford University Press, London 1957, Chap. 9, p. 120.)

[3] Exter, op. cit., p. 27. On a previous page, however, the author of this very proper warning seems to have come rather close to disregarding it himself, since amongst his opening words occurs the statement 'Perhaps no single factor can do more to influence the welfare and growth of a community than the flow of money.' (Ibid., p. 1) On the peculiar dangers of inflation for an under-developed territory see *Methods of financing economic development in*

It is impossible, then, to consider the merits or disadvantages of the sterling exchange standard for under-developed countries in terms of orthodox general credit control of the kind used to maintain stability in a highly developed economy. In the under-developed countries of the world the basic cause of poverty is not unused capacity of the Keynesian kind but the *lack* of productive capacity, a lack which cannot be made good by purely monetary measures and changes in overall demand.

Nor would it be correct to argue that the sterling exchange standard necessarily involves the currency supply in a mechanical and inflexible relationship with the balance of payments. If it were true to argue, for example, that a surplus on the balance of payments of a country on the sterling exchange standard auto-matically involved an expansion in the supply of money, and *vice versa*, a serious situation would obviously exist. At a time of a surplus on the balance of payments the internal pressure on resources is particularly high, and the danger of inflation is especially great; if in such circumstances an expansion automatic-ally occurred in the currency issue, some additional stimulus to this inflationary pressure would undoubtedly be given. Similarly, if a country is running an import deficit, there will naturally be a deflationary influence at work in the economy; a contraction of the currency issue at such a time would give additional impetus to this downward pressure.

In fact, the connection between the issue of a sterling exchange currency and the balance of payments is by no means wholly automatic and mechanical, primarily because the total volume of credit in most countries operating this system can be influenced by the banking system as well as by the currency authorities. Although a surplus on the balance of payments would be one factor operating towards an increase — or, rather, *permitting* an increase — in the issue of currency, the operations of the banking system may be such as to offset this tendency wholly or partly.[1] Indeed, it has been asserted that 'the controlling factor in the

under-developed countries, United Nations, New York 1949, Introduction. See also A. Hazlewood, 'The economics of colonial monetary arrangements', *Social and Economic Studies*, Vol. 2, December 1954, Section VI.

[1] Pre-war Uruguay provides an example of compensatory action by the banking system in the face of marked oscillations in export earnings — see B. Brovedani, 'Latin American medium-term import stabilisation policies and the adequacy of reserves', *I.M.F. Staff Papers*, Vol. IV, No. 2, February 1955, p. 272.

colonial money supply, cash and credit, is not foreign exchange but commercial bank resources'.[1] There is therefore some justice in describing as 'inaccurate and misleading' the proposition that the currency circulation under this system is automatically responsive to the balance of payments.[2] An important criticism of the sterling exchange standard is indeed implicit in this key role of the commercial banking system. The criticism is not that the currency system is inflexible but that 'it depends for its flexibility not on any official authority but on the actions of private profit-seeking institutions'.[3] It is also important to bear in mind that the commercial banks can introduce this flexibility into the monetary system only in those sectors of the economy with which they concern themselves — which may prove to be in fact a fairly restricted sphere.[4]

There is another aspect of the sterling exchange standard which is perhaps more important. It has been argued that the propensity of the public to hold part of its wealth in the form of notes or coin implies a sacrifice of consumption which they are prepared to forego in order to obtain currency. In a closed economy with an independent monetary system, the resources corresponding to the consumption so foregone would be handed over to the monetary authorities, who would be free to employ them as they thought fit. The community as a whole would be no poorer as the result of the issue of currency; the resources sacrificed by one part of the community are merely transferred to another part of the same community. The essential fact about the sterling exchange system, however, is that the resources sacrificed by the community in increasing its holdings of currency are not retained within the same community; the requirement that London sterling — United Kingdom or other Commonwealth government securities — be

[1] I. Greaves, 'Colonial trade and payments', p. 49.
[2] Gunasekera, ibid., p. 150. See also Hazlewood, 'The economics of colonial monetary arrangements', Sec. IV. At the same time, it would be going over-far to argue that, given the existing international banking structure, 'there is generally all the elasticity of reserve cash necessary to allow as much credit expansion as the local bankers are willing to sponsor' — R. S. Sayers, 'Central banking in under-developed territories', p. 114. There is evidence that in Nigeria, for example, the banks have adopted a passive policy and have thus tended to 'follow' the balance of payments — D. Rowan, ' Banking in Nigeria: a study in colonial financial evolution', *Review of the Banca Nazionale del Lavoro*, Vol. V, No. 22, July–September 1952, pp. 164–5.
[3] Gunasekera, ibid., p. 149.
[4] W. T. Newlyn and D. C. Rowan, *Money and banking in British colonial Africa*, Oxford University Press, London 1954, Chap. 9, p. 191.

held against additional issues of currency notes means, in effect, that overseas governments acquire the command over resources which the colonial community has sacrificed in order to hold currency.

In general, therefore, the sterling exchange standard has involved the dependent territories in lending to the government of the United Kingdom (or to a lesser extent other Commonwealth governments) that element of their national income which in any year they wished to add to their stock of currency, or, in more recent years with the relaxation of the 100 per cent rule, a substantial element of it. It would be perfectly true to say that this has not necessarily involved the colonial territories in a sacrifice of imports: the fact that their currencies are for all practical purposes identical with the British pound sterling means that their note issues are used to purchase locally produced output equally with imports. The resources locked up in the currency reserve, in other words, could have been used to finance local expenditure just as much as to purchase goods and services from overseas. Hence there is no necessary connection between the size of a territory's currency reserves in sterling securities and its capacity to import, as opposed to its capacity to consume.[1] The essence of the matter is that the territory concerned has abandoned a claim to resources in general equal to the value of the securities purchased in London.[2]

The fact that some of the sterling against which currency is issued may have been provided in the first instance by an overseas enterprise operating within a colony has no particular relevance to this general proposition. An expatriate trading company which finances the purchase of goods and services within a territory by means of sterling from its own resources would need to obtain local currency in order to do so whatever currency system prevailed. The special significance of the sterling exchange system is that funds used to purchase local currency, whether by residents or foreigners, are withheld from the government of the territory

[1] Greaves, ibid., pp. 56–7.

[2] It is incomplete, rather than incorrect, therefore, to say that the sterling exchange standard system 'reduces the funds available to a colony for external expenditure'. (Hazlewood, 'The economics of colonial monetary arrangements', p. 295.) The system reduces *all* potential expenditure, not merely *external* expenditure. Similarly, the comparison of the sterling exchange system with a 100 per cent reserve gold standard, while not without some validity, cannot be pushed too far. (J. Mars, 'The monetary and banking system and loan market of Nigeria', *Mining, Finance and Commerce in Nigeria* (ed. M. Perham), Vol. II, Faber and Faber, London 1948, Part 2, Chap. 4.)

concerned and are instead put at the disposal of the Government of the United Kingdom.[1]

It is inevitable, therefore, that in searching out sources of finance for economic development in a territory operating this currency system attention must be devoted to the possibility of replacing it, at least in its original and rigid form, by one more suited to the development of the territory. This means, in effect, the reduction of the extent to which the currency reserve is held in the form of securities issued by other governments, and the transfer of some of the funds so released into the securities of the government of the territory concerned — or into such other channels as will enable it to use the funds for its own development. As was shown above, this is a process which has been under way for a number of years, but as yet has attained only very modest dimensions; it is argued below that it needs to be pushed substantially further. The accumulation of savings represented by currency reserves is too important an element in the supply of domestic savings for its optimum use in development to be left to go by default.

3. *The repatriation of currency reserves*

An under-developed territory seeking to obtain capital for development would be well advised, then, to look to its currency reserves in order to discover the contribution which it is possible to obtain from the repatriation of overseas assets and their conversion into local securities. This is particularly the case with the territories operating the sterling exchange standard; to some degree it is true also of other countries whose currency systems have been based on a similar principle of dependence on another currency and the retention of large external reserves. The magnitude of the contribution which can be obtained from this source, of course, must not be over-estimated; it will depend on, first, the size of the currency issue and, secondly, the extent to which it is considered advisable to retain a proportion of the currency reserve in the form of external assets of one sort or another.

The government of an under-developed country usually has little control over the first of these factors; the volume of currency

---

[1] It is of course true that there is nothing inherently incompatible between colonial lending to London for one purpose (currency backing) and simultaneous borrowing from London for another purpose (development) — King, op. cit., p. 720. On the other hand, such simultaneous borrowing and lending *as a long-term practice* makes sense only on special assumptions about the dependent territories which become increasingly unrealistic as the years proceed.

is substantially determined for it by the extent to which its citizens have developed the use of currency for their everyday transactions. Its rate of growth in the future will depend on the shifts which may occur in spending habits — away from barter transactions and towards currency transactions, and in turn away from currency transactions to bank credit transactions — and on the rate at which the general level of incomes and prices rises as the years proceed.

The second factor is one requiring careful consideration by the authorities of each individual territory. The extent to which repatriation of currency reserves involves a risk so far as the solvency and stability of the currency are concerned will naturally vary from one territory to another.[1] It would be pointless to deny that some element of risk will almost always be involved in the repatriation of external currency reserves; this is no more than to say, however, that the movement of a territory towards independence, whether political or economic, is a development with which risk is inescapably connected. In most senses a colonial territory is always a safer proposition from the investor's point of view than a territory which has some significant degree of control over its own affairs. On the other hand, if the economic development of a territory is unnecessarily retarded — and lack of finance may be a factor working in this direction — it is possible that the risks involved in a partial repatriation of currency reserves would be less dangerous than the risk of the political upheaval which might be the result of an unnecessarily slow rate of growth of income.

It is for this reason that United Nations reports have deplored the fact that the currency system operating in some territories has resulted in government hoarding because local currency notes (or savings bank deposits) are backed 100 per cent by foreign exchange. The reports point out that this high percentage 'unnecessarily sterilizes foreign exchange to the extent of that part of the money supply which the government will never be required to redeem in foreign exchange'[2] and that in such cases 'domestic monetary reform may be an important method of providing

[1] Much also depends on the philosophy of outside observers. The ultra-orthodox reaction to Ceylon's decision to move away from the Currency Board stage was not merely that risks were involved but that the policy was 'necessarily fraught with great dangers' — 'Ceylon's central banking experiment', *The Banker*, Vol. XCV, No. 294, July 1950, p. 33.

[2] *Measures for the economic development of under-developed countries*, United Nations, New York 1951, Chap. VI, para. 99, p. 36. See also Exter, op. cit., p. 5, and Hazlewood, op. cit., sec. VII.

finance for economic development'.[1] The hoarding of foreign exchange, and its consequent retarding of economic growth, is in itself a risk against which the risk of repatriation has to be measured. It is not a question of whether a risk should or should not be taken; the matter at issue is whether the risk involved in one course of action (repatriation of currency reserves) is smaller or greater than the risk run by the lack of such action (possible retarding of economic growth).

In considering the magnitude of the overseas reserves which could safely be repatriated and invested in local securities, it is clear that no real risk is run with that part of the currency issue which it is certain will never be presented for conversion into some other form.[2] The maintenance of a 100 per cent foreign backing to a currency can be justified logically only on the assumption that the possibility exists that every single currency note outstanding might be presented to the issuing authority for conversion into some other currency. Such a possibility seldom exists in the real world. The problem which arises, however, is the assessment of the magnitude of the basic element in the currency issue which is of a completely stable, non-convertible kind. The proportion will vary from territory to territory, and is likely to be largest where the use of money is most advanced and of longest standing. There is no reason why a careful study of the statistics of currency redemptions and issues, month by month and year by year, should not yield a fairly reliable guide to the degree of instability which exists in any given currency system. To the extent that, say, 25 per cent of the currency can safely be presumed to be the basic minimum without which it would not be possible for the economic life of the community to proceed, then this proportion of the currency reserve is clearly eligible for repatriation without any risk whatever.[3]

Over and above this hard core of currency which will never be presented for redemption, there remains the proportion of the

[1] *Methods of financing economic development in under-developed countries*, United Nations, New York 1949 (1949, II, B.4), Introduction, p. 21. See also W. A. Lewis, op. cit., Chap. V, pp. 246–7.

[2] Hazlewood, op. cit., Sec. VIII.

[3] A practical point of some importance, however, is that the 'local' backing for the currency should be specified in terms of an absolute figure rather than a percentage. The use of a percentage regulation would involve the monetary authorities in embarrassing and unnecessary sales of local assets whenever the total currency issue fell, however temporarily. (Newlyn and Rowan, op. cit., pp. 259–60.)

currency issue which, while not normally likely to be presented for repayment, is nevertheless to some degree liable to be brought to the currency authority for conversion. Here it becomes relevant to consider the type of crisis which is being envisaged. If the postulated movement out of currency has as its object the acquisition of some other locally obtainable asset — e.g. local bank deposits or locally issued securities — the problem is a relatively minor one. As and when the movement occurs it will be the task of the local monetary authorities to offset the shift in public preference by a corresponding shift in the supply of assets.[1] This presupposes the existence of a central bank, or some other institution with corresponding functions and powers, which can stand ready to meet crises of this sort when they occur. The implications of this aspect of financial development are considered in later chapters of this essay.

More serious and complex problems arise, however, when the authorities are contemplating the possibility of a shift out of a locally issued currency and into foreign currencies, whether to finance the purchase of current imports or to hold assets abroad in substitution for local assets. Here it is clearly necessary that the government of a territory should hold, either in the form of a separate currency reserve or in general national foreign exchange reserves, external assets of such type and magnitude as to enable it to meet any such shift by providing the requisite foreign exchange to the public. (This assumes, of course, that the full convertibility of the currency is being retained; as is noted below, the repatriation of currency reserves by no means implies that the convertibility position of a currency is at all affected.) The problem of calculating the minimum volume of foreign reserves which it is prudent to retain in order to guard against this contingency is an exceedingly difficult and complicated one. Much will depend on the extent and nature of the foreign trade of the country concerned, on the relative movements of imports and exports through the various seasons of the year, on their liability to sudden and substantial movements in prices, on the probability of shifts in the demand for, or supply of, goods bulking large in its foreign trade, on the propensity of its citizens to lose confidence in their own economic system and to seek refuge in foreign financial centres, and so on.[2]

[1] A. W. Plumptre, *Central banking in the British Dominions*, University of Toronto Press, Toronto 1940, Introduction, pp. 30–2.
[2] Greaves, *The Colonial sterling balances, passim.*

Clearly no single rule can be adequate to cover the cases of all the under-developed territories of the world, with their infinite variations of character and stages of development.[1] There would not appear to be any good reason, however, for applying to the foreign backing of the currency issues of under-developed territories the type of technique used in connection with the general official reserves of a developed economy. It does not appear relevant, for example, to argue that certain countries which do not possess deposits of gold or silver find it necessary to retain foreign exchange reserves amounting to 100 per cent or more of the currency issue.[2] Nor does it appear relevant to express the problem in terms of a given number of months' imports, as has been done in connection with the Federation of Rhodesia and Nyasaland and the Gold Coast.[3] The irrelevance of these comparisons springs from the fact that the countries with which comparison is being made possess independent monetary systems, their reserves being held not specifically against the currency issue but against all contingent demands for foreign exchange, whether through the means of currency or otherwise. These countries would include in their foreign exchange reserves not only the external assets held by the note issuing authority (which in the case of the United Kingdom would be virtually nil) but also those held by, or subject to the influence of, all official agencies. They might well also include the foreign assets held by the commercial banking system. The relevant comparison, in so far as it is applicable at all, would thus be between the total foreign exchange reserves of these independent countries, on the one hand, and, on the other hand, the total foreign exchange

---

[1] After a study of the statistics relating to East and West Africa, for example, Newlyn and Rowan conclude that anything up to 50 per cent for the currency reserve could safely be repatriated. (Op. cit., p. 202.)

[2] Greaves, 'Colonial trade and payments', p. 57.

[3] S. I. Katz, 'Development and stability in Central and West Africa: a study in colonial monetary institutions', *Social and Economic Studies*, Vol. 5, No. 3, September 1956, p. 282. Another writer advances the doctrine that 'the greater the volume of imports, the greater the required holdings of foreign reserves are likely to be' with a total disregard of other variables such as the level of exports or capital movements. (E. A. Birnbaum, 'The cost of a foreign exchange standard or of the use of a foreign currency as the circulating medium', *I.M.F. Staff Papers*, Vol. V, No. 3, February 1957, p. 487.) The same writer's attempt to assess the adequacy of currency reserves against the incidence of exchange restrictions or the resort to devaluation — quite apart from its implicit value judgement as to the relative merits of internal growth on the one hand and external liberalism on the other — would cast doubts on the solvency of a good many eminently respectable developed countries.

c

reserves of not merely the currency authorities but of all official agencies, in the under-developed territories being considered — in other words, the reserves would have to be defined so as to include those held by the central government itself, by Marketing Boards, and by other institutions such as Savings Banks and Development Finance institutions.[1]

The truth of the matter is that the variables entering into the question of the adequacy of foreign exchange reserves are far too complex to permit the formulation of an answer in a simple and mechanical form. We are told that in the hey-day of the gold standard the British authorities managed sterling — 'which in practice meant the good management of a whole constellation of currencies' — with a gold reserve which was usually of the order of £20 million; this could be compared with a contemporary reserve (i.e. in 1951) of some £1200 million — 'which is deemed so low as to spell perdition'.[2] The precise extent to which at any time the currency of a territory is liable to be presented for conversion into a foreign currency is one which can be determined only by the authorities of each individual territory itself, using all the available statistics of its experience in recent years and — most important of all — in the light of its own informed judgement as to the liability of its balance of payments to wide and adverse swings in the years immediately ahead. It is clear that the risk involved in the considerations just discussed can never be wholly obviated. Indeed, as has been suggested earlier, it is a question of deliberately incurring this risk in preference to what is almost certainly the greater risk of an avoidable retarding of the rate of economic growth.

It is implicit in all this that there exists a method by which the richer economies of the Western world can stand ready to help the less developed territories — both those within their imperial influence and otherwise — in accordance with their often-stated

[1] Thus Currency Funds amounted to only 28 per cent of the sterling balances of the British colonies at mid-1960 (*Quarterly Digest of Colonial Statistics*, No. 47, H.M.S.O., London 1960, Table 55, pp. 62–3). It is therefore startling to read the statement that 'the foreign asset reserves held by Currency Boards, under a 100 per cent exchange standard, probably constitute the greater part, if not the whole, of official foreign exchange reserves of the country or colony' — the inaccuracy of which is scarcely corrected adequately by a footnote qualification that 'The marketing Boards and other government agencies of certain British colonies, however, also hold relatively large foreign exchange reserves'. (Birnbaum, op. cit., pp. 481–2.)

[2] Sir Roy Harrod, *The Pound Sterling*, Essays in international finance, No. 13, Princeton University Press, Princeton, New Jersey, February 1952, p. 3.

intention of giving all possible aid to such territories. Since the risk involved in currency-reserve repatriation cannot be completely eliminated, the richer countries could offer insurance against it in the manner of an insurance company insuring clients against the risk of fire or theft. The central banks of the richer countries, that is, could assist the economic development of their poorer neighbours by underwriting the risk of a 'crisis' run on their currencies which exceeds the latters' capacity for providing foreign exchange. Just as the developed countries have, in the International Monetary Fund, an institution from which they can obtain stand-by credits to meet balance-of-payments crises, so the central banks of the United Kingdom, the United States and similar countries could make available to the poorer countries of the world stand-by credit facilities which would become operative in the event of large-scale movement out of their currencies.

It is likely that little real burden would be imposed on the central banks extending such facilities; the chances are that a movement out of an 'under-developed' currency will be inspired by an attempt to obtain the currency of one of the richer countries — in all probability to obtain capital assets within those countries. The central banks giving stand-by credits would therefore be doing no more than making available to the debtor territory the monetary resources which in any case would be flowing from the citizens of that territory. Furthermore, the knowledge that such stand-by credits existed would almost inevitably prevent many psychological crises developing in the first instance. The knowledge that a policeman is on his beat may deter the criminal from the crime which he might otherwise have committed; similarly, the knowledge that the government of a territory has at its disposal a stand-by credit from a powerful foreign central bank could convince would-be refugees from its currency that flight was neither necessary nor fatally embarrassing to their monetary authorities.

This would seem to be a method by which help could be given to under-developed countries, therefore, with little or no burden on the assisting country. Such an opportunity — to assist poorer countries without undergoing any real sacrifice — is one which occurs so infrequently that it is unfortunate that advantage has not already been taken of it. The central banks of some Western countries often show a peculiar resistance to suggestions of this kind, presumably because of fears that facilities granted to one country would automatically be sought by others. The truth of the matter is, however, that just as an insurance company reduces its own risks by increasing the number it insures against any given contingency, so the central banks of the developed world would be reducing their contingent liabilities by spreading their safety-net as widely as they possibly could.

4. The status of a currency

In the preceding discussion there has been no suggestion that the repatriation of part — even a major part — of the overseas assets held against a currency previously on a sterling exchange or comparable standard would involve the creation of a new currency, or the severing of ties previously existing between a dependent territory and the richer, metropolitan country. It is often suggested that these consequences are inseparable from a movement by an under-developed territory towards monetary reforms of the kind under discussion. Thus it has been argued that if a central bank is created in a colony previously on the sterling exchange standard, it will represent not merely an addition to the monetary system but a completely and fundamentally new departure. The central bank, it is suggested, would be issuing a new currency, which would necessarily involve for the first time the problem of its relationship to foreign currencies, and hence create a convertibility problem.[1] It has also been argued that the other facilities previously obtainable in the metropolitan financial centre would be withdrawn from the territory concerned if it created its own central bank. Thus a colony repatriating its currency reserves would be threatened with the loss of its powers to borrow on the metropolitan capital market, the sacrifice of any favourable status previously given to its bonds and the loss of other comparable facilities (e.g. the Joint Colonial Fund in London).[2]

[1] I. Greaves, 'Central Banks for new Dominions', *The Banker*, Vol. CVII, No. 379, August 1957, p. 512.

[2] Greaves, 'Colonial Trade and payments', p. 57. A similar implication seems to be contained in the United Nations report *Domestic financing of economic development*, New York 1950 (1951, II, B1), pp. 22–3. So far as London is concerned, the practical significance of this threat is in any case diminishing fairly rapidly. To many colonial governments there is a distinctly antediluvian sound about such statements as 'The colonies have always been able to float their securities on the London market, and it is doubtful if the time will come when reasonable quantities of such securities will be unsaleable, provided there are the safeguards which usually attend a sound government borrowing programme and development plan'. (King, op. cit., p. 721.) A good deal depends, of course, on how the word 'reasonable' is defined.

None of this would appear to be necessary. Repatriation of some of the assets held against a colonial currency has in itself no direct bearing on the relationship between that currency and others. There is no reason, for example, why a currency previously backed 100 per cent with sterling securities but now backed as to, say, 50 per cent by local securities, should cease to be fully convertible at par into the pound sterling. There are many reasons why the territory concerned would be wise to retain its previous exchange relationship with the metropolitan area. In this respect it would be in the same position as, for example, the new Dominions included in the Sterling Area; these retain the general characteristic of having a currency freely convertible into the British pound sterling, but nevertheless possess independent and effective central banks.

The question of repatriation of currency reserves, in other words, is distinct and separate from that of changing the basis of the foreign exchange value of a currency. The same is true of the suggestion that the other facilities of the metropolitan capital market would have to be sacrificed. If such a consequence did result, it could only be because of an arbitrary decision of the metropolitan country itself; there would be no reason inherent in the changed structure of the currency system of the erstwhile dependency why such a result should necessarily follow.[1] It need hardly be added that a decision of this kind on the part of a metropolitan country would clearly be contrary to the expressed aims of the richer countries of the world to assist their poorer neighbours, and would be a proceeding fraught with risk for the stability and amicable development of the world economy.

[1] Newlyn and Rowan, op. cit., Chap. 10, p. 224.

Chapter 2

THE ROLE OF CENTRAL BANKS

1. *The purpose of central banking*

The creation of central banks in under-developed countries has been widespread in the years since the war. This is often regarded as being a sign of the desire of newly self-governing countries to assert their independence; it has been interpreted as a political rather than an economic development. Most central bankers themselves appear to be opposed to the establishment of central banks in many of these newly independent territories, ostensibly on the ground that such institutions can play no useful part in the development of the territories concerned and may indeed do much harm. This represents a reversal of opinion since the 1920's and 1930's, when central bankers tended to favour the establishment of central banks with the primary object of protecting the value of the national currency, a notable case in point being the resolution passed by the International Financial Conference at Brussels in 1920 to the effect that countries which had not already created a central bank should proceed to do so forthwith.[1] The change in attitude is explicable partly by the fact that the gold standard no longer exists — so that the maintenance of the stability of the value of money has become less of an automatic central banking function — and partly by the fact that central banks have increasingly become instruments of wider and more general economic policy, and to this extent agencies of the government.[2] In effect, the contemporary view reflects the increasing concern of bankers at the extent of political intervention in the activities of central banks.

The widespread scepticism concerning the usefulness of central banks in under-developed territories seems to have originated in the doctrine that the major function of the modern central bank is to control the overall credit situation, the object of which is

[1] M. H. de Kock, *Central banking*, 3rd ed., Staples Press, London 1954, Chap. 1, p. 19.
[2] Sayers, 'Central banking in under-developed countries', p. 110.

taken to be to prevent wide fluctuations in the level of prices; many observers fear the possibilities of serious damage to the economic system as the result of inexpert and ill-considered applications of this power. Although bankers seem to be generally antagonistic to the creation of central banks in under-developed countries, however, others are convinced that such institutions have certain limited uses in maintaining the stability of incomes and prices in the countries concerned.

It is important to note that even amongst those who are prepared to welcome the creation of central banks in under-developed countries there is still a marked tendency to visualise the role of such banks in traditional terms. The main function of a central bank is still regarded as being the control of the commercial banking system with the object of stabilising the economy. Thus, disinterested observers reach such conclusions as that 'an agile central bank can do something to moderate the swings of income, if only by checking the commercial banks in their natural tendency to accentuate the swings';[1] the usefulness of a central bank is assessed in terms of its ability to eliminate instability. Basically, therefore, such observers are retaining a traditional view of central banking.

It may indeed be true that a valuable contribution can be made by a central bank which moderates the purely monetary effects — as opposed to the broad economic effects — of balance-of-payments oscillations through the use of a statutory reserve ratio or similar techniques.[2] Nevertheless, this traditionalist approach is in danger of neglecting the possibility that the role of a central bank in an under-developed country at the present time may be fundamentally different from its role in the developed economies of Western Europe and North America. To a large extent the general view as to what is, and what is not, the proper function of a central bank has been conditioned by recent experience in the industrial economies of the world. Historically, however, the functions performed by these banks have been those which fell to them by reason of the circumstances and conditions in which they were created and in which they evolved. The older central banks in general developed at a time when the money supply was thought to be best regulated by some largely automatic mechanism, and when commercial banking — and a gradually expanding

---

[1] Sayers, ibid., p. 131.
[2] S. N. Sen, *Central banking in under-developed money markets*, Bookland Ltd., Calcutta 1952, Chap. IV, pp. 67–8.

network of other credit and financial institutions — already existed at a fairly high level of sophistication. It is natural, therefore, that the main purpose of a central bank has come to be regarded as the administration of the money supply and the regulation and supervision of a more or less adequate structure of credit institutions in the economy. Central banking is now seen as essentially the art of influencing and controlling the activities of commercial banks, the level and structure of interest rates, the activity of money and capital markets, and so on. To translate conceptions of this kind to territories in which the indigenous credit system is either non-existent or at an extremely rudimentary stage, however, is surely to be guilty of historical insensitivity.

The needs which central banks met in Western Europe and North America were the needs of developing complex credit systems; in countries where a credit system does not exist the need to be met by a central bank must be essentially and radically different. The primary requirement of the under-developed territories of the world (in the context of monetary matters) is not the regulation and control of a complicated and mature financial system, but the encouragement of long-term development in the basic sectors of the economy. Heretical though it may perhaps be held to be, it is in fact only historically sound to argue that a central bank must meet the most urgent need of the monetary situation in which it comes into existence and develops. For the under-developed territories of the world the usefulness or other- wise of a central bank must therefore be assessed first and foremost in terms of its ability to assist the process of economic growth and capital formation; the contribution it can make to the regulation, direction and guidance of such credit institutions as may exist at the time must be a secondary and lesser consideration. As has been observed in the context of colonial Africa,

> where economies are highly dependent and under-developed, a central bank should not be considered primarily as a potential stabilisation device but as a potential development agency of a rather unusual variety.[1]

2. *The functions of a new central bank*

In view of what has been said in the preceding paragraphs, it would be inadequate, and possibly misleading, to discuss the

---

[1] Newlyn and Rowan, op. cit., Chap. 10, pp. 225–6.

functions of a central bank in an under-developed economy solely
in terms of the traditional functions of the older and more familiar
type of central bank. These are well known. Amongst them are
usually included, first, the issue of currency, secondly the discharge of banking services for the government and for the
commercial banks, thirdly the preservation of the reserves of the
banking system and the external reserves of the economy as a
whole, and fourthly the provision of facilities as a lender of last
resort and the foundation of the liquidity of the financial system.[1]

Although several of these functions may be performed by the
central bank of an under-developed territory, many of them are
scarcely possible in a country with only a rudimentary credit and
banking system. Observers conscious of this limitation have
therefore drastically reduced the scope of activities which in their
view could be successfully undertaken by a central bank in such
circumstances. The more limited functions nowadays suggested
for a new central bank are thus little more than the provision of
advisory and technical services to the government — and possibly
to commercial banks — in the field of foreign exchange, the
encouragement of the growth of a sound commercial banking
system, the development of capital and money markets, and the
gradual evolution over time of techniques of monetary control
suited to the economy in which it operates.[2] Many of these
functions can be performed only to a limited degree, and their
full exercise may be achieved only slowly over a period of many
years.

It is reasonable to suppose, however, that some of the more
important traditional functions can usefully be performed by a
central bank in an under-developed economy. It is true that its
effectiveness in these matters, in the sense of its power of
independent action, may be extremely limited in the first instance.
However, no-one proposes to create a central bank merely because
of what it can perform in the next year or two; its establishment
is essentially a long-run matter in which the responsible authorities
naturally and properly look to the growth and development of its
functions over generations into the future. What it may do today
to only a limited extent is obviously not the same as what it may
be able to do in twenty or thirty years' time, given a start at the

[1] See de Kock, op. cit., Chap. I, pp. 20–5, Plumptre, op. cit., Introduction,
pp. 14–6, and Newlyn and Rowan, op. cit., Chap. 13, pp. 269–70.
[2] E.g., Sayers, ibid., pp. 114–5.

present and given the normal development of the economy over the years.

There is every reason, for example, why a newly created central bank should become the administrator of the currency issue in the traditional fashion. The moral importance of this is immense; in a developed economy the note issue is usually the only form of legal tender in existence, and it therefore constitutes the fundamental basis of the credit system. Because of this, the essential characteristic which marks off a modern central bank from all other banks, and is the foundation of its position of authority, is not its supervision of commercial banking or its role as bankers' bank[1] but its ultimate power of note issue. In most under-developed territories this power can give moral rather than practical strength, since it is admittedly the control over commercial bank reserves which counts in practice[2] and these often take the form of foreign assets rather than local currency. But the moral influence is in itself vital; the practical significance of the local currency issue, on the other hand, will increase over time as the economy develops.

A second important consideration in this connection has already been discussed at some length in the previous chapter — namely that a good deal can be done by way of financing development by relatively minor adjustments in the nature and operation of the currency system, particularly one like a sterling exchange standard currency which has previously been backed by reserves largely or wholly held in some foreign centre. It is natural and convenient that when such changes occur the old type Currency Board should be replaced by the Currency Division of a central bank. The separation of a central bank into a Currency Division and a Banking Division is one which has little justification in logic, but it may well be that the psychological needs of the investing public, or the public at large, will indicate the wisdom of retaining the traditional — and in principle meaningless — distinction between the two parts of a central bank. Although there may be no logical reason why it should be so, the confidence of the public in the soundness of a currency issue might be undermined if the assets forming the backing to the currency were no longer shown separately, and if the currency was included as merely one of the various liabilities of the central bank (which indeed it is), with

---

[1] Ibid., p. 120.   [2] Plumptre, op. cit., p. 33.

the assets corresponding to the currency issue included amongst the other assets held by the bank and indistinguishable from them.

Whether the currency assets are shown separately or not, their transfer to a central bank undoubtedly constitutes an important source of funds available to the bank for various purposes. The major functions of central bank in these circumstances are argued below to consist of, first, the (indirect) financing of long-term development within the economy and, secondly, active and positive encouragement of the growth of local capital and money markets. It would probably be advantageous from a psychological point of view if the assets held in the Currency Division of the central bank (that is to say, the assets constituting the backing to the note issue) were used for the second purpose rather than the first.

Another traditional function of the central banks of more developed economies which could usefully be taken over by a new central bank from its inception is that of acting as banker to the government itself. The central bank would normally be the executive agency of the government in managing the public debt and in arranging its transfers into and out of foreign currencies; there are obvious and important advantages in having the conduct of these matters in the hands of the same institution as that which handles the general revenue and expenditure accounts of the government. A close co-ordination of debt policy and fiscal policy is nowadays universally accepted as necessary, and this can be attained more easily and effectively by a central bank handling both the government's ordinary banking business and its transactions on capital account. An incidental advantage, which some might regard as being of considerable importance, is that this would also enable the staff of the central bank to become familiar with the processes of day-to-day banking and the handling of payments into and out of ordinary bank accounts.[1]

One aspect of this matter is that the administration of accounts as active as those of a central government — the average idle balances held in which are not likely to be very considerable — is often a fairly expensive business. It is improbable that a central bank would generally be able to acquire any but short-term assets to correspond with the balances held by it in its capacity as

[1] Sayers, ibid., p. 120.

government banker.[1] Despite this, there can be little doubt that the advantages lie with the use of the central bank as banker to the government. As will be suggested below, official banking business may be shared with commercial banks for the purposes of monetary control, but it is conducive to the maintenance of the prestige and position of the central bank if it has responsibility for the accounts of the government itself.

When the other traditional functions of a central bank are considered the outlook seems less favourable. For example, the crucial function of the orthodox central bank — on which the whole power and influence of the bank rests — is the provision of an ultimate source of liquidity in the economy. In a banking system which is largely an internal organisation concerned with payments to and receipts from other institutions within the economy, there is little difficulty in principle in establishing a note-issuing central bank as the lender of last resort and the basis upon which the entire credit system is constructed. In most under-developed territories, however, the great international banks tend to look outside the economy for their needs when a demand for liquid funds arises suddenly, and the problem of ultimate liquidity and control becomes exceedingly complex. This and other aspects of commercial banking in under-developed territories are discussed at more length in the following chapter. It is sufficient to observe here that, insofar as indigenous banks are developing, a new central bank can and will play an important part as lender of last resort; for the established, imperial banks, however, its power to play this role will inevitably be drastically limited.

It is only by drastic legislative measures that a central bank could be forcibly built into this position *vis-à-vis* the imperial banks. For example, if the international banks were forbidden to invest their funds abroad, or, alternatively, were required by legislation to hold balances with the central bank, then in a real sense a new central bank could be made into a lender of last resort. But it is idle to suppose that without measures of this fairly extreme type a new central bank could hope to

---

[1] Nevertheless, government balances do not appear to be invariably unprofitable by any means. They have been used to meet private credit needs in Syria, Iraq, and the Lebanon (Ali, op. cit., p. 63), while one writer attributed the profits made by the State Bank in the Gold Coast (now Ghana) solely to the interest on investments made possible by substantial government deposits. (J. W. Williams, 'State banking in the Gold Coast', *The Banker*, Vol. CVII, No. 374, March 1957, p. 172.)

become the centre of the credit system after the fashion of the central banks of developed economies if the commercial banking in its territory rests predominantly in the hands of large international banks. In many under-developed regions the major commercial banks are parts of international organisations whose resources — in terms of political influence, perhaps, as well as finance — are considerably greater than those of the central bank, or even the region's government itself. Hence there is little real substance in the argument that under a Currency Board system, where the great Imperial banks are concerned, 'the banks are vulnerable, for without a central bank they have nowhere to turn for help in case of need'.[1] A new central bank will be fortunate if it escapes a situation in which it finds the boot very much on the other foot.

Nevertheless (as is argued below) for reasons of control, even if this control is largely prospective rather than actual, and — more important — in the interests of the finance of development within the country, it is probable that the central banks of most under-developed territories would find it necessary to possess statutory powers by which commercial banks operating in their territory could be required to maintain deposits with it. By this means the central bank can establish a relationship with the commercial banks which has at least some similarities with the traditional position of a central bank in a developed economy. The question then arises of the use to which a central bank will be able to put these assets so long as there is any question of it acting as lender of last resort to the commercial banks, or to any other part of the credit system. As was argued in the previous chapter, the possibility of a crisis in the monetary system does not imply for a central bank — as it does for commercial banks — that a high degree of liquidity must necessarily be maintained in its assets. If the crisis in question consists of a demand for local funds, i.e. local currency, then there is no necessity for the central bank to hold liquid assets against the contingency; in fact, in such a situation the central bank will need to *expand* its assets rather than realise them, since it will be issuing currency notes, lending to commercial banks or purchasing securities in the market in order to meet the demand for liquidity on the part of the public.

[1] Exter, op. cit., p. 5. It is surely going much too far to suggest that in such a situation the establishment of a Central Bank can 'make the banking system almost invulnerable in time of crisis'. (ibid., p. 6.)

There would be no point in holding liquid assets which are convertible in some other market in order to meet such a situation. On the other hand, if the crisis were to take the form of a demand for foreign exchange, then the same considerations are likely to arise as were discussed in the previous chapter in connection with the currency issue.

3. *Central banks and commercial banking*

The general subject of commercial banking in an under-developed territory is discussed in some detail in the following chapter. It is argued there that in an economy of this kind the traditional functions and powers of central banks *vis-à-vis* commercial banks are liable to be largely, if not wholly, inappropriate. It is generally agreed that the failure to appreciate adequately the implications of the differences between the state of evolution of the United Kingdom or the United States and that of many developing countries has resulted in the establishment of unsuitable and ineffective central banks in recent years. The traditional weapons for controlling the credit basis of commercial banks — open-market-operations and the use of bank rate — were unthinkingly and slavishly adopted by central banks for which such powers were wholly inappropriate. In one country after another, remarks one writer,

> open market operations were just a dream because there was no market in which to operate. The member banks were powerful institutions; many of them were free to draw off their offices in the world's leading financial centres and never needed to go near the central bank, whose free discount rate was made completely inoperative, published in the pious hope that someone would sometimes notice what it was.[1]

In other words, the conception of a central bank as an institution which operates in the short-term money market and gives a lead to the credit system by delicate changes in its discount rate is wholly inapplicable to a developing territory in which security markets are either extremely narrow or non-existent and in which the credit basis consists not of the liabilities of the central bank but of assets held in some foreign centre.

It by no means follows from this, however, that control of the commercial banking system by a new central bank in an under-

[1] Sayers ibid., pp. 112–3.

developed territory is impossible; the means by which this may be achieved are discussed at some length in the next chapter. It is sufficient to note at this stage that the most appropriate technique adopted for eventual control over the overall level of bank credit — the statutory reserve ratio — endows the central bank with certain resources which form part of the total assets available to it for the finance of development and other purposes. On the other hand, an important function of the central bank is the indirect encouragement of development through the application of selective credit controls.

A second consideration in this context is the need for a central bank to ensure that the commercial banks operating in its territory are being conducted on a reasonably sound and prudent basis. In countries having a highly-developed commercial banking system, special legislative provision for this purpose is often unnecessary, and this will also be broadly true of branches of old-established international banks operating in under-developed territories. Where indigenous banking is at an early stage of development, however, the authorities will usually find it advisable to adopt special commercial banking legislation which is conveniently administered on their behalf by the central bank. The main instrument of control will normally be a minimum liquidity ratio, a device which historically originated as a means of protecting the interests of bank depositors but which has since been adopted in developed financial systems as a weapon of general credit control.[1] The legislation might also be extended, however, to cover minimum capital provisions, deposit-capital ratios, directors' qualifications, prohibited assets and so on.[2]

An important question which arises at this point is whether powers to prevent the emergence of unsound banking and to protect the interests of depositors in financial institutions — or, for that matter, the 'policy' powers of general and selective credit control discussed in this and the succeeding chapter — should also be made applicable to other types of financial institution, such as building societies, insurance companies, investment trusts, finance houses, credit co-operatives, savings banks and thrift and

[1] P. G. Foussek, *Foreign central banking: the instruments of monetary control*, Federal Reserve Bank of New York, New York 1957, Chap. V, p. 57.
[2] The Nigerian experience provides a good illustration of the problems which can arise in the development of indigenous banking — Rowan, 'The native banking boom in Nigeria', *The Banker*, Vol. XCVII, No. 309, October 1951.

provident societies. Such institutions are frequently incorporated under special legislation which render further supervisory measures unnecessary, while some may be, like the banks, branches of international organisations whose probity and solvency cannot be called into question. Nevertheless, some indigenous institutions in these various categories may remain or emerge in the future, and it will be important to ensure that the growth of these peripheral credit agencies takes place on a sound and healthy basis. Further, as the Radcliffe Committee has stressed in connection with recent British experience, credit controls cannot be confined to commercial banks; to be effective they must extend to those institutions which are partial substitutes for banks and which may indeed be brought into existence by the application of controls on bank credit.[1] Hence the authorities will be well advised to follow the example of, say, Israel, and empower its central bank to apply its banking controls to such other categories of financial institution as it may define from time to time.[2]

One other aspect of the relationship between central and commercial banks may be considered in some detail at this point. It is sometimes argued that a newly-established central bank would do well to undertake a limited amount of ordinary commercial banking business along with its central banking functions. In the first place it is suggested that this would have the advantage of familiarising the staff of the central bank with the routine processes of day-to-day banking, and would also enable the bank to acquire direct knowledge of, and keep in constant touch with, the general state of the economic life of the country in various regions and at all commercial levels.[3]

Secondly, and perhaps more important, it can be argued that a central bank may be able to discharge its vital function of correcting distortions and closing gaps in the existing credit system only by actively entering the market place itself. Thus, the encouragement and extension of the use of suitable credit instruments — e.g. trade bills or crop liens — may be achieved only if the central bank actually proceeds to discount them on favourable terms. Again, an undue concentration by commercial banks on highly profitable foreign exchange business to the neglect of the ordinary

[1] *Report of the Committee on the working of the monetary system,* Cmd. 827, H.M.S.O., London 1959, Chap. VI, paras. 504–11.
[2] See *Bank of Israel Law,* Bank of Israel, Jerusalem 1954, Part 13, Sec. 70.
[3] Sayers, ibid., pp. 118–9.

credit needs of the economy may be held to justify the entry of the central bank into foreign exchange business with the general public, the primary object being to reduce the profit margins on such business and encourage commercial banks to pay more attention to internal credit operations.[1] Finally, it may be thought that an inadequate supply of credit to particular sectors of the economy — e.g. agriculture or small businesses — can be corrected only by the direct provision of credit by the central bank itself.

Against these advantages must be set certain serious objections. First, since commercial banks will probably be required to maintain reserve balances with the central bank, on which little or no interest will be paid, equity requires that the central bank should not then proceed to compete against the commercial banks for their ordinary business.[2] To some extent this objection must be moderated by the consideration that the banks will derive considerable general advantage in the long run from the existence of a central bank, and it is thus only proper that they should make some contribution to its resources and its income.

More important is the objection that the pursuit of ordinary banking business may cause the central bank to lay itself open on occasion to an internal conflict between its interests as a commercial operator and its responsibilities as central bank. This is of some especial relevance in the type of economy with which this study is concerned; if the private operations in question are designed to fill gaps in the credit system, the central bank may well find itself with loans which would be peculiarly difficult to call in (or, for political reasons, peculiarly difficult to refuse) if credit contraction became necessary in the public interest.[3] Not unnaturally, in actual practice central banks are no more insensitive to the attractions of sound and profitable loans, or the unattractiveness of those with poor profit prospects, than their commercial

[1] Exter, op. cit., p. 6.
[2] Sayers, *Modern Banking*, Oxford University Press, 5th edition, London 1960, Chap. 11, p. 265, and *Domestic financing of economic development*, p. 68.
[3] Similar embarrassment may be caused in the sphere of orthodox credit control, of course. Nicaragua provides an example of a central bank finding it difficult to refuse re-discount facilities to commercial banks (when it wished to do so), because such facilities were in fact being enjoyed by its own banking department to which the public had direct access — E. Laso, 'Financial policies and credit control techniques in Central America', *I.M.F. Staff Papers*, Vol. VI, No. 3, November 1958, pp. 430–1.

D

colleagues. Observers of several central banks with commercial lending powers remark that

> it is often difficult to find any substantial differences between the lending policy of the banking department of the Central Bank and that of the private banks. In some instances the banking department has been a leading contributor to an excessive expansion of credit.[1]

At the same time it must be remembered that to some extent this argument is valid *whatever* assets, public or private, the central bank may acquire. For example, the sale or purchase of government securities at disadvantageous terms may be necessary at any time in the course of open-market operations in a developed financial system, or in the interest of stabilising or promoting local securities markets in a less developed system. Similarly, credit policy may necessitate a reduction in the central bank's overall level of assets and liabilities — with a consequent loss of earnings — at a time when its own profit position might be a delicate one. The withdrawal of a central bank from ordinary commercial business, in other words, does not relieve it entirely from this potential conflict between private and public interest; the conflict is inherent in the nature of central banking, and only a complete indifference to rates of profit can dispose of it. The absence of private business may well influence the degree of the problem: it does not dispose of it altogether.

A third objection to the conduct of ordinary banking business by the central bank, however, is much more fundamental. This is that, quite apart from the private interests of the central bank, the pursuit of competitive banking business is likely to compromise the standing of the central bank in the eyes of the commercial banks. A newly-created central bank is almost certain to be regarded with disfavour and suspicion by old-established commercial banks which have been operating in the territory concerned for many years. They will be sceptical of assurances that the aim of the newcomer is solely to serve the best public interest, and that it is in no way proposing to use its necessarily extensive statutory powers in order to damage the prospects and profitability of existing commercial banks. Nothing is more likely to lend substance to such doubts and suspicions than the endowment of a central bank with powers to compete with them for

---

[1] R. Goode and R. S. Thorn, 'Variable reserve requirements against commercial bank deposits', *I.M.F. Staff Papers*, Vol. 7, No. 1, April 1959, p. 28.

ordinary business from its position of especial strength and authority. To put it no higher, a grave risk would be run that the already difficult task of building up the moral position of a new and inexperienced institution would be rendered more difficult. The inadvisability of such a proceeding is apparent when it is remembered that the acquisition of respect and leadership by a new central bank is probably the crucial test by which it may ultimately succeed or fail; that a central bank in a territory of this kind will almost certainly

> make its influence felt more effectively through the development of day-to-day relations of confidence and understanding between itself and the various banking institutions than through the exercise of all the powers given to it. . . .[1]

Against the advantages which may accrue from the incursion of a central bank into ordinary commercial banking, therefore, must be set several disadvantages, and especially this crucially important consideration of the risk of compromising its moral position. In the circumstances of an under-developed country establishing a central bank there is a strong probability that this latter consideration will be conclusive — especially when it is remembered that there are several other courses open to a central bank seeking to achieve the advantages which may somewhat doubtfully be claimed for its entry into commercial banking.[2] The experience of routine banking practice may be gained by its staff through the operation of government accounts or by recruitment from, or secondment to, other financial institutions, including commercial banks. Distortions in the flow of credit can be filled either by statutory controls over commercial banks or by the support of official credit agencies — the creation of separate State banking agencies in competition with private commercial banks,

[1] Exter, op. cit., p. 1. See also Plumptre, op. cit., Chap. XIX, pp. 425–7. de Kock goes so far as to make the non-conduct of ordinary banking business one of the requisites of a 'real' central bank, laying stress on the importance of maintaining good relations with commercial banks — op. cit., Chap 1, pp. 22–3. At the same time, the case must not be over-stated; Libyan experience appears to suggest that it is not impossible for a central bank discharging certain heavily circumscribed commercial banking functions to retain friendly relations with the private banking system — see Chandarvarkar, op. cit., p. 8.
[2] That these disadvantages have generally been found to be conclusive in practice is shown by the fact that in recent years it has 'become increasingly accepted that central banks should not, in general, engage in ordinary commercial banking. . . .' Foussek, op. cit., Chap. II, p. 14.

for example, may well be a salutary process all round.[1] An adequate assessment of the day-to-day state of the financial system should not be impossible through the establishment of an efficient intelligence system and the normal liaison procedures of a central bank. The moral position of the bank, however, can usually be secured only if it is not merely above the market-place struggle but is clearly seen to be so.

4. Constitutional issues

An important question in the establishment of a new central bank is that of its relationship with the government. To some extent the treatment of the question is dependent on the political philosophy of those responsible for the creation of the bank; advisers inclined towards what may loosely be called right-wing views will lay heavy stress on the virtues of independence of thought and attitude in a central bank, while those of left-wing opinions will stress the inevitability of a high degree of integration between the monetary measures applied by a central bank and the levels of income and employment, for which ultimate responsibility must clearly rest with government and cannot be devolved on any independent agency.

In practice the balance of advantage would seem to lie somewhere between the two extremes, although probably closer to the official-agency position than the independent-body position. It is interesting to observe how several of the old central banks have gravitated towards this common point; thus the Bank of England, which began as a wholly private institution, has steadily evolved into a quasi-official, although independent, body, while the Commonwealth Bank of Australia, which began as a wholly state-controlled body, has tended to shift back towards a position of more independence.[2]

The rationale of this compromise solution is not difficult to see. On the one hand, governments have come to undertake an

[1] As has been shown, for example, in Ghana. The reluctance with which the innate solicitude for private banking in certain quarters is subordinated to the need to expand and invigorate the financial services of an under-developed territory, however, is very profound. A recent Colonial Office report contains the following illuminating remark: 'The Seychelles [Government Savings Bank] was able to withdraw certain quasi-commercial banking facilities following the establishment of a branch of Barclays Bank (DCO) in the colony'. (*The Colonial Territories, 1959–60*, Cmd. 1065, H.M.S.O., London 1960, para. 589, p. 98.)
[2] For a discussion of this trend towards 'nationalised' central banking see Sir Theodore Gregory, *The present position of central banks* (The Stamp Memorial Lecture, 1955), University of London, The Athlone Press, London 1955, pp. 7–12.

increasing degree of responsibility for the level of employment —
and thus for the levels of prices, income and output — and a
parallel narrowing of the freedom of action which could be allowed
to a central bank has inevitably occurred. In the words of the
Radcliffe Report,

> monetary policy, as we have conceived it, cannot be envisaged as a
> form of economic strategy which pursues its own independent
> objectives. It is part of the country's economic policy as a whole,
> and must be planned as such. . . . It follows that this policy, whatever
> form it may take from time to time, must include the general planning
> of monetary policy and monetary operations and that the policies to
> be pursued by the central bank must be from first to last in harmony
> with those avowed and defended by Ministers of the Crown respon-
> sible to Parliament.[1]

On the other hand, most of the day-to-day operations of the bank
— the tactics, as opposed to the strategy, of monetary policy —
while not of a policy-making nature are nevertheless of a highly
specialised and technical kind, so that the official government
machine is suited neither by the training of its personnel nor by
its procedural arrangements to discharge them effectively.[2] Nor
can a central bank without a minimum degree of independence
hope to operate effectively in the private financial sphere — 'It
must enjoy prestige, and it must have real powers, otherwise it
will not enjoy prestige'.[3]

A compromise is therefore indicated, with the central bank
operating as an independent corporation so far as its staffing,
administration and day-to-day policy are concerned, but with
ultimate control for its broad strategy firmly and clearly vested in
the government. This control is most unambiguously achieved by
the authorities if the majority of the bank's equity capital is
contributed from public funds; at the same time, this does not
preclude either the participation of private investors in financing
the bank or the appointment of a Board of Directors — and
especially a Governor — capable of formulating and advocating
policy measures as well as administering them.[4] While it would
be true to say that the directors of such a bank are 'more likely

---

[1] *Report of the Committee on the working of the monetary system*, Cmd. 827,
H.M.S.O., London 1959, Chap. IX, para. 767.
[2] Exter, op. cit., p. 13. [3] Gregory, op. cit., p. 19.
[4] Nor, conversely, does this exclude the possibility of having high-level
official representation on a predominantly independent Board of Directors.

to act as a shock-absorber than as a steering gear',[1] it is also important to remember that the recruitment of really able people to the Board of Directors, and the acquisition by the bank of status and prestige in the financial world, will depend to a large degree on the extent to which the governing body of the bank is able to express its independence, and on the seriousness with which its recommendations, whatever they may be, are treated by the government of the day.

All this raises a difficult and crucially important problem of balancing independence against effective responsibility. In the particular circumstances of an under-developed economy, of course, there is the additional consideration that capital for a central bank is not likely to be forthcoming on an adequate scale from private sources in the first instance. In its nature a new central bank cannot promise to make large profits,[2] and will therefore have relatively little appeal for the ordinary investor. There might indeed be a case for persuading commercial banks to subscribe to the capital of a central bank in these circumstances but unless the banks are to be allowed a voice in the policy of the central bank — a patently unlikely supposition — they would hardly be willing to make the investment voluntarily. A compulsory investment of bank funds in the capital of a central bank, on the other hand, would certainly be a procedure which would augur ill for the future relationship between central and commercial banks.

There is one other aspect of the constitutional position of a central bank which is of some practical and psychological importance in an under-developed territory. As has already been remarked, a newly-established central bank must expect to be the object of some suspicion by the commercial banks operating in its territory, particularly as regards its intentions towards themselves. It is also likely to face suspicions on the part of the wider financial and investing world concerning the intentions of present and future governments with regard to the monetary stability of the territory. Not without some reason in view of past experience, a substantial element of the investing population both inside and outside the territory concerned is liable to visualise a new central bank as an engine of credit-creation for governments seeking to

---

[1] Plumptre, op. cit., p. 29.
[2] Except possibly through the currency issue, in the context of which private capital participation scarcely arises.

escape the irksome limitations on spending imposed by the need to raise corresponding revenues — 'the milch cow of an improvident Government'.[1] A chain reaction of deficit budgets, central bank lending, currency expansion, inflation and monetary anarchy is therefore conjured up; serious repercussions can obviously follow on the propensity to invest in the territory in question.[2]

However unjustified such suspicions may be in a particular case, the designers of a new central bank would probably do well to pay homage to it by writing into the bank's charter provisions designed to give assurance that such a role will not be played by the new institution. The potential danger of the suspicion is so great that it is not enough to merely ignore it; in any case, a prudent and responsible administration will have no intention of abusing its central bank and will therefore suffer no real loss by declaring such abuse to be illegal. The provisions in the charters of many recent banks prohibiting the extension of central bank credit to the government except within specified and usually fairly narrow limits are therefore justified abundantly by considerations of expediency, however pointless they may be in principle.[3]

[1] 'Ceylon's central banking experiment', *The Banker*, July 1950, p. 38.

[2] This is especially important, remarks one observer, in the under-developed territories crying out for capital expenditure; 'here the central bankers must be ready to fight hard for the distinction between capital and money' (R. S. Sayers, *Banking in the British Commonwealth*, Oxford University Press, London 1952, Introduction, p. xvi). It would be seriously mistaken to draw from this statement, however, the inference that the ability to make (or fight for) the distinction in question is a prerogative of central bankers in these territories. This inference seems to be present in the suggestion that if a central bank is established immediately after political independence, rather than some time before it, the result will be 'the familiar and disastrous confusion between the ability to create money and the ability to create capital'. (Newlyn and Rowan, op. cit., Chap. 13, p. 279.) A report of the O.E.E.C. indeed, has not only described the distinction between 'capital' and 'credit' as frequently illusory, but has remarked on the fact that it is by no means always recognised by 'practising bankers' — *The supply of capital funds for industrial development in Europe*, quoted by W. Diamond, *Development Banks*, Economic Development Institute, John Hopkins Press, Baltimore 1957, p. 8.

[3] For example, the Central Bank of Ghana is permitted by its constitution to extend credit to the government only to a maximum of 10 per cent of the government's expected revenue for the year in question, and such credit has to be extinguished by the end of the same financial year; the constitution of the Central Bank of Ceylon contains a similar limitation, except that loans to the government must be repaid within six months; the Central Bank of Rhodesia and Nyasaland is limited by its constitution in its government lending to a maximum of 20 per cent of the government's estimated revenue for the year, such lending having to be repaid within three months of the end of that year; the Central Bank of Israel may lend up to 20 per cent of budget revenue, but the advances must be repaid by the end of the financial year in which they are made. For details of restrictions in other countries see Foussek, op. cit., Chap. III, p. 32.

It is obvious that legal provisions in themselves can ultimately give no real protection to investors against the abuse of a central bank's powers. No sovereign government can bind its successors; what has been written in one law can always be changed, or eliminated, by another. In the last resort, investors have to rely only on the good sense and probity of the government of a territory and on nothing else; solvency and sound finance cannot be provided by statute. As one commentator has observed 'Nothing except the good judgement of the central bank and wise abstention on the part of the government can provide an adequate safeguard against the deliberate misuse of central bank credit'.[1] At the same time, it is seldom easy to change laws quickly; legislative provisions do at least give the cautious investor the assurance that matters can be changed only after the (usually cumbrous) process of legislative enactment has been duly observed — with all its publicity, debate and opportunity for pressure, protest and perhaps escape. This is as much as any investor, anywhere, can reasonably hope for in an unstable and uncertain world.

5. *Conclusion*

Assuming the existence of a central bank with the general features described in the preceding sections, what exactly will be its role in assisting economic development? It was emphasised at an earlier stage that it is according to the answer to this type of question, rather than in relation to the sophisticated techniques and functions of old-established central banks, that the usefulness of the institution will primarily be judged in the environment of an under-developed territory. The answer is best set out under three headings — first, the direct finance of development, secondly its indirect finance, and thirdly the provision of what might be called the financial infrastructure of development.

The various means by which the central bank may contribute directly to development have already been examined. The resources at its disposal will comprise, first, its own capital and

---

[1] Sen, op. cit., Chap. IV, p. 72. In actual fact restrictions of this sort proved to be contrary to the best public interest in New Zealand, the Netherlands, India, Switzerland, South Africa and Canada and had to be relaxed subsequently — de Kock, op. cit., Chap. XII, pp. 210–1, and Foussek, op. cit., Chap. III, p. 32.

such undistributed profits as it may accumulate; the greater part of this is likely to take the form of a budgetary allocation, and its magnitude will therefore depend on the government's fiscal position. It is not impossible, however, that loan capital will be attracted into the bank from private sources after the course of time, since a successful institution will display what could be a formidable combination of government-guaranteed status and independence of administration. Secondly, the bank will have at its disposal the investible portion of the currency backing — a source of funds which will probably expand from year to year. Finally, it will have command over any commercial bank deposits required for the observance of the reserve ratio regulations referred to briefly above and discussed at some length in the following chapter. The sum total of these various contributions to its resources may not be immense, but they are unlikely to be trivial.

The use of these resources will naturally be subject to certain reservations. In the first place, long-term development projects will not represent the only claimant on the bank's funds. If it is to gradually move towards a position in which it acts as lender of last resort to the commercial banks — although it has been stressed that this situation cannot be effectively established for many years so far as the great expatriate banks are concerned — a certain proportion of its assets will need to be held externally in order to guard against contingencies involving an external drain of funds. (The adoption of the system of stand-by credits referred to in the previous chapter, however, would much reduce the need for liquidity under this heading.) Again, if the central bank is to play its proper role in encouraging the development of local money and capital markets it will certainly need to hold resources in a relatively liquid form so as to conduct the security operations necessary to establish and preserve a smoothly-functioning market mechanism. Finally, as banker to the government it will need to be able to make short-term advances for the normal and desirable financing of temporary deficits.

A second point requiring emphasis is that the resources available to the bank will by no means wholly represent a net addition to the supply of capital funds available to the economy. To the extent that resources are drawn from budgetary allocations or currency reserves, the bank will merely be administering funds which would in any case have been available to the authorities, at least in principle. Some (conceivably, but improbably, all) of the funds obtained by commercial bank reserve deposits would also have been invested within the economy. It does not follow that no advantage is gained by having these funds channelled into a central bank, however. The advantages arising from having a number of relatively small streams of investible funds channelled into a single institution are too well known to require repetition here; many things become possible with a single magnitude which would have been impossible (or at least improbable) so long as its component parts remained individual and uncoordinated entities. Administration through a central institution does at least facilitate the allocation of official capital funds between sectors on a rational and consistent basis.

Thirdly, the description of this part of the bank's role as 'direct finance of development' is perhaps somewhat misleading in that there are formidable objections to the detailed administration of individual loans by a central bank. Its staff will scarcely have the expertise involved in the management of industrial or agriculture credit; the type of assets acquired in such lending would not always be appropriate to the type of liabilities incurred by a central bank; day-to-day participation in lending transactions might well convey a suggestion that it was competing with the commercial banks for ordinary banking business, the serious disadvantages of which have already been stressed. Hence the channelling of funds by a central bank into development would most conveniently take the form of the purchase of securities issued by, or advances to, specialised official lending agencies of the type described in Chapter 4 below.[1] Funds will still be channelled directly into economic development, but the assets obtained in the process, having gilt-edged standing, will be of a kind more suited to a central bank. The bank can still discharge its important function of securing a proper allocation of official capital funds through its decisions concerning the volume of credit to be channelled to the various lending institutions, and the proportion of available funds to be used in this way rather than on the other responsibilities with which the bank is charged.

[1] See also Diamond, op. cit., p. 64.

What may be called the indirect finance of development can be summarised under two headings. First, by the deployment of selective credit controls over commercial banks — and possibly other lending institutions — the bank can attempt to influence the pattern of private lending in the way which it believes to be in the best interests of the community. Secondly, it is possible that the bank will be able to assist development finance institutions through its guarantees to attract external capital more easily and on better terms than would be possible for the sponsors of the several individual projects seeking finance.[1]

Finally, a central bank can play a vital role — and perhaps it is the only type of institution which can undertake it — in building up the financial infrastructure of future economic development. The creation of local money and capital markets is an obvious and important activity under this heading. Another is the administration of any necessary measures to ensure the soundness of commercial banking in its area, and perhaps the development of indigenous banking. A third is the use of its controlling powers to moderate the credit swings associated with balance-of-payments oscillations in under-developed territories, to which so many observers have called attention.[2] A fourth is the establishment of an expert and objective intelligence service seeking out and publicising data on the important variables in the economic system; without continued and informed research of this kind the formulation of intelligent policy, whether public or private, is scarcely possible.

The role of a central bank in an under-developed economy is therefore an extensive and complex one. The fact that it has neither the means nor the opportunity for the marginal delicacies of discount rates and open-market-operations is scarcely relevant; such refinements are appropriate only to an economy which has reached the point at which growth becomes dependent primarily on indigenous and cumulative factors. Its major task is of a more direct and basic kind during the long years before the point of

---

[1] It is worth noting that the literature circulated by the United States government to prospective borrowers concerning its Development Loan Fund makes clear that an application for a single loan to a development bank of some kind, for subsequent allocation amongst a number of separate projects, would be much better received than a multiplicity of small applications amounting in total to the same value.

[2] Exter, op. cit., p. 5; Sayers, 'Central banking in under-developed countries', p. 131; Sen, op. cit., Chap. 4, pp. 67–8; Guneskera, op. cit., p. 150.

maturity is attained. And it is difficult to resist the conclusion that the contribution it can make during that intervening phase may be considerably more substantial and long-lived than any it will make after that phase has ended.

Chapter 3

COMMERCIAL BANKING

1. *The nature of colonial banking*

In some respects, the organisation of commercial banking in many under-developed territories has effects similar to those of the colonial currency system. The greater part of commercial banking in such territories frequently rests in the hands of expatriate international banking organisations with head offices outside the region concerned. Just as the sterling exchange currency system has had the effect of making a colonial territory part of the monetary system of the metropolitan country, so the organisation of commercial banking in these territories has operated as if they were in fact part of the metropolitan area; the banks operating in them have been branches in a position fundamentally identical with that of branches of the same banks in the home country itself. As one writer has observed of the colonial banking system,

> There is no reason to assume that the head offices operate their branches as independent units working to any rigid rules regarding cash or liquidity ratios. Their management is probably more akin to that of a branch bank operating in the same country as the head offices.[1]

Another commentator has likened a bank operating in the territory then known as the Gold Coast to a branch operating in a residential London suburb 'where the local branch — because the local demand for loans is limited — accumulates excess funds which are transferred to, and loaned out by, more active branches'.[2] The whole effect of international banking administration in colonial territories has been to integrate the latter into the branch banking system of the metropolitan country.[3]

Except when required to do so by local legislation, therefore, until the recent past at least, the expatriate banks operating in colonial territories have not regarded those territories as separate

[1] Guneskera, op. cit., p. 146.   [2] Katz, op. cit., p. 289.
[3] W. T. Newlyn, 'The Colonial Empire', *Banking in the British Commonwealth* (ed. R. S. Sayers), Oxford University Press, London 1952, Chap. 13, pp. 436–8; Greaves, *Colonial monetary conditions*, Chap. 3; Bell, op. cit., Chap I.

areas so far as their banking operations were concerned. The banks have operated as single international entities; the deposits acquired in the territories in which each functions have been shown collectively on a single balance sheet, and assets have been acquired against those liabilities without regard to the location of origin of the deposits which were being applied. During the past few years some signs of change have been visible in this respect; individual banks have been showing rather more regard to the needs of the particular territories in which their deposits originate before remitting funds elsewhere. Nevertheless the position remains substantially that British colonial banks, for example, operate as branches of their head office in the same way as branches of a similar bank would operate in a particular county of Great Britain.

One result of this has been that the policy adopted by the expatriate banks in colonial territories has been determined by their head offices primarily with regard to monetary conditions prevailing in the country in which the head office was situated. That is to say, if interest rates were raised in, say, the United Kingdom as a result of a rise in Bank rate and the usual accompanying measures, interest rates would be raised more or less equally by all the branches of that bank operating throughout the world, without any special reference to the needs or circumstances of the individual overseas territories involved. Similarly, the total volume of business undertaken in any particular territory by one of the expatriate banks would be determined by decisions in its head office, and would have no necessary connection with the demand for credit, or the state of output and employment, in the overseas territory. It should be emphasised that this has not been a wholly disadvantageous situation from the point of view of the under-developed areas. Integration into the money market of richer countries has implied that a benefit was felt in the form of generally lower interest rates than would have prevailed if the under-developed countries, with a capital situation in a state of famine rather than shortage, had found themselves in a position of financial isolation.[1] Their economic growth could not hope to

[1] A point not given due weight by most critics of the expatriate banking system — but see U Tun Wai, 'Interest rates in the organised money markets of under-developed countries', *I.M.F. Staff Papers*, Vol. V, No. 2, August 1956, p. 265. Commercial banks operating in French colonies have also been able to lend at longer term than would otherwise have been possible because of their ability to rediscount medium-term paper through the facilities of the metropolitan money market — see Hanson, op. cit., Chap. III, p. 64.

prosper, however, so long as the flow of credit to them ebbs and flows in sympathy with conditions prevailing in distant, and very different, metropolitan areas.

A second feature of commercial banking in under-developed territories as carried out by the international banks has been that — again until recently — they have tended to concentrate their local lending on the expatriate industries operating in the territories concerned — usually those involved in the cultivation and export of primary products — and have also laid stress on the business of foreign exchange transactions, especially between the currency of the local territory and sterling or, occasionally, other currencies.[1] That this has been so is hardly surprising, since the commercial banks were originally drawn to these territories by the attraction of the business to be obtained from the expatriate enterprises being set up in them, and for which the colonisation of the territory was in the first instance undertaken. Further, it has been true until relatively recently that for all practical purposes the only major industrial activity in these territories — that is to say, the only productive processes involving the use of bank facilities — has been that carried on by these large expatriate enterprises. Indigenous industries, apart from small-scale crafts for which bank credit was often neither required nor appropriate, scarcely existed until recent times.

In general, it would appear that the extension of commercial banking activities has not kept pace with the potential growth of local manufacturing industries in these areas; by and large the main fields in which credit is extended by the international banks has continued to be commerce and the expatriate exporting enterprises. Further, so far as securities are concerned, the expatriate banks have in general shown little inclination to use funds for the purchase of local issues. The volume of such securities

---

[1] Hazlewood, 'The economics of colonial monetary arrangements', Sec. VI; I. G. Patel, 'Selective credit controls in under-developed economies', *I.M.F. Staff Papers*, Vol. 1, No. 4, September 1954, p. 73; J. H. Adler, 'The fiscal and monetary implementation of development programs', *American Economic Review* (Papers and Proceedings), Vol. XLII, No. 2, May 1952, p. 595; Hawkins, op. cit., pp. 339–40 and 343; Katz, op. cit., pp. 291–2; E. Laso, 'Financial policies and credit control techniques in Central America', *I.M.F. Staff Papers*, Vol. VI, No. 3, November 1958, p. 433; Silcock, op. cit., Chap. 2, p. 102; Rowan, op. cit., p. 166; Ali, op. cit., pp. 53 and 60; Williams, op. cit., p. 172; *Domestic financing of economic development*, p. 60, fn. 33, pp. 104, 115, 188. Dr. Ida Greaves dissents from this general view, but her judgement seems to have been largely based on conversations with bank managers and 'the business community' — 'Colonial trade and payments', pp. 47–8.

has not been large, of course, and their marketability has not been great; to a large extent, however, this is a circular situation — the lack of interest on the part of the banks in local securities has discouraged their use, resulting in a small volume and restricted marketability so limiting the banks' interest in them still further.

Once again it would not be accurate to make this point without simultaneously noting the signs of policy changes in recent years. Several of the great international banks have established development corporations as subsidiaries in the past decade, for example, for the specific purpose of making long-term loans to indigenous industries in overseas territories in which they operate. The modest dimensions which the activities of such corporations have attained indicates that policies and conventions may still be inappropriate to the circumstances of most of the territories involved, but the acceptance of the principle is a welcome development. Another example of the changed approach was provided by the recent appointment of Nigerian directors to the board of Barclays D.C.O. with the object of assisting the branches of that bank within the Federation of Nigeria in meeting the region's needs.

A third important feature of the policy of the expatriate banks has been the retention in overseas territories of conventions and standards to which the banks had become accustomed in their native countries and which they exported to the overseas territories in the same way as the colonisers exported their currency and their capital.[1] Again, this is not surprising in view of the fact that until recently these banks regarded themselves as concerned primarily with the finance of expatriate enterprises, usually from their own country. It was no doubt appropriate to apply to such enterprises more or less the same type of treatment, and to require the same credit standards, as would have been required if both the bank and the enterprises were operating within their native country.

The application of similar conventions and habits to local enterprises in under-developed territories, however, is a fundamentally different proposition, and one which is difficult to defend. In general, few local enterprises are able to conform to the standards of credit-worthiness, or to provide the type of collateral security, which banks would be entitled and accustomed to demand in the

---

[1] Guneskera, op. cit., p. 153; *Domestic financing of economic development*, p. 62; Diamond, op. cit., p. 13.

more highly developed industrial economies.[1] The local industries are almost invariably small scale, and their ability to provide conventional security is often strictly limited. The absence of a formal system of legal title to land in particular often renders it extremely difficult for a farmer in an under-developed territory to produce the mortgage security which would be common in a more developed economy with a highly formalised system of land tenure.[2] Further, the predominant need of such industries would be for relatively long-term, or certainly medium-term, capital of the type which industry in a developed economy would normally expect to raise on the capital market or from long-term lending institutions. The restriction of bank lending to working capital requirements which is customary in, say, the United Kingdom would be peculiarly unfortunate in the light of the needs and nature of the industries struggling to establish themselves in under-developed territories where no long-term capital market exists.

In other words, the local industries and agricultural organisations with which the expatriate bank needs to be dealing in territories of this kind would be essentially similar to the type of borrower which such banks would have encountered in their home territories in the eighteenth or nineteenth centuries. Unfortunately, the banks have tended to apply to such borrowers the conventions which they are adopting, and the standards they are requiring, in the second half of the twentieth century, rather than those they would have applied in the nineteenth. There is general agreement that as a result the needs of the large expatriate exporting and trading concerns have been more or less adequately met by the commercial banking system in colonial territories while there has been a distinct lack of credit of the appropriate kind, and on suitable terms, available from the banking system to locally developing industry.

The broad result of all these features of colonial banking — the integration of all branches of the bank into a single unit administered from head office, the concentration of credit on expatriate

[1] See Newlyn and Rowan, *Money and banking in British Colonial Africa*, Chap. 10, pp. 211-9, Guneskera, 'Banking arrangements in Ceylon', *Banking in the British Commonwealth*, pp. 407-8, Rowan, op. cit., p. 167, and 'The native banking boom in Nigeria', *The Banker*, Vol. XCVII, No. 309, October 1951, pp. 244-5, Williams, op. cit., p. 172.
[2] *Domestic financing of economic development*, p. 83; U Tun Wai, 'Interest rates outside the organised money markets of under-developed countries'; *I.M.F. Staff Papers*, Vol. VI, No. 1, November 1957, p. 88.

E

primary-producing or trading enterprises, the application of conventions and standards exported from the home country — was at least until quite recent years an inadequate rate of expansion of credit for new development in most dependent territories. The banking system had the effect of channelling funds away from

Table III: COMMERCIAL BANKS OPERATING IN
BRITISH COLONIAL TERRITORIES [a]

£ million

	End of year					
	1954	1955	1956	1957	1958	1959
LOCAL LIABILITIES						
Deposits - - -	433	392	403	457	493	529
Other [b] - - - -	113	121	132	107	136	150
TOTAL - - - -	546	513	535	564	629	679
LOCAL ASSETS						
Loans and advances -	183	209	225	256	262	297
Other [c] - - - -	187	152	173	185	224	242
TOTAL - - - -	370	361	398	441	486	539
Total as % of local liabilities - - -	68	70	74	78	77	79

[a] Excludes Hong Kong, Falkland Islands, St. Helena, Seychelles, Western Pacific H.C. territories, North Borneo, Brunei, Sarawak, and Somaliland Protectorate.
[b] Mainly amounts due to other local banks and currency issues. In the territories covered by the table, this latter item is very small.
[c] Mainly cash on hand, balances due from other local banks and securities. Insofar as the latter include non-local issues (e.g. British Government securities) the total for local assets is over-stated; the volume of such holdings, however, is not believed to be very significant.
SOURCES: As for column (2) of Table II.

local industrial development and towards the country in which the banks' head offices are located.[1] The limited outlets resulting from the concentration on expatriate enterprises, the rigorous credit standards, the disinclination to take up locally-issued securities — all inevitably implied that as deposits rose there was a surplus of funds

[1] As Newlyn puts it, *'given the banks' lending policy,* the investment opportunities for banking funds are not equal to the supply of such funds, and the surplus which arises has perforce to be employed outside the colonies' — 'The Colonial Empire', *Banking in the British Commonwealth,* Chap. 13, p. 438. (Italics added.) See also A. Hazlewood, 'Central banking in Nigeria', *The Bankers' Magazine,* Vol. CLXXXVI, No. 1373, August 1958, p. 115.

in some territories which the bank proceeded to repatriate to their head office or the money markets of their native countries.

Many colonies were therefore at one stage in the position of credit-exporting areas as a result of the peculiar organisation and attitude of the commercial banking system.[1] The data set out in Table III provide evidence of the extent to which this process had been carried in British colonies until recently, and also of the progress which has been made towards a correction of the position by the banks themselves in the past five or six years. At the end of 1954, more than 30 per cent of the funds collected by the commerical banks over the British colonies as a whole had been remitted out of the colonial territories, almost wholly to London head offices or money market. By the end of 1959 the proportion had fallen to little over 20 per cent, although it will be observed that most of the reduction occurred during 1955–7, little change being visible during 1958–9. Although the drain of new funds from poor to rich through the banking system has been reversed in recentyears, therefore, the colonies remain, so to speak, net losers. At the end of 1959 the assets held in the British colonial territories by the commercial banks still amounted to some £140 million less than their liabilities in the same territories.

This is surely a paradoxical and undesirable situation. Underdeveloped territories are by definition in need of large amounts of capital for basic development, and almost all of them make great efforts to raise loans from foreign sources because of the inadequacy of the supply of savings within their own locality. For a banking system operating in such a situation to have had the effect of funnelling savings into relatively wealthy and well-established enterprises, and even out of the economy towards the richer countries from which they originated, is clearly a reversal of the natural order of things — and of the state of affairs which is essential if the development of overseas territories is to be encouraged and accelerated.[2]

[1] Not only colonies — the 1950 United Nations report *Domestic financing of economic development* observed the same phenomenon in Egypt, Mexico, and Haiti (p. 65, fn. 39). It is scarcely coincidental that a recent study of capital flows within the sterling area in the post-war years reveals that the broad pattern has been 'perverse' — i.e. towards countries at a high level of development rather than those whose need was greatest. See A. R. Conan, *Capital imports into sterling countries*, Macmillan, London 1960, Chap. I, p. 37.
[2] It is surely complacency to argue that in dependent territories there is a 'cross-flow of capital, which usually results in a net inflow into the underdeveloped areas' (*Domestic financing of economic development*, United Nations,

As with the currency system, however, it would be inaccurate and unfair to omit reference to the immense benefits which these territories have secured through their possession of a commercial banking system which has established and retained extremely high standards so far as stability, integrity and safety are concerned. It is by no means obvious that if the international banks had never operated in these countries any really adequate local banking would have emerged instead; local banking in many of them has had an unhappy history of improvident operation and inefficient administration which has ultimately resulted in bank failures and has scarcely been conducive to confidence in banks and banking on the part of the local population. The expatriate banks, by contrast, can point to a long history of reputable and completely dependable banking; consequently, the habit of banking has become established, and a tradition of integrity and efficiency has been built up which will serve these territories well in the years ahead.

This is a fact of immense importance; just as the long record of currency stability is one from which the overseas territories will continue to benefit in the future, so the tradition of sound and efficient banking, and of complete safety and honesty in the administration of deposited funds, is one which could hardly have developed in such territories without the operation of the expatriate banks, and one which will be of great importance in the future.[1] These are highly significant gains from the existence of expatriate banking, and they constitute a substantial offset to the disadvantages which have been outlined in the preceding discussion. The true position with expatriate banking is not that it has been innately unsuitable and disadvantageous to the territories in which it has operated. A more accurate statement of the truth is that the under-developed territories have gained immensely from the operations of these banks, but now seek to alter to some degree the nature of their policies, primarily because the territories themselves have moved to a different stage of economic development. This is a fact which many of the expatriate banks have

New York 1950, p. 22). There is no evidence for supposing that the funds invested in the dependent territories are necessarily connected with the funds which the banking system has busily exported, and unless some such connection can be established the fact must remain that the potential supply of development capital to the under-developed areas is being unnecessarily restricted.

[1] Another point not always given due weight by writers on the expatriate banking system — for an exception see Ali, op. cit., p. 57.

shown rather too little inclination to appreciate despite the changes which many of them have made in recent years; hence most of have been over-reluctant to adjust their practices and policies accordingly.

2. *The implications of political independence*

While a territory remains a colonial extension of a metropolitan country, with no substantial control over its own affairs and no machinery for the formulation of its own political and economic policy, the system of colonial banking was a logical and consistent adaptation in the financial and monetary sphere of the state of affairs prevailing in the political sphere. Without internal self-government, and without a separate and distinct economic policy, a colonial territory has little need of a self-contained, controllable commercial banking system of the kind familiar in most developed economies. The imperial country tends to regard its colony, from an economic point of view, primarily as a source of foodstuffs or raw materials and as an outlet for its own exports. A commercial banking system which concerns itself primarily with the credit needs of expatriate exporting enterprises in these territories, and with the finance of foreign trade, is therefore not merely sufficient but wholly consistent with the underlying economic relationship.

With a movement towards self-government, however, the needs and position of the economy are fundamentally altered. The mere maintenance of supplies of raw materials and foodstuffs to another country, and of a market for imports, cease to constitute an adequate economic policy for the region; the needs of the metropolitan country now become subordinate to those of the dependent territory itself. Given the poverty of most of them, the emphasis in economic policy is of necessity shifted towards the development of agriculture and industry within the territory itself, and the raising of the incomes of its own population. This is not to say, of course, that the export industries cease to be of importance; for many years to come, perhaps permanently, those industries will be an important and even fundamental element in the economic system. Nevertheless, the shift in policy is clear and unambiguous; the needs of the whole population, both as producers and as consumers, now enter into economic policy in their own right, and indeed become the predominant consideration. Inevitably, therefore, a banking system which is of its nature geared to the original colonial-type economic policy becomes inadequate and unsatisfactory.

The first feature of the colonial banking system which must of necessity be altered is its complete integration with an overseas head office and its inability to formulate or administer a specific policy for the territory in which it is operating. It is not merely that the banking system must adopt new policies. The whole point is that the commercial banks in a territory must for the first time develop a policy peculiar to that territory; this may or may not be consistent with the policy which its head office would otherwise have adopted for the operations of all its branches. So long as the banks are acting merely as branches of an international organisation, and have no policy-making machinery other than their head offices — which are in no way subject to the government of a particular territory — the integration of the banks into an economy's development policy is clearly impossible. In order to ensure this integration, the chain of policy control from an overseas head office must be broken, or at least modified to whatever extent is necessary to this end.

No modern government is able to abdicate from its responsibility for the maintenance of such stability as is attainable or, in the particular context of under-developed territories, from its responsibility for stimulating rapid economic development. Further, no government charged with such responsibility can tolerate the presence within its country of economic influences as fundamental as those of a modern banking system which are not consistent with the policy it is attempting to follow, whether that policy be wise or otherwise as judged by some outside standard. Commercial banks operating in the economically advanced countries do not expect to be able to pursue whatever policy they wish, regardless of its compatibility or incompatibility with the economic and monetary policy of the government of the day. And they can scarcely demand in under-developed countries a degree of freedom and power which they would not dream of expecting in their own country. The extension of some measure of control over the policy adopted by the branches of a bank operating in an under-developed territory is therefore inevitable, and indeed only logical, once that territory has been granted any effective measure of self-government.

The second, and related, feature of the commercial banking system operating in most under-developed countries which must inevitably disappear as those territories draw up economic development policies of their own is the external investment of accumulated funds in the way described in the preceding section. So long as the territory had no independent policy of its own, but merely existed as a dependency in all senses of the word, it was largely a matter of indifference that the savings of its own people were being invested abroad rather than within its own borders. With the assumption of responsibility for economic development by the government of the territory, however, the existence of a mechanism by which funds originating within the territory are in fact used abroad — despite the overwhelming need for every possible source of capital finance which would exist in the territory — is clearly inconsistent with governmental responsibility for the achievement of the maximum possible rate of economic growth.

Apart from the question of the formulation of banking policy, therefore, the acquisition of responsibility by the government of an under-developed territory for its own economic development implies a duty to attain the maximum rate of capital formation, and therefore of savings. The exploitation of all sources of internal and external finance available to it will thus be one of its primary tasks. It would not be reasonable to expect such governments to continue borrowing from abroad — at relatively high rates of interest — investible funds which have in fact originated within their own territories, been deposited in their own banks (at low rates of interest) and then transferred abroad. The tendency of the expatriate banking system to hold abroad funds which originated in undeveloped territories is scarcely consistent with internal responsibility for economic development in those territories.

The third feature of the banking system which needs to be changed with the devolution of responsibility for policy to an under-developed territory is the concentration of credit facilities on expatriate and trading enterprises. Independent policy implies a programme of development for agriculture and industry, designed to provide for the needs of the whole population rather than for those of an imperial power only. Once this is being pursued, it is hardly possible for commercial banks to continue to concentrate their credit almost wholly on the expatriate exporting sector or on the finance of wholesale and retail trade. Necessarily, the banking system will be a major instrument for transferring funds from the saving public to investment in different sectors of the economy; it would be inconsistent with a general development programme if the financial mechanism — by which the programme must be applied in practice — is operating in a direction different from the priorities laid down by the government's economic policy. In a monetary economy, the allocation of resources between sectors depends on the acquisition of funds by producers in the sectors concerned; it would be futile for the government of a territory to draw up a development programme which implied that resources were to be allocated in a particular way if it did not ensure, at the same time, that financial resources were distributed according to a corresponding pattern. The financial system, therefore, is intimately bound up with the general programme of economic development desired by a government; it is inevitable that measures should be adopted to ensure that the banks are so employing their monetary resources as to ensure an allocation of physical resources which is in accordance with that programme.

3. The overall volume of bank credit

Since it is necessary for commercial banking in under-developed territories to change in these various ways as each territory moves towards a position of self-government, it is relevant to consider the means by which the alterations may be secured in the first instance and maintained with the passage of time. It is clear that the usual control devices established and developed in the advanced economies of Western Europe and America are inappropriate and ineffective in the environment of an under-developed economy — an economy under-developed not only in terms of output but also in terms of financial institutions. The primary mechanism of orthodox banking control in the Western world — the use of open-market-operations by the central bank to control the banks' cash reserves — has little or no applicability in an economy which has no developed money market or securities exchange. Open-market-operations achieve the control of cash reserves by the sale of securities in a competitive securities market, and in most under-developed economies no such markets exist. Even where they do exist, they are too narrow to withstand severe oscillations of prices, so that any aggressive selling or purchasing by the authorities would have highly injurious effects on the marketability of securities in that economy; it would in fact create a serious risk of fatally damaging the market itself.[1]

It does not necessarily follow from this that the technique of controlling commercial banks by operating on their cash reserves is not available at all to an economy having no highly developed money market or stock exchange. The essence of open-market-operations is the increase or reduction of balances held at the central bank by the commercial banks. The purchase or sale of securities is the means by which adjustments to these balances are usually secured, but it is not the only one. The same effects could be secured if the government held balances with commercial banks as well as the central bank, and so regulated payments into and out of them as to influence balances held in the commercial banks in whatever direction was desired — a procedure adopted to a limited extent in the United States. For example, if government balances are held in commercial banks and it is desired to reduce the banks' cash reserves, it could be done by financing current government expenditure rather more from balances in commercial banks and rather less from balances at the central bank; similarly, the reduction could also be secured by crediting revenue receipts rather more to accounts at the central bank and rather less to the accounts held in commercial banks. By adjusting official payments and receipts as between accounts held in commercial banks and those at the central bank, exactly the same effects are secured on the cash reserves of the commercial banking system as would be secured by the purchase or sale of securities.[2]

It is true that this method of control requires that the government should hold balances of sufficient magnitude with commercial banks, which may not always be a practical possibility. The significance of this limitation is somewhat reduced, however, by the fact that it is the *net* relationship between all credits and debits which needs to be adjusted, rather than the absolute level of

[1] See Sayers, *Modern Banking* (5th edition), Oxford University Press, London 1960, Chap. 11, pp. 254-5.

[2] The technique described here should not be confused with the use of fiscal policy to influence the level of aggregate demand by means of budget surpluses or deficits. Such a policy is not within the control of the central bank. Further, it is one which operates directly on the level of income, any monetary effects being incidental to this; the procedure outlined in the text is a purely monetary device. For a critical comment on the use of this technique in the U.S. see Milton Friedman, *A program for monetary stability*, Fordham University Press, New York 1960, Chap. 3, pp. 55-6.

cash balances. By merely spending rather more from one account and rather less from another, or by having receipts paid rather more into one type of account than to another, considerable effects could be secured on bank reserves so long as the government's current receipts and expenditures were at all significant. Provided the commercial banks operating in the territory accept their balances with the central bank as cash reserves, either by convention or as a result of legislation, the adjustment of government working cash balances in this way would secure the required effects. The system, indeed, has the advantage that the cash reserves of individual banks could be regulated as required — something not feasible with open-market-operations in which the purchaser or seller of securities in the market may be a customer of any one of the banks operating in the country. It could in fact be a more direct and efficient means of control than open-market-operations, and might well justify further study and development in practice.

Its immediate applicability to under-developed territories is limited, however, by the crucial fact that commercial banks operating in many of them have not regarded in the past, and will not readily regard in the future, their balances at the central bank of the territory as cash reserves. In the nature of their organisation, the international banks regard balances at head offices as their operative reserve, and the head offices will regard balances in their own central bank as the cash reserves which are important so far as their own policy is concerned.[1] The balances which branches may hold with the central bank of an under-developed territory will be regarded in all probability merely as unremunerative assets which they have been compelled, either by law or by moral pressure, to sacrifice to the authorities involved, and which are for all practical purposes completely frozen assets. (This objection, of course, is equally valid against the use of traditional open-market-operations, assuming such operations to be practical.)

In view of this, it has become common for the device of a statutory reserve ratio to be used in substitution. The commercial banks operating in a territory are required to deposit with the central bank a specified proportion of their total assets, this being held by the central bank in the form of bankers' reserve balances. The ratio may be changed from time to time in accordance with

[1] Foussek, op. cit., Chap. II, p. 26. See also A. K. Cairncross, 'Banking in developing countries, *The future organisation of banking*, Institute of Bankers in Scotland, Blackwood, Edinburgh 1958, pp. 82–3.

the needs of the prevailing situation, being raised at a time when the central bank wishes to restrict the volume of bank credit available in the economy. It is usual for the legal provisions governing changes in the reserve ratio to contain safeguards from the point of view of the commercial banks — i.e. changes are permitted only within specified limits, and furthermore are permitted only after a period of notice has been given. In some countries different ratios may be applied to different types of bank deposit, the most common practice being that a low ratio is required in the form of reserve balances at the central bank against deposits withdrawable only after a period of time, and a relatively high ratio is required against deposits on which calls may be made without notice. (In a system of expatriate banking it might well be necessary to specify a separate ratio for balances due to banks abroad in order to be able to sterilise funds brought in from overseas with the object of circumventing local credit policy measures.) The essential difference between this technique and the cash-ratio type of control for an under-developed country is that it is the *absolute size of the balances withdrawn* from the commercial banking system which is important, not any multiple secondary effects of the kind experienced in a banking system operating on a high deposit-cash gearing.

The use of this system has a fairly considerable history in a large number of countries, although in many cases it is used as a variant of open-market-operations aimed at secondary, multiple deposit changes rather than for the purpose of adding or withdrawing resources directly into or from the banks. In recent years it has been subjected to a certain amount of criticism, primarily on the ground that it is a relatively 'blunt and inflexible instrument'.[1] Practising bankers regard it as impracticable to vary ratios except by fairly substantial amounts, since the administrative difficulties involved in enforcing a ratio expressed to three or four decimal places are considerable. As a result, it is often said, the changes which are possible are necessarily of a substantial magnitude, and this makes marginal and delicate regulation of bank credit extremely difficult. Open-market-operations can be carried out, if desired, in relatively small amounts so as to produce only fractional changes in the cash reserves of the banking system; reserve ratios,

[1] Statement of the Chairman of the Board of Governors of the Federal Reserve System before the Congressional sub-committee on general credit and debt management, *Federal Reserve Bulletin*, April 1952.

on the other hand, can only be used to change the reserve balance requirement by, say, a half per cent at a time.

There may be a good deal of substance in this point when applied to a highly developed financial system where the central bank is able, and indeed required, to concern itself with delicate short-run adjustments to the credit system.[1] It would appear to have considerably less force, however, when applied to an under-developed economy, where in the nature of the case the central bank will be content to secure only relatively broad adjustments at infrequent intervals. This kind of adjustment is all that can reasonably be expected in such an environment; the economic structure of most under-developed territories is usually such — being highly dependent on primary products with an inelastic output in the short run — that infrequent and broad changes are precisely those which will be required. Further, against this dis-advantage of variable reserve ratios in the highly sophisticated credit systems of developed economies, there must be put its overwhelming virtue of being operable without a developed market in securities, or without the need to indulge in potentially de-stabilizing operations in a market of a delicate and elementary kind.

Another suggested disadvantage of the variable reserve ratio is that it does not enable the authorities to adjust the credit position of different banks to different degrees, so that a change in the reserve ratio which might be of little significance to one bank may be sufficient to cause acute embarrassment to another. This objection is equally valid, of course, against open-market-operations or any other system of control over cash reserves which operates in a general fashion. Further, the reserve ratio system actually has the technical advantage that it is at least possible to specify different reserve ratios for different banks, precisely in order to take account of different situations within the banking system;[2] at the same time, it must be observed that although such discrimina-tion as between banks is a technical possibility, it is by no means always practical from a political point of view.[3]

[1] The issue is carefully discussed by J. Aschheim, 'Open-market-operations *versus* reserve-requirement variation', *Economic Journal*, Vol. LXIX, No. 276, December 1959, pp. 697–704.

[2] Differing ratios have been laid down for different categories of banks in the United States, in the Special Deposit scheme recently inaugurated in the United Kingdom, and in many other countries.

[3] For an excellent survey of practices adopted in connection with reserve ratio requirements, see Foussek, op. cit., Chap. IV, pp. 45–56, and Appendix I, pp. 102–5.

A central bank which has adopted a system of reserve ratio control will inevitably face the question of the use to which the bankers' deposits held by it may be put, a problem which was discussed in general terms in the preceding chapter. At one extreme are those who would suggest that since reserve balances are repayable whenever commercial bank deposits should decline they must be held in a highly liquid form against the possibility that the funds so repaid will be converted into foreign exchange. At the other extreme are those who would regard the reserve deposits of the commercial banking system as more or less permanent, since the central bank will never reduce the reserve ratio below the minimum stipulated in the enabling legislation. This permanent element of the reserve balances, it is argued, could be used for relatively long-term investment by the central bank. Alternatively, if the question of converting the central bank's liabilities into foreign exchange does not arise, credit (or currency) can be created to effect repayment and the illiquidity of assets purchased with the original deposits becomes irrelevant.

The truth would appear to lie somewhere between these extremes, one suggesting that reserve balances must be held liquid and largely in foreign reserves, and the other that they may be largely invested at long-term; the extent to which policy approaches either extreme will depend in practice on the circumstances and conditions of individual territories. It would seem reasonable that in the majority of cases a substantial part of the balances could in fact be used to finance medium-term investment; there is considerable force in the argument that there will be a minimum level below which the central bank is unlikely to reduce the reserve ratio, so that its liability to convert these balances into foreign exchange would be confined to the contingency of a fall in the general level of bank deposits. The likelihood of this would not appear to be great in most cases. Nor would such repayments and conversion into foreign exchange be likely to occur with such magnitude that the consequences would be beyond solution — for example, through resort to other external balances which the central bank is likely to have at its disposal. At the same time, there is also force in the suggestion that the central bank will not be in a position to invest, other than at short-term, reserve balances held over and above this basic minimum; it will be liable to repay, and convert, such balances whenever it is desired to ease credit conditions within the economy as well as in response to a fall in bank deposits.

In practice, therefore, it is likely that most of the funds deposited under the reserve ratio provisions will be available to the central bank for medium and long-term investment, the probability being that the ratio in application will almost always be somewhat above the minimum permitted by legislation; a small margin will remain which the bank will need to hold liquid against the possibility of repayment and conversion into foreign exchange. In this way the central bank will not only establish its means of control over the commercial banks for immediate or prospective credit policy requirements; it will also obtain a fairly substantial volume of funds for the finance of development agencies in its territory. Further, the authorities will have ensured that as the economic system progresses and develops, and as bank deposits rise with the general growth of incomes, a constant fraction of these additional deposits will continue to accrue to the central bank for channelling into development. In other words, the commercial banking system will be so organised as to ensure that a part of all domestic savings taking the form of bank deposits will be contributed to the basic economic development of the territory — development upon which the higher incomes and larger bank deposits are themselves ultimately dependent.[1]

For the purposes of credit control the reserve ratio needs to be variable, and it will usually be advisable for the central bank to retain the right to enforce a reserve ratio of up to 100 per cent in respect of bank deposits in excess of a total reached at some point in the recent past or near future. This power to levy reserve ratios of a high order must necessarily be restricted to increments to banks' deposits — e.g. to increases after the date on which the high marginal reserve ratio is to become effective; the possibility of punitive reserve ratios would otherwise be a constant nightmare to

---

[1] A relevant, although less fundamental, consideration is whether the commercial banks should receive interest on their reserve balances. Newlyn and Rowan are definite in their view that interest should be paid (op. cit., Chap. 13, p. 288), on the grounds that such balances will be replacing income-earning assets. On the other hand, it could be argued that the short-term and (more important) the long-term benefits enjoyed by the commercial banks from the existence of a central bank will be sufficient compensation. The answer in any particular case will probably depend on political rather than economic factors; in Canada, for example, commercial banks receive no interest on their ordinary reserve balances with the Bank of Canada, and are also required to meet the costs of their own annual inspection by the Inspector of Banks.

the commercial banking world. Even the mere possibility that a high reserve ratio could be enforced by the central bank in such a way that the obligation could be honoured by banks only through the enforced sale of assets on a substantial scale would be an element of such danger and instability in the system as to represent a serious threat to the practicability and solvency of commercial banking itself.

Although the use of the reserve ratio system permits broad control to be secured over the total volume of bank credit in an economy, it is unlikely that this power will be either particularly useful or completely adequate in the circumstances of an under-developed country. By and large, the problem of the central bank in a country of this sort will be to ensure that credit is available on a sufficiently large scale and directed to the most urgent needs of the economy, rather than to ensure that credit is restricted within a certain limit. An under-developed economy may be faced, of course, with violent movements in its balance of payments, par-ticularly those which follow upon fluctuations in the prices of primary products on world markets. These may well require immediate and drastic action on the part of the central bank in an attempt to prevent undue variation in the volume of bank credit arising from large export earnings or overseas deficits; credit movements of this kind may be large enough to set up serious secondary repercussions within the economy.[1] Nevertheless, these will be essentially short-run problems. The long-run object will be to ensure that the maximum credit is used to the maximum advantage; taking one year with another, its control over the volume of bank credit will in general be aimed at ensuring that it is as great as possible, rather than otherwise. It is for this reason that suggestions that statutory reserve balances must be used *either* for control *or* for investment betray a lack of appreciation of the nature of the problem. First things first: as long as an economy is seriously backward the emphasis must be on develop-ment. The emphasis need shift to the control aspects of reserve balances in the orthodox sense when the economy has developed sufficiently for it.

4. *Selective controls*

Having done what it can to establish a means of ultimate control over the total volume of credit it is important from the point of

---

[1] Guneskera, 'The money supply and balance of payments in Ceylon', p. 150.

view of development that the central bank should ensure that such credit as is available (and this will usually be inadequate in comparison with the total need for it) is used in the optimum way. So long as commercial banking remains in private hands — and nothing in the present study is intended to be a judgement upon this essentially political question — the authorities must be content to leave the detailed administration of bank credit to the commercial banks themselves; it would be an unwarrantable interference in the operation of the banking system for the authorities to attempt to do otherwise. On the other hand, the authorities have a clear duty to ensure that the distribution of bank credit, like the distribution of physical resources in the economy, is broadly consistent with the basic pattern of development which they themselves believe to be in the interests of rapid economic progress. Hence the central bank needs powers to ensure that, so far as it is possible to do so, the various sectors of the economy are given proportions of the available financial resources which are consistent with the general scheme of economic development which it is hoped to establish.

In addition to its reserve ratio powers to influence the total volume of credit, therefore, a central bank in an under-developed country needs to possess powers over the distribution of bank credit. The use of selective credit controls is customary in many highly developed financial systems, and it would be difficult to argue that commercial banks in under-developed territories should dispose of their supplies of credit with a greater degree of freedom than they would possess in an advanced country. On the contrary, the need for and scarcity of capital is so much greater in under-developed areas that the imposition of some degree of broad official control over its allocation is only to be expected. In nature, the controls would be similar to those familiar in Europe and America; they would usually specify that bank advances to certain sectors should not exceed a particular sum, or a given proportion of all bank advances, or expand at more than a specified rate.

Obviously, commercial banking could not be carried on where powers of this kind are used by the authorities in such a way as to place banks in the position of being forced to *expand* credit in any given sector; the most that the authorities can reasonably expect to attain, and the least that commercial banks must be willing to concede to them, is a general power of encouraging credit to flow towards especially important sectors whose growth is being hampered by a lack of appropriate forms of finance, and of preventing it from exceeding a certain maximum in other sectors.[1] Such a maximum would need to be defined so as to make it impossible for a commercial bank to be placed in a position in which it had no option but to suddenly recall some of its loans, or to realise some other illiquid assets, in order to comply with the law. It is generally believed that these controls, being essentially negative, can play only a minor and supporting role in the broad monetary policy of the authorities; they cannot be expected to make any significant positive contribution.[2] They can be used, however, to ensure that undue credit is not given to activities such as real estate speculation, in which a great deal of capital is apt to be employed in under-developed territories with results which may be seriously disadvantageous to their general economic development.[3] As has been noted by the International Bank for Reconstruction and Development, the experience of many under-developed countries in recent years has shown that there has been

> a lack of the right type of financial institutions, and also an excessive diversion of their resources into short-term, often speculative, types of activity, with little contribution to the types of investment most needed by the economy.[4]

One final type of control over bank credit which can play an important part in the financial aspects of development is the power to impose a local assets ratio on banks operating within a territory. Unlike the controls which have been discussed in the preceding paragraphs, a local assets ratio is a device by which the volume of credit available in an economy may be increased, and not merely one which seeks to ensure a proper and reasonable distribution of credit. The local assets ratio involves a regulation which is such

[1] Controls of this kind, however, have undoubtedly succeeded in stimulating the flow of credit into agriculture for example — see U Tun Wai, 'Interest rates outside the organised money markets of under-developed countries', *I.M.F. Staff Papers*, Vol. VI, No. 1, November 1957, p. 89, and E. Laso, 'Financial policies and credit control techniques in Central America', *I.M.F. Staff Papers*, Vol. VI, No. 3, November 1958, pp. 436–7.

[2] They are also undoubtedly subject to severe administrative difficulties — see Foussek, op. cit., Chap. VI, pp. 69–81, and Cairncross, op. cit., pp. 84–7.

[3] Guneskera, ibid., pp. 153–4, Patel, op. cit., pp. 73–80; *Domestic Financing of economic development*, p. 57.

[4] Statement by the International Bank for Reconstruction and Development, *Methods of financing economic development in under-developed countries*, U.N. Department of Economic Affairs, United Nations, New York 1949 (1949. II. B4), pp. 92–3.

F

that the commercial banks operating in a country are required to utilise a minimum proportion of the deposits collected within it for the purchase of local assets of one form or another. With the aid of this weapon central banks can ensure that one feature of many dependent territories in the post-war years — i.e. the export of considerable supplies of capital to a highly-developed metropolitan country — can be gradually reduced in extent with the progress of time.

Once again, there are certain safeguards which it is only proper to give to the commercial banks themselves. It would clearly be unreasonable, for example, to impose on the commercial banking system a local assets ratio which was considerably higher than the actual ratio of domestic assets to total deposits prevailing at that particular moment. In order to comply with such a requirement, the commercial banks would be forced to dispose of a substantial volume of external assets, possibly involving considerable losses or reducing their external assets to so low a figure as to cause them serious and legitimate concern. In the not-very-long period, conduct of this kind can only result in creating such anxiety and lack of confidence amongst commercial bankers regarding the stability and intentions of the country in question as to lead them to reduce, or certainly to cease expanding, their business in that country.

On the other hand, a reasonable and cautious policy by which a central bank establishes the local assets ratio at an initial level equal to, or only slightly higher than, the prevailing ratio of local assets to total deposits in its commercial banks, and gives a considerable period of notice before the new ratio becomes effective, may do much to correct a distorted state of affairs in which bank credit is being drawn away to richer territories. Commercial bankers, being human, are naturally liable to enforce standards and conventions which they find convenient to themselves, and these tend to become identified in their minds with those which are essential to sound and prudent banking. The imposition of a local assets ratio presents the banks with the alternative of either finding suitable outlets for their credit locally or holding a significant part of their resources in the form of idle balances within the territory. This is liable to cause striking developments both in concepts of what is and what is not a suitable banking asset and in the energy with which the banks address themselves to the task of discovering suitable assets within the territory.[1] The banks having been brought gradually in this fashion to a given local assets ratio the process can be repeated, the ratio once again being raised slightly, until the external assets held by the banking system are no more than the level which is strictly necessary for the sound conduct of banking business, rather than that which is most lucrative in relation to imported concepts of credit-worthiness.[2]

5. The benefits of a central bank

The broad impression emerging from what has been said in the preceding section may be that the controls which must be exercised over commercial banking in under-developed territories operate in almost every case adversely to the commercial banker himself; the inference may be drawn that banks are called upon to make sacrifices and changes, all of which — while no doubt valuable from the point of view of the development of the territory concerned — involve them in inconvenience and possibly financial loss. This would not be a realistic or fair conclusion. The creation of a central bank, and the endowment of it with the powers which have been described in the previous sections, is in the long run a development which is undoubtedly in the interests of the commercial banks themselves. Nothing is more likely to contribute to banking of a profitable kind, and on an increasing scale, than the healthy economic development of the territory in which the banks operate. Speaking of the experience of the great exchange banks of the Far East since the war, for example, one writer refers to the short-run problems created for the banks by a series of enactments which have substituted self-government for British rule in several territories; despite these short-run problems of adjustment, however, he affirms the view that in the long run 'these statutes probably strengthen the position of British overseas enterprise'.[3] Hence it may well prove to be in the banks' own

[1] For this reason a local assets ratio which leaves the choice of assets to the commercial banks is preferable to the powers given to the Irish central bank to call for deposits *with itself* if local commercial bank assets are too low — see N. J. Gibson. 'Ireland's evolving central bank', *The Banker*, Vol. CX, No. 413, July 1960, p. 455.

[2] It is worth noting that legislation with a similar aim has been introduced in Mexico and the Philippines in connection with insurance companies — *Domestic financing of economic development*, pp. 66–7.

[3] G. Tyson, 'Bigger groupings for Eastern Banks'. *The Banker*, Vol. CX, No. 418, December 1960, p. 805.

interest to make some contribution towards the establishment and administration of measures which have considerable potentialities for stimulating the economic growth of the territory concerned.

It would be idle, of course, to pretend that a newly established central bank can directly add to the strength and solvency of old-established banks operating in a territory. As was stressed in the previous chapter, many of the international banks are enterprises whose total resources are considerably greater than those of the central banks of particular territories. For many years to come, whatever internal banking legislation may be adopted, such banks are likely to continue to regard their balances at head office, and their short-term investments in overseas money markets as their actual working reserves, as opposed to the local reserves required by the legislation of the overseas territories in which they operate. Nevertheless, looking further ahead, the far-seeing commercial bank will realise that the central bank in an under-developed territory, however weak and inexperienced it may be in the first instance, can ultimately contribute greatly to the economic stability and prosperity of the area. It can therefore be regarded as being as much in the best commercial interests of the private banks as, say, the London clearing banks would now regard the Bank of England — for many years their highly suspect competitor.

The major advantages which international banks can hope to gain from the establishment of a central bank, and from its acquisition of powers of control over their own activities, are necessarily of a long-run kind. This is not to say, however, that there may not be other, although lesser, advantages which will accrue more or less immediately. One example of these is the provision of clearing facilities by the central bank. In some overseas dependencies in which international banks are operating, it is necessary for indebtedness between the different banks operating in any given territory to be settled by means of drafts on London. This is a clumsy and frequently expensive process, since clearings executed by means of drafts on balances held thousands of miles away may involve fairly considerable sums in the process of collection at any one time. Even in a highly developed country like Canada, the establishment of a central bank and its provision of clearing facilities brought considerable benefit to the commercial banks since it enabled them to operate with smaller reserves of cash. (The provision of central clearing facilities is said to have enabled Canadian banks to reduce their holdings of cash for clearing purposes by 5 per cent of total deposits.) In territories far removed geographically from the head offices of the banks involved, a similar economy could be gained through the establishment of facilities which obviated the need for clearing by means of international drafts. This real advantage accruing to commercial banks must therefore be set off against any losses they may sustain in, for example, maintaining reserve balances at the central bank.

This is not an argument which can be pushed too far, nor is it one which is susceptible of statistical measurement, because of the special position of branches of overseas banks so far as head office balances are concerned. The branches of a bank operating in different territories will not need to hold their own individual reserves for clearing at head office. More precisely, a head office will be able to offset clearing losses in respect of some territories against clearing gains experienced by branches in other territories; the total amount which a head office needs to hold in cash in order to meet daily clearing obligations will thus be smaller than the total which would have to be held by all its branches if they were operating independently. Hence the gain to any given bank from the establishment of clearing facilities in an overseas territory is somewhat less than would be the case if the branches operating in that territory had been separate banks. Nevertheless, to some extent a gain must remain.

A second immediate advantage to the commercial banking system from the establishment of a central bank with adequate powers is that the latter will be able to develop at least the rudiments of a short-term money market within its territory. As a result, the commercial banks in the territory may find that short-term assets of a suitable degree of liquidity and credit-worthiness become available, and that facilities for marketing them emerge. This will enable commercial banks to find local assets of a type which they need, and which hitherto they had sought only in some international financial centre. The ability to hold short-term funds in a highly liquid form and yet on a lucrative basis within its own territory will clearly be advantageous so far as a commercial bank is concerned.[1]

[1] See Sayers, *Modern Banking* (5th ed.), Chap. 11, p. 267, Sen, op. cit., Chap. 3, p. 23, Guneskera, op. cit., p. 148, Plumptre, op. cit., Introduction, p. 11, and A. Rudd, 'Ghana and the Sterling Area', *The Banker*, Vol. CVII, No. 374, March 1957, pp. 170–1.

A third advantage which a well-established and prudent commercial bank will secure from the creation of adequate central control over the banking system will be the prevention of the development of unsound banking practices in its territory. Such a development might occur either with overseas banks or the locally-established banks which are almost certain to appear in increasing numbers in countries of this kind. If banks are allowed to develop in these territories without some official control over their liquidity position and general banking practices, credit crises would be almost inevitable. Although an individual bank might not be involved directly in such incidents it is common knowledge that a crisis anywhere in the banking system is bound to injure all the constituent banks in the system. The protection of the public from unsound banking through central control and inspection will therefore be a direct and important advantage to every prudent bank operating in the territory.

In conclusion it is necessary to return to the fundamental point made earlier. Assuming that a properly equipped central bank can make a contribution — even though many will no doubt believe it to be a relatively small one — to the rapid and healthy economic growth of a territory, it must follow that its establishment is something which any far-seeing commercial banker will welcome. Banking is peculiarly dependent upon the general level of prosperity, and is especially liable to increase in importance and prosperity if incomes and output rise steadily and rapidly. No institution has a greater or closer interest in well-established, expanding and successful industry and agriculture than a commercial bank; anything which contributes to economic development contributes to the growth and prosperity of commercial banking. As a report of the United Nations puts it, 'developmental improvements, once achieved, provide better safeguards for banks than orthodox rules of operation'.[1] Unless it is believed as a matter of faith that a central bank can make no contribution whatever to the economic welfare of a country, however powerful it may be and however wisely and intelligently its powers may be employed, therefore, the commercial banker, like everyone directly or indirectly concerned with stimulating the growth of under-

---

[1] *Domestic financing of economic development*, United Nations, New York 1950 (1951. II. B1), p. 57.

developed territories, should welcome the introduction of central banking powers and do everything possible to assist the bank in its establishment and throughout the career of practical policy which will lie ahead of it.

Chapter 4

THE CREATION OF LENDING INSTITUTIONS

1. *The need for lending institutions*

In the more highly developed economies of the world, specialised saving and investment institutions are a familiar feature. Over a period of years the forces of market evolution have resulted in the establishment of institutions concentrating on either the collection of investible funds from a variety of sources or the disposition of such funds between various outlets. The advantages of specialised institutions of this kind are well known. In the first place, the channelling of savings through them, rather than direct investment in productive enterprises by individual savers, enables funds to be collected from a wide range of different sources, each of which could individually account only for sums which would be too small for worthwhile investment, or whose investment would be so costly as to make the effective rate of interest unduly high. In modern times, the amalgamation of these relatively small individual flows from a large number of separate sources can result in substantial aggregations of funds; it is likely that much of this flow would have been lost to useful investment without some medium through which the small saver could dispose of his funds cheaply and safely. In the second place, and related to this, these institutions enable the investor to spread his risks in a way which would not have been possible if all investment had to take place directly. The placing of funds in an investment trust, for example, in effect enables the holders of small amounts of capital to distribute their funds over a wide range of industries and enterprises, and this distribution achieves a significant reduction of the risk to which capital is exposed in the course of investment in industry.

On the investing side equally there are advantages to be gained from the allocation of capital between different sectors by institutions specialising in particular types of credit. The disposal of funds in manufacturing industry, in housing, in government

72

securities or in foreign assets all involve their own different types of expertise; it can naturally be effected with considerably greater efficiency by institutions with long experience of a narrow range of investment outlets than by an individual investor with no specialised knowledge of any. Hence the growth of various types of lending institutions such as building societies specialising in housing credit, agricultural banks specialising in farm credit, finance houses specialising in consumer credit, merchant banks specialising in the channelling of capital to particular types of industry and particular branches of trade, and so on. In both the collection and the distribution of investible funds, then, there exist economies of specialisation comparable with those obtainable in productive processes in industry or agriculture.

In most industrial economies these institutions have evolved through the normal processes of market pressure, and have acquired their organisation and functions only after a long period of development and experiment. It is true to say that in exceptional cases, where marginal needs have not been met, official agencies have often been established — or private institutions established with official support and encouragement — in order to fill some particular gap in the credit structure. These agencies are exceptional in that they usually provide only a small proportion of the total volume of credit flowing from savers into investment; in general they have been established to deal with sectors of the economy where the risk, expense or difficulties of administration have been such that the private institutions dealing with the bulk of the credit flow have proved unwilling to extend their activities into them. Just as a privately-owned electricity supply system, left to itself, will not usually extend its services into areas where population is thinly spread over relatively large distances, so private investment institutions have found certain areas of the economy of such difficulty or peculiarity as to create expectations of only small profit, or none at all. In general, it is only to fill the gaps resulting in this way that official institutions have been set up in the world of investment finance.

The significance of all this for the under-developed economy is fairly clear. In the first place, the pressure of poverty in them is so intense (and the vulnerability of popularly elected government so great) that the need for specialised agencies for the finance of investment cannot safely be left to the processes of slow evolution.

What in earlier generations could have been allowed to develop over scores, if not hundreds, of years must now of necessity be created in a much shorter space of time. Secondly, the sectors of the economy where conventional profit expectations are highly uncertain, or relatively low, are not so much exceptional as customary. In a highly-developed industrial economy official agencies are needed only for marginal and relatively unimportant fragments of the economy, profit expectations in the major part of the system being sufficiently powerful to stimulate an adequate amount of privately-financed activity; in the under-developed economy, on the other hand, the reverse is the case. Certain limited sectors of the economy (typically the export of primary produce) will hold out sufficient profit expectation to ensure that adequate finance is forthcoming from banks and other sources; for the rest of the economy, however, profit outcomes are so uncertain and far-distant that private capital is reluctant to flow into it of its own volition.

In a word, an economy is under-developed precisely because the greater part of its productive capacity has not proved an attractive investment for private funds; institutions to channel funds into those sectors have therefore failed to evolve from the spur of ordinary market forces. Hence if the savings available to the community — and such other funds as it may be able to obtain from abroad — are to be used so as to attain maximum growth in the economy, the institutional framework to assist and stimulate the flow must be deliberately created and supported by the government of the territory concerned.[1] To leave this task to unassisted market forces is to incur a serious risk that it will not be performed except after intolerable delay.

2. *The role of lending institutions in an under-developed economy*

The tasks of financial institutions in an under-developed territory are therefore almost self-evident. In the first place, their purpose is to provide a collecting point for savings of a relatively small average amount from a large number of individual sources. So long as the means to utilise savings safely and profitably are not available within an economy, funds will either be diverted abroad, sterilised in useless hoards of cash or precious metals, or,

---

[1] The importance of this is stressed heavily in the United Nations report *Methods of financing economic development in under-developed countries*, pp. 3–8, 74–5, and 92–3.

more likely still, will not accumulate at all.[1] However poor an economy may be there will be a need for institutions which allow such savings as are currently forthcoming to be invested conveniently and safely, and which ensure that they are channelled into the most useful purposes. The poorer a country is, in fact, the greater is the need for agencies to collect and invest the savings of the broad mass of persons and institutions within its borders. Such agencies will not only permit small amounts of savings to be handled and invested conveniently but will allow the owners of savings to retain liquidity individually but finance long-term investment collectively.

The second point follows closely from this. Given the high degree of risk inherent in investment in an economy of the kind under discussion, it may prove essential that the institutions established to collect and invest the savings of the community should be supported by a guarantee of its government just as public utilities in industrialised countries are financed with the aid of government guarantees. It is inherent in an under-developed economy that the risk attached to investment in local enterprises is large; private individuals cannot reasonably be expected either to assess the extent of this risk fairly, or to take it entirely on their own shoulders. It is a proper function of government in such circumstances to provide some guarantee against these risks; it is the only organisation which is able to spread its own risk over the entire economic life of the community, and it is in fact the only part of the system whose function it is to accept the uncertainties inherent in the development of the economy as a whole.

A third important function of the framework within which savings flow from individuals to enterprises is that the specialised institutions can ensure that proper advice, guidance, information and general investment consultancy accompanies capital wherever necessary. It is generally beyond the responsibility or means of a purely private institution to take upon itself the function of ensuring that enterprises utilising its funds are adopting proper methods of accountancy, production techniques, marketing arrangements and so on. Yet control of these matters is an essential part of the investment process in an under-developed economy; it is crucially important that when capital is invested in an enterprise such measures as are humanly possible are simultaneously

[1] On this last possibility see Lewis, op. cit., Chap. V, p. 229.

adopted to ensure that it will be used properly and efficiently. Under-developed economies cannot afford the luxuries of capital wastage and over-employed bankruptcy courts. Only a relatively large-scale and disinterested agency can be expected to provide these services and to make them generally acceptable, however, and it is therefore a highly desirable function of investment institutions in an under-developed economy to secure and administer management consultancy of this kind — in the words of the central bank of Rhodesia and Nyasaland, to provide 'both ante-natal diagnosis and after-care'.[1]

Finally, the creation of development finance institutions can make a contribution to the solution of the general problem of ensuring that scarce supplies of capital are distributed in accordance with the best interests of the development of the economy as a whole. A private institution, must naturally be guided in making its decision by the profitability of different avenues of investment over the reasonably near future. But it hardly needs to be argued that the resulting pattern of investment may not coincide with that allocation of resources which is conducive to greatest long-run expansion in the economy. A central lending institution allocating investible funds becoming available from private and official sources is therefore a fundamental necessity in an economy where capital is so extremely scarce, and where the need for growth so pressing, that the wastage of capital in terms of the best economic development of the community cannot be tolerated.[2] This by no means implies that the financing of investment needs to be barred altogether to private initiative; it does imply, however, that a central agency disposing of a substantial proportion of the total capital flow will be necessary to augment and complement the work of private investors.

[1] Bank of Rhodesia and Nyasaland, *The financing of economic development in the Federation of Rhodesia and Nyasaland*, Salisbury, May 1959. See also Diamond, op. cit., pp. 57–60. Examples of the dismal consequences which can follow from the absence of such supervision may be found in W. A. Lewis, *Report on industrialisation and the Gold Coast*, Government Printer, Accra, 1953.

[2] United Nations experts favoured the creation of special agencies for the disposition of public capital funds to the private sector, but mainly on the ground that official administrative machinery was not well suited to the direct investment of such funds — *Domestic financing of economic development*, pp. 44–5. In recent years the I.B.R.D. has actually encouraged borrowing countries to establish development banks for the specific purpose of assisting industrialisation — preferring, however, that they should not be government agencies. See A. K. Cairncross, *The International Bank for Reconstruction and Development*, Essays in International Finance No. 33, Princeton University Press, Princeton, New Jersey, March 1959, pp. 22–3.

It would not be appropriate in an essay of this kind to attempt to discuss the detailed form of organisation which development finance institutions should adopt.[1] In general it may be said that the balance of advantage will probably lie with a separation of the two functions of collecting investible funds, on the one hand, and their investment in specific enterprises, on the other, into two distinct institutions. The former function is best left to organisations specifically designed to meet the peculiar circumstances of the country concerned — official or semi-private savings banks, insurance companies, thrift and provident societies etc. — which could transmit funds to the lending agencies by taking up securities issued by the latter or through the medium of the public debt, a subject discussed in the following chapter. Little need be said about the collecting agencies by way of detail, therefore; their form will depend almost entirely on the individual characteristics of each territory, and their number will naturally depend on the magnitude of the potential flow of funds.[2] (It is scarcely necessary to add that the practice whereby a large — perhaps the greater — part of the assets of official Savings Banks in many Commonwealth countries are invested overseas obviously requires modification. The issues involved are essentially similar to those discussed in Chapter 1 in connection with the currency system, and that discussion need not be repeated here.)

Just as commercial banking control and inspection is usually desirable in under-developed countries to prevent the growth of unsound banking institutions, central banks in territories of this kind will probably find it necessary to require other institutions inviting deposits from the general public to be registered with it and to observe general regulations concerning capital structure, liquidity, management, reserves etc., laid down with legislative force.[3] One or two points of principle concerning the policy of agencies responsible for the disposition of funds amongst individual investment projects, however, are discussed in the following sections.

[1] Those wishing to examine the detailed problems involved in designing institutions of this kind are well served by two excellent studies published under the auspices of the I.B.R.D.: W. Diamond, *Development Banks*, John Hopkins Press, Baltimore 1957, and Shirley Boskey, *Problems and practices of development banks*, John Hopkins Press, Baltimore 1959. A somewhat more critical survey of several development banks is given in Hanson, op. cit., Chaps. VII and VIII.

[2] On this subject see *Domestic financing of economic development*, United Nations, New York 1950 (1951. II. B1), pp. 16–20.

[3] See Chapter 2, section 3.

3. *The ownership of development finance institutions*

The decision as to the location of ultimate control of a financial institution concerned with the channelling of funds into predominantly private enterprises is a matter which will be decided primarily on political rather than economic and financial grounds. Nevertheless, it seems clear that in an under-developed economy the normal considerations which would apply to the ownership of institutions of this kind in a developed industrial economy lose much of their force. By definition, the need for specialised institutions arises because under the prevailing circumstances the profit mechanism cannot be expected to result in the optimum allocation, or even the maximum encouragement, of the savings of the community. Although funds may be invested predominantly in privately-owned enterprises, the essential aim of the institutions is to ensure that financial resources are used in a manner consistent with the long-run interests of the development of the community, and it is difficult to argue that responsibility for that development can be divorced from government.

If governments assume responsibility for drawing up, in some sense, development plans for their countries, the distribution of resources by development finance institutions can be in full harmony with these official plans only if the institutions have clearly decided that the criteria to be adopted in deploying funds are those accepted by their governments, rather than those which would arise from consideration of commercial profit and loss. Because the unassisted profit mechanism does not work adequately and satisfactorily in an economy of this kind, a development finance institution can operate effectively only if it is in such close touch with its government as to make private control of it largely illusory in substance if not in form.[1] One detailed survey of the experience of such development finance agencies has concluded that they

> normally cannot be established on a sound financial basis unless the government is prepared to extend generous financial support.[2]

And it would scarcely be reasonable for any government to be expected to provide 'generous financial support' without a substantial degree of control over the uses to which public funds were being put.

---

[1] A related consideration given heavy stress by the United Nations experts is that official control will also be needed to ensure that borrowing from the market for various investment projects takes place in an orderly and co-ordinated manner, *Domestic financing of economic development*, pp. 47–9.

[2] Boskey, op. cit., Chap. I, p. 8.

Another consideration leading to the same conclusion is that a major function of this type of institution must be to provide a suitable outlet for the funds accumulated by official and semi-official bodies such as the central bank (including currency reserves), official Savings Banks, and even commercial banks operating in the territory. The investments held by institutions of this sort must of necessity be extremely high-grade and of the kind commonly described as gilt-edged. That is to say, they must be government obligations or something close to them. In any case, as was noted earlier, the granting of a government guarantee to the liabilities of such an institution is almost certain to be highly desirable, if not essential.[1] Another comprehensive survey of the experience of development finance institutions throughout the world has affirmed that

> while some development banks have been successful in raising funds in domestic bond markets, the success of many has undoubtedly depended either on their official position or on official support.[2]

But if, for example, a government guarantee as to the capital sums invested in such an institution is to be given, it is not easy to see how it could be reconciled with any really effective degree of private ownership of the institution. Private ownership would imply at least a possibility of conflict between the policy of the government and that decided upon by private share-holders; if such a conflict is possible, it is difficult to envisage how a government could enter into a guarantee concerning the capital invested in the institution.

Another important function of the institution will be the attraction of external capital; the supply of investible funds within an under-developed territory is seldom adequate to meet the full possibilities of its investment programme. Once again, the achievement of this end is not always as easy to reconcile with private ownership as it might be in a richer and more advanced economy. Investment in an under-developed territory by foreign investors has such a high degree of risk subjectively attached to it that it is unlikely that private investors, or even foreign public investors, would willingly commit funds to an institution of a purely private

---

[1] For example, the bonds issued by the industrial development corporation of Mexico carry a federal guarantee, and are virtually government issues. On the other hand, such guarantees are not normally considered necessary for the issues of similar corporations in Puerto Rico or India, even though their capital is subscribed by the government — ibid., p. 49. See also Cairncross, 'Banking in developing countries', p. 91.

[2] Diamond, op. cit., p. 68.

kind, its obligations might be defaulted upon, and its operations must inevitably be liable to governmental control in a way which might be regarded as adverse to the interests of the foreign investor.[1] The history of international capital movements in recent decades suggests that capital will generally be invested in private enterprises (other than those which are foreign-owned) in under-developed territories only on such conditions as to make the process distinctly expensive or onerous in other ways from the borrower's point of view. The risk inherent in investing in the private enter-prises of a foreign country are such that this must almost necessarily be the case. To the foreign investor, the liability of the government of another territory to interfere arbitrarily with externally-owned capital assets is always so real a threat (and to be honest, the attitude is not without some justification in the light of past experience) that the flow of capital is inevitably restricted.[2] Only a government guarantee of sufficient extent and duration to take care of considerations of this kind can hope to stimulate the flow of foreign capital into the territory, and this sort of guarantee would in general be so far-reaching in its implications as to make a substantial degree of official control of the policy of the institution concerned a practical necessity, whatever the institution's form of ownership.[3]

[1] The Articles of the International Bank of Reconstruction and Development, indeed, *require* that loans to private borrowers must carry a governmental guarantee. Nevertheless, when encouraging the establishment of development banks, the Bank insists that wherever possible such agencies should be private corporations or have private representation on their Boards. This is not an inflexible rule however; I.B.R.D. loans have been made to government develop-ment agencies in the Netherlands and in Ethiopia — Cairncross, *The Inter-national Bank for Reconstruction and Development*, pp. 22–3.

[2] *Measures for the economic development of under-developed countries*, Chap. XI, paras. 257–8, p. 81.

[3] However, some governments have chosen to make institutions of this kind wholly privately-owned, although sometimes (as in the case of the Rhodesia and Nyasaland Development Corporation) giving a guarantee in respect of its external borrowing. Presumably the advantages of government control sum-marised in the text were not thought sufficient in these instances to overcome a political disinclination to involve the government in the affairs of private enterprises. As Diamond puts it, prime importance is attached to 'the independence of the management of the institution from pressures both private and bureaucratic' (op. cit., p. 61); similarly the I.B.R.D. view is simply that 'industrial development is best left to private enterprise' (Cairncross, *The International Bank for Reconstruction and Development*, p. 23). Clearly, there are some nicely-balanced considerations here, but it is difficult to see how both a complete integration of investment policy *and* independence of management can be achieved. Each government has to decide for itself which of these two *desiderata* is to be given priority. The point is fully argued by Diamond, op. cit., pp. 70–6.

4. *Agricultural credit*

In principle there would be a great deal to be said for the creation in an under-developed territory of a single development finance institution charged with the allocation of its supplies of credit to all sectors of the economy, whether privately-owned or otherwise, and with the administration of all the capital funds which could be made available to it for investment by either the government, through its current revenue surplus, or private savers and institutions in the territory. In the first place, the creation of the single institution would ensure that administrative skill and talent was concentrated and not dissipated over several competing institutions. In the second place, the granting of a virtual monopoly of the credit available from sources other than the established institutional investors (e.g. the commercial banks or insurance companies) would help towards the familiar aim of ensuring that scarce supplies of capital were allocated between broad economic sectors, and between marginal enterprises in different sectors, in a logical and consistent fashion. If the need for capital was greater in one sector than another, an institution controlling a substantial part of the total supply available could ensure that the disposition of funds was adjusted accordingly.

It would follow from this that the government of an under-developed territory seeking to stimulate the collection and invest-ment of the savings available would be well advised to create a single development finance institution, carrying its guarantee, controlled and administered by directors nominated by it, and drawing up its policy in close consultation with the organs of government responsible for the formation of overall economic policy. Such an institution might well become the major single source of capital outside the banking system for all enterprises in the agricultural, mining, manufacturing and commercial sectors. Nevertheless, there are serious disadvantages in having a single institution of this kind to provide finance not only to the broad range of manufacturing industry but to special categories such as agriculture, small businesses, and commercial organisations.

The case of the last of these can be disposed of briefly. By and large, the finance of trade is not a problem in under-developed territories; indeed, one of the major complaints which can be laid at the door of the expatriate commercial banks is precisely that

G

they have over-supplied the commercial sectors of the economy with credit, concentrating on financing foreign or internal trade transactions and neglecting indigenous industry. Furthermore, the finance of commercial transactions is a function which does not go easily with industrial investment. It is more than mere accident that in the highly developed economies of the world it is usual for these two types of credit business to be kept distinctly apart; funds are drawn for each of them from different sources and disposed of through different forms of securities.

The problem of agriculture is of a quite different order. There is widespread agreement that in almost all the under-developed territories of the world the supply of credit to agriculture is inefficient and inadequate.[1] In particular, the expatriate banks have almost universally stood aloof from agricultural finance (other than the provision of working capital for the expatriate enterprises producing for export) largely because of the difficulties presented by communications, the lack of conventional forms of security — especially mortgages — and the small-scale nature of most of the indigenous agriculture of these countries. The need to provide adequate credit to agriculture is certainly of the highest priority in all of them. Nevertheless, it would not appear wise for the provision of this type of credit to be combined with the provision of credit to the general field of manufacturing industry.

The main reason for this is that in almost every country of the world the support of agriculture is by way of being a political, as well as an economic, matter. It is almost invariably found expedient to provide farmers, especially the small-scale farmers typical of these countries, with credit at abnormally low rates of interest, on terms which are distinctly generous so far as maturity and redemption conditions are concerned, and against a type of security which would probably not meet ordinary commercial standards. Further, extension services of all kinds are almost invariably equally essential as the provision of credit; these need to go much further than the type of advice and consultancy mentioned earlier in connection with industrial investment. Reflecting on the

[1] See Sen, op. cit., Chap. 10, pp. 210–1, Ali, op. cit., p. 60, and E. Laso, op. cit., p. 433. One investigator has concluded that agriculture accounts for less than 10 per cent of total commercial bank lending in most under-developed territories — U Tun Wai, 'Interest rates outside the organised money markets of under-developed countries', *I.M.F. Staff Papers*, Vol. VI, No. 1, November 1957, p. 94.

experience of agricultural credit in India one commentator observes that

> Cheap and easy credit has often enough been the ruin of the thriftless individual farmer, who has used this double-edged sword to his own undoing. What he requires is cheap, but controlled credit. . . .[1]

The institution involved in agricultural finance must thus also be concerned with a range of services well outside the strictly financial sphere, usually taking the form of the provision of equipment, seeds, marketing facilities etc., all at something well below their true cost.[2] Experience provides overwhelming proof that such supervision and control of agricultural credit is essential even on grounds of common financial prudence, and it is unfortunate that they are in fact substantially absent in most under-developed countries.[3] In addition to this, the assistance of the small-scale farmer is a matter of political and social importance, quite apart from its economic significance. In the words of a United Nations report,

> . . . the abolition of the small farmer was neither feasible nor desirable. The issue was therefore both an economic and a social one, and the credit problems involved could not be solved as an independent technical problem outside the general framework of social and economic policy. . . . Part of the assistance might be given with the idea of eventual repayment and part of it without hoping to be reimbursed, more as a relief measure than as an extension of credit. . . .[4]

As a result of all this, any institution involved in the provision of credit to agriculture almost inevitably needs to be subsidised in some way or another. Whatever the economic rights and wrongs of the question, agricultural credit is in reality a subsidised service in most parts of the world, and will probably continue to be so for as long as can be foreseen. It would therefore be extremely difficult for a development institution to utilise funds on an economic basis and simultaneously associate itself with a type of lending which is universally known to be uneconomic in any real

---

[1] *Domestic financing of economic development*, p. 133.

[2] All this, as Diamond remarks 'makes the problem of farm credit quite different in kind from that of industrial credit'. — op. cit., p. 16; see also p. 48. Agricultural credit in such countries, remarks another writer, 'is not only a technical and banking problem but also a social one — Ali, op. cit., p. 67.

[3] U Tun Wai, ibid., p. 93.

[4] *Domestic financing of economic development*, p. 84.

sense of the word. It is important that the finance institution should be seen to be operated on reasonably sound, economic lines if it is to hope to attract capital from private investors both within and beyond its borders.[1] It is impossible for it do this if part of its investment activity takes the form of credit which cannot be justified on the ordinary economic standards which would be applicable to industrial investment, even standards resting on the sort of basis referred to above — namely, one taking a distinctly long-run view and measuring profit-outcomes in a distinctly broad sense.

It would appear to be best, therefore, for agricultural credit to be administered by a separate institution which could itself be closely integrated with the various other agencies of agricultural policy in the country. This would have the disadvantage that a part of the credit flow would be administered separately from the remainder, so that there would be no guarantee that the proper allocation of scarce capital between individual industrial and agricultural projects would be secured at the margin. Nevertheless, the danger of confusing industrial investment with subsidised agricultural credit is so great that this penalty seems to be well worth paying.[2]

5. *The finance of small business*

Another sector to which comparable considerations apply is that of small-scale business, meaning by this enterprises which are at an early stage of development and which involve probably only a single proprietor and a small number of employees. This is a type of enterprise which also involves political issues as well as economic considerations. The protection and encouragement of small-scale enterprise is usually regarded as being a matter of social importance, and is a policy aim which most governments regard as being outside the bounds of a strictly economic calculus. Because of the administrative expense and high default-probability involved, it is an almost universal experience that institutions involved in the lending of funds to small-scale business find themselves doing so at a loss. There is a point below which the size of loan simply

[1] Diamond, op. cit., p. 81.
[2] For a survey of the agricultural credit problem see H. Belshaw, *Agricultural credit in economically under-developed countries*, F.A.O. Agricultural Study No. 46, Columbia University Press, New York 1960, and Hanson, op. cit., Chap. IX, pp. 258–78.

cannot be economically carried; beyond this the costs of servicing and collecting interest and capital repayments are so high, and the incidence of default so great, that the provision of such credit becomes quite unprofitable.[1] Any institution concerned with the finance of small-scale business can therefore scarcely hope to conduct its business on economic lines. The parallel with agricultural credit is thus almost exact; a development finance institution seeking to hold out to investors the promise of the use of funds on reasonably economic lines, and of being profitable at least in the long run, cannot hope to achieve this end if it is involved with the provision of credit to small business. Such business is simply incompatible with the operation of an institution on a break-even basis, let alone a profitable one.

Despite the disadvantages of separating one element of the flow of credit from 'social' investment finance over the economy as a whole, therefore, practical considerations again suggest that separate arrangements be made to meet this particular need. If this is not possible — and it might certainly involve a duplication and wastage of administrative resources — then it is essential that the finance institution should conduct its lending to small businesses as an entirely separate and distinct part of its total activity, using separate funds and drawing up a separate balance sheet for it.[2] The element of subsidy in this part of its business could then be seen clearly and responsibility for it could be passed to the government, where it belongs. In this way the institution could assure the investor that this particular part of its activities — if it ran counter to ordinary economic considerations — was entirely separate, and was not financed with funds collected from private sources to which strictly economic principles were applied. The funds used in loans to small businesses would be only those

[1] Hence the astonishing estimate that the Reconstruction Finance Corporation in the United States lost nearly $6000 on each loan of $1000 it made, and the agonised remark of one of its directors that 'There is no way for a corporation which operates with our checks and balances to make a $1500 GI loan and make any money on it. I am sure we would be better off if we wrote them a check and called it a day'. (Saulnier, Halcrow and Lacoby, *Federal lending and loan insurance*, National Bureau of Economic Research, Princeton University Press, Princeton 1958, Appx. B, pp. 512–3.) Similarly, the Industrial and Commercial Finance Corporation in the United Kingdom has found that loans of less than £15,000 show no profit and are probably losing propositions if full account is taken of investigation and administration costs — Diamond, op. cit., pp. 48–9.

[2] The United Nations report *Domestic financing of economic development* (p. 58) stresses the aggravation of the scarcity of qualified personnel which follows from a multiplicity of credit institutions; it therefore pronounces in favour of subsidy or direct assistance for small businesses.

especially set aside for the purpose by the government; similarly, the assets acquired against them would be separated off and any losses on them distinguished in the operating account of its main business.[1] This would at least eliminate the fear — ever present in the mind of the private investor in a situation such as this — that an institution set up to collect and invest savings would be forced into uneconomic and unprofitable lines of business in the interests of political pressure-groups and official government policy.[2]

---

[1] This type of procedure has been adopted in Mexico and Puerto Rico; in countries such as India and Pakistan, on the other hand, lending to small concerns has been hived off to separate institutions — see Boskey, op. cit., pp. 58-61.

[2] More or less identical arguments as those presented in this and the preceding section apply to the provision of finance for housing, another field in which social considerations and subsidies appear to be universally applied. The construction of low-cost housing is often administered directly by a government department, however, and development finance institutions are seldom saddled with this responsibility.

Chapter 5

THE DEVELOPMENT OF CAPITAL MARKETS

1. *The importance of liquidity*

In discussions of under-developed territories pride of place is usually given to the absolute shortage of capital — both in the sense of real physical assets and of the funds with which their construction is financed — as a factor underlying the low levels of income and rates of growth. The vicious circle of under-development has become an extremely familiar concept; productivity and incomes are low largely because of an inadequate volume of capital per head, but the stock of capital and the rate of capital formation are low precisely because incomes are low. Thus the under-developed territories are caught in a situation from which there is no easy escape; inevitably and properly, stress has been laid on the need to break into the circle by means of capital from external sources. The truth of this general doctrine is undeniable, and an important role of the new institutional relationships discussed in this study may well be to make the flow of capital into an under-developed territory from outside sources easier, more efficient and cheaper.

Apart from the absolute shortage of capital, however, a feature of many under-developed territories which was noted earlier is the inappropriate distribution of the available supply of funds amongst various types of investment. Capital is not only scarce, but often used in ways which are not conducive to the maximum rate of economic expansion. A good deal of capital, for example, has been remitted out of under-developed territories in the past and invested in international financial centres where safety and liquidity are secured but where the need for capital is considerably less pressing than in the territories from which the funds came.

Even if this export of capital does not occur, funds are frequently channelled into forms of expenditure which are not those which could be given a high priority in a rational allocation of scarce resources; in particular, the insistence of investors on safety has tended in the absence of well-organised and reputable financial institutions to divert a substantial proportion of savings into real estate development and comparable forms of investment.[1] In an advanced economy land is not usually regarded as a particularly liquid asset, but the concept of liquidity is essentially relative. Where active security markets and a whole network of institutions offering safe and liquid forms of investment exist, land is relatively illiquid; in an under-developed territory with few of these domestic investment outlets, land is frequently amongst the safest, most profitable and most marketable assets in which an investor can hold his savings. As a result, a great deal of the available investible funds (and much of the scarce supply of entrepreneurship also) may be absorbed into real estate projects, frequently with a consequential and harmful inflation of land values; productive investment in agriculture and industry may meantime be held back because of the scarcity of funds and high cost of land.[2]

Because of the importance of liquidity in the allocation of savings, therefore, the creation and encouragement of rudimentary markets in long and short-term loans within under-developed territories is a task of the first importance. At first sight it might seem extravagant and inappropriate for a badly under-developed territory to be indulging in the luxury of the creation of stock exchanges and comparable institutions; in fact, such a policy would be rooted in common sense, and might even prove essential to the success of other measures of development. Unless local investors

---

[1] Or, of course, into hoards of gold or other 'precious' substances. It has been suggested that in some countries of South and South-east Asia and the Middle East private gold hoards amount to 10 per cent of the national income — *Measures for the economic development of under-developed countries*, Chap. VI, p. 35. One report has estimated the value of gold hoards in Syria alone at about $150 million in 1949 — see A. Bonné, *Studies in economic development*, Routledge and Kegan Paul, London 1957, Chap. X, p. 197. Traditional forms of 'conspicuous consumption' may also absorb badly-needed resources; thus Professor Arthur Lewis writes of under-developed countries in which 'productive investment is not small because there is no surplus; it is small because the surplus is used to maintain unproductive hordes of retainers, and to build pyramids, temples and other durable consumer goods, instead of to create productive capital'. (Op. cit., Chap. V, p. 236.) See also Ali, op. cit., p. 52, N. Rosenberg, 'Capital formation in under-developed countries', *American Economic Review*, Vol. L, No. 4, September 1960, pp. 707–8, and S. Kuznets, *Economic change*, Heinemann, London 1954, pp. 175–6.

[2] It is of course true that the over-valuation of land does not in itself absorb resources which would otherwise be available for capital formation, unless the capital profits are absorbed into conspicuous consumption, but in practice the speculative profits arising therefrom show a marked propensity — for fairly obvious reasons — to migrate rapidly. On all this see N. Rosenberg, op. cit., pp. 711–4, and Hanson, op. cit., Chap. II, pp. 35–6, and Chap. III, p. 65.

are able to secure the kind of investment outlets which they are seeking, capital will continue to be diverted out of a territory or inappropriately used within it; only when the available capital has been channelled in the right directions will the maximum rate of development become possible. Growth, as one study remarks, often depends more on where and how capital is invested than on the absolute quantity of savings.[1] Hence the development of capital markets may be a necessary prerequisite of agricultural and industrial development, not a result and reflection of it.[2] Furthermore, by ensuring that assets of a proper kind and having a reasonable degree of liquidity are available to local investors, the authorities will not merely encourage the direction of the internal flow of savings to the most suitable and most important ends; the rate of saving itself may well be stimulated in time by the knowledge that attractive, safe and lucrative outlets exist for the employment of savings.

In developing local capital markets the government, and its foremost agent the central bank, must necessarily play the main role. Only a governmental institution has both the resources and the responsibility for shouldering the risks implicit in increasing the liquidity of investment within its territory. No private institution, however great its resources and however far-seeing its management, can be expected to take upon itself the task of underwriting the development of the economy as a whole, a development which may yield material returns only after the passage of many years. It is the government and its agencies which must take the initiative in the creation of local markets and the encouragement of the supply of local assets of such a kind as to give investors confidence in their marketability.

The process is one which implies the shouldering of a good deal of risk; liquidity can be conferred on assets only by some form of implicit or explicit guarantee that in the event of a crisis the redemption of local investments will be possible on reasonable terms at all times. This risk is one which a private institution working primarily and naturally for profit would be eminently

---

[1] T. C. Cochran, 'The entrepreneur in American capital formation', *Capital formation and economic growth*, N.B.E.R., Princeton 1956, p. 372, quoted by Diamond, op. cit., p. 11.

[2] It has been suggested, for example, that the absence of local liquidity may induce commercial banks operating in under-developed areas to hold unusually large cash reserves and pursue especially conservative lending policies — Birnbaum, op. cit., p. 480.

unlikely to undertake. Since the shouldering of it may play an essential role in the development of the economy, it follows that it is a serious responsibility resting upon the government and upon the agencies through which it exercises its monetary and fiscal measures. An appreciation of this fact is exemplified by the statement of the Governor of the Bank of Canada in 1954 that

> As part of our programme to improve and broaden the money market for the benefit of lenders and borrowers and of our financial structure as a whole, the Bank of Canada has been a constant trader in Government of Canada securities since we opened our doors in 1935 . . . we have endeavoured to help make a market for all Government issues. . . .[1]

2. *Short-term credit markets*

Outlets for the profitable and reasonably safe use of funds at short term, comparable with those existing in the discount and money markets of more developed economies, are particularly lacking in under-developed territories. Many territories in this category have a fairly high proportion of activities with different seasonal patterns and may thus have a substantial volume of short-term funds seeking temporary investment from one season to another. Without a local short-term market, funds available on a temporary basis of this kind will probably be remitted overseas, through the banking system or otherwise, or hoarded in a sterile form internally. It might happen that local investors would be prepared to hold local assets for the purposes of long-term investment, knowing that their relative illiquidity would not be an overwhelming disadvantage for an operation aimed primarily at the acquisition of a flow of income over a long period; if those same investors had only short-term funds at their disposal, however, they would be very reluctant to commit them to local long-term assets for which no active market existed. Yet if sufficient short-term funds are available at any one time, the provision of suitable assets may convert a series of short-term investments into a supply of relatively long-term finance. The turnover of short-term assets may be fairly high for individual investors, but for the economy as a whole a substantial volume of them may well be permanently demanded, so opening up a source of long-term finance.

[1] Mr. Graham Towers, quoted by Foussek, op. cit., Chap. III, p. 37. Official finance agencies such as those discussed in the previous chapter have also an important contribution of a similar kind to make — see Diamond, op. cit., p. 55.

An important step in the construction of a market which can lead towards this result is therefore the encouragement of a supply of local short-term assets, comparable to the emergence of commercial bills which led to the creation and prosperity of London's discount market. The use of private trade and finance bills may indeed be encouraged by the authorities as a means by which local enterprises can finance working capital needs or the holding of stocks.[1] On the other hand, it is essential that the market should be constructed on the basis of assets with which the territory is familiar, rather than on those which happen to have played a major part in similar developments in different countries and in earlier periods of history. Hence a short-term credit market might be built more easily and firmly on instruments which would appear unfamiliar and perhaps outlandish to an observer from Europe or America — such as warehouse warrants, crop liens, or notes secured on bills of lading. The establishment of a money market in Australia in 1959, for example, seems to have been stimulated to some extent by the appearance of a growing volume of short-term hire-purchase paper.[2] The essential point is that the instruments upon which the market is developed should be those suited to the peculiar needs of the economy involved — if possible, those which already circulate in the area, even if on only a modest scale. The encouragement of the use of these instruments, both by borrowers and lenders, can often best be given by the central bank and the commercial banks operating in the territory through their acceptance as collateral security against overdrafts, or a willingness on the part of the banks, central and commercial, to re-discount such paper freely and cheaply.

The use and encouragement of local private assets of this kind is no doubt the ideal from many points of view. Nevertheless the fact remains that such instruments may not be forthcoming in sufficient quantities to establish an active market, or may not prove acceptable to the potential suppliers of short-term funds. In many cases, therefore, a leading role must of necessity be played by the Treasury bill or its equivalent — that is to say, by a security issued by the government and repayable at par in a short time. For

[1] Attempts to establish money markets in India, Pakistan and Burma on the basis of commercial paper, however, do not seem to have been as successful as efforts elsewhere to build on the foundation of short-term government securities — see Foussek, op. cit., Chap. VII, pp. 96–7.

[2] C. T. Looker, 'Australia's evolving money market: how the market works', *The Banker*, Vol. CX, No. 412, June 1960, p. 386.

generations to come the existence of a market in short-term funds will be an unfamiliar and somewhat delicate element in many under-developed territories, and it may very well be that only the use of securities carrying the highest possible credit-standing will enable such a market to flourish and expand. Since the gains to the economy as a whole from the growth of a market in short-term funds will be considerable, it is proper that the government should accept the fact that it has a vital, and possibly somewhat costly, part to play in this process. The issue of Treasury bills will often be highly desirable, and indeed essential, if a short-term market is to be established at all, whether the government needs to raise funds at short-term at any particular moment or not.

In this connection, the adoption of a tender system of issuing Treasury bills is perhaps the only way in which a market rate of interest on short-term loans, fluctuating from week to week and month to month in response to conditions prevailing in the market, may be established — as many countries, from Canada to Thailand, have found. The process of offering Treasury bills at short intervals is one which the authorities can handle relatively easily and with little administrative cost; at the same time, it provides a means whereby the current market conditions may quickly and clearly reflect themselves in the rate of interest at which the bills are taken up. Furthermore, by adjusting the amounts of Treasury bills for which tenders are accepted, the authorities can even out fluctuations in the overall volume of bills outstanding, or adjust it upwards or downwards in accordance with the current needs of the economy.

This obviously implies that government policy with regard to short-term borrowing will need to be formulated on a considerably wider basis than the mere consideration of raising funds when needed at the lowest possible cost. The needs of the market in short-term funds may dictate an expansion in the volume of Treasury bills even if this means an avoidable increase in the government's debt service charges.[1] It is desirable, also, that the central bank should offer re-discount facilities of a fairly generous kind to purchasers of Treasury bills, so that investors will know

---

[1] An over-zealous effort to keep Treasury Bill rates low has probably discouraged the commercial banks from participating in the tender in Egypt and Pakistan and has therefore retarded the growth and development of the money market in those countries — see Ali, op. cit., p. 74.

that it is always possible for them to secure repayment at short notice and with little or no capital loss.

The experience of many countries supports these conclusions. In Canada, the introduction of a three-month Treasury bill issued by means of a tender system, together with a re-purchase guarantee by the Central bank, have done a great deal to establish an active and expanding money market. As a result (between 1953 and 1955 especially) the growth of the Treasury bill issue has been paralleled by a substantial increase in the volume of private short-term paper in circulation as market institutions have become stronger and more familiar.[1] In India the issue of Treasury bills by tender was adopted shortly after the establishment of the Reserve Bank, and the latter offered re-discount facilities from 1937. Considerably more progress in the creation of a market seems to have been made from 1952 onwards, however, when re-discounting facilities at preferential rates and stamp duty concessions were offered in respect of commercial bills, including those embodying credit previously extended to the private sector by the commercial banks in the form of loans and overdrafts. Similarly, the issue of Treasury bills by tender and the creation of re-discounting facilities date back to 1927 in South Africa, but relatively slow progress was made in the creation of a market largely because of the hostility of the commercial banks towards what they conceived to be a threat to their own time deposits — a practically universal occupational hazard of the builder of short-term credit markets.[2]

Two more recent experiments in the creation of money markets may perhaps be mentioned. In Australia an attempt by the Commonwealth Bank to develop a market through the issue of Treasury bills to the public in 1936 was effectively defeated by this same hostility on the part of the commercial banks.[3] In 1959, however, another attempt was made by the granting of re-discounting facilities to four — subsequently seven — approved dealers whose total liabilities, under the impact of the new arrangements, rose from £34 million in March 1959 to £80 million in March 1960. The hostility of the commercial banks continues but

---

[1] de Kock, op. cit., Chap. XII, pp. 212–3, and Foussek, op. cit., Chap. VII, pp. 91–3.

[2] On the South African experience see de Kock, op. cit., Chap. XII, p. 215, and G. F. D. Palmer, 'The development of a South African money market', *The South African Journal of Economics*, Vol. 26, No. 4, December 1958.

[3] de Kock, op. cit., Chap. XII, p. 215.

the market is growing nevertheless.[1] Similarly, the introduction of a tender Treasury bill system by the government of Jamaica in 1958, together with generous re-discounting facilities at the Treasury itself, was followed by a growth in the volume of Treasury bills outstanding from less than £1 million at the end of 1957 to nearly £5 million by the middle of 1960.

The availability of attractive re-discounting facilities has been a key element in all these attempts to establish a short-term credit market. Yet it appears to be common experience that, in the event, relatively little call is made on them. The effect of their introduction, in other words, seems to be to attract funds into Treasury bills and keep them there, rather than the reverse. It is one of the paradoxes of the world of investment that the easier it is for investors to get out of a security, the more willing are investors to move into and stay in such a security.

It must again be stressed, however, that to ensure the creation of even a rudimentary short-term credit market on which a continued expansion may be founded, the government must so formulate its policy as to accept costs of borrowing which may be in excess of the minimum possible. Governments will find it necessary to issue Treasury bills from time to time when their own borrowing needs are nil, or even when they are in a position to redeem existing short-term debt. Investors will never develop the habit of purchasing Treasury bills and comparable securities regularly and in any significant magnitude unless they can be assured that an adequate supply of such assets will always be available. A Treasury bill issue which fluctuated widely from a large amount to practically nil within any given year would be valueless as an instrument for the development of a stable credit market. Similarly, governments may find themselves in the position of having to pay a relatively high rate of interest on Treasury bills in order to maintain an adequate volume of bills in the market.

The gains accruing from the development of the short-term market are neither immediately visible nor confined to any particular sector of the economy; they consist of 'external' economies for which governments must nevertheless make due allowance in framing debt policy. The gains to the economy from the existence of a healthy market in short-term debt, in other words, may justify what amounts to a hidden subsidy in the form of borrowing at rates above

[1] C. T. Looker, op. cit., pp. 385–91.

those which could be secured, and of borrowing on occasions when the government itself may have no need of finance. Indeed, it is implicit in all this that a vitally important role of the public debt in an under-developed territory is to secure funds, not for the government itself, but in order to establish a regular and acceptable channel by which private investors may obtain suitable assets within the economy and local enterprises may obtain access to funds which would otherwise have been lost to investment within that territory.

3. *The long-term capital market*

This latter point has even greater significance when the discussion is switched from short-term to long-term capital. Traditional concepts concerning the function of long-term public debt are particularly inappropriate to the needs and aims of an under-developed economy. If local private assets are such that investible funds possessed by local investors would not be attracted into them because of their lack of liquidity, then it is eminently desirable that the public debt should provide a mechanism by which local enterprises may receive funds and local investors may simultaneously achieve the liquidity which they require. Once again the issue of public debt cannot be determined solely by considerations of the current state of the government exchequer. Public debt is, of course, a means by which a government can borrow for its own current or capital purposes, and in many instances governments find themselves having to undertake capital expenditure programmes which would be carried out in the private sector of a more advanced economy, either because of an inadequate supply of entrepreneurship or because no-one other than a government can obtain the necessary funds.[1] The role of the public debt in an under-developed economy, however, extends far beyond the financing of government expenditures themselves; it is also a device whereby funds can be obtained from local investors, channelled into official accounts and transferred, primarily by means of the type of institution discussed in the preceding chapter, to private as well as public enterprises for the finance of real capital formation.[2]

[1] E. R. Black, 'The age of economic development', *Economic Journal*, Vol. LXX, No. 278, June 1960, p. 271.
[2] It is essential, of course, that this should be appreciated by overseas observers in order to dispel the attitude reflected in H. C. Wallich's generalisation: 'In under-developed countries, with their often rudimentary capital markets, the suspicion that government bonds on bank statements reflect fiscal

Similarly, the types of security issued by the government cannot be determined solely by the particular needs of the government itself. The public debt can be used in an under-developed economy to stimulate saving and local investment; hence the securities issued will often need to be designed primarily with the needs of the investor in mind, rather than with those of the borrower — i.e. the government itself — whether the government is acting on its own account or on behalf of others in raising the loan concerned. It may be, for example, that the type of investor possessing investible funds at a particular moment is such that only a long-term security will be an acceptable asset; this might well be the case with insurance companies operating in the territory. Unless the government is prepared to issue long-term securities, therefore — whether the borrowing needs be long-term or otherwise — the funds potentially available from such sources will in fact be lost to the territory altogether. There is little point, after all, in offering a long-term investor short-term assets of a kind which do not meet his particular investing needs. Conversely, if funds are available predominantly from investors who seek short-term securities, then the public debt should contain a predominance of short-term assets of the kind which such investors are desiring, even if it is the intention to use the funds at long-term. In fact, a succession of short-term issues will be used to obtain funds which are to be invested on a long-term basis; a straightforward issue of long-term securities would be inappropriate to much of the capital which happens to be available at that time.

From time to time, indeed, the public debt will need to be expanded by issues which combine various maturities and other terms of repayment; a given volume of public debt, that is, may be offered to the public in several alternative forms, the investor being left to decide for himself which particular type of security, and what volume, he is prepared to purchase with the funds currently at his disposal. As with Treasury bills, it may also be necessary for a government to issue different securities from time to time even if its own borrowing needs are nil. From the investors' point of view, a regular supply of securities is as important as acceptable terms and interest rates; a bank, a building society, an insurance company, or any other prospective investor of funds, will need to

straits becomes virtually a certainty'. — ' Under-developed countries and the international monetary mechanism', *Money, trade and economic growth* (Essays in honour of J. H. Williams), Macmillan, New York 1951, p. 22.

be assured not merely that a suitable investment outlet is currently available, but that comparable assets will continue to be made available at intervals in the future, as and when additional funds become available for investment. Without the assurance of a regular and adequate supply, investors will continue to look outside the economy for investment outlets.

A parallel need for an under-developed economy is the establishment of a market in which public debt securities may be regularly traded at prices which do not fluctuate between wild extremes from week to week, even if the market initially takes a very rudimentary form. When an investor is seeking suitable assets, he will need to be assured not merely that they are currently available, but that it will be possible to dispose of them without calamitous loss or extreme difficulty if at some time in the future it should prove necessary to realise the investment. Liquidity, in other words, must be given to long-term as well as short-term government debt by means of marketing facilities.

The establishment of a market in long-term securities is usually considerably more complex, and involves more risk, than would be the case with short-term credit. It would be absurd to suggest that anything as sophisticated as the stock exchanges of London or New York could be established within the foreseeable future in any of the under-developed territories of the world. On the other hand, it is unlikely that anything as refined and complex as this is at all necessary in the environment of such territories. All that is needed is some elementary machinery by which multilateral trading in government securities can occur between the major buyers and sellers from time to time. The arrangements may be no more complex and expensive than a weekly meeting of representatives of the institutions and individuals active in the purchase and sale of securities, possibly in an office made available by the central bank or by one of the leading institutional investors. At such a regular meeting it would be sufficient for the prospective buyers and the prospective sellers to come together through the medium of their representatives, and for a kind of clearing-house to be established for them. The price level of securities emerging from such machinery would naturally fluctuate from time to time, but it is in no sense necessary for fluctuations to be entirely absent from a securities market in order that those securities should have an acceptable degree of liquidity. So long as investors know that

H

they are likely to secure a price within a reasonable range of the purchase price, they are likely to be content; few will demand an absolute guarantee that the price will never fall below par at any time.

Nevertheless, it is almost certain that in the early stages of the development of such a rudimentary stock exchange the authorities will need to play a major part by way of a stabilising force in the market. It is likely to prove necessary for the authorities to maintain a market in their own securities, offering to purchase its public debt issues at a lower range of prices and to sell at an upper range. This is no more than is commonly done by many central banks in order to maintain a reasonably stable exchange rate for their own currency in guaranteeing to buy and sell within a range of prices announced from time to time and, of course, modified from time to time to take heed of current market conditions.[1] The suggestion is obviously not that a government should undertake the responsibility of permanently stabilising the price level of its quoted debt. All that is necessary is that basic support to trading in the public debt should be given by the authorities; no guarantee to buy or sell need be given except at minimum and maximum prices which could both be considerably removed from the level which is likely to prevail in normal conditions.

Naturally, only experience can show how far such a range of prices would need to extend; it seems inevitable, however, that in the early stages at any rate some such active participation by the authorities will be absolutely necessary if regular and systematic trading is to develop. Once investors become familiar with the fact that it is possible to dispose of government securities at reasonable prices without undue difficulty at intervals of, say, a week or a month, then — as happens with Treasury bills carrying generous re-discounting facilities — those investors will not normally seek to dispose of their securities at all. Liquidity must be provided by the government itself; not complete liquidity at some immovable guaranteed price, but reasonable liquidity in the sense that the market in securities is never entirely frozen, even if moderate price differences have to be accepted.

Much stress has been laid on the role of public debt in the establishment of securities market. For the reasons outlined in

---

[1] A procedure widely used by, for example, the South African Reserve Bank. A similar policy, although on a less formalised basis, is pursued by the central banks of Australia, Ceylon and Pakistan — Foussek, op. cit., Chap. III, pp. 41–2.

connection with the short-term credit market it seems clear that in the early stages of a rudimentary stock exchange the public debt, and government operations in it, will play a fundamental role in the development of the market.[1] With the passage of time, however, and the increasing familiarity of institutional and private investors with the fact of active dealing in securities and relative stability of prices within short periods of time, it is likely that securities issued by other public authorities and, ultimately, private corporations within the economy will also be actively dealt in.[2] When this happens, it will become possible for enterprises to contemplate raising capital locally by the issue of securities as has long been done in the advanced industrial economies of the world. Until some active trading is a possibility, however, it is extremely unlikely that enterprises within an under-developed territory will be able to issue securities to raise funds locally except perhaps to a very limited circle of the entrepreneur's friends and relations. The expansion of the economy presupposes an adequate flow of capital to the productive enterprises of the country. In the first instance this is likely to be done to a large degree through the medium of the public debt. With the development of trading facilities in securities, the possibility of the issue of private securities directly to local institutional investors becomes a reasonable one, and the flow of capital will be stimulated and expanded.

4. *The institutional framework*

It is evident that in the developments which have been discussed in this chapter the ideal would be to build upon the individuals and institutions, as well as the assets, which are to some degree already familiar in the economy concerned. That is to say, it is desirable that both the market in short-term and long-term securities, while initiated and in the early stages supported by the government or the central bank, should ultimately be handled and

---

[1] This differs from the view adopted by the United Nations experts in *Domestic financing of economic development* (pp. 70–6), in which the stress is laid heavily on the marketing of private securities. They considered it necessary, indeed, to consider whether government securities should be traded at all on a rudimentary stock exchange. This surely misses the essential point that local security holding and trading are in themselves unfamiliar experiences in most under-developed territories and that (in their own words) in the advanced countries 'Private stocks were traded in only after sufficient public confidence had been created by prior experience with government bonds'. (p. 76.)

[2] The Central Bank or development finance institutions, for example, may be able to assist the growth of the market by issuing its own obligations. See Boskey, op. cit., Chap. VIII, pp. 103–4.

administered by persons and institutions already established within the economy as investors and brokers; if such institutions are not in existence, in all probability they will begin to emerge as profitable and reputable security markets establish themselves.

It is perhaps necessary to stress, however, that the institutional framework within which such markets can be created and developed in any particular economy will by no means be necessarily modelled on the particular institutional arrangements to be found in the old-established markets of London or New York. For example, since the markets in both short-term and long-term capital will almost inevitably be small-scale for many years, there would appear to be no particular reason why a sharp division of function between short-term and long-term security dealings should necessarily be imposed upon brokers. One would envisage that representatives of the major institutional investors (e.g. insurance companies or commercial banks) and of private lenders (e.g. local brokers or security dealers, or even lawyers and money lenders) would deal in both long-term and short-term assets, if they were so disposed. The specialisation familiar in London and elsewhere may very well prove to be neither practicable nor particularly desirable for the completely different environment and smaller scale of an under-developed economy.

While the encouragement of local enterprise and local participation in the institutional arrangements is to be welcomed — and regarded as the ultimate aim — the fact remains that, as has been repeatedly stressed, in its initial stages the development of credit markets in an under-developed territory will be largely the responsibility of the government, usually working through its agency the central bank. Only the government can accept the risks inherent in the provision of re-discounting facilities or a price-stabilisation mechanism. Such provision may well involve losses from time to time, whether they take the form of relatively high interest rates on new issues of public debt or of capital losses occurring in connection with the purchase or sale of long-term securities in the interests of an active securities market. It would be unreasonable to expect such losses to be carried by any private institution. On the other hand, the improved flow of funds into the various sectors of the economy, and the stimulus to the creation of savings, following from the development of active security markets are likely to be so considerable — even if widespread and intangible — that a government would be fully justified in shouldering the risks and bearing these possible losses.

Indeed, there is a responsibility resting upon a government in this context which is as serious as those in the fields of, say, public health or education, which no contemporary government would attempt to repudiate. The economic progress of an under-developed territory does not rest upon the rate of capital formation alone; the rate of capital formation, in turn, does not rest on the flow of finance alone. In the words of a United Nations report, 'Good financial organisation cannot by itself produce development; bad financial organisation can hamper it'.[1] The flow of credit, in adequate amounts and in a logical pattern of distribution, is only one of the many vital links between, on the one hand, growth and development in the economy and, on the other hand, the activities of individual private citizens. Like all links in a chain, this particular link cannot be regarded as having a superior importance in relation to any other. As with any other chain, however, a particular link in the chain of economic relationships cannot be neglected if a community is to be lifted from a state of under-development to — ultimately — a high and expanding level of output through which its welfare is raised to the highest level attainable with the human and material resources with which it is endowed.

[1] *Domestic financing of economic development*, p. 1.

EPILOGUE

THE nature of the subject discussed in this essay is such that a concluding chapter of the conventional kind could do little more than repeat a series of individual points which have already been made in the preceding pages. There would be little useful purpose in such a procedure. Yet, in a sense, the core of the argument reduces to a single theme — just as recent thought has come to stress more and more the essential unity of monetary systems which at first sight appear to be collections of distinct and separate, and often distantly-related, organisations and institutions. That theme would be the critical importance of a change of attitude towards the functions and purposes of financial systems operating in areas of economic under-development — or, to be more precise, the importance of an absence of attitudes inherited from other environments, and the willingness to think out the problems from first principles and without preconceived doctrines.

Where, then, is this change of attitude required? In the first place, surely, in the under-developed areas themselves. They do not lack advisers anxious to stress the limitations of financial measures or the awful dangers which await them if the monetary apparatus is not handled with all due reverence and caution. But have the wise and knowledgeable amongst their citizens — and the incidence of these is certainly no lower than in the regions from which advice pours in such profusion — perhaps become so impressed with these risks and dangers as to lose sight of the important gains which can be secured from a proper ordering of their financial arrangements? Perhaps, also, the habits of thought of Europe and North America have spilled over into these developing regions, so that almost unwittingly the potentialities of monetary weapons are assessed in traditional terms of anti-cyclical policy and delicate marginal adjustments, rather than in the more appropriate terms of basic growth and development.

Obviously attitudes must change amongst the operators and administrators of monetary institutions also, both in the under-developed and richer areas. All too often one encounters evidence of resistance to new measures — be it the creation of a central bank, the application of commercial banking regulations, or the establishment of a money market — on the part of those engaged in the business of making a living from the day-to-day operation of the financial system. At worst such opposition can be construed as a hostility to any interference in the process of private profit-maximisation; at best it must be taken as a manifestation of the inability of the persons or institutions involved to perceive either that wise policy for the development of a territory may originate outside themselves or that their own interests must ultimately coincide with such policy. The latter is undoubtedly nearer the truth; as one percipient observer has remarked,

> It is the nature of bankers, including central bankers, to be conservative rather than adventurous. But economic growth is essentially an adventurous conception.[1]

This conflict of approach is an inescapable fact of life, but it is one which will have to be reduced in magnitude if the growth of under-developed territories and the long-run interests of institutions operating in them are not both to suffer. To be fair, there are many signs of change in the attitude of commercial banks and other institutions towards a bolder and more positive policy. But as yet the change is lamentably small in both area and degree.

Finally, and perhaps most important, a drastic change of attitude is still necessary amongst those of the richer countries who bear responsibility for ruling, assisting or even merely advising the under-developed areas. All too often the desire of dependent territories to carry out monetary reforms is treated in terms normally reserved for a child wishing to play with a lethal weapon; commentators describe the creation of new financial institutions as a rather adolescent attempt to assert new-found sovereignty, not to be taken too seriously; official advisers commence their reports with the words 'Central banks are notoriously expensive institutions', or some such, a statement which, leaving aside its accuracy, usually implies that this sort of thing is suitable only for more mature and sophisticated countries (such as that from which the adviser has himself emerged).

To some extent attitudes of this sort originate in cultural or racial prejudices the discussion of which is obviously beyond the

[1] C. R. Whittlesey, 'Relation of money to economic growth', *American Economic Review* (Papers and Proceedings), Vol. XLVI, No. 2, May 1956, p. 200.

scope of this work. To a substantial degree, however, they arise from a purely technical inability to see financial institutions, in their form and their function, except in terms of the particular phase of evolution which they happen to have reached in the industrialised societies of Europe or America. The error is elementary; but it is nonetheless firmly-rooted and dangerous.

It is only right and proper that the final emphasis should thus be laid on human rather than physical or institutional factors. In the last resort the raising of standards of living depends not on capital, nor on technology, nor on institutional arrangements, but on men and women. Economic arrangements exist merely in order to permit the optimum expression of human potentialities, and if they fail to do this no other justification for their existence remains. This is not to say that the much-advertised dangers of inexpert tampering with the monetary system are without substance; such dangers emphatically exist. It is rather to act as a reminder that there also exists an opposite danger; that when conventional methods of administration, or concepts of prudence, or channels of control, have positively begun to hinder and hamper the improvement of standards of human life where that improvement is most needed, then priorities have become improperly reversed and institutional arrangements must be altered.

No-one believes that monetary arrangements or techniques can in themselves conquer poverty; their most fervent exponent would not claim that they could make more than a modest contribution — but a not insignificant one — to that end. But the least that can surely be demanded is that they should not stand in the way of advancement, and should make what contribution they can. For if the Sabbath was made for man, and not man for the Sabbath, how much more is this true of mere coins and counting-houses?

BIBLIOGRAPHY

ADLER, J. H., 'The fiscal and monetary implementation of development programs', *American Economic Review* (Papers and Proceedings), Vol. XLII, No. 2, May 1952.

ALI, A., 'Banking in the Middle East', *I.M.F. Staff Papers*, Vol. VI, No. 1, November 1957.

'ANALYST' 'Currency and banking in Jamaica', *Social and Economic Studies*, Vol. 1, No. 4, August 1953.

Banker, The, 'Ceylon's central banking experiment', Vol. XCV, No. 294, July 1950.

BANK OF RHODESIA AND NYASALAND, *The financing of industrial development in the Federation of Rhodesia and Nyasaland*, Salisbury, May 1959.

BELL, P. W., *The sterling area in the post-war world*, Oxford University Press, London 1956.

BELSHAW, H., *Agricultural credit in economically under-developed countries*, F.A.O. Agricultural Study No. 46, Columbia University Press, New York 1960.

BIRNBAUM, E. A., 'The cost of a foreign exchange standard or of the use of a foreign currency as the circulating medium', *I.M.F. Staff Papers*, Vol. V, No. 3, February 1957.

BOSKEY, S., *Problems and practices of Development Banks*, I.B.R.D., John Hopkins Press, Baltimore 1959.

CAIRNCROSS, A. K., 'Banking in developing countries', *The future organisation of banking*, Institute of Bankers in Scotland, Blackwood, Edinburgh 1958.

CHANDAVARKAR, A. G., 'Central banking in Libya', *The Banker's Magazine*, Vol. CLXXXIX, No. 1395, June 1960.

CLAUSON, G. L. M., 'The British colonial currency system', *Economic Journal*, Vol. LIV, No. 213, April 1944.

DE KOCK, M. H., *Central banking*, 3rd ed., Staples Press, London 1954.

DIAMOND, W., *Development banks*, Economic Development Institute, John Hopkins Press, Baltimore 1957.

EXTER, J., *Report on the establishment of a central bank for Ceylon*, Sessional Paper XIV, Ceylon Government Press, Colombo 1949.

FISHER, J. L., *Report on the desirability and practicability of establishing a central bank in Nigeria for promoting the economic development of the country*, Government Printer, Lagos 1953.

FOUSEK, P. G., *Foreign central banking: the instruments of monetary policy*, Federal Reserve Bank of New York, New York 1957.

FUERST, E., 'Liquidity control of banks within dependent monetary systems', *The Bankers' Magazine*, Vol. CLXVII, No. 1266, September 1949.

GOODE, R. and THORN, R. S., 'Variable reserve requirements against commercial bank deposits', *I.M.F. Staff Papers*, Vol. II, No. 2, April 1952.

GREAVES, I. C., 'The sterling balances of colonial territories', *Economic Journal*, Vol. LXI, No. 242, June 1951.

GREAVES, I. C., *Colonial monetary conditions*, Colonial Research Studies No. 10, H.M.S.O., London 1953.

GREAVES, I. C., 'Sterling balances and the colonial currency system: a comment', *Economic Journal*, Vol. LXIII, No. 252, December 1953.

GREAVES, I. C., *The colonial sterling balances*, Essays in international finance No. 20, Princeton, New Jersey, September 1954.

GREAVES, I. C., 'Colonial trade and payments', *Economica*, Vol. XXIV, No. 93, February 1957.

GREAVES, I. C., 'Central banks for new dominions', *The Banker*, Vol. CVII, No. 379, August 1957.

GREGORY, SIR T., *The present position of Central Banks*, Stamp Memorial Lecture 1955, University of London, Athlone Press, London 1955.

GUNASEKERA, H. A. DE S., 'The money supply and balance of payments of Ceylon', *Review of the Banca Nazionale del Lavoro*, Vol. VII, No. 30, September 1954.

HANSON, A. H., *Public enterprise and economic development*, Routledge and Kegan Paul, London 1959.

HAWKINS, E. K., 'The growth of a money economy in Nigeria and Ghana', *Oxford Economic Papers*, Vol. 10, No. 3, October 1958.

HAZLEWOOD, A., 'Sterling balances and the colonial currency system', *Economic Journal*, Vol. LXII, No. 247, December 1952.

HAZLEWOOD, A., 'Colonial external finance since the war', *Review of Economic Studies*, 1953–4, Vol. XXI(1), No. 54.

HAZLEWOOD, A., 'Sterling balances and the colonial currency system: a reply', *Economic Journal*, Vol. LXIV, No. 255, September 1954.

HAZLEWOOD, A., 'Memorandum on the sterling assets of the British colonies: a comment', *Review of Economic Studies*, 1954-5, Vol. XXII(1), No. 57.

HAZLEWOOD, A., 'The economics of colonial monetary arrangements', *Social and Economic Studies*, Vol. 3, No. 4, December 1954.

KATZ, S. I., Development and stability in Central and West Africa: a study in colonial monetary institutions', *Social and Economic Studies*, Vol. 5, No. 3, September 1956.

KING, F. H. H., 'Sterling balances and the colonial monetary system', *Economic Journal*, Vol. LXV, No. 260, December 1955.

LASO, E., 'Financial policies and credit control techniques in Central America', *I.M.F. Staff Papers*, Vol. VI, No. 3, November 1958.

LOOKER, C. T., 'Australia's evolving money market: how the market works', *The Banker*, Vol. CX, No. 412, June 1960.

MACRAE, N. A. D., 'Experiments in central banking: a study of San Domingo's new bank', *The Banker*, Vol. XCI, No. 273, October 1948.

MARS, J., 'The monetary and banking system of Nigeria', *Mining, finance and commerce in Nigeria* (ed. Perham), Vol. II, Faber and Faber, London 1948.

NEWLYN, W. T., 'Central bank for Central Africa', *The Bankers' Magazine*, Vol. CLXXX, No. 1347, June 1956.

NEWLYN, W. T., and ROWAN, D. C., *Money and banking in British Colonial Africa*, Oxford University Press, London 1954.

NICULESCU, B. M., 'Sterling balances and the colonial currency system: a comment', *Economic Journal*, Vol. LXIV, No. 255, September 1954.

NURKSE, R., *Problems of capital formation in under-developed countries*, Blackwell, Oxford 1953.

PALMER, G. F. D., 'The development of a South African money market', *The South African Journal of Economics*, Vol. 26, No. 4, December 1958.

PATEL, I. G., 'Selective credit controls in under-developed economies', *I.M.F. Staff Papers*, Vol. IV, No. 1, September 1954.

PATON, G. D., *Report on banking in the Gold Coast*, Government Printer, Accra 1948.

PATON, G. D., *Report on banking in Nigeria*, Government Printer, Lagos 1948.

PLUMPTRE, A. F. W., *Central banking in the British Dominions*, University of Toronto Press, Toronto 1940.

ROSENBERG, N., 'Capital formation in under-developed countries', *American Economic Review*, Vol. L, No. 4, September 1960.

ROWAN, D. C., 'The native banking boom in Nigeria', *The Banker*, Vol. XCVII, No. 309, October 1951.

ROWAN, D. C., 'Banking in Nigeria: a study in colonial financial evolution', *Review of the Banca Nazionale del Lavoro*, Vol. V, No. 22, July–September 1952.

ROWAN D. C., 'The monetary problems of a dependent economy', *Review of the Banca Nazionale del Lavoro*, Vol. VII, No. 31, December 1954.

SAYERS, R. S. (Ed.) *Banking in the British Commonwealth*, Oxford University Press, London 1952.

SAYERS, R. S., 'Central banking in under-developed countries', *Central banking after Bagehot*, Oxford University Press, London 1957.

SEN, S. N., *Central Banking in under-developed money markets*, Bookland Ltd., Calcutta 1952.

SHANNON, H. A., 'The modern colonial sterling exchange standard', *I.M.F. Staff Papers*, Vol. II, No. 2, April 1952.

SHENOY, B. R., 'The currency, banking and exchange system of Thailand', *I.M.F. Staff Papers*, Vol. I, No. 2, September 1950.

SMITH, W. L., 'Monetary-fiscal policy and economic growth', *Quarterly Journal of Economics*, Vol. 71, No. 1, February 1957.

TREVOR, SIR C., *Report on banking conditions in the Gold Coast and on the question of setting up a National Bank*, Government Printer, Accra 1951.

TRIFFIN, R. F., 'National central banking and the international economy', *Review of Economic Studies*, Vol. XIV(2), No. 36, 1946–7.

UNITED NATIONS, *Methods of financing economic development in under-developed countries* (1949. II. B4), New York 1949.

UNITED NATIONS, *Domestic financing of economic development* (1951. II. B1), New York 1950.

UNITED NATIONS, *Measures for the economic development of under-developed countries* (1951. II. B2), New York 1951.

UNITED NATIONS (ECAFE), 'Mobilisation of domestic resources for economic development and the financial institutions in the ECAFE region', *Economic Bulletin for Asia and the Far East*, First quarter 1950, Vol. I, No. 1, August 1950.

UNITED NATIONS (ECAFE), *Mobilisation of domestic capital*, Reports and documents of the second Working Party of Experts, Bangkok 1953.

WAI, U TUN, 'Interest rates in the organised money markets of under-developed countries', *I.M.F. Staff Papers*, Vol. V, No. 2, August 1956.

WAI, U TUN, 'Interest rates outside the organised money markets of under-developed countries', *I.M.F. Staff Papers*, Vol. VI, No. 1, November 1957.

WALLICH, H. C., *Monetary problems of an export economy — the Cuban experience, 1914–1947*, Harvard University Press, Cambridge, Mass. 1950.

WALLICH, H. C., 'Under-developed countries and the international monetary mechanism', *Money, trade and economic growth* (Essays in honour of John H. Williams), Macmillan, New York 1951.

WATSON, G. M. and CAINE, SIR S., *Report on the establishment of a central bank in Malaya*, Government Printer, Kuala Lumpur 1956.

WILIAMS, J. W., 'State banking in the Gold Coast', *The Banker*, Vol. CVII, No. 374, March 1957.

WILSON, J. S. G., 'Money and banking in British colonial Africa', *The Bankers' Magazine*, Vol. CLXXIX, No. 1331.

INDEX

PRINTED IN GREAT BRITAIN BY
ROBERT MACLEHOSE AND CO. LTD
THE UNIVERSITY PRESS, GLASGOW